"Benítez writes with passionate sensitivity, sharp political insight, courage, and honesty."

—*Detroit News/Free Press*

"A compelling read."

—*Boston Sunday Globe*

"It's hard not to get hooked."

—*St. Louis Post Dispatch*

"Addictive...Mesmerizing in its simplicity and frankness."

—*Publishers Weekly* (starred review)

"Luminously rendered...Memorable...[A] vivid chronicle of strong women facing the challenges of living in sad and violent times."

—*Kirkus Reviews*

"Engaging and involving...packed with exquisite detail...entirely captivating."

—*Austin American-Statesman*

"Moving, engrossing...the novel is rich in hope, determination, and the slimmest promise of happiness.... *Bitter Grounds* is a remarkable story well told."

—*Hartford Courant*

"Sandra Benítez has penned a powerful epic."

—*Buzz*

BITTER GROUNDS

▼

Also by Sandra Benítez

A Place Where the Sea Remembers

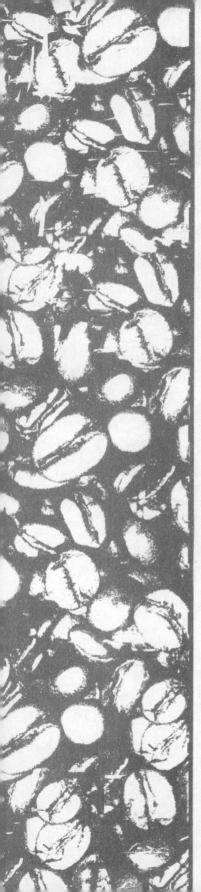

Bitter Grounds

Sandra Benítez

PICADOR USA  NEW YORK

For information on Picador USA Reading Group Guides, as well as ordering, please contact the Trade Marketing department at St. Martin's Press.
Phone: 1-800-221-7945 extension 488
Fax: 212-677-7456
E-mail: trademarketing@stmartins.com

ISBN 0-312-19541-9

First published in the United States by Hyperion

First Picador USA Paperback Edition: September 1998

10   9   8   7   6   5   4   3

Para Anita y Carlos Emilio
y para el pueblo salvadoreño,
quienes lo vivieron

ACKNOWLEDGMENTS

▼▼▼

Deep, heartfelt thanks to Jim Kondrick, Judith Bernie Strommen, Martha and Jim Ables, Anita and Dr. Carlos Emilio Alvarez.

In equal measure, thanks to Ellen Levine, Louise Quayle, and Leslie Wells.

To the Spirit, eternal gratitude.

▼▼

This is a work of fiction. All characters and their stories have been forged by my imagination. While attempting throughout the tale to stay within the framework of Salvadoran history, I have, to best suit the telling, taken creative license with Salvadoran geography and topography. I trust the reader will forgive these liberties. In the name of fiction, I have endeavored to invent the truth.

Bitter Grounds

Listen, for all your words
you cannot know.

In Salvador, coffee is
red-roofed estates,
high walls crowned with shards of glass,
uniformed servants hurrying over marble
toward a buzzing at the door.

In Salvador, coffee is
trips abroad,
languid Miami shopping:
dewy hands
plunged between
voile and cambric and silk.

You say, but for the golden hope of coffee
few men would get ahead.
I say, when the people harvest,
all they reap is bitter grounds.

In Salvador, coffee is
filled berry baskets
tied around waists;
bloodied fingertips
wrapped with strips of rag;
sisal arms
reaching up again to pick.

In Salvador, coffee left
in tins, pottery mugs, china cups,
never grows cold.

In Salvador, coffee steams while it sits.

Alma del Pueblo
(Soul of the People)

PART ONE

▼

MERCEDES AND ELENA

▼▼

Izalco, El Salvador
January 1932

The parakeets ascended in a rustling roar of wings from the amate and primavera trees. Chattering rowdily, they hailed the rising sun. They flew toward the southern sea cresting in a line of shimmering foam that broke and then evanesced along the black volcanic shore. The birds wheeled, banking in a long graceful turn before heading back over the forest they had roosted in; they soared toward breakfast in maicillo fields twenty kilometers away. Jabbering, the birds glided and dipped over the alluvial plain furrowed by rivers and streams coming down from the highlands. Across the plain, they trailed a hasty shadow over squares of cattle ranches and rectangles of scattered farms; they sailed past the spot where, four hundred years before, don Pedro de Alvarado and his conquistadores defeated the mighty army of the Pipil. But such a victory exacted its toll, for in the fierce skirmish, Alvarado took an arrow in the leg, a wound from which he would never recover. The parakeets flew on. Over the green patches of pepeto and madrecacao trees. Over the deeper green of coffee trees flourishing beneath. Over volcanoes evincing the land's periodic rage. When they reached el Izalco, the birds swooped a wide path around the fire and smoke spewing from its crater. They sailed around its blackened cone rising like a fist clenched toward God himself.

On a path below, Mercedes Prieto noted the passing birds. She hurried toward the stream that was minutes from her hut. The morning was cold and humid. Ash from the volcano settled like gray moths over the dewy scrub. Along the path, patches of mist formed filmy shapes, and these apparitions both perplexed and alarmed her.

Bound against her back in a shawl sling was Justino, her two-month-old son. Thankfully, Tino was sleeping. The night before he had tossed fitfully. Twice she had risen to tend to the dry cough that had plagued him for a week. Trailing behind them was her daughter Jacinta. Back at the hut, her husband Ignacio still slept. The women took the path several times a day for water. Mercedes preferred the later trips over these. At dawn, the mist played tricks with her.

She narrowed her eyes. Was that a pair of guardias springing up in the mist behind the lemongrass? Earlier in January, thirty kilometers away, coffee pickers had rebelled against patrones, and now there was talk of guardias prowling even this countryside. Mercedes imagined the men in their khaki uniforms and tan-colored sun helmets; she pictured their long cruel rifles, and these thoughts churned into fear. She rubbed her eyes to see more clearly. No one was there; she was being foolish. If strangers were about, the yellow mutt would let her know. Tzi trotted ahead. He stopped now and then to poke his snout into the scrub. Her heart went out to him, he was such a sorry sight. His ribs protruded under ragged fur. If only there was more to feed him than a handful of beans and a wedge of tortilla each day.

Mercedes adjusted the empty water jug balanced on her head. She pulled her shawl more tightly over her nose and mouth, a protection against the cunning spirits hovering in these early hours. She glanced over her shoulder to make sure Jacinta had not fallen behind, but her daughter was only steps away. Tall and slim, she wore her dark tapado draped over her head and falling loosely over her shoulders. She had not covered half her face as Mercedes had insisted. Just turned thirteen and already so defiant, Mercedes thought.

"I'm coming," Jacinta said, giving the end of her shawl a little flick. She disliked these early treks for water. Each day her mother shook her awake, laying a finger over her own mouth to counsel silence. Each day Jacinta dressed quickly and crept from the hut to leave her father asleep inside it. How she wished she were given this same consideration. Last night she had been dreaming of Antonio Ochoa, reliving their first sweet kiss, when her mother placed a hand upon her shoulder.

Reaching the brook, Mercedes set the jug down on the bank. At water's edge, she gathered her long skirt up and squatted beside the stream. Through the dissipating mist, she trailed a hand in the bracing water. Beyond the opposite bank, new light flashed through the quavering leaves of the ironwoods. It was over there that the best kindling lay. Over there, among the shadows, where Jacinta would have to forage.

"I'm going across now," Jacinta said. She spoke in Nahuatl, the language of the Pipil. Mercedes's family spoke Spanish, of course, but it was Nahuatl they preferred. In these disordered times, Pipil ways had to be preserved.

"Let me," Mercedes said. "Today you stay on this side and see to the water jug."

Jacinta lowered her shawl to her shoulders and rolled her dark eyes. "With Tino on your back, you can't bend over for kindling, Mamá." Jacinta wore her hair pulled back into two braids. Her skin was the color of taffy, and though she was not pretty, her round face had an intense look that made her quite uncommon. This, however, she did not know about herself.

"Very well," Mercedes replied. "But take the mutt with you. And don't you stray too far."

Jacinta lifted her skirt and stepped into the clear, shallow brook, shuddering a bit at the chilliness of the water. "You worry too much, Mamá," she said over her shoulder. "You allow too many things to frighten you." She crossed the river in a half-dozen paces and then turned back to face her mother. "I myself am not afraid of anything." Jacinta gave three sharp claps that reverberated like shots in the air. "Come, Tzi," she said.

Mercedes watched the two go off through the brush and start toward the ironwoods. She scooped a handful of water onto her face. Perhaps the girl's right, she thought. The countryside was calm. Other than Jacinta there was no one in sight. Soon the sun would fully rise. Toward noon the land would shimmer in its warmth. In the distance el Izalco groaned, and the volcano's familiar voice was a reassuring sound.

Mercedes dried her face with a corner of her shawl. She dragged the jug close. She had tipped it down into the brook and it had begun to fill when she heard Tzi bark.

Mercedes looked out across the stream, leaving the jug to bob gently in the water. She could see Jacinta's shoulders, her head poking out over some scrub. "What is it?" Mercedes called, but the only response that came was the alarming yelps of the dog. Mercedes sprang into the brook. At midstream she went down on one knee, but she picked herself up and waded clumsily to the other side, the front of her skirt soaked through and weighty. Tino fidgeted against her back and began to cry, but Mercedes went on. She stumbled over the incline of the opposite bank, then scrambled through the undergrowth. Out of breath, she reached the trees. Tzi ran up, yapping and leaping around her. Jacinta stood rooted to the ground.

"What?" Mercedes said.

Jacinta pointed to a blanket of fallen boughs lying at her feet. From under the boughs, two legs encased in canvas leggings protruded.

"La guardia," Mercedes whispered.

"He has no head," Jacinta said.

A blood-spattered torso lay under the loose covering of branches and twigs. A silvery belt buckle emblazoned with the notorious coat of arms glinted at her. She pushed away the thought of a detached head lying somewhere under there. Tzi poked his snout through the boughs, and Mercedes picked up a switch and struck out at him. "Get," she said, and the mutt tucked his tail between his legs and whimpered off.

"We have to tell Papá," Jacinta said.

"No," Mercedes said, surprised at her own fervor. "We mustn't involve ourselves in this." Tino cried in earnest now. Mercedes could feel his little fists flailing against her. "Sush, sush," she said, bouncing on the balls of her feet to quiet him.

"But what if another guardia comes, Mamá? You know they work in pairs." Antonio Ochoa spoke frequently about the Guardia; he told stories of their brutality, how for money and in quest of power, the Guardia had turned against their brothers, not that Jacinta had need of such confirmation. Once Antonio had sworn her to secrecy: his father, Goyo Ochoa, had killed two guardias in an ambush. Was this killing don Goyo's doing, too?

Mercedes spun around and scanned the land for other men, but there was no one. Pink and blue serpentines streaked the sky. In the trees overhead birds warbled. Mercedes lifted a few branches from the guardia's body. She squatted to touch his thigh. The flesh was unyielding.

Jacinta dropped down beside her mother. "What are you doing?"

"He's been dead for some hours," Mercedes said, the memory of Cirilo, her firstborn, flooding her mind. He had lived for five months. When he died, she had sat under the laurel tree that grew beside her hut, clutching his lifeless body against herself. She could not give him up—how could she give him up?—and so she clung to him until his tender frailness hardened into stone.

Mercedes looked at Jacinta. "We have to hide the body. There must be no sign of a guardia's death on land so near our hut."

Jacinta bunched a hand over her mouth. "But shouldn't we get Papá?"

"No. Knowing will endanger him." If Ignacio learned of this, he would turn to Goyo Ochoa. Goyo, the compadre whose hut lay a few minutes from their own and who believed in insurrection and rebellion.

"But what about us, Mamá? If we do this, it will be you and me who are in danger."

Mercedes was silent. In her forty years, she knew two things with certainty: From the minute we are born there is danger. In the end, it is up to the women to shield and protect.

She cast aside the boughs covering the corpse. "Quickly, Jacinta," she said. "We must work very quickly."

▼▼

CHAPTER TWO

The two dragged the guardia—without his head, which was nowhere to be found—from under the ironwoods toward a cave that Jacinta once had stumbled upon. Surprisingly, despite the stiffness in the dead man's limbs, his arms were not difficult to extend. But the body was heavy. They dragged it over uneven terrain, jerking it around clumps of broad brush, down one side and up the other of a dry arroyo that cut a narrow cleft in the field. As they worked, Tino fussed and squirmed against Mercedes's back, but this time Mercedes did not try to quiet him. Up ahead was the mound that marked the cave.

Mercedes pushed aside the trumpet-flowering vines obscuring the cave's entrance. She looked quickly at the guardia, struggling to keep her eyes from resting on the gruesome stump of his neck, from the blood that had turned his khaki tunic, and even a length of his uniform breeches, into a crusty maroon.

They dragged the guardia in, sprinkling him with what little earth they could hastily dig up from the cave floor, covering him as best they could with scrub brush. Outside again, Mercedes hungrily inhaled the fresh morning air. "We've done all we can."

They turned back to their chores. Jacinta gathered up the wood, and then they both recrossed the stream to where the jug lay filled with water. Tino had quieted, and Mercedes was thankful for the respite. With a grunt, she hoisted the pot onto her head, cushioning its weight with a circle of cloth. The two set off for home. They did not speak. Even Tzi, as if understanding the gravity of what had transpired, trotted silently before them. Once home, Mercedes and Jacinta squatted beside the blackened pottery comal set over coals in the kitchen lean-to that, years before, Ignacio had built next to the hut.

The odor of cook smoke and brewed coffee soon permeated the air. Light sneaked past the vine-wrapped saplings that formed the walls. It fell in slender lines across the dirt-packed floor. Mercedes looked out toward the clearing surrounding them, taking comfort in the familiar sights: her laurel tree and its circle of shade, the low rock wall spanning the distance between road and hut, the hedge of crimson poinsettias bordering one side of it. At any moment, the smell of coffee would bring Ignacio from his mat. When he came near, Mercedes thought, would he also catch a whiff of the rusty scent of the guardia's blood? She smoothed a hand over her face and stirred a pinch of salt into the beans heating over the fire. She glanced at Jacinta, who was laying a freshly made tortilla next to four others cooking on the comal. A twitch pulled at the corner of her daughter's mouth.

"We did all we could," Mercedes said.

Jacinta squeezed off a ball of masa from the mound of corn dough. She slapped one hand against the other, turning the dough against her palm. "We didn't find the head," she whispered. Later, she thought, when they were picking coffee, she would escape the watchful eye of the foreman and seek Antonio Ochoa out. There under the coffee trees, she'd ask him to his face what he knew about the killing. Did your father behead a guardia? she would say. If he did, where's the man's head? These were bold questions, to be sure, but she was not too shy to ask them.

Mercedes swallowed hard. The knowledge of the severed head, of it lying who knew where, that such a thing could give them all away, stunned her.

Presently, Ignacio Prieto appeared in the doorway. He wore roomy white pants and a white cotton shirt. He worked at taming a tuft of hair that sprung from the crown of his head. The stamp of sleep was still on his face, and it gave him a soft and vulnerable appearance.

"Your coffee's ready, Papá," Jacinta said. Her father grunted an acknowledgment and went off down the path toward the river.

"Are you telling him?" Jacinta asked when her father was out of hearing range. She poured coffee for the three of them.

"Didn't you hear what I said? We have to keep quiet about all this."

Jacinta shrugged. "I think we should tell him."

When Ignacio came up the path, Mercedes shot Jacinta a warning glance before Ignacio hunkered down beside them. "There's a bit of panela left," Mercedes said. "I saved it for both of you." She broke up the small piece of brown sugar, crumbling some into two cups. Usually it was her man who got the last of the panela, but today Jacinta clearly needed something sweet.

"How's the boy?" Ignacio said, turning his head toward Tino's hammock. He made circles with his coffee cup to help dissolve the sugar.

"He has a bad cough," Mercedes said. "Last night, I covered his chest with vinegar and camphor."

Ignacio nodded. He took a noisy sip of coffee. In the distance the volcano rumbled. "The mountain has a lot to say." He accepted the tortilla Mercedes held out to him and topped it with a spoonful of beans, over which he sprinkled a pinch of salt. After a moment, he said, "Today we won't be picking."

"What!" Jacinta exclaimed.

"We won't be picking. That's all." Ignacio took a bite of tortilla.

Mercedes, too, was taken aback. Her husband had made a similar announcement only weeks earlier, after the Guardia had suppressed a demonstration at a coffee plantation in Ahuachapán. "Are they demonstrating at don Pedro's finca?" she asked, knowing that it was not a woman's place to question her man's decisions.

Ignacio finished his tortilla and took another sip of coffee. He wiped his mouth with the back of a hand. "I don't know anything about that." He knew plenty, of course, but it was not something to be discussed with a woman.

Mercedes readied a second tortilla and handed it to him. Overcoming her hesitation, she asked another question: "Are the others not picking today?" It was the compadre Goyo Ochoa whom she had in mind. And his wife, la comadre Pru. Their three sons, too.

"It's up to them to do what they will." Ignacio went to stand in the doorway, and the pig came to snort and root around his feet. The rooster and the hens joined the pig. They pecked at tiny pebbles peppering the ground. Even Tzi, who earlier had been given his tortilla, whined for more. "These animals should be fed," Ignacio said, kicking out at the pig. He motioned for Jacinta to start her chores, and then he took a spot beside the laurel.

Mercedes went out to sit on the bench under the tree. She waited until Jacinta was out of sight before speaking to Ignacio. There were questions to be raised, and she would risk her husband's anger and pose them. "Does Goyo Ochoa have anything to do with our not picking today?"

When Ignacio didn't answer, she questioned him again. "Does our not picking have something to do with the Federation of Workers?" She knew about Goyo's business, about the compadre's efforts to recruit men into the group that met secretly once a week. These men called each other by names that were not their own, and once, while she visited Pru, la comadre, she heard a man call Goyo "camarada."

Ignacio remained silent. He preferred silence to explanations, not that he had any explaining to do.

"Have you joined Goyo's men? Have you gone to their meetings?"

Ignacio let out a burst of air to show exasperation. He dropped down on his haunches, his back against the tree trunk. He picked up a stick that was close by and scratched at the dirt between his feet with it. He decided to say a little something to put an end to the interrogation. "I haven't joined Goyo's men. I haven't gone to any meetings."

"But Goyo comes over frequently to get you to join. Forgive me, husband, but I have heard him ask you this."

"Goyo comes to ask, and the priest comes to say I must not join, but I do what I wish to do."

It was true about the priest. El padre had come on more than one occasion to caution them against the band of godless ones that sought to disrupt the tranquility of their lives.

"Goyo Ochoa is a communist," the priest had said on one of his visits. "As one, he shall lose the kingdom of heaven, for he is an unbeliever and a heretic and the fires of hell will be his punishment." El padre Castillo's face flushed with vehemence. His jowls flapped a little as he spoke.

To show respect, Mercedes had lowered her gaze, but the priest's words confused her. Goyo was not an unbeliever. Mercedes and Ignacio had known Goyo and Pru for twenty-five years, and the compadres believed, as she and Ignacio did, in the gods of their people. In Xipetotec, the god of corn. In Tláloc, the god of rain. In Tzultacah, the god of the earth.

"You must not heed Goyo Ochoa's words, Mercedes Prieto," the priest had continued. "You must listen to me, for I am the representative of the one true God." She knew this God, the one called Jesus. She knew that many of her people now believed in him, too, but Mercedes could not rest all her faith in Christianity. She listened to el padre Castillo, and she agreed that you must love Jesus because he loved so much more in return. But Mercedes still prayed to the gods of her people. If Jesus was compassionate, he would not let her risk angering her gods through inattention.

Next to the rock wall, Tzi began to bark. Up the road, Goyo Ochoa came this way. "See what I mean," Mercedes said, pointing toward him. "Here comes el compadre."

Ignacio drew himself up from beside the tree and went into the hut. Soon he came out again, his hat on his head, his machete hilt strapped to his waist.

Goyo Ochoa had a machete, too. As he neared, it bumped against his leg. When he reached the hut, he raised a hand to his sombrero in greeting. Mercedes nodded. "Buenos días, compadre," she said. And so it begins, she thought.

In the hut, Tino started bawling. Mercedes gave a sigh and went to him. When she laid him down earlier, she had swaddled him in a blanket square, but he had kicked the blanket loose. Now one foot had wormed its way through the hammock netting. As he struggled to free it, he coughed a dry, hacking cough that darkened and contorted his face. Mercedes quickly worked his foot free. She picked him up and placed him over her shoulder, rubbing circles against his back. "Ya, ya, mi niño," she murmured, her mouth on his cheek.

He smelled warm and smoky like the inside of the hut. There was also about him the pungent smell of the poultice she had spread on his chest late in the night. She stood in the dusky light, soothing and stroking him, and soon his coughing stopped. She wrapped him back up and took him out under the laurel, where she offered him a breast. While he nursed, he gazed into her eyes, his expression deliberate and grave. He had a shock of black hair that stood out in all directions, and were he not so somber-faced, he might have looked comical. She softly traced the birthmark that stained his right ear. Who could explain such damage? For nine months, she had made a wide path around the deformed, for it was well known that a woman with child placed her baby at risk if she let her eyes rest too long on the lame. For nine months, she had not directly breathed in the harmful air of daybreak. And never, never had she allowed those cursed with the evil eye to gaze upon her. Not knowingly, of course. Still, she knew the old belief: El sol pone, la luna quita. The sun adds, the moon subtracts. And so it must have been the sun that had marked her little child.

A few meters away, the men talked beside the rock wall, each looking off down the road. Mercedes kept her eyes on her son, her ears strained toward the men's conversation.

"So what do you think?" Goyo was saying.

"I don't know," Ignacio replied.

"You have to decide, hombre. Tonight we strike. At midnight we take military barracks, police stands, and guardia stands. Tonight we strike out against all oppressors."

"I don't know, compadre," Ignacio said. "Everywhere you turn, there's the guardia. It's as if they're waiting for rebellion to start. Look at Farabundo Martí. Already he's been captured. If they can take el líder, just think what they'll do with the rest of us."

"We mustn't let our leader down, compadre. We must strike out in the name of Farabundo Martí."

Mercedes looked quickly up to see Ignacio shake his head.

Goyo went on, "Don't you want to keep your rancho? Your milpa?"

Ignacio said, "I have kept them all these years. When others sold their plots of land, I held on to mine."

"I tell you, compadre, it'll not be yours for long. You know these bastard landowners. They offer a pittance for the land of our ancestors. Or they take our land by force."

"I'll never sell my land. I won't allow anyone to take it."

Mercedes noted the strength in Ignacio's voice. The land he owned, it was not much, but it was all he possessed: a parcel of earth stretching over rocks and pebbles, the small plot on which he'd built their hut.

"You're a fool to think so, compadre," Goyo said. "I tell you, you should have joined the federation. If you'd come to the meetings, you would know the truth—how land is taken, how we're all fools for picking coffee for mere centavos a day."

"I've told you before. I don't want to involve myself in politics."

Oh yes, Mercedes thought.

Goyo said, "This is not a matter of politics. It's a matter of survival. It's a matter of keeping your land, of living your life like a human being. Look at your woman. Doesn't she deserve more than she has? And what about your boy? Doesn't he deserve to have a future? No, hombre, this is about survival."

"What's planned is dangerous," Ignacio said.

"What we gain tonight is worth any danger we face. Come to my place after nightfall, compadre. What do you say?"

At the question, Mercedes looked toward the men. Ignacio had his back to her. She watched his hand tap a slow rhythm against the wall, and for a moment this gave her hope. But then he dropped his hand to his side, and the gesture crumbled the barricade she'd piled up inside her against the door of inevitability. It's no use, she thought. In this world, fate always has its way. She stiffened, waiting to hear her man's reply.

"I'll go," he said after a moment. "I'll do it for my family."

Under the tree, Mercedes fingered the three red agates threaded on the jute cord circling her son's neck. The stones bestowed health and longevity. For added power, they had been blessed by el cacique, don Feliciano. Each of her children had possessed similar amulets. In her forty years, Mercedes had been with child nine times. Of the babies, only Jacinta and Tino remained.

Goyo Ochoa tipped his hat to his neighbor and went back down the path again. Ignacio walked over to his son, who stopped nursing when his father bent over him. Tino furrowed his brow in concentrated study of his father's face. For an instant, Ignacio rested the curve of a brown finger against his son's cheek. "He will be a serious man," Ignacio pronounced. He straightened up. "I'll go check on Jacinta's progress with the animals."

Mercedes watched him go off toward the field. Is there a special stone to keep a family safe? she asked herself.

Mercedes settled herself on the straw petate that was all she possessed for a marriage bed. Tino was logy from nursing, and she placed him facedown on her stomach. She softly patted his behind. Looking around, she took inventory of her belongings: the chair that had been her mother's favorite resting spot when she was alive, the table that Ignacio's mother had given them before she died. Against a hut wall, near the door, was her grandest possession, the dresser Ignacio had made from scraps of wood he'd gathered from don Pedro's coffee finca. The dresser had three drawers, each made from different woods. On the dresser top was the oval hand mirror with the pearly handle Ignacio had given her on their wedding day. Also on the dresser was the tall votive candle she always kept lit. It cast a glow over a portrait of the Mother of God, on the row of small frames lined against the dresser back. Ignacio had made the frames himself. Each contained locks of hair she'd snipped from her dead babies' heads.

Mercedes struggled to comprehend the portent of the conversation she'd overheard. What would she do if she lost her husband? She laid her sleeping baby down on the mat and went to sit on her mother's chair. Sometimes, when life was hard—and life was often hard—she sat in the chair and willed the spirit of her ancestors to come. "What should I do, Mamá?" she asked the shadows in the room. Because her mother never failed her, a hint of a plan began to form itself in Mercedes's mind. She saw herself wrapping Tino tightly in banana leaves just as she had wrapped Ignacio the time he was so sick. He had needed a cleansing sweat to cure him then, and the banana leaves had done it. A small grove of trees stood halfway between her hut and la comadre's. If Mercedes hurried, she could gather the leaves she needed before her family returned. A machete was hanging by its leather thong on a nail by the door. She took the knife down, glancing quickly at Tino to make sure he was sleeping. She left the hut propelled by the insight her mother's spirit had clearly shown her: If Tino broke out into a fever, if his cough became worse before it got better, Tino would keep his father home tonight.

▼▼

CHAPTER THREE

By the light of the moon, Ignacio Prieto made his way along the mat of tangled grass lining the riverbank. In the distance, el Izalco rumbled. Throughout the day, the volcano had thrown off a cloud of ash that now lay like a gray shroud over the countryside. Ignacio listened to the volcano, for its thunderous voice bolstered him and eased his anxiety. Tino was burning up with fever. Each time his boy coughed, his body convulsed. Back in the hut, Mercedes and Jacinta had concocted first this new poultice and then another. When all the remedies brought no relief, Ignacio knew he must renege on his promise to el compadre and hasten to don Pedro instead. Ignacio's family had picked coffee for don Pedro for many years. El patrón had medicine. El patrón would certainly help them.

Ignacio reached the slope that led to the road he would soon have to cross. He scrambled up the slope, twigs and bracken crackling under his weight. When he reached the top, he lay on his belly, peering down the road in both directions. Goyo Ochoa came into his mind again. Ignacio pictured the knot of men Goyo must be leading into Izalco. Ignacio imagined their machetes waving furiously above them; he saw them rushing toward the plaza, stopping in sudden silence at the doors of the garrison that would surely be shut against them. Ignacio himself was on a mission clearly as ur-

17

gent. In his heart he knew that his hope for a better future lay with the child he sought aid for tonight. Sometime back he had told Goyo that a man could better raise himself if he had sons to help him do it, but Goyo had scoffed at the idea. "Look at me," he had said. "I have three sons. In the end, that's three more mouths to feed. The trouble with you, compadre, is you dream too much. Dreams can be treacherous."

Ignacio scrambled up and hurried across the road. On the other side, he went down a lane lined by coffee trees. He kept under the trees, laying a reassuring hand on his machete now and then. After a time, he reached the entrance to don Pedro's coffee finca. Moonlight washed over the gates that were flung open as if beckoning him to enter. Although time was essential, he did not quickly start through the gates. He watched from the road for signs of guardias. Each season, don Pedro hired several pairs of them to keep order during picking time. Usually two men were posted at the gate as pickers arrived. Other guardias customarily stationed themselves around the finca office ready to quell fights that sometimes broke out on payday. At this time of night, guardias could be anywhere, so Ignacio looked and listened before he darted past the gates and onto don Pedro's property.

His hand on his machete, Ignacio Prieto went down the gravel road that led to the main house. Walking along, he rehearsed what he might say to the patrón, groping for the words he would use to explain his presence out here in the night. "It is my sick son I come about," he would say, and the patrón, because he was a man who understood the worth of sons, would help him and his woman.

Up ahead the road ended in a group of wooden buildings that formed a buttress against don Pedro's house. Even at this late hour, lights blazed around it, illuminating these buildings and the big office attached to them. Ignacio stepped under a tree. He listened for unfamiliar sounds that might warn him of danger. But there was only the bark of a faraway dog and then the yelp of another joining in.

Abruptly, out of the corner of his eye, he caught a slight movement, but he was not immediately frightened, for it could have been the breeze playing on the leaves of the madrecacaos, or it could have been the skittering shadow a cloud casts upon the earth as it drifts across the face of the moon. It could have been these things and others of equal harmlessness, but still he unsheathed his machete, for only a fool was caught unprepared.

A new sound sprang up, one Ignacio quickly recognized: From somewhere on the road came the crunch of boots on gravel. La guardia, Ignacio thought. He edged closer to the tree trunk, tightening his grip on his weapon. It was then he felt the unmistakable jab of a rifle barrel against his back, then that he heard the exultant cry of victory erupting behind him. "¡Ajá! Look what we have here!"

Ignacio jerked his head around to get a better look. Where had the guardia come from? Had he been perched in the tree above him? From the road came the sound of running, and soon another guardia covered him.

"Turn," the one ordered. "Drop the machete."

Ignacio turned slowly, but he held on to his weapon. An indio without his machete might just as well be dead.

"Drop it," the other one barked. He swung out with his rifle butt, catching Ignacio's wrist, sending the big knife flying out of his grasp. Ignacio's hat dropped to the ground also, and one of the men stepped on the hat, crushing it under his heel. A searing pain flowered at Ignacio's wrist. He could feel his hand begin to swell.

Using their rifles, the men prodded Ignacio out from under the tree and into the road. One of them spun him around, and wrenching his arms behind his back, the man tied Ignacio's thumbs together with a length of henequen. The agony in his injured hand was severe, and soon his thumbs, swelling quickly against their restraint, felt thick and hot.

"Movete, hij'ueputa," one man spit out. "Indios de mierda," the other one said. The two taunted and nudged Ignacio up the road, past buildings and the office and into the sprawling courtyard surrounding don Pedro's house. El patrón himself stood on the porch that girdled the house. He held a revolver in his hand.

"What is it?" don Pedro yelled when the three came up. El patrón was large, middle-aged, and corpulent. He took by twos the wide steps that led from the porch. A sleek, black dog came bounding after him.

"We found this pendejo, patrón. He was hiding under a madrecacao. God knows how many more are with him."

What? Ignacio thought. Because his arms were tied behind him, he tossed his head to make his point. "No, no, patrón," he said. "There is only me. Sólo yo, patrón."

"What is your name?" don Pedro asked.

"Ignacio Prieto. A sus órdenes, patrón."

"Are you a picker? Do you work for me?"

"Sí, patrón. I have picked for you for ten years." The length of his service surely gave him the right to be heard out. Ignacio thought of his woman and his daughter, how both had worked beside him for almost as long.

"My family has also picked for you," Ignacio added, hoping to add weight to facts that might aid him.

"Why are you here?" Don Pedro held his revolver against his thigh. "Why are you out at such a late hour?" Don Pedro's eyes narrowed. For days there had been alarming reports coming from the capital. The wires were filled with news of imminent rebellion. Though Farabundo Martí had been captured, and President Martínez had ordered a roundup of all known radicals, the rebellious indios were assembling. Was this hijo de puta one of them?

Ignacio felt his blood rush in warning. The volcano spoke again: *Choose your words carefully, Ignacio Prieto, lest you be misunderstood.*

"It's my son I come about. Mi niñito, Justino Prieto. The child has the cough. He needs medicine."

"If there's truth in what you say," don Pedro said, "why not go into Izalco? There's a curandera in Izalco." As though to mark the rhythm of his thoughts, el patrón slapped the revolver against the side of his trousers.

Ignacio looked down at his bare feet. He could not answer these questions. How could he admit that it was a rebellion that had kept him from town? He could not say these things, and though he knew his silence would somehow be used against him, he said no more.

From somewhere behind the house, a volley of rifle fire erupted and Ignacio ducked instinctively. Don Pedro raised his revolver and jabbed at the air with it. "¡Hombres!" he yelled. "Go to the back. I'll keep this indio covered here."

The two guardias ran off, their rifles at their chests. Don Pedro's black dog ran after them. Soon all three disappeared around the corner of the house.

Left behind, Ignacio trained his eyes on the revolver pointed at him. "Patrón," Ignacio said, because it was time to speak out. "My being here, it's not what you think. I have come for my son. Tino is very small, and now he's very sick. But with your help, patrón, my boy will get well. Thanks to you he will grow, and one day he'll be big. Big enough to pick for you, patrón." Ignacio watched a cord of muscle tighten along the side of don Pedro's face, and he knew it was no use. It had come to this: For ten years Ignacio and his family had picked the coffee that had made don Pedro rich, and it was all for nothing. In the end, a decade of servitude would not buy him even a moment of mercy.

New shots reverberated. Shouting sprang up, too. The night was filled with the frenzied barking of dogs.

A voice called from beyond the house. "Patrón, come quick." Another voice, this one huskier than the first, yelled, "We have more indios, patrón."

Don Pedro leaped across the space that separated him from Ignacio. "I knew it!" he exclaimed. "For weeks Martínez has been warning us of revolt. Well, el presidente was right." He wheeled Ignacio around, propelling him in the direction from which the shouts had come.

Ignacio found it hard to keep his balance, pushed as he was, his arms secured behind his back. He rounded the side of the house, hearing don Pedro's ragged breathing behind him. Goyo Ochoa's words came suddenly to mind. *Tonight we will strike out against all oppressors.* Ignacio understood it all now. Groups of men had headed for the town's garrison while others had taken their rage to the homes of the rich themselves. He looked frantically about, searching for an avenue of escape, but there was none. Up ahead, in the glare of lights perched high above the courtyard, three guardias circled a band of four men. Four men dressed in Indian clothing. Pipil Indians come to revolt.

When they were almost upon the group, don Pedro threw an arm around Ignacio's throat, bringing him up short a meter or two from the others. The sour odor of el patrón's sweat assailed Ignacio's nostrils. He tried swallowing the stench away, but don Pedro's stranglehold kept him from it.

The guardia with the husky voice said, "There were others, patrón, but we drove them off." He gave his rifle a quick forward jab as if demonstrating the way in which he'd repelled the rest.

"¡Hij'ueputa!" el patrón cried, his mouth close to Ignacio's ear. "You let the others get away. How many more of them were there?"

The guardia did not answer don Pedro's question. Instead, he ran his hand up and down the slender barrel of his rifle.

With a grunt, el patrón shoved Ignacio into one of the men the guardia was covering. The man reached out for Ignacio, keeping him from tumbling to the ground.

"You indios are all alike!" don Pedro bellowed. "You're not to be trusted. Look at you; you're nothing but ingrates. I give you work. I feed you, and this is how you repay me?" Don Pedro gestured wildly; sweat stained large circles under his arms.

"They are murderers, too, patrón," said a guardia who had a droopy mustache and wide-set eyes. "One of these savages killed Tomás." He pointed to the edge of the yard where the gravel ended and where the grass and low brush began to rise. As if pinned in place by the harsh light flooding the courtyard, the body of a guardia lay there, his head cleaved neatly down the middle by a single blow from a machete.

Ignacio turned his eyes away. He looked at the men around him. They had been stripped of their weapons, and these were piled on the ground nearby. Ignacio recognized the men. They were all pickers who worked here on don Pedro's plantation. The one named Chema had been wounded. Chema's face was gray and he was shirtless. He had laced his hands over his stomach as if to keep his entrails from spilling. Blood seeped between his fingers. It stained the front of his trousers a brilliant red. Another man held Chema up. He seemed unaware that his own trousers were soaking up Chema's blood.

Ignacio looked to these indios who did not cry out, and their valor lessened his fear. He was with his own people now. He was buoyed by them and by the hatred for the enemy that shone in their eyes.

The dogs had stopped barking. A few stretched out, yawning because of the hour.

"What should we do with them?" a guardia asked. He kicked at a dog who sniffed at the canvas legging covering his calf.

Don Pedro looked around the courtyard. "Flores," he said, "take them to the office. Lock them up in there."

Flores, the guardia with the mustache, clicked his heels together. "Sí, patrón. As you say."

Don Pedro tucked his revolver into his waistband. "I'm going in to call the garrison," he said. He strode to the back of the house and disappeared inside.

Silence fell over the yard. In the lull, Ignacio heard the volcano thunder. This time the mountain had no words for him.

"Vámonos," Flores ordered. "You will march to the office."

Prodded into a line, the five men trudged onto the grass, past the slain guardia's body. They tramped the distance between the yard and the stretch of buildings Ignacio had passed earlier. Guardias marched at the side of the column, shouting insults and jabbing shoulders and buttocks with their rifles. The dogs tagged along, too, and because they were dogs and did not know any better, they trotted merrily as if they were on an outing. When the group reached the office, the guardias ordered them to stop.

Flores spoke up. "Tonight you indios have forgotten your place. This error will cost you." He walked slowly in front of the men, pausing to look at one and then another as he spoke. "One of you killed a guardia tonight. This will not be tolerated."

Flores stopped in front of the man with the wound in his belly. "Although it was you who killed Tomás, it will not be you who pays, for you'll be dead soon enough."

Flores continued down the line until he stood in front of Ignacio. "I think it will be this man who pays." He grasped Ignacio's shoulder and jerked him out of line.

Flores's hand was a brand on Ignacio's shoulder.

"I picked this man because picking him made no sense," Flores said. "Senselessness begets senselessness, and one of you was senseless tonight."

The image of Tino swam hazily at the forefront of Ignacio's mind. "I have a son," Ignacio said. "His name is Justino."

"Kneel," Flores commanded.

Ignacio slowly knelt upon the earth and the earth felt cool against his legs even through the fabric of his trousers. He bent his body toward the earth so his forehead rested finally upon it. Tzultacah, he thought, god of the earth, you are with me now as you have always been. In your mercy protect my women and in your goodness grant that my son will cherish and work your soil as I have done.

Ignacio Prieto, indio pipil, willed his mind to draw itself back into that place where nothing could reach it. "Justino," Ignacio said, speaking against the earth his son's name even as the rifle barrel dug into his neck. Even as the very air exploded around him.

▼▼

CHAPTER FOUR

In the glow of the candles burning in the hut, Mercedes sat in her mother's chair and kept watch over Tino bundled in his crib at her feet. In the three or so hours since Ignacio had left, Tino had gone from bad to worse, and now he'd taken another turn, this one for the better. Minutes earlier he'd been in her arms, and he'd thrown up a ball of phlegm and sour milk. Now his fever seemed to be breaking. His eyes were dazed as he looked up at her. Mercedes was wet from his perspiration. Her tapado reeked of vomit.

"Jacinta, fetch me a little water from the jug," Mercedes said, lifting the shawl away from herself. Jacinta was crouched beside the crib. Next to the doorway, Tzi began to growl. Mercedes looked out the doorway into the night.

"Papá's come back!" Jacinta said, her face brightening. She jumped up. "I'll go meet him."

"Gracias a Dios," Mercedes said, weak with relief.

Tzi's wagging tail beckoned Jacinta down the path to the road. She made her way through settling volcano ash. Ahead, the dog reached the crossroad, his tail tucked in a half circle between his bony legs. From somewhere the slightest noise came. Papá? Is that you? Jacinta thought. She could not say what kept her from voicing this, or what impelled her to spring off the path and take cover in the brush. She peeked out through the brambles.

A few meters away, two guardias moved stealthily up the road in her direction. The men were two long shadows, but their rifles were well-defined and each man held his at the ready. Tzi went stiff at the sight of the men. A low growl rumbled in his throat before he yapped and lunged. The dog caught one man unaware, but the guardia quickly recovered. He batted the dog away with his rifle butt. There was a dull crack as wood met bone; then the dog collapsed onto the road. The second guardia took aim and emptied a shot into Tzi. The blast lifted the dog off the road before he dropped in a heap back down again.

Jacinta darted toward home, staying low behind the poinsettia hedge, fully expecting to be cut down. She was breathless when she reached the hut. Her mother stood framed in the doorway. She had strapped Tino to her chest with her tapado.

"Mamá, la guardia! They killed Tzi."

Mercedes slumped against the doorway, her face crumpling.

Jacinta took her mother's arm and pulled her into the yard. "Vámonos, Mamá, or they'll kill us, too," she ordered, knowing that at this time she must be strong enough for both of them.

Mercedes, with Tino close against her, and Jacinta crouched behind a patch of saw grass a short distance from the hut. The two guardias were fifty meters or so away. "Salgan de allí," one of them yelled. "Come out of there, indios comunistas." Rifle fire peppered the shack.

The rifle volleys caused Tino to cry softly. "Keep him quiet," Jacinta whispered fiercely, wild with the thought the baby would give them away. Mercedes jiggled and patted him.

"Come," Jacinta said, and they went off again, keeping low to the ground until they came to the arroyo. Dropping down into it, the two looked homeward over the berm of the riverbed. A spark flashed. An instant later, the hut was burning. The fire crackled and crept up the sides of the hut until the flames reached the top before they leaped to catch the laurel tree. Mercedes watched the laurel leaves shudder and then curl up in the heat. She watched her little kitchen collapse; she watched her hut as it seemed to sigh and then fall in upon itself. She watched her world burning up: Tino's crib, her mother's chair, the hand mirror that had captured her image, the babies' coils of hair.

The guardias charged the edge of the saw grass. "Those indios must be somewhere," one of them said. "They're probably out there in the brush."

"Let's go," Jacinta ordered.

"No," Mercedes said. She could not leave this place. Across the field the billowing smoke filled the night with the scent of all her days.

"We have to go," Jacinta said, pulling Mercedes and Tino down the length of the arroyo.

"Where?" Mercedes gasped.

"To la comadre's."

Mercedes allowed herself to be led, for she had no strength to resist. As they fled, she looked back only once, and running on, she thought that she had seen, in the plume of smoke spiraling from the hut, the face of Ignacio rising.

When they reach Pru's hut, Mercedes dropped down on a bench under a tree while Jacinta hurried to the doorway of the hut and called out for la comadre. No answer came from the dark interior. "Where is everybody?" Jacinta said after a moment. Antonio! she wanted to cry. ¿Donde estás, Antonio?

Mercedes could not even muster a reaction to Jacinta's question. She opened her tapado and inspected her son in the moonlight. Because she'd had no time to wrap him, Tino lay naked against her. His skin was cooler now than it had been. He was awake and he frowned up at her as if asking for an explanation of the chaos around him. Mercedes lifted her blouse and poked a nipple into Tino's mouth, the only thing she had to offer. The baby suckled for a moment, but then he fell asleep.

"Mamá," Jacinta said, "here comes someone." For an instant Jacinta thought her heart would stop at the sight of the shadowy bundles coming toward her. When she recognized la comadre and the children, she was flooded with relief. Then she thought, But where's Antonio?

"It's me," Pru said, going up to Mercedes. Two little ones huddled next to their mother. The smallest rubbed sleep out of his eyes.

"Ay, comadre," Mercedes said. "La guardia. They burned everything. Everything's gone."

"They killed Tzi," Jacinta said.

Pru nodded. "I heard the shots. We were hiding in the ravine." She thrust her chin in the direction where they had been. "I saw the fire light the sky."

"The boy's been sick. Last night Ignacio went to don Pedro's for medicine." She said no more, for what else was there to say?

"It'll soon be morning," Pru said, her face no longer a shadow. In the light of the dawn, she looked almost youthful with her braids crisscrossed over the top of her head. "Goyo and Antonio left last night. Tiburcio Leonidas came to get them. Tiburcio killed a guardia. He cut off the guardia's head with his machete."

So there it was. Had only a day passed since the trip to the stream?

Tino began to fidget, and soon he wet himself. "Ay, el niño se meó," Mercedes said, unwrapping him from the tapado. Urine soaked hot through her skirt.

"Here, let me have him." Pru plucked Tino from Mercedes's lap. "Comadre, you go down to the river and wash yourself off. Jacinta, take your mother down there." Pru held Tino upright against her shoulder. "Manolo, go inside and get a blanket for the baby."

Mercedes stood. "No, let me have him. I'm just a little wet, that's all."

"You're more than wet, Mamá," Jacinta said. "There's vomit on your shawl. Come, I'll walk you to the stream. It's only a minute away." She took her mother's arm.

"When you get back, we'll leave," Pru said. "Goyo told me I should take the boys away if he and Antonio hadn't returned by morning."

"But what about Papá?" Jacinta said. She looked past the clearing as if her father might be stepping into the yard.

"Your father will take care of himself," Mercedes said. "If he were here, he would want us all to go." These words were difficult to voice. Her husband was gone. He would not be back. She had seen his face rise up to the heavens.

"Where will we go?" Jacinta asked. How could they leave with her father and Antonio still gone? It wasn't right to leave here.

"We'll go to my sister Chenta Gómez's place in El Congo," Pru said. "It's to the north. Past the volcano. Past the lake of Coatepeque. When this is over, Goyo will find us there."

"Vaya, Mamá," Jacinta said, prodding her mother in the direction of the river.

Reluctantly, Mercedes yielded to reason. She leaned against her daughter's shoulder.

Together the two struggled off toward the stream.

▼▼

CHAPTER FIVE

T he two guardias turned off the road and started down a trail that was certain to lead to another hut. Dawn was not far off. In the weak light, volcano ash was a charcoal carpet around them.

"This time let's get some indios," said Flores, the one with the hardened eyes. Earlier, the two had set fire to a hut and it had infuriated Flores that the hut was empty, that no indios had fallen under his rifle blasts. Rolando Morales had learned not to cross his partner. When he's enraged, I wouldn't care to be on the other side of his rifle barrel, Rolando thought.

It had been a long and exhausting day. In the afternoon, they had found the headless corpse of a fellow guardia. The body was hidden in a cave, but the stench had given it away. The smell still lingered in Rolando's nostrils, so he stopped and placed a finger against the side of his nose and blew out heartily. He repeated the procedure with the other nostril and then he hurried to catch up. Later, when the sun was high, he and Flores would return for the body and search for the head. This was not a thrilling notion. Still, despite the unpleasantness that sometimes accompanied his job, Rolando Morales was proud to be part of those who brought peace to the countryside. Each morning, as he slipped the leather puttees over

his calves and donned his riding breeches, a feeling of importance
and power were renewed in him. Each morning, when his woman
handed him his khaki tunic with its shiny brass buttons, her eyes
gleamed, for she, too, felt the pride that comes with being the wife
of a guardia nacional.

"I think we're in luck," Flores whispered. In the pale morning
light, a hut showed itself up ahead. A voice came from somewhere
beyond it.

Flores laid a finger over his lips. "We'll surprise them," he said
under his breath. "You go right. I'll go left."

Rolando Morales, his rifle at the ready, circled the hut just as
his partner came around the other side of it. A solitary tree stood
in the clearing. A large woman with braids atop her head was under
the tree. She held a bundle to her breast. The woman turned, and
even though she was in shadow, Rolando Morales saw her eyes
widen. She raised one hand as if to drive them back. "No," she said.
Only that.

A rush of sound came from the hut. Flores whirled and fired a
volley of shots into the doorway.

The woman lunged. "¡Mis hijos!" she cried. Then, as if something forgotten was remembered, she turned and started to run.

Rolando Morales squeezed the trigger of his rifle.

For a fleeting moment there was no sign of the bullet's impact,
but then the woman's head jerked forward and she swayed. Her
knees buckled. She pitched forward, landing a few meters beyond
the tree.

Somewhere a child wailed.

"¡Puta!" Flores said. "There's more of them in there." He sprang
into the hut, firing wildly as he went. The odor of gunpowder filled
the air.

The morning went quiet, but Rolando Morales stood his
ground. He would fire in the direction of any new sound.

Flores came out of the hut. "Two boys were in there. They'll not
grow up to own machetes." He cleared his throat and then spat on
the ground. With two quick strokes, he smoothed the ends of his
mustache.

A child wailed again.

The two guardias looked at each other.

"The sound's coming from there," Flores said, pointing to the woman. The two crossed to the spot where she lay.

With a boot, Rolando Morales nudged the woman onto her back. The bullet had entered the base of her skull. As it exited, it had taken with it her throat and a portion of her jaw. There was a baby under the woman. The baby cried fiercely.

"Looks like we found us a very young communist," Flores chuckled. "It's a boy." He poked the tiny penis with the tip of his rifle barrel. The baby wailed more loudly.

"What shall we do with him?" Rolando Morales asked.

Flores said, "Kill him."

Rolando Morales's conscience gave a tug. In his mind he saw his woman who, a few months before, had given birth to his first son. The child had looked remarkably like this one: the same round face, the squat nose, the same shock of coarse black hair. "No," Rolando said, because something came over him that forced him to say it.

"Even the smallest traitors should be eliminated," Flores said.

Rolando Morales shook his head. "Not this one. This one I'll take to my woman. Only weeks ago, she lost a child. She will raise this one to be a guardia, a great guardia like the two of us."

Flores said nothing. He slid his rifle barrel up the baby's torso until it rested against the temple of his little head.

"You're a fool to want him," Flores said. Abruptly he jerked the rifle back upon his shoulder. "Let's get out of this pigsty. I need to get some sleep."

▼▼

CHAPTER SIX

Mercedes and Jacinta stumbled over a path that wound around the madrecacaos growing in one of the region's many coffee fincas. Though the day was warm, Mercedes was chilled. She felt disembodied as she moved under the trees. Her boy was missing, and nothing she had ever experienced prepared her for the anguish of it. She had lived with death, and she had lived with the bleakness that accompanied living, but not knowing where her son was, not knowing his condition, brought her a pain so weighty there were no tears, no gestures to express it.

The horror of the past night would never leave her. If she lived twice-over the years she had already endured, the sound of rifle shots would still reverberate in her ears. She had run all the way back from the river. Dashing into the clearing of Pru's hut, she had stumbled upon the sight of la comadre's body, of the bloodied bodies of Pru's children. But what of her own son? Where was he in all the carnage?

She had searched for her Tino. For hours, she and Jacinta had picked their way through the scrub and trails surrounding Pru's hut. So certain was Mercedes that at each new bend they'd discover Tino's body, that a scream lay waiting in her throat. But alive or dead, she had not found her son.

At Jacinta's insistence, they were moving now in a northerly direction, toward El Congo, the place where Pru's sister lived. The volcano was their guide. Izalco was a gray-black cone, its sides devoid of vegetation. It was a barren sight that mirrored Mercedes's own desolation. Though she placed one foot ahead of the other, she felt herself fading by slow degrees. Perhaps in an hour or two, somewhere along a trail, she would simply cease to exist.

Mercedes looked at her daughter trudging beside her. Jacinta's cheeks were smudged with dirt and tears. Strands of hair escaped the confines of her braids and stood in wisps about her face.

Jacinta stopped short. "Listen," she said. They were at a spot where bracken and brushwood grew densely among the madrecacao and coffee trees. Jacinta pulled Mercedes under a sheltering canopy of undergrowth. No sooner were they out of sight when two guardias tramped by. Mercedes placed an arm around Jacinta as if to anchor herself. She wanted to burst from their hiding place and run out onto the path. Where is my son? she would scream out to the men. Who has taken him and why? That the guardia would surely fire did not frighten her. If she were alone, she would welcome their bullets.

"Let's try to sleep," Jacinta said. "Too many guardias are out for us to travel now." She said this for her mother's sake. She herself must stay awake, remain alert to the dangers around them. Before the massacre at Pru's hut, she had been staunch in the belief they must not abandon their land, but the crack of rifle fire, the sight of what rifle fire can do, changed everything. Though she had not seen them killed, she knew with a certainty she could never explain that her father and don Goyo and even Antonio were now gone. Her brother, Tino? His disappearance was a mystery, but she could live with this mystery if they got far enough away. She must survive so she might return again to solve it.

Half dozing, the two nestled against each other until late afternoon. As daylight weakened, they came out from under the trees and continued on, walking warily lest they give themselves away. At the end of the trail, they climbed a steep slope to the shoulder of a road, grasping clumps of grass to pull themselves up. Nettles stung Mercedes's legs. The jagged ends of dried twigs cut into her arms and feet.

At the side of the road, they dropped down behind a thick growth of teasel. Mercedes rested her cheek against the ground. She could go no farther. If only she could sink into the earth until it covered her. As if to oblige, the earth began to tremble. A tremor traveled the length of Mercedes's body. Jacinta felt it, too, and she opened her mouth in alarm. The rumble became a roar as three trucks rolled by. In the back of each truck, a crowd of armed soldiers stood jammed together. The trucks flung gravel from under their wheels, and Mercedes quickly covered her head with her tapado. She reached to shield Jacinta from the debris pelting them. Dust rolled in from the road. The two choked and sputtered as it washed over them.

"It's the army," Jacinta said when the trucks had passed. "As if the guardia weren't enough, now the army's out." They darted across the road, scrambling down a slope steeper than the one they had just climbed. Mercedes felt the ground give way, and she slid down the incline. Jacinta tumbled alongside her. They lay without moving for a few seconds just short of a barbed wire fence. "Are you hurt, Mamá?" Jacinta asked.

Mercedes shook her head. Her breath was ragged in her throat. Something heavier than blood coursed through her veins. "No puedo más, hija. I can't go on."

Jacinta nodded. Beyond the fence stretched a pasture. On the pasture there was a corral and a small stable. "Look," she said, pointing to it. "A place to rest."

The madness that had come over the world was thankfully absent from the stable. Here, there was the sweet odor of hay and the pungency of manure. Here, the waning sun spilled through the wall slats and lined up in stripes across the wooden stalls. They had entered the place stealthily, grateful to see that it was empty. They were crossing toward one of the stalls when something rustled in a corner. Mercedes stiffened, praying the sound was only scuttling mice.

A woman's head popped up from over the side of a stall.

Mercedes took a step back.

"Don't be frightened," the woman said, coming out into the

open. "I'm Rufina Fermín. We saw you come in." She spoke in Nahuatl. "My husband and son are with me." The woman pointed behind her, and the rest of her family rose into view.

There was Vicente Fermín, the woman's husband. He plucked off his hat and gave Mercedes a nod. He had a machete at his side. It was reassuring, Mercedes thought, to be with a man who had a weapon. And there was Basilio, their son, an eleven-year-old boy with narrow shoulders. He muttered, "Buenas," and did not take off his hat when he said it. His mother made a disapproving cluck and poked him into a proper greeting.

"It'll soon be dark," Rufina said. At her invitation, Mercedes and Jacinta went to a water spout that, while it produced only a tepid trickle, refreshed them nonetheless. They washed their hands and faces, then drank from cupped hands. Soon they were settled in the stall with the best view of the stable door. Vicente took the front position the better to keep a watch on any visitors. Rufina unwrapped the end of her shawl and produced two tortillas. She tore them up and handed them around. Mercedes tried to eat her little meal, but it tasted like dust. Her breasts cramped and leaked with the need for her baby to suckle them. She handed the tortilla wedge to her daughter. "You have to eat, Mamá," Jacinta said, handing it back.

Mercedes slumped against Jacinta's shoulder. The others exchanged stories, but all Mercedes could do was cup a breast under her tapado. She tried to focus on what the group said and not on the image of her baby, out there in the night somewhere, whimpering for the milk seeping warm between her fingers.

Rufina and her family were from Nahuizalco, she said. This was across the river an hour or so away from Izalco. To the northwest, the village of Juayua had been taken, the woman added. Vicente told how bands of rebellious workers had burned the guardia garrison, the town hall, the telegraph station. Hearing the news and fearing repercussions, most of the townspeople had fled, he said. Some had hidden in ravines and caves, the boy pointed out. Vicente said, "But there are others like us who are heading farther away."

The group spoke in hushed tones about the peril in their lives and the meagerness of their future. Their talk bound them together, and they decided to join forces. Because they were exhausted, they would stay here until dawn. It was as safe a place as any, Vicente said. There were no animals in sight outside. No chance someone would be leading them in for the night. In the morning, they would leave the stable. Starting tomorrow, they would seek shelter under trees by day and travel only at night. And they would go to El Congo. Vicente Fermín knew the route. They would go around the village of Tunamiles, past the volcano, and then on to Lake Coatepeque. Once at the lake, El Congo was very near, Vicente said.

"I'm going back," Mercedes said, speaking for the first time since the conversation had started.

Jacinta gave a start. "What are you saying, Mamá!"

"In the morning, I'm going back. I have to find Tino." Mercedes's breasts had stopped cramping. The top of her dress was soaked through and cooling.

"If you go back, then I'll go back," Jacinta said.

Vicente Fermín held up a hand. "Un momento. The chance of survival is slim if you go back. Are you sure you want to put your daughter in that kind of danger?"

"But my Tino . . . ," Mercedes said, and her words trailed off.

Jacinta reached an arm around her mother's shoulders. It was she who told about Justino and how it was that her brother came to be missing.

"All the more reason not to go back," Vicente said after Jacinta had spoken. "If you go back, you not only put yourself in danger, but you put your son in danger, too." Vicente shook his head. "No. These are terrible times. Let the danger pass; then you can go back and look for your son."

To Mercedes, it was as if Ignacio himself had spoken. She looked more closely at Vicente, but in the gloom that had settled around them, all she could make out was a shadow with a hat.

"When it's time," Jacinta said, "I'll go back with you, Mamá. Together, we'll find our baby." When she said this, fear pinwheeled in her stomach. She pulled her mother closer.

"Maybe you're right," Mercedes said, patting Jacinta's hand lying on her shoulder. Fatigue had permeated Mercedes's bones so that lifting an arm seemed too great an effort. She dropped her arm onto her lap and leaned heavily against the side of the stall.

"But now we have to sleep," Jacinta said, and her pronouncement caused the talk to die away. Mercedes curled up beside her daughter. She willed her mind to go blank, focusing on the slow, rhythmic breathing of those around her. At length, she, too, gave in to sleep.

Outside, the morning mist had nearly vanished. The sky was pink. The air was chilly and fresh smelling. As the group assembled, they stood at the door, silently looking out over the field they had to cross.

The pasture was wide and long and unfortunately free of scrub that might conceal them. A barbed wire fence surrounded it. To the left, past the fence, rose the high road over which the army trucks had traveled; to the right, beyond the section of fence, there lay the fringe of trees that would be their cover.

Vicente pushed his hat back from his forehead. He pointed to Mercedes and Jacinta. "You two go first," he said. "Basilio will go with you. Find a place through the fence; then we will come."

For a moment the boy hung back, but then his mother gave him a push. "Go," she said.

"Hurry," Vicente said. "Let's go before it gets too light."

Jacinta stepped out the door. She broke into a run and Mercedes followed. Over her shoulder, she heard Rufina speak to Basilio again. "Go on," Rufina said, this time more sharply. Soon Mercedes heard the boy running up behind her.

Mercedes's heart boomed in her chest when she reached the fence. Jacinta had found a slack section of wire, and she had climbed over it. She raised it for Mercedes, who crossed under as quickly as she could manage. Mercedes, in turn, lifted the wire for Basilio, who spread a hand over the crown of his hat as he scrambled through.

From under the trees, the three looked past the fence. Vicente and Rufina were crossing the field. They were halfway to the fence when the droning began. Mercedes looked beyond the pasture to the road, and to the place down the road where she was certain a cloud of dust would signal approaching trucks.

But the road was undisturbed.

In the field, Vicente looked up to the sky. He yelled something out and broke into a run. Rufina came hurrying after.

The droning grew into a sonorous throb. As if shot from a cat-apult, an airplane roared over. Basilio sprang past Mercedes, his hat fluttering to the ground. He scrambled along the fence, searching frantically for the place where the wire was slack. Mercedes tugged him back toward the trees, but he held the fence wire so tightly that she could not pull him away.

Pinpoints of fire exploded from the airplane. Bullets rained over the yellow stubble of the field. When Vicente and Rufina were hit, they were both looking up. When the bullets struck, each gave a little jerk and then collapsed as though they were puppets and their strings had gone slack. An instant later, the airplane trailed its shadow over the road and then over the thicket of trees that Mer-cedes and Jacinta had traveled through only yesterday. The sound of it grew dim, then dimmer still. The silence left behind was a sound in itself.

Basilio wiggled through the fence and ran hard toward his par-ents. When he reached them, he darted from one to the other. At his mother's side, his knees buckled. A panting Mercedes joined the boy and knelt beside him while Jacinta's voice at the fence was an incomprehensible howl.

▼▼

CHAPTER SEVEN

El Congo
March 1932

For days after arriving at Chenta Gómez's place, Mercedes Prieto's mind refused to settle itself into the cramped, windowless room that was all of Chenta's home. At times, she felt the presence of Jacinta fussing over her. At others, it was Chenta spooning soup into her mouth. Frequently, Mercedes's vision was blurred. Colors were indistinct. Occasionally, when Jacinta or Chenta spoke, their voices changed into those of Ignacio or Pru. Of one thing Mercedes was certain: Basilio Fermín, curled up and silent, lying in the thumbnail of space between the wall and her petate.

The boy seemed never to move, though Mercedes knew this was impossible. Now and then, she would pat the slender curve of his back, and when she did, he twitched a little and moaned as if he were a dog sleeping through a nightmare.

While Mercedes lay on her petate and convalesced, stories drifted in. Stories about la matanza, the massacre. Almost thirty thousand had been killed, it was said. Indian men, women, and children. So many dead that corpses had been dumped into massive, common graves. So many dead in the south and in the west that the air reeked with the stench of them. So many dead, so hastily buried, that rooting pigs or marauding dogs would sometimes carry home a piece of human flesh, a length of bone. And it was said that those not killed during the revolt had been hunted down and shot when found.

For days after hearing this, Mercedes took to talking to herself. She spoke low, under her breath, mouthing sentences such as, If he was alive when we left, he's surely dead now. Once—it was very dark in the room when this happened, so it must have been night— Ignacio's face appeared to her and she asked him about Tino. Have you seen him, husband? Is our boy alive or dead? But Ignacio had not spoken. It was Jacinta, lying beside her, who responded, "Sush, sush, Mamá. Dormite ya. Go to sleep now."

This news, too, spread quickly through town: Additional squads of guardias were now in El Congo. The men watched with sharp eyes for Indians here who might duplicate the actions of their brothers in the south. Fearing reprisals, Indians ceased to speak Nahuatl and to wear their native dress. Gone were the long skirts in lavender and sky-blue and soft persimmon. The contrasting sashes that set off the waist. In their place came plain, short dresses of somber colors. Silenced were the lilting sounds of the Pipil.

Today, Mercedes sat in the covered gallery at the rear of Chenta's room. There were twenty rooms in the mesón, all surrounding a large, grassless patio. A tall maquilishuat tree, abloom with bright pink blossoms, grew in the center of the patio. These days, she felt stronger. Weeks back, when she'd first arrived, Chenta had offered work at her food stand in the market. "But only when you're ready," Chenta had said. For Jacinta, Chenta had found a fruit vendor who needed help along the roadway. The boy Basilio was a different story.

Now he came out of the room and shuffled off across the patio to the shed in the back that contained the toilet. Although he was eleven, he was as tall as Jacinta. He was a homely boy with a broad flat face dark as a roasted coffee bean. Minutes later, he came out of the shed and used his thumbs to hike up his trousers. He came and hunkered down beside Mercedes.

"Buenos días, niña Meches," he said. He called her "niña," the word meaning "girl." It was used by most people to show respect and endearment for women of all ages. But he also called her "Meches," the shortened form of Mercedes. Only he had ever called her that, and this tender familiarity touched her.

Mercedes said, "In a few days, I'll be going to the market to work with Chenta."

"Me, too." Basilio kept his eyes on a spot across the patio.

"You can't work at the market," Mercedes said. "There's a job for you at the church. El padre Donacio needs a helper." It was Jacinta who only days before had learned of el padre's need. Once a week, on Tuesdays, she carried a basketful of fruit to the church so that la Gerónima, the priest's cook, could make easy selections.

"I don't want to work at the church."

"El padre is a good man." Mercedes did not know him personally, had only seen him at mass, but she relied on Jacinta for information about the priest. He would take the boy in. Make a spot for him in a corner of the sacristy.

"El padre has work. You can sweep the church. Whitewash the walls. You can even ring the bells."

"I don't want to ring the bells."

Mercedes rubbed her eyelids with two fingertips. There was so much weighing on her. So much weighing on the boy. You can ring the bells. What a tawdry inducement. As if their lives merited any kind of celebration. "I'm sorry, Basilio, but you can't stay here any longer," she said, deciding it was time to be blunt. "Chenta has been more than kind." Truth was, there was only so much space. And there was the question of Jacinta, who was troubled, she said, by the way Basilio's eyes followed her when she was home.

"I want to go back," he said.

Mercedes drew herself up in alarm. "You can't go back now. It's too dangerous to go back."

"Quiero regresar a mi tierra." What would he find if he returned to his land? His mother was gone. His father. They had dragged their bodies back across the killing field and into the stable. Covered them with loose hay, all they could find for burial. Yes, he would go back. He would kneel beside them, dropping his head in reverence like his mother had taught him to do when they made trips to the camposanto to visit the family graves. Basilio stood up and went into the room. He lay down in the middle of Mercedes's petate.

After a time Mercedes went in after him. The coffee she'd made this morning on the charcoal burner in the corner was still hot. There were two tortillas wrapped in a square of cloth resting over the top of the coffeepot. She poured the boy a cup and brought it to him with the tortillas. "Here's your breakfast," she said, squatting down near him.

He propped himself up on an elbow in order to take the cup she offered. He took a long sip and then one of the tortillas and ate it in four bites, swallowing hard after each bite.

Toward the end of May, the rains soaked the countryside, melting away layers of dust from trees and fence posts, from the broad backs of oxen tethered along the road. Cobblestones lining the streets of El Congo absorbed the moisture and took on a rich hue that pleased Mercedes as she walked over them. Each morning the air was bright and clean smelling.

Since March, Mercedes had worked alongside Chenta at her food stand. On this early dawn, the two women, both bundled in tapados, made their way to the center of town to the market. Soon the villagers would arrive, and many would take their first meal at Chenta's comedor.

Chenta Gómez had worked hard to establish her food stand. She had named it La Cucharona de Chenta, Chenta's Ladle. After only two years it had become so profitable that she'd hired Emiliano, the artist, to sketch a large green ladle on the wide lintel that framed the top of the booth and served as its marquee.

The two crossed the plaza fronting the church as its bell began to peal. Mercedes pictured Basilio tugging at the rope that sent it ringing. He rang the bell for the Angelus at daybreak, at morning mass, and then again at noon and sunset. In the months since the boy had worked at the church, he seemed less morose. Every evening, he walked over to Chenta's mesón to sit for a while with the women. Most times he had little to say, though the women liked to talk. They asked questions such as, What does the priest's cook fix for him? Does she feed you well, too? Is el padre demanding? Or they made comments about how working in la casa de Jesús gains a soul a plenary indulgence, or how a boy who sleeps in a sacristy could well grow up to be a priest. These two comments had come from Chenta, who was devoutly religious, she said, although she frequently missed mass.

In the market, the vendors had stacked fruits and vegetables into pyramids on the counters of their booths. While Chenta started up the fires that would cook today's meals, Mercedes went from stand to stand selecting the ingredients. Into her basket went green and red peppers, prickly pears, and long, pointed chiles. She added fat bunches of cilantro and chipilín, a firm head of cabbage to be shredded for curtido. She walked to the left side of the market, past red-eyed iguanas whose short legs were tied to wooden stakes, and went directly to the chicken stall, where she chose a pair of ready-to-cook hens to drop into the soup pot.

The sight of all this food, and the fact that she was able to buy a basketful, gratified Mercedes. In Izalco, on those few occasions when she had gone to market, she had needed only her hands to contain her purchases.

She was folding the fragrant leaves of chipilín into the soup when the priest's cook came into the mercado. She was not carrying a basket as she usually did when marketing, and she hurried toward the booth. Mercedes laid down her spoon and wiped her hands on her apron. "What is it?" she asked when the cook was standing at the counter, her face drawn tight like a fist. She was large and solid, a woman of indeterminate age. A mole sat like a tiny dark insect on the corner of her lip.

"El muchacho se fue."

"What do you mean the boy left?"

"Every morning, after he rings the Angelus, Basilio comes into the kitchen and has his breakfast. This morning he didn't come. After a while, I went looking for him, but he wasn't in the bell tower. He wasn't in the sacristy. He wasn't anywhere in the church. He's gone. It was me who rang the bell for mass. When el padre finds out, he won't be happy."

"Maybe Basilio went to Chenta's," Mercedes said, refusing to be alarmed.

"No. I went to the mesón and he wasn't there. I think he went off to Nahuizalco. Lately, that's all he's talked about. Anyway, I thought you should know."

Nahuizalco was his village. It was a day's walk away from Izalco. Mercedes saw the boy tramping, alone and vulnerable, over that harsh terrain they'd traversed to come here.

"How long has he been gone?"

"A few hours, más o menos. Anyway, I thought I'd come tell you. You're like his mother, so I thought you should know."

Mercedes untied her apron and folded it up and set it on the little table next to the comal. She turned to Chenta, who'd been keeping track of the conversation. "I have to find him," Mercedes said.

The boy had left the church after the Angelus bells, just as morning was breaking. He remembered the route that had brought him here, every stone it seemed. Every clump of brush. Every tree. The rains had turned the countryside very green. The brooks he passed gurgled with rushing water that was high almost to the tops of the banks. He had been traveling for three, four hours. His machete was sheathed at his side and he had provisions: a gourd canteen filled with water, and an alforja into which he'd stuffed what he'd filched from the cook's kitchen. Some time ago he'd left the road that led out of El Congo and he had made a wide loop around the lake of Coatepeque. Now he followed a worn path that meandered up the skirts of the volcano. El volcán de Santa Ana. He remembered going around it back in January. Today he would climb and cross it because he was in a hurry. Since the rains had come, the path was no longer dusty. Every now and then he looked back to see his footprints bold on the rich black earth, a true sign that he was doing this thing that for months he had been dreaming about.

He did not know exactly what he would do once he reached Nahuizalco. Before getting home, he would stop at the stable. He saw himself, standing in the slanted light, approaching what was left of his mother and his father. He swallowed down the lump in his throat, deciding it was best to put what he imagined out of his mind until he actually faced it.

The sun was high. It had already burned the dew off the lush clumps of wild mint and manzanilla and off the stiff spines of the magueys. The day had turned hot, and he was glad for the brim of his hat that kept his face shaded. It was his father's hat he wore. It had a squared-off crown and a tooled leather band, and there was never a day that his father had not worn it. The hat was his now.

Basilio had picked it up off the field where it had lain after the assault. On the back brim the pale straw was splotched dark, and once Jacinta had suggested he should scrub the stain away, but he would not consider it. It was his father's blood there and he would honor it. Honor, too, the sweat of his father's brow that, from years of labor, had turned the inside of the hatband dark as blood.

He trudged higher up the volcano. When the path he followed petered out, he picked the best of the pebbly trails before him. The terrain grew rough and hilly with mounds that sent him scrambling up and sliding down. Periodically he looked back to see where he had been, noting the great patches of pale grassy land, these framed in an intense green by wide stands of timber. From time to time, the furrowed brown configuration of a cornfield stood out. Here and there he saw thatched huts or sometimes the glinting tin roofs of more prosperous owners. Small smooth stones were sprinkled along the trail, and it surprised him to find that his feet were tender as he went over them. Although the soles of his feet had been thick with calluses, over the months his feet had softened. How could it be otherwise? All that was required of him now was that he scurry over the cool tiles of the church and of the sacristy.

He did not like working at the church. He did not like working for any man, even if the man he worked for was a man of God. Until all the trouble, he had worked with his father on the rancho. Each day they went out to the milpa, tended the corn, saw to the steer, the horse, the half-dozen pigs. Until the trouble, it was just himself and his father working all day to return at noon and then at eveningtime to the hut and to his mother.

Basilio reached what he thought was the top of the volcano. What he saw there took his breath away. This volcano did not peak. Santa Ana rose up to a flat broad plateau that spread a verdigris like moss toward a crater that was the great gaping mouth of the mountain. Around the edge of this mouth, the earth was blackened and bare, and there were deep rents in the earth like terrible scars. A billowy cloud had gathered in the crater, and for a moment Basilio thought the volcano was spewing smoke. He dropped on his haunches, the better to collect himself. He looked beyond the cloud and then he saw it, rising off in the distance: his own volcán, Izalco.

Stretched past it, as far as he could see, was the green expanse that was his home.

He hunkered down there for a very long time, allowing his eyes to rest on the panorama. He took it all in: Izalco, haughty and impassable, the grand sweep of his land that was like a spread of rumpled blanket. All of it running off into a horizon of clouds and sky. There were no milpas there. No huts. No shacks. No tin roofs to reflect the sun. Spreading before him was nothing to suggest that which he could remember of his life. The cook had been right. "You can't go back," she'd said on many occasions. "There's nothing left back where you came from." And it was true. He could see it now. Nothing was left. Nada.

Mercedes came around a bend of the crooked road she had used to skirt the lake when she saw the boy appear. She stopped and stood still for a moment, first because she was relieved to see him, but also because the sight of him marked the end of her searching. She had been walking for hours. It was well past noon; she could tell from the way her shadow lay long against the earth. She had left El Congo with nothing to eat, with only her tapado to keep the sun off. It was foolish, she knew, to have set off so unprepared, but maybe, in some deep way, she had known that it would not be long before she found him.

A leafy mango tree grew by the side of the road. Mercedes went over to sit down in its shade. Minutes later the boy came up and sat beside her. They remained like that, in silence, for quite some time, and then the boy unstopped his gourd canteen and offered Mercedes a drink. She drank deeply, thankful for the water.

The boy opened his alforja and foraged around inside it. "Here's something to eat," he said. "Pupusas. I took two this morning. Want one?"

Mercedes nodded and took the tortilla the boy offered. They ate, both watching the road, the sun on it, the creek meandering across the way.

"You're coming back," Mercedes said after she had taken another swallow from the canteen.

"I went to the top of the world," the boy said at length. "I looked out and saw there is nothing left of our home."

Mercedes nodded.

"I'm coming back because there's nothing left to go to."

"Así es," Mercedes said. "That's right."

After a time, the two stood up and brushed themselves off. "Vámonos," Mercedes said.

▼▼▼

CHAPTER EIGHT

It was Basilio Fermín who first thought of celebrating Jacinta's saint's day. Because he worked for el padre, Basilio often touted church information such as santos and holy days of obligation. He had arrived at the mesón early in August, bringing the news that the feast of San Jacinto fell on the seventeenth. He repeated what el padre had said: that it was fitting to mark a person's santo with some kind of celebration. Hearing this, the women had readily agreed. Life had been hard. It was time for a party, Chenta said. In all her years, Mercedes had attended but one party, and that was on her wedding day. She remembered long ago when she'd paraded from her mother's hut into town to obtain the blessing of don Patricio, Izalco's old cacique. How remarkable it had been! Mercedes striding down the road with Ignacio on one side and her mother on the other, the guests trailing along behind them. Mercedes had cradled the oval hand mirror, Ignacio's wedding gift, all the way to the chieftain's door. Now Mercedes wished Jacinta could seek a saint's day blessing from don Feliciano, Izalco's present-day cacique. But given the times, that day seemed long off.

Tonight Mercedes was out on the gallery, as were most of the neighbors of the mesón. A few regulars from Chenta's Cucharona were also here. The neighbors had dragged chairs out from their rooms; they had brought candles, too, and these glowed up and down the gallery. Jacinta sat in the patio under the maquilishuat tree. She wore the dress her mother had bought at Tiburcia's booth in the mercado. The dress was lavender with capped sleeves. Jacinta's dark, thick hair fell past her shoulders. A purple ribbon—a gift from Chenta—was tied in a bow at her temple. Mercedes recalled years gone by, and how there had been no money for trinkets and gifts. Presently, while Mercedes's payment for working with Chenta was a roof overhead and food on the table, the money Jacinta made at the fruit stand provided them with something extra that they might spend on a few frivolities. Still, Mercedes was careful to set money aside. In the clay pot lying in the bottom of Chenta's wardrobe, there were now four one-colón bills, three five-cent pieces, and two cuartillos.

Jacinta opened gifts, a little smile pulling at the corner of her mouth. Paula Díaz from room number 5 gave Jacinta a turquoise tapado she had made herself. Jacinta gave a whoop and wound the shawl around her shoulders, doing a pirouette to show off the present. Zoila Pérez, from number 2, offered dulces de camote, sweet-potato confections. Paco López, from number 8, who was called el Peche because he was as thin as the edge of a five-centavo piece, approved of Zoila's gift. "Candy is just the thing," he said, reaching out with a long finger for a sweet in a twist of pink tissue paper. Old toothless Josefa from number 12 made a sucking sound and said, "Peche, keep your hands off the girl's candy."

"My gift is the music," Joaquín Maldonado proclaimed. He was from number 20, the room next to the cantina. Joaquín was the only neighbor who had a radio. That there was no electricity in the mesón had not stopped Joaquín from providing music to his neighbors over the years. Joaquín had made a deal with don Angel, the owner of the cantina. Joaquín had bored a hole into the soft adobe of his wall and threaded a crude cord through it into the cantina. When he wished for music, he had only to rap on the wall for don Angel to plug him in. For this service, don Angel was paid an undisclosed amount, which Joaquín could readily afford, considering he charged each of his neighbors a fee just for listening. But not tonight. To-night, in honor of Jacinta and because he believed that periodic goodwill was a proper investment, Joaquín allowed his neighbors to listen for free. A rowdy ranchera was now playing, and it lent gaiety to the festivities. In the mesón, Joaquín Maldonado was considered a clever businessman. That he sometimes had a heart gave the neighbors something extra to admire.

Despite being the instigator of the occasion, Basilio stood apart from the others. It was not until there was a lull in the conversation that he judged it time to make his move. He went to Jacinta. "I, too, have something for you," he said, poking a finger into the pocket of his shirt.

"What is it?" she asked, taking the offering from him.

"It's a holy card. Of San Jacinto."

"Oh," Jacinta said. "Just last night I was asking about him. I wondered what he looked like, but nobody could say." She peered at the card and then smiled broadly at Basilio. "Where did you get it?"

"From el padre."

"Gracias, Basilio. I'll add this to Chenta's saint shelf." On one of the walls in the room, Chenta had constructed a little altar. There was a framed picture of la Virgen de Guadalupe, a rosary coiled around a tin crucifix, a large print of the Sacred Heart of Jesus. On the shelf, too, were tall votive candles that Chenta always kept burning and a manteca can sprouting a spindly marigold. "See," Jacinta said, handing the card over to Conchita from number 3.

Conchita set her baby girl down on the ground and gave the saint a close examination. "It's a good card," she said finally.

Jacinta passed the gift around. The guests murmured their approbation. When it reached the hands of old Josefa, she peered at the card and then thrust her chin out before speaking, "This saint looks like my first husband." She smacked her lips in confirmation.

Basilio beamed at the stir his gift had caused. On the radio, "Adelita" was playing. He caught the song's refrain: "Si Adelita se fuera con otro, la seguiría por tierra y por mar." Truth was, if Jacinta ever went off with someone, Basilio would follow *her* over land and over sea. She is lovely today, he thought, in her violet dress and with Chenta's ribbon in her hair.

Luis Martínez, the young man Jacinta worked for, was sitting next to the door of number 7. He sauntered over to Jacinta and extended a square packet wrapped in blue crepe paper. "Here," he said. Jacinta slowly unwrapped the package and then looked quizzically at him. "It's a pair of earrings," Luis said. He went on to tell how they were fashioned from the pits of two marañones that had come from his own fruit stand. Jacinta flashed Luis a coy smile before holding the gift up for others to see. Each marañon pit was the length of a thumb and was shaped like a kidney. Each was yellowish brown and lacquered so highly it shone like a golden stone. Old Josefa crooked a finger and said, "A ver," and Jacinta handed the earrings over. Josefa narrowed her eyes in inspection and then narrowed them more to squint at Luis. "Humph," she uttered, before passing the earrings on.

Mercedes had to admit a gift like that could set a person to thinking. Moreover, it was the way Jacinta had smiled at Luis that gave her the most to think about. Mercedes glanced at Basilio, who had retreated to lean against the gallery wall. He was no longer beaming. When Chenta walked out of number 10 carrying a plate stacked with squares of semita and announced, "Here's the cake," Mercedes was glad for the interruption.

"I'll get the coffee." Mercedes went into the room to the charcoal brazier. She had been busy for five or ten minutes when the church bell began to ring. She paused in her preparations because it was not usual for the bell to ring so late. She stuck her head out the door and looked toward the spot where Basilio had stood, but the boy was no longer there. On the gallery and out in the patio the neighbors went silent. All listened to the bell. "What could be wrong?" el Peche asked. "It's hours past bell time." The wild clanging stopped and a series of short, clear strikes began. After a moment, Joaquín took up the count, his chest thrust out like a peacock's.

"... ocho, nueve, diez, once, doce, trece. That was thirteen strikes," Joaquín said, the last bell echoing over town.

"I'm thirteen," Jacinta said, looking over in Mercedes's direction. "Mamá, is that Basilio? Did he ring the bells for me?"

Something sweet and sad turned in Mercedes's heart. "Sí. Lo hizo para tí."

Joaquín Maldonado hooked his thumbs into his belt. "The boy is a clever man," he said to all the neighbors.

▼▼

CHAPTER NINE

I t was el Día de los Muertos, the Day of the Dead. Despite the nature of the feast, El Congo was brimming with festivity. Vendors lined the dirt road leading to the cemetery.

This afternoon, while Chenta worked at the market, Mercedes had set up a brazier and comal on the strip of grass under the trees across from the cemetery. She offered pupusas y curtido—tortillas stuffed with cheese or frijoles and a vinegary cole slaw—treats to those on their way to decorate graves. She had two pails of drinks: one filled with horchata and the other with fresco de tamarindo. She had made a pot of coffee. Jacinta worked across the street, heaping fingers of pineapple, orange, and papaya into paper cones to sell to passersby.

In the cemetery, candles lined the graves. At night they would glow like the tops of birthday cakes. Freshly cut dahlias, chulas and amor seco were spread like blankets over graves. Draping the headstones were gaudy paper flowers. Some, because they were close to candles, burst into flames that quickly died away.

Mercedes envied these people on their way to the cemetery. How fortunate were those who could visit their dead. Since la matanza, this comfort had been denied to her and Jacinta. The graves marked with the name Prieto were back in Izalco, and these, like all their past possessions, were but a memory in a faraway place.

Joaquín Maldonado walked up to the brazier. "Muy buenas, niña Mercedes," he said. He wore his usual pair of tan-colored trousers, but the shirt he had on was one she had not seen before. It was black and had full sleeves. Mercedes shook her head. It was just like Joaquın to wear something priestly on such a sacred feast. She wondered if el padre had passed the shirt on to him. She pointed out to Joaquín his choices for lunch.

"Give me two pupusas." He pointed to the ones filled with beans; then he squatted down next to Mercedes. "I'll take some of that curtido. And a little coffee, por favor."

Mercedes stacked two tortillas on a square of paper and heaped on the curtido. She poured coffee into a tin. "How's business, Joaquín?" she inquired. She referred to the money-making scheme the man ran each year. On the Day of the Dead, he offered the town his expert help. Capitalizing on his ability to read and write, Joaquín would, for a fee, inscribe the names of souls in a special notebook. "It's the written name upon a page that allows souls to come home," he explained. "Entrust a name to me, and you'll assure a soul a year in which he'll not wander about in darkness." Mercedes disapproved, of course. Every year, on November second, the souls of her own journeyed back to her. Every year, she saw each one of them distinctly. She did not need another person to help conjure them up.

Joaquín pushed his hat back from his forehead and knitted his brows together. "Business? You refer to my holy work with souls as business?"

"Here's your lunch," Mercedes said, sorry she'd brought the subject up.

Joaquín took the food, but the prospect of eating did not silence him. "The souls whose names are in my notebook will speed home tonight. Those inscribed know their destination. Fortunate for them, they'll not be lost in twilight."

Mercedes nodded, and held her tongue. For more seasons than she wished to count, her dead had journeyed back to her. She did not have the words to describe how she envisioned this travel. All she could say is that she pictured herself linked to her dead by lengths of silvery thread, threads as shimmery and delicate as the filaments of spiders.

That night, while Jacinta slept beside her, Mercedes lay on their mat, eyes open to the candlelight she'd readied to guide her dead home. To quench thirsty souls after their journey, there was a jug of water on the shelf tacked to the wall. There were ears of maíz to remind them of home. Amor seco, with its papery blossoms, was bunched in a manteca can. And there was the lingering smell of incense that had burned itself to ash.

Mercedes watched her mother come. Death had been kind to her. It gave her back the unlined face she'd had when she was young. Mercedes remembered the day her mother died, recalling how pain had distorted her face. The evil spirit gnawing at her mother's belly had fed upon her face as well. But that was long ago. Tonight, as in all the years since her death, her mother appeared untouched.

Ignacio rose up before her. He came across the room and knelt down at the foot of the mat. Mercedes propped herself up on an elbow and reached out for him, but he lowered his head until it rested on the floor before he disappeared.

Cirilo, her firstborn, came next. His hair stood in a spiky crown above his head. He was her reyecito, her little king. He cooed as she gazed at him, his mouth wet and glistening. When her six daughters appeared, they did not make a sound. They looked her way with large, woeful eyes. She kissed them each and they went peacefully to sleep.

Mercedes waited anxiously for Tino, the loss of him new again. When he found his way to her, she would take him in her arms. She would breathe in his sweet smoky smell. Even the sight of the birthmark on his ear would be a comfort tonight. Mercedes lay quiet as stone, knowing that in silence she would catch his journeying. But the candles flickering in the room grew dim as morning dawned. And still Tino did not come.

Light had seeped in around the frame of the door when a thought, shadowy and unsubstantial, occurred to Mercedes. Slowly, it took form and then burst into her head.

The thought she had was this: Her boy was not dead. Her Tino had not come tonight because he was alive.

▼▼▼

CHAPTER TEN

After el Día de los Muertos, Mercedes thought of little else but that her son was alive. The next afternoon, she and Chenta were returning from the market when Mercedes blurted out, "What would you say if I told you I know my boy's alive?"

They had just crossed the park. Chenta stopped in midstep after hearing Mercedes's question. "What are you saying?" Chenta asked, reaching up to steady the basket balanced on her head. "How do you know this? Who told you?"

Mercedes gripped harder the edge of her own basket. "No one told me. I just know it, that's all."

Chenta stared at Mercedes for a moment and then said, "He's not alive. Forgive my bluntness, comadre, but your boy is dead, just like my sister Pru is dead. Just like Goyo and my three nephews are dead." She started off again, walking at a brisker pace. Over her shoulder, she said, "That is the truth. What good is it to think otherwise?"

Chenta's words were underscored by the stiff way she carried herself. Mercedes thought, I've been wrong to tell her this. My words have awakened the pain of her own loss.

"Maybe you're right," Mercedes said. In the future, she would keep this matter to herself. She would go back to find her son, but the trip would be a solitary pilgrimage. Though Jacinta had promised to accompany her on the return, Mercedes would place only herself in danger.

She considered various ways to begin the search but could not settle on any one way to conduct it. She had walked to El Congo, then halfway back when she had gone after Basilio, so she could not envision traveling those roads again. Besides, she needed a faster way to make the trip. For that, there was the bus. And there was the train. In her life, she had never used either. A train came through El Congo—each morning she awakened to its doleful whistle—but she did not know where it went. She knew even less about the cost of train travel. There were many unknowns and so many questions that she decided to ask Joaquín Maldonado for advice. Joaquín Maldonado would have ideas. Ideas for a price, of course.

Two days passed before she could speak to him alone. Mercedes waited until Chenta and Jacinta had left the mesón. She waited until most of the neighbors were away, too. It was a sign, she thought. The mesón was almost empty, yet there sat Joaquín, just inside the gallery on the crate he used for a chair. Mercedes crossed the patio and went under the maquilishuat toward him. A pair of chickens pecking around the toilet shack scattered when she went by.

"Buenos días, Joaquín."

Joaquín Maldonado stood when she addressed him. "Buenos días, niña Mercedes."

"Siéntese, siéntese." Mercedes motioned for him to sit again. "Tell me about the train," she said. "Where does the train go that comes into El Congo?"

Joaquín Maldonado did not sit back down as she had asked him to do. "You want to know about the train. Well, the train comes through here from Santa Ana. It's on its way to San Salvador."

"Does it go to Izalco?"

Joaquín shook his head. "If you switch trains, you can go to Sonsonate. Sonsonate's not far from Izalco."

"Yes," Mercedes said. She and Ignacio had walked to Sonsonate. That last time Cirilo was so sick, they had taken him to a curandero who lived there. In the end, the trip had been for nothing.

"How much does it cost, the trip to Sonsonate?"

"Fifteen cents. Each way."

Treinta centavos, Mercedes thought. For all expenses, she had less than five colones.

Joaquín Maldonado hooked a thumb into his belt. "Are you thinking of taking the train yourself, niña Mercedes?"

"Is it safe to travel now?" she asked, ignoring his question. "Are there guardias on the trains?"

Joaquín Maldonado studied her before he spoke again. "There are guardias everywhere, niña Mercedes. But a woman dressed like you would be safe on the train."

She was wearing one of her two dresses. This one was dark green and had a skirt that ended at midcalf. There was not a spot of Pipil decoration on the dress. "Can you help me get the train? I need to go very soon."

"How soon?"

"Mañana." She had not known how eager she was until she spoke this. Having said it, tomorrow seemed too long a wait.

"Of course I can help you. But we'll have to be at the station very early. No later than six o'clock."

"Mañana, pues." Mercedes went back across the patio. Tomorrow she would be home again. Tomorrow she would begin to comb the countryside asking for her child. She would step into huts and into white adobe houses, ever on the lookout for a baby with a birthmark identifying him as her own.

She had gotten to her door when she remembered she had not paid Joaquín for his help. She hurried back to number 20, where he was still sitting on his crate. "How much do I owe you?"

Joaquín made a little dismissive gesture with a hand.

"Mañana," he said. "We'll settle up tomorrow."

El Congo's train station consisted of a modest square building and the wide covered platform that was parallel to the tracks on which the incoming and outgoing trains ran. Mercedes and Joaquín were on the platform, at the ticket counter with its ornately barred window. It was Joaquín who bought the tickets for Mercedes. "Dos tiquetes a Sonsonate. Round trip." Mercedes poked a finger into the neckline of her dress and extracted a pañuelo in which she carried her money. The coins and bills were knotted up in a corner of the handkerchief. She untied the knots and counted out thirty centavos. "Here you are," she said, handing over the coins.

They stood at the edge of the platform. "Once you get on the train, it will stop first at Sitio del Niño," Joaquín said. "At Sitio del Niño, you'll change to the train for Sonsonate."

"What?" Mercedes said. She could not believe what he had said.

"First Sitio del Niño. Then Sonsonate." Joaquín went silent. Then he leaned closer to Mercedes before continuing. "Señora, are you ill?"

Mercedes steadied herself against a nearby post. Sitio del Niño. The Place of the Child. It was a sign. The best sign of all that she should make this trip. "No. No. I'm fine," she said. "My boy disappeared during la matanza. I'm going back to look for him."

"Ay," Joaquín said, lightly touching her arm.

"Please give a message to Jacinta for me," Mercedes said. She had left the mesón on the pretext of going to early mass. "Tell Jacinta about my trip. Tell her she mustn't come after me. Tell Basilio that, too. And tell Chenta that I'll return when I can. Tell them all not to worry."

The rumble of the train far down the track set the platform vibrating. "Oh, and how much do I owe you?" Mercedes fished the handkerchief out of her neckline again.

Joaquín Maldonado took a step backward. "Señora, por favor. There are things a man does that he doesn't do for money." He waited until the train whistled and steamed into the station. Then he helped Mercedes onto the train, walking her down the aisle until she found an empty seat.

Had the purpose for the trip not been so grave, the setting not so disorienting, Mercedes might have found the train ride enjoyable. She sat in the next-to-last car, where the narrow seats were wooden and unpadded and where no glass stretched across the windows to keep the engine smoke from billowing in each time the train chugged around a curve. Mercedes was seated beside a window, next to a young woman named Telma, who had immediately introduced herself. Of the two, Mercedes got the worst of the smoke. Though it made her cough, this was the least of her worries. Her main preoccupation was a pair of guardias who periodically picked their way through the people and the baskets and the chickens in the aisle. A guardia went by now, swaying slightly in counterpoint to the movement of the train. Mercedes kept her eye on the bobbing helmet until it disappeared in the section between the cars.

Telma gave Mercedes a soft poke with an elbow. "La guardia," she whispered, though she had to whisper loudly because there was the sound of the train and of the people and the animals on it. "If we ignore them, they won't bother us."

Mercedes nodded, repositioning the string bag resting on her lap. In the bag was a whole semita, a stack of pupusas, a small papaya, and a few bananas. Part of the food would sustain her on the trip. Part of it was a gift of appreciation for whomever it was that had kept her child safe.

"Are you getting off at Sitio del Niño?" the woman asked.

"I'm going to Sonsonate."

"Yo también. Sonsonate es mi pueblo. If you want, we can change trains together."

"Muy bien." While Mercedes appreciated the girl's friendliness, she did not wish to be drawn into conversation. She watched out the window as the train rolled through coffee lands, then past flatlands on which cattle grazed and pigs nosed along the fence lines. Although Mercedes said hardly a word, the girl continued chattering. She had been working in Santa Ana for two years. She was a laundress there, at the house of doña Elena de Contreras. La niña Elena was the best of patronas, and she, Telma, would never have left such a job, had she not, silly girl, gotten pregnant. So now, here she was, going back to Sonsonate to have her baby before she could start working again. Though maybe after the baby came, she would stay in her pueblo instead of going back to the city.

Mercedes turned to the girl and said, "Is this your first?"

Telma laid a hand on her belly. "Sí. Mi primero."

"After it's born, never let it out of your sight," Mercedes said.

It was almost noon when Mercedes left Sonsonate and started walking toward Izalco. The girl Telma had kept her word. She had helped Mercedes make the change to the southwest-bound train and had stayed with her for the hour it took for the train to arrive. Mercedes was thankful for the girl's company. The two had made themselves comfortable on one of the benches on the platform, and the girl continued to tell about la niña Elena and her husband, don Ernesto, and how el señor y la señora, and all the Contreras family, would soon leave their house in Santa Ana to spend the coffee-picking season in the big farmhouse on their finca, La Abundancia. The plantation was not far from Santa Ana; it was spread prettily, the girl said, along the skirts of el volcán. She told how she loved the four months la familia lived in la casona, the big house, on the finca. She said it was like a vacation to be there, and even though last picking season had been a horrible time, just a horrible time, she had been looking forward to this season and to the stay at the finca. But then, here came the baby, and when la niña Elena learned about it, that was that, no more finca time. At this point in the recitation, Telma leaned conspiratorially into Mercedes and said, "La señora, may God bless her, gave me ten colones for while I'm waiting out my time." Telma had patted the area above her heart, the place where she, no doubt, had tucked her money cache. For her help, Mercedes gave her a banana and two pupusas.

Now Mercedes walked the gravel road that paralleled the stream running near her hut. There was no one on the road. In years past, before the trouble, this road had been well traveled. Taking it, you could see carts drawn by oxen prodded by boys with long sticks. Horses, their sides and backs stacked with bundles of kindling, frequently plodded along. But most of all, it was women and girls who used the road. Gracefully balancing water jugs or baskets on their heads, the women gossiped and the girls giggled. And there was always a dog or two on the road. Sometimes one had to skirt a noisy herd of cattle before continuing. Today the only thing to be seen was el Izalco rising up in welcome on the horizon.

Mercedes came to the trail that led directly home. When she got there, she saw that nothing was as she'd imagined it would be. Weeds sprouted from the chinks in the rock wall. The poinsettia hedge was wildly overgrown. She followed the crimson blaze of the hedge right up to the blackened branches and trunk that were all that was left of her laurel tree. Mercedes slumped against the wall. Her hut was gone. Of course her hut was gone. She had seen it burning, nine months back, on that terrible night of rifle shots and flames. Now she had returned. And only this stillness which was almost as terrible greeted her.

For a time, Mercedes stayed next to the wall, gathering support from the solid rock she leaned on. When she felt strong enough, she walked over to the sooty circle that once had marked the boundary of her private world. Since the burning, a rainy season had come and gone. The rains had washed cinder and ash away from the charred remains of her possessions. Here were a few pottery shards that were surely pieces of her water jug or her comal. There were the three sooty stones on which her comal had rested.

Mercedes picked up a pottery shard no larger than her palm, rubbing away some of the soot covering it. She held the shard for a moment between her hands before dropping it into one of the deep pockets of her dress.

She looked across the clearing, toward the clumps of lemongrass growing obliviously in the sun. She looked beyond the arroyo, and Pru's hut rose up in her mind with such force that it jolted her.

Mercedes crossed the clearing. She went down the arroyo and then up the trail that spilled directly into Pru's yard. La comadre's hut was still standing. Pru's mango tree slashed the hut with shade. Mercedes dropped the string bag and entered the hut. She looked around in the gloom. The hut was bare, and what she had seen the last time she was here caused her mouth to go dry: Juancho and Manolo in a bloody tangle by the door. Mercedes went out to stand on the spot where Pru had died, realizing that, coming here, she'd expected to find dead bodies. No matter how much time had passed, how illogical it seemed, she had thought, when she returned, she would come upon Pru's body. The children's bodies. And she would come upon her son, too. But her son would be alive. Miraculously, he would be here, under the mango tree, where she had left him, alive and trusting she would return.

Mercedes walked up Izalco's main street to the plaza across from the church of La Asunción. Most of the Pipil Indians of Izalco lived in the surrounding barrio, which was named after the church. It was past noon—the church bells had struck the hour sometime before—

and few souls were on the hot streets now. For a while, Mercedes walked aimlessly around the square under the spare shade of the olive trees. The plaza was ringed with white adobe houses. Some of their walls bore gray pockmarks from the impact of bullets. Though the evidence of la matanza's violence chilled her, she drew strength from her goal: finding Tino. But how to do it? ¿Cómo, cómo?

It occurred to Mercedes that she was hungry. She had left the mesón quietly in the morning, not taking the time to eat for fear she would awaken Jacinta and Chenta. On a bench under the trees, Mercedes took a pupusa out of her string bag but ate only half before wrapping it back up and putting it away. How could she take time to eat when her boy was calling out to her? She went across the street, to the side of the church, and drank deeply from a water spigot there. She wiped her mouth with the heel of her hand, looking away from the church to Izalco in the distance. She thought of Tláloc, the god of rain, who lived in the volcano, and he blessed her with an idea. She must rely on her own people to help her find her son. Yes. She would enlist the help of don Feliciano, the Pipil chieftain of Izalco. Don Feliciano had succeeded don Patricio, who had been the cacique when Mercedes was young. Caciques mediated disputes; they counseled those who brought them problems. Caciques blessed the tribe's marriages; they sent tribe members into the afterlife with prayers and invocations. When Mercedes's mother had passed away, don Feliciano had stepped into Mercedes's hut to lay his hand over her mother's corpse in ritualistic benediction. And when Cirilo had died and Mercedes could not release him, it was el cacique himself who had gently pried the baby from her fierce embrace.

Mercedes hurried down a side street toward don Feliciano's house. She turned at his corner and collided with a guardia stationed in front of el cacique's door. Up the street was a second guardia posted at the corner.

"Ay, perdone, señor guardia," Mercedes said to this one, steadying herself. She looked down at her bare feet, shifting her string bag from one arm to the other.

"¿Dónde vas?" the guardia asked.

Where was she going? Mercedes looked up, to the small store a few meters away. "A la tienda," she said, motioning in the store's direction. Her heart pounding, she went off before the guardia could say more.

She escaped into the cramped interior of the store and went to lean against the glass-topped counter that was only a step away from the door. There was a very large woman sitting on a stool behind the counter. Mercedes had never seen the woman before. In the past, it was la niña Generosa who ran the store.

"Ay, Dios," Mercedes said.

"What's wrong?" the woman asked.

"La guardia," Mercedes said, pointing feebly out the door.

"Oh, that's Rolando Morales," the storekeeper said. "Is there a woman with a little boy out there, too? Sometimes his woman comes while he's on guard. When she comes, she always brings the boy in here." The storekeeper thought of the child, of that dark splotch covering his little ear. Every time the storekeeper saw him, she thought, This child's mother was careless when she carried him. But she only thought it. She would never say such a thing.

"No. There's only two guardias out there," Mercedes said.

"Well, I'm sure one of them's Rolando Morales. Ever since they hanged don Feliciano, Morales stands watch at el cacique's door."

As if she had been prodded, Mercedes gave a jump. "They hanged don Feliciano?"

The storekeeper nodded. "Yes, back in January. They hanged him in the plaza. From one of the olive trees there. Pobrecito, don Feliciano, may he rest in peace. What can I get for you? As you see, we don't have much of anything these days." She gestured with a hand, indicating the walls with floor-to-ceiling shelves, each stacked meagerly with merchandise.

"Nada, nada. Gracias," Mercedes said. She went back out and up the street, away from the guardia. She turned the corner, and before she knew it, she was back at the church again. She went inside, partly because she wanted to be out of the sun but mostly because she needed a place where she could safely collect her thoughts.

The church was cool and shadowy. It appeared to be empty. Along the walls were the familiar niches, each the home of a different saint: There was San Antonio and San Vicente, San José and San Rafael. Banks of candles flickered next to the niches. Mercedes slipped into a pew, setting her string bag beside her. Over the main altar, the carved figure of la Virgen greeted her. Our Lady rose up from a blue crescent of moon into a froth of clouds and radiant stars. Rosy-cheeked angels helped in the assumption. Mercedes allowed the church's silence to envelop her. El cacique was dead. Why had she not known this? How had this news escaped her?

The parish priest came out of a side door next to the altar. He looked in Mercedes's direction and then walked down the main aisle until he stood next to her pew. "Hija," he said, "it's been months since you were here."

Mercedes stood, but she did not look at him. He called her "daughter." Because he was younger than she, this form of address had always troubled her. "I've been away," she said.

"Oh yes. So many fled. So many died."

"I heard don Feliciano died." When she said this, she looked up at the priest. In Izalco everything had changed, but el padre had not. He was still round and robust. His face looked like one of la Virgen's angel's.

"I'm sorry to say this is true. The cacique was hanged from one of the olive trees in the square. The man was a communist. He was wearing a red tie when they hanged him."

Mercedes said nothing, for in her mind there was nothing but the image of don Feliciano swaying from an olive branch in the plaza. Earlier today, had she sat under the tree that held him?

"Are you back on your rancho?" el padre asked. "How did your family fare in the rebellion?"

Mercedes ran a slow hand along the top edge of the pew beside her. She looked past the priest, at Our Lady rising up above his shoulder. "I've come looking for my son," she said, and then she blurted her story out, but not to him—no, not to him. She told the story to la Virgen.

The priest dropped down on the pew after Mercedes went silent. For a long moment the priest was silent, too, but then he took a deep breath. "I'm sorry to have to say this, but your son is not alive, Mercedes Prieto. He cannot be alive." The priest went on to tell a story of his own. Days after the rebellion, he said, surviving Indians had come and filled the plaza. A certain general had sent a message: "Lay down your machetes, and there will be safe-conducts for women and children, and men as well." And the families had come, the priest said. They waited out in the sun for the general who was to speak to them of peace and new prosperity.

The priest stood up as if impelled to do it by his confession. He stepped into the aisle, then turned to face Mercedes. "And the general arrived," the priest went on. "And so did the trucks filled with soldiers. They started to shoot, and the shooting went on and on. I heard it myself, for I was here, in the church. When the shooting stopped and it was safe to go out, it was a nightmare that greeted me. There were so many bodies, so many children. . . ."

"Por favor," Mercedes said, holding up a hand. In her head were the houses set around the square, the bullet holes marring some of the walls. In her heart, the final unbearable understanding: Her boy was dead. The priest had told her so. "Please. Not another word," Mercedes said, picking up the string bag. "Con su permiso, padre" she added, before sidestepping down the pew and going out the church.

Back in the little store again, Mercedes placed a five-centavo coin on the counter. "Give me ten candles," she said to the woman, who had not moved from the stool. "I'll take the tall white ones. And a few of the flowers." Clusters of paper flowers in various colors hung down over the counter.

The woman gave a grunt and hopped down from the stool. She gathered up the candles, wrapping them in a square of brown paper. "¿Y de qué color las flores?"

Mercedes pointed out the whites and the yellows and the pinks.

"I see you're going to the graveyard," the woman said. She bunched the flowers into a bouquet.

"La niña Generosa. She used to be the owner," Mercedes said in answer.

"If you're going to el camposanto, la Generosa will be there. Most everyone in Izalco now rests in the graveyard." The woman pushed a one-centavo piece across the countertop toward Mercedes.

Mercedes pocketed the change. She collected her purchases and walked into the street. She held her head high as she went past the guardia standing at don Feliciano's door.

▼   ▼   ▼

El camposanto, the Pipil graveyard, was at the end of a road that stretched two kilometers from town. Although el Día de los Muertos had come and gone, tonight Mercedes Prieto was at the graveyard remembering her dead again. The sun had set hours before. A half-moon shone over grave mounds and simple crosses. The moon lit the tokens of homage still abounding in the cemetery: Hardly a grave was not dotted with candle stubs, paper blossoms, and withered flowers.

Few were here this night, each lost in private recollections. Mercedes was at her own family's gravesite. She had spent the afternoon clearing debris and picking weeds that had sprouted from the mounds during the time she had been gone. Mercedes's tapado was wound around her shoulders. Over the years, this tapado had covered her in times of joy and despair; the substance of her life seemed woven into its fibers. And so it was tonight. Wrapped in her tapado, she sank the stems of paper flowers, the ends of candles into the soft earth of her plot. The candles glowed over six graves, each topped with a painted wooden cross on which a name and date were scrawled. There was a cross for her mother, Apolonia; one for Cirilo; and four more for her daughters Segunda, Grata, Ursula, and Digna. And there was Benita and Inocencia, whom she had lost when she was only months along. Though their bodies were not here and there were no crosses to represent them, Mercedes had lighted candles for them, too, because they had been her babies whom she had named to make them real.

Mercedes settled herself beside the mound of Cirilo's grave, the earth cooling beneath her. The moon slipped behind a cloud. She reached into her pocket and extracted the pottery shard she'd saved from the ruins of her home. The shard was slippery with soot; its edges were sharp as flint. She used this sharpness to cut a hank of hair from the top of her head. She wound the hair round and round the shard, tucking the end in to keep it from unraveling. Clasping the shard between her hands once more, she held on tight to this final evidence of her past. When the moon came into view again, the spirits of her dead vibrated in its light. She used the shard to dig a small pit in the mound of Cirilo's grave. She placed the shard in the pit, positioning it this way and that until the shard itself told her to stop.

Mercedes opened her hands and held them over the pit. "Ignacio Prieto," she said softly, voicing her husband's name because there is the power of manifestation in things that are spoken. "On this night, I bury you next to our first son, Cirilo Prieto. On this night, I lay our second son, Justino Prieto, beside both of you." Using a burning candle, she drizzled nine drops of wax over the surface of the shard. She pressed a finger to each wax drop before proclaiming, "May this husband and son, may this father and brother join, at last, those long ago departed." When she said this, Mercedes pictured the spirits of her mother, Cirilo, and all the girl babies sweeping down in a rush for Ignacio and Tino. For a long time, Mercedes clung to this comforting image. Then she filled the pit up again with cool moist earth, patting the ground till it was smooth.

This done, Mercedes Prieto unwound her tapado. She draped it over her head, then enshrouded herself in it once more. She curled up in the midst of her family's graves. Dawn was not far away. When the night had passed, she would rise and return to Sonsonate, where she would catch the train that would take her to Jacinta and Basilio, to those people who needed her the most. In the meantime, she would lie here, handing over her past, surrendering herself to the knowledge that in this world there were things she could not know, loved ones she would not see again.

▼▼

CHAPTER ELEVEN

Finca La Abundancia
outside Santa Ana, El Salvador
February 1933

I n the bedroom of la casona, the big house sitting at the edge of her husband's coffee plantation, Elena de Contreras was startled awake by a dream in which her teeth tumbled around inside her mouth like so many stones. In the dream, she had spit the teeth out, one by one, into her hand. Elena propped herself up on an elbow. It was sometime after dawn, and she used the grainy light to look into her hand, expecting to find molars and incisors lying in her palm. None were there, of course, and she fell back against the pillows.

"Ernesto," she said softly, turning to her husband, who slept on his side, away from her. She scooted over to him, molding herself around the substantial curve of his body. He was warm, and he smelled of the musky fragrance he splashed on each morning after he shaved. "Ernesto," she repeated, throwing a slender arm over him and giving him a shake. "I had the dream again."

"Umm," Ernesto muttered.

"Amor, I dreamed my teeth fell out."

Elena waited for him to come fully awake. When he did not, she allowed him to sleep on. It was nearing the end of coffee-picking season, the first since the uprising the year before. All day he was jostled on the horse. All day he and Neto and Alberto, their two

69

sons, rode over La Abundancia, all carefully watchful for signs of unrest among the workers. Each night Ernesto dropped heavily into bed.

Elena snuggled closer to him. She had dreamed this dream before. On three occasions, to be exact. After each dream, misfortune had followed. Hardly a week after the first dream, Elena's mother discovered a growth in her breast that had led to her untimely death. The second dream foretold the slow deterioration of her father's mind. And only a year ago, the dream had come again. A few days later, campesinos south of here, rebelling against the very families that sustained them, turned a January night into a bloodbath. During the revolt, Armando Aragón, a close friend of the family's, had been butchered.

Elena rolled away from her husband. She nestled into the softness of her bed and her down pillows. Their brass bed was set beside a window that reached down to the floor. The window was screened against insects and had shutters on each side to protect against the rain. Through the screen came the fresh smell of morning and the gurgle of the brook only meters away. Outside, the new light filtered through the branches of pepetos and madrecacaos; its glow nudged into the room.

Twenty-two years ago, shortly after she and Ernesto married, they had begun to live in La Abundancia during the four months of coffee season. Back then, she had selected this bedroom as theirs because, of all the rooms of the house, it alone allowed nature to come inside. What a difference from their main house in Santa Ana. That house, just five kilometers away, was bordered by four city streets, and only in the patio was there a semblance of the greenery at la casona.

Elena ran her tongue over her teeth, still surprised to feel them intact and in her mouth. The dream had been so real. The dread of apprehension pressed down on her. What did *this* dream foretell? Was this one solely about herself? In a nearby tree a dichosofuí warbled. Dichoso fui, the bird trilled, singing of lost luck and faded happiness. Was this another omen today? Elena had lived an enchanted life. Indeed, in her life, she'd been more fortunate than most. She had been her mother's only daughter; before her father's decline, she had been the light of his eyes. And she was Cecilia's soul mate and Ernesto's one true love. But years had passed and life took its turns. She was forty now, and this fact preoccupied her. She admitted it was a petty fixation, especially given the times. In the country, coffee prices had never been lower. Though the campesinos had quieted, hatred still shone in their eyes. In the world, a depression raged. Of late, she was depressed, too. She had always been beautiful. She had been a beautiful child. Despite her age, she was still a beautiful woman, she was told. But after forty, could a woman count upon her looks for long?

But enough of gloomy thoughts and premonitions. Outside the sun would soon be shining. Elena threw back the embroidered sheet. She swung her legs over the edge of the bed, probing under it for her slippers. The polished tiled floor was cool to her feet. Last night, she had tossed her silk robe across the chaise longue, and she retrieved it now, pulling it over her gown, the sleeveless one with the tucks and gathers. At the dresser, with its tilting oval mirror, Elena searched for the gold clasp Ernesto had surprised her with on her saint's day. She poked around perfume bottles, fishing in saucers spilling with the faux jewelry that don Valdemar, the jeweler, made specially for wearing at the finca. Finding the clasp, she secured her hair in a coil atop her head. She did not look at her image in the mirror before going out the door.

In the hall, the sound of her father's voice greeted her. Elena sighed deeply. "Nononononono," her father intoned, the word like a mantra traveling down the dim corridor transecting the house. As was its custom, Coffee, Ernesto's German shepherd, was sprawled in the hallway against the door. The old dog heaved itself up after Elena stepped over. It yawned and wagged its tail, trailing Elena past Neto and Alberto's door, past her daughter Magda's door, past the room in which Cecilia de Aragón and her daughter, Isabel, slept as well. Elena entered her father's room, leaving Coffee in the hall.

The morning light had chased the night's shadows halfway up the walls and up the massive armoire in the corner. On the night table, a lamp cast its shine along the edge of the bed and on her father, don Orlando Navarro, who was propped upright by a bank of pillows. He wore his blue pajamas. His arms were crossed against his chest; his shoulders were hunched to his ears. His eyes were shut so tightly they had almost disappeared. "Nonononono," he chanted, his mouth an O.

"Papi, ¿qué te pasa?" Elena said, smoothing the sheet bunched around his waist. Besides herself, her father had two other children, her older brothers Mario and Carlos. Growing up, they had christened Elena with a nickname. They called her la Consentida, the Pampered One. After a time, they had shortened the name to la Conse. La Conse always gets what she wants, one brother would say. La Conse never has to do anything, the other one would add. Elena hated the name. A few years back, when her father's first symptoms appeared, it was decided that because she was the daughter, it fell to her to care for him. "Papá will move into la Conse's house," Mario had said. "It's time for la Conse to pamper someone else." Elena had readily accepted the responsibility for her father's care, but she had threatened her brothers with not speaking to them if they used the name again.

"Your father won't take his pills," the night nurse said. She wore a white uniform and stood on the opposite side of the bed. A stiff little hat was pinned to the top of her head. She held a glass and tablets of different shapes.

"Papi, you have to take your medicine."

Don Orlando let his shoulders drop. When he saw Elena, he snapped his eyes shut again, hugging himself more fiercely than before. "No quiero la medicina."

"Papi," Elena said, using her singsong voice because sometimes this calmed him. "Don't you want to get well?" He was not going to get well. He could take small pills, large pills. No pills could ever cure his ailing mind.

The nurse said, "Mercedes came in a minute ago. She went to get ice."

Elena nodded. For weeks her father had been asking for ice. He liked to suck on long fingers of it that Mercedes chopped from the block. "La Nana is getting ice for you, Papi."

Mercedes hurried in with a bowl. "Buenos días, niña Elena." Coffee took advantage of the open door and slipped inside. The dog sniffed around the bed before flopping alongside it.

Don Orlando opened his sea green eyes when he heard the dog.

He threw an arm out, feeling with an open hand along the bedside. "¿Dónde está la Pepa?" he said.

It was his pet hen he asked about. The hen was at home, in Santa Ana. She had been his pet for more than ten years. She laid an egg for him every day. At night, she roosted on the crossbeam at the foot of his bed. "La Pepa is at home, where she's safe in the patio," Mercedes said. El señor asked about the hen every day. Every day he was given the same answer.

Mercedes made room for the ice bowl on the night table crowded with jars and vials. "After you take the medicine, you can have the ice," she said, reaching for the glass and pills the nurse still held. Mercedes offered each to don Orlando, who smiled an infantile smile as he obeyed. The nurse gave a grunt of displeasure and went around the bed. "It's time for my breakfast," she said.

"Gracias, Mercedes," Elena said after the nurse had left and Mercedes had laid the bowl in her father's lap. "I don't know why I bother with all these nurses." Since her father's illness two years ago, Elena had employed half a dozen women. Each had fled after only a few months. "Don Orlando is a difficult man," one nurse had muttered before turning on her heels. Another, after a period in which don Orlando hurled all food brought to him across the room, had bolted from the house in the middle of her shift. "El señor es un loco," she shouted for all the house and the world to hear. Since the illness set in, its progression being a slow train pulling into the station, there had been a multitude of comments, all stated in various degrees of frankness, all amounting to one and the same thing: Caring for don Orlando was a trial, and it was only Elena who could calm him and reason with him. The last being true until Mercedes Prieto came along.

Elena sat in a chair and watched Mercedes. The servant was solicitous, tender. In her loose, black dress, she seemed ageless and unflappable. She wore no shoes, and in fact was opposed to the notion. Back in November, when Mercedes had appeared at Elena's house in Santa Ana, she had been shoeless. Back then, Elena was catching up on her correspondence on the wide veranda facing the heart of the house: the interior patio with its pretty tiled fountain, with the lemon and orange trees, with the roses and the jasmine shrubs as well. Clara, called the inside girl because she did the cleaning and the food serving, led Mercedes in. "She's coming about Telma's position," Clara had said, and almost immediately Elena broached the subject of shoes as a way of cutting the interview short, for she was not in the mood to be hiring today. All the help wore shoes, Elena said. Wearing shoes was sanitary. Perhaps this is true, Mercedes said. But she had never worn them, and at her age, she was not one to begin. What's more, Mercedes had said, I come about laundry work, not about inside work. Laundry work is done outside and under the sky. Shoes are not practical for a laundress to wear. Elena recalled the matter-of-factness in Mercedes's voice. Something about her said: Take me as I am. You will not regret it. Three months ago, Elena had.

Although she had been hired for the laundry, Mercedes frequently helped Elena with don Orlando. From the beginning, her father had taken more than a liking to Mercedes. He had first seen her the afternoon she carried in an armload of fresh linen to store in the armoire. Don Orlando had been in his armchair, gazing out the window, while Elena read to him from *Las mil y una noches*, the only book that held his attention. When Mercedes came in, he looked her way, then back out the window, before turning to her again. "Nana," he said, pulling himself up dottily from the chair. Elena realized then how much Mercedes resembled la Tere, her father's venerable nursemaid who had died only last year.

"Do you believe in dreams?" Elena said to Mercedes, surprising herself for speaking out so frankly to a servant, a relatively new one at that. Outside the window, the sun was high now. "I had a bad dream last night," she added as explanation.

"Sometimes dreams appear to be bad when they're really not," Mercedes said. She was thinking about the times Ignacio came to her. About the times when she dreamed about Tino and she would awaken, her heart racing because she had seen her baby again. These dreams caused her grief, but they were not bad dreams.

"This one was bad," Elena said. "I've dreamed it before, and each time something bad happened." Why was she saying this? Perhaps in voicing the fear, she might dispel it.

"Ah," Mercedes said. She used a napkin from the night table to blot don Orlando's chin.

"I dreamed my teeth fell out," Elena blurted, instantly regretting this disclosure. It was as if she'd set something on its course when she spoke.

Mercedes looked in Elena's direction. She had dark, deep-set eyes. Along her forehead, there were furrows even when she wasn't frowning. Now she frowned when Elena told her about the teeth.

"I know it's bad," Elena said, looking out the window again. "Dreaming about teeth falling out is bad."

Mercedes nodded. "No es bueno. After a dream like that, one must be careful. Hay que tener cuidado."

The main charm of la casona was the wide, columned porch that lay across the front of the house and stretched around the west side, where it was screened for evening sitting. Elena preferred to take breakfast on the screened wing because it was bright and airy, and because the brook was so near that its moisture helped to dampen and plump the skin. From here, she could observe the courtyard and, beyond it, the buildings that comprised the finca office and the beneficio, the coffee-processing plant. Growing in the middle of the courtyard was the ancient ceiba, the silk-cotton tree, with its twisted trunk as thick around as a dozen men put together. The tree branched out high on its trunk, and under its canopy, the horses stood patiently tethered to their posts. Although it was only eight or so, the dogs of the finca were already sprawled and dozing in its shade.

After visiting her father's room and after she'd bathed and changed into daytime clothes, Elena was on the porch with Cecilia de Aragón. Elena had rung the bell for breakfast, and the two waited for Clara to bring it.

Elena and Cecilia. The two had been best friends since childhood, when their names were Elena Navarro and Cecilia Muñoz. In appearance, they were opposites: Even as a child, Elena was elegantly slender and pale. Tiny freckles dusted her long legs and upper arms. Cecilia was petite and softly round. After only a bit of sun, she turned a coppery color that was stunning. Elena's hair was the color of caramels; she preferred to wear it long. Cecilia was a brunette, with a feathery cap of curls around her face. Elena had the same green eyes as her father; Cecilia, black fiery ones.

In temperament, they were just as opposed. Elena was sensitive and sentimental. In most situations, you could predict what she might do. At a party, she preferred to sit on the side and observe the goings-on. Cecilia, on the other hand, was bold and outlandish. At a party, people made a ring around her when she danced. What people thought of her was never much of a concern. To show how different they were from each other, the families liked to tell a story about the two. Once, when they were five or six, the girls had been on an outing at don Orlando's hacienda in the eastern part of the country. Elena's father strode into the room shouldering a rifle and looking very sportive in his safari wear. "I'm going to hunt some rabbits," he announced to the girls. At the news, Elena had bolted from her chair and run to the door. "I'm going to warn all the rabbits to hide before you can get to them, Papi," Elena said, her lower lip quivering. Cecilia marched over to don Orlando's side and looked up at him. "Can I come with you, tío Orlando?" she said.

Together, Elena and Cecilia had attended primary and secondary school at La Asuncíon, the Catholic girl's school in Santa Ana run by the Sisters of the Assumption. In their classes, they had insisted on side-by-side tables, but soon the nuns, in the interest of education, put a stop to their closeness. After school, the girls made up for daytime deprivations. They raced home to change out of their starched navy uniforms with the silly white pinafores, and then met under the vanilla growing in Cecilia's patio. The tree had a slender twisted trunk that looped around here and there to form what the girls thought looked like arms held out in an embrace. To amplify its loving appearance, the leaves of the tree were pale green hearts. Under the vanilla, the girls gossiped and conspired. Under the vanilla, the nanas a glance away, the girls took afternoon snacks: fresco de tamarindo for Elena, and fresco de avena for Cecilia. When they became señoritas, they strolled into the elegant salón of the Casino Santaneco dressed in crisp linen dresses of complementary colors. They crossed the polished floor toward their customary table where they were served café con leche in thin china cups.

In Santa Ana, la Elena y la Cecilia's friendship was legendary. La una es la sombra de la otra, their parents said. One is the shadow of the other. When they married, each the other's primera madrina, they moved into houses on Calle Número 9, directly opposite one another. Each day, when the double-door gate of one of the houses opened, it was as if greeting the gate across the street. Still, the friendship was not an exclusionary one. The women joyously embraced their marriages, but both Ernesto Contreras and Armando Aragón understood, though it went unspoken, that the bond the women shared was one they must never attempt to weaken.

Last year, after the attack at La Merced, their friendship grew even stronger. Last year, at Armando Aragón's finca in Ahuachapán, Armando and his administrador had been slashed to death with machetes by coffee pickers in revolt.

This morning Cecilia was settled on the wicker sofa with her legs drawn up against herself. She and her only child, Isabel, had taken refuge for the coffee season in la casona.

Clara came in with a silver tray laden with breakfast. Sweet rolls and rounds of crisp toast were heaped in a basket. Softened butter and French confitures had their own little saucers. On a platter glistened crescents of papaya. Icy orange juice formed a moist sheen on a pitcher. There was a small pot of esencia—espresso—and another larger pot of hot milk. Coarse-grained sugar lay golden in a bowl. Clara arranged the food and the tableware on a wicker table and left.

Elena poured esencia into a cup, joining the stream of coffee with another of milk. The coffee was thick and flavorful. It was processed on the finca, and it was a treat to have it, given that practically all of La Abundancia's coffee was shipped away for export. Elena poured a second cup, heaping two tablespoons of sugar into Cecilia's cup just as she liked it. She added no sugar to her own.

"Tu café, Ceci," Elena said.

Cecilia placed the cup and saucer on her lap. She smiled and looked down into the cup. She was grateful to be here. Strange that she could feel safe at this finca, a finca so much like her own. To that place she would never return. But here, in the loving presence of Elena and Ernesto, she was turning into herself again.

"Did you sleep well?" Elena asked. When they were girls and they spent the night at each other's houses, a rare occurrence in other families, the first thing they did on awakening was talk about their dreams. Lying in the darkened room with only the little night table between them, they whispered back and forth about the images sleep brought them.

Cecilia shrugged. "You know how it is, Nena. Some nights are worse than others." Cecilia always called Elena "Nena."

Elena said, "I had a bad dream last night." She couldn't hold the news back. She needed to tell Cecilia. She needed Cecilia to say "All will be well."

"Last night, I dreamed I saw Armando." Cecilia made circles with her fingertips against the side of the cup. "In the dream, he was at La Merced. He was wearing that favorite sombrero of his."

Elena nodded. She could see Armando in his leather hat with the wide brim. At the finca, he wore it all day long. She and Cecilia liked to tease him about the way his hair looked after he took it off. Another memory came to her about him. "Remember when Armando went off on that hunting expedition?"

"¿Cuál?"

Elena took a sip of coffee. She nibbled at a corner of a piece of toast. "The one to Lake Guija. The one where he shot the alligators. Remember the alligator skins he brought back? Remember how we had purses made? He wanted to have a hat made. What you said made me remember."

Cecilia set the cup and saucer down on a side table. "Mando almost got killed on that trip. Remember, one of the hunters shot him by accident."

"Oh, God, what was I thinking? Forgive me, Ceci. I can't believe I caused you to remember that."

"It's not your fault," Cecilia said. "There's hardly a thing you can say that won't make me remember something about him." She was silent for a moment, and then she said, "That trip was years ago, when Isa was two." She turned her eyes on Elena. "Armando could have died then, Nena, fifteen years ago. We had all those years together after that trip." What a marriage they had had. He was the only man she knew who allowed his wife to be herself. In her life, there would never be another man like her Mando.

"Yes," Elena said. Armando Aragón's death was as vivid in her mind as when she first heard of it. Cecilia and Isabel had seen it all. For weeks afterward, over and over, Cecilia spoke of little else: We heard them coming. The dogs began to bark, and then we heard the shouts. Barking and shouting. It was all like a howl. Howls along the road and across the yard. Howls over the steps, right up to the door. Armando threw his back against the door. His back, can you believe it, Nena? The revolver was in his hand and he shot and shot again, but that didn't deter them. The machetes clattered through. They pushed their way in. Armando screamed to me and Isa, Get back. Get back. Where in God's name is la guardia? What in God's name is happening? It was dark, but you saw the machetes. You heard the whistling sound machetes make before they strike flesh.

Ernesto Contreras joined the women on the porch. He wore pressed khaki pants and a starched white shirt. Over his shoulder hung the leather holster from which a revolver butt protruded.

Elena stood and went across to greet him. "Buenos días, amor," she said, kissing him on the mouth. I'm so happy you're alive, she thought.

▼▼

CHAPTER TWELVE

Moments later, Neto and Alberto appeared. Neto was twenty; his brother, nineteen. The first of Elena's sons, although named after his father, was tall and slender like his mother. Alberto, instead, favored Ernesto, who was a compact, solid man. The brothers greeted their mother with a kiss. They smelled of the same aftershave their father used. Both were fresh and robust, their hair damp from their showers; the path of the combs' teeth was still evident through it. The brothers greeted Cecilia, too, bending over her, calling her "tía" because she was like an aunt.

"Did you have breakfast?" Elena said.

"We had something inside," Neto said, straightening up and adjusting his revolver, which he preferred to carry poked into his waistband. It was easier to get at, carried in this way.

"We all had something inside," Ernesto said. He went over and gave Cecilia a peck on the cheek, too. "I met with your accountant," he said to her. "You and I need to talk." Ernesto, at Elena's suggestion, was helping Cecilia with her finances. "But I can't do it today. Tomorrow is payday." Payday always fell on Saturday. There were more than two thousand coffee workers at La Abundancia. It took the better part of a day to get them all paid. Ernesto pointed to his sons. "Today, the boys are seeing to the guardia. I'm driving to the

80

bank." Customarily, four guardias were stationed around the finca. On payday, their ranks tripled, a protection against brawls that often started. Pickers fought over gambling debts, over women. With money in the pocket could come a bottle of guaro in the hand. Pickers and liquor were always a bad mix.

Out in the yard, Samuel Vega, el administrador, called out to el patrón. Samuel Vega had managed operations for more than twenty years. During that time he reported to don Ernesto. Now it was required he report to the patrón's sons as well, a situation Samuel Vega resented. The men in the house went out and joined him. Elena watched them all gather under the ceiba. Two guardias stood there, too. Neto and Alberto mounted their horses and trotted off. Ernesto and Samuel Vega walked across the compound toward the Cadillac stored in the shed. The automobile was a 1931 Town Sedan. It was shiny black, with gray fenders and running boards. Ernesto had paid eight hundred dollars for it, almost half that amount to have it shipped by boat from the United States. Elena thought owning it was an extravagance, although she had to admit it was a handsome sight.

Magda, Elena's seventeen-year-old daughter, came out onto the porch. She wore a long white nightgown and was barefoot. Her black curly hair was wild around her face and along her shoulders.

"What are you doing up so early?" Elena lifted a cheek to her daughter's kiss. Magda and Cecilia's daughter were on school vacation, and they liked to sleep late. In a few weeks, both of them would start their last year at La Asunción, the same school their mothers had attended. "Where are your slippers?" Elena said.

"Y la Isa?" Cecilia asked.

"She's still asleep. Coffee kept scratching at the door. He woke me up." Magda kissed Cecilia and then dropped down beside her. She lifted her feet and wiggled her toes. "The floor is so cool. It feels good on my feet." She leaned toward the coffee table and poured herself a cup. "I'm going into Santa Ana today. I want to get the mail."

"Your father just drove off. He and Samuel went to the bank."

"Oh no," Magda said, placing the coffeepot back on the table. "Papi won't think to check the mail." She was newly engaged to Alvaro Tobar, who was working the cotton season on his own family's hacienda across the country, in Usulután. Magda hadn't seen Alvaro for nearly a month. It would be two more weeks before they met again. On December 2, after she received her bachillerato, Magda and Alvaro would be married.

"Didn't Papá bring three letters just the other day?" Elena asked.

"That was then," Magda said. Alvaro wrote almost every day, a rare thing for a man. But then, Alvaro was like that. Thoughtful. Sentimental. It was he who invented their special riddle. What do 65 and 59 add up to? (The figures represented the number of letters in their first and last names: Alvaro [6] Tobar [5] and Magda [5] Contreras, [9].) The answer was 83, not 124 as it was logical to believe. Eighty-three stood for the number of letters in the two words that made up the phrase "nosotros dos," which meant we two.

Magda lifted a papaya crescent from the serving plate and plopped half of the fruit into her mouth. "Um," she said because the fruit was sweet and creamy.

"And how is Alvaro?" Cecilia said.

Magda licked her fingers, accepting the napkin her mother handed her. "He's wonderful. He's working very hard, he says." In his letters he also wrote he couldn't wait until they married. He said, "Come December 2, I'll spend the rest of my life making love to you." At the thought, a delicious thrill of expectation shot through her. They would honeymoon for a month, not in Europe as was the custom, but at El Refugio, her grandfather's rustic getaway to the north, in the piney mountains of Chalatenango. The change of venue had been dictated by the economic bad times. Magda was not fazed. Whether crossing on the *Ile-de-France*, staying at the Ritz in Paris, or lodging at her grandfather's cozy cabin, it came to the same thing: she and Alvaro in bed together at last.

Cecilia stood and stretched. "Let's take our walk."

"Why don't you come?" Elena said to Magda.

Magda stifled a yawn with a hand. "You two go on. I'm going back to bed."

Elena and Cecilia left the house through a rear door that opened up to the ample yard where Mercedes did the laundry. Stylish imported scarves covered their heads and were tied jauntily under their chins. The dog came along, too. Ernesto insisted on it. In addition, he had instructed a caporal to trail them on their walks. Elena didn't mind the man as long as he kept at a respectable distance so that she and Cecilia could talk openly.

Today they kept to their customary routine. They crossed the yard and went under the ceiba, then past the cluster of wooden structures that comprised the administration building. They passed the open sided cookhouse abuzz with women tending the wood fires over which the day's meals were being prepared. Breakfast had been served hours ago. At noon, the cooks would haul tortillas and coffee out to the fields. At dusk, the pickers would come in for supper: thick chewy tortillas ladled with beans flavored with chiles. Daily, ten thousand tortillas and ten cauldrons of beans were prepared. Coffee was always plentiful. From dawn to dusk, large sooty ollas simmered on all the hearths.

Most pickers lived in long, low buildings that were now empty, given the hour. Each family had a room and a washtub. This morning, a few small children romped gleefully in the road that served as their yard. Many had bellies so distended they appeared larger than their heads. As Elena and Cecilia went by, a woman in one of the rooms poked her head around the length of cloth serving as a door. She clapped to get the children's attention. They stopped playing and scurried home, not once looking back toward the women when they passed.

Not far from the buildings, and sitting quaintly in a clearing ringed by coffee bushes and the narrow paths snaking around them, were a dozen or so ranchitos, small dwellings with red tile roofs. In front of the ranchos, groups of pickers had come in from the trees, and were bunched around mounds of bright coffee beans, ready now for loading. A barranco, a gully, was not far away. It was here that the latrines were set, and though they were not visible, the smell alone marked their presence.

A few meters down the road, the women went by the classroom and the clinic. Both appeared deserted. The clinic attendant was leaning against the door frame in his smudged white smock, and he stepped back inside when he saw the two.

Farther on, at the right of the road, loomed the beneficio. It was a hub of activity, for if coffee was the blood of the finca, the processing plant was its heart. The beneficio was built beside a stream because water was elemental to coffee processing. After the pickers stripped the plump red berries—el café en uva—from shrubs into baskets lashed around their waists, they dumped load after load into mounds and then into costales, henequen sacks. All this was done under the scrutiny of caporales who, armed with dull pencils and small ledgers, kept a record of all pickers and their measures. These reports were handed to Samuel Vega in time for la planilla. Once in costales, el café en uva left the fields and was brought by oxcart to the beneficio.

Elena and Cecilia passed a dozen carts, all loaded with sacks of coffee; they passed broad-shouldered men unloading the sacks. Many dogs milled about. Some trotted up to Coffee and sniffed at him, but Coffee was a tolerant dog and didn't allow this intrusion to impede his progress down the road.

The women neared the water tanks where coffee soaked to help loosen pulp from bean. After a day, the berries were greatly softened, yet still they were run through the pulping machine with its huge paddle wheels to finish the job the water had begun. Once free from the bean, the pulp floated off. Elena and Cecilia broke into a run to get quickly away from the stench of fermenting coffee. The dog, too, picked up his pace, but he was old and the women soon left him behind. He caught up with them again when they slowed to go past the tendederos, the vast cement patios where the berries went tawny in the sun. This café en oro was a pretty sight, and Elena relished seeing workers in their wide-brimmed hats rake and turn and level Ernesto's coffee. Next to the tendederos were the long sheds under which dried coffee rattled and jiggled along conveyor belts to the sorting tables where sharp-eyed women examined the beans and plucked out imperfect ones.

Elena and Cecilia arrived at the place where the stream made a crook. Now the banks of the stream flattened, and stones and pebbles, boulders and flat rocks made up the riverbed. Meters from the stream, thickets of álamos and ironwoods rose up; their leaves fluttered gray and then green in the little breeze.

The two made their way across the stony bank. They headed for the one flat rock, large as a table, that was the destination of all their walks. Coffee stepped gingerly over the stones, too. He went to lie in the sliver of shade the table rock provided. The women scrambled up onto the rock while the caporal stayed under the trees. He leaned against an álamo, his machete at his side, his left boot raised against the tree trunk.

Elena untied her scarf and draped it around her shoulders. She stretched out on the rock, feeling its warmth over the length of her body.

Cecilia stretched out as well. She closed her eyes, and after a moment, the sun made little pinwheels of light under her eyelids. "When we were on the porch, you said you had a dream. Perdóname, Nena, I know I cut you off."

Elena sat up and pulled her knees to her chest and hugged them. She looked at Cecilia's face framed by the edges of her scarf. Cecilia's thick lashes were dark little half-moons against her cheeks. "I dreamed my teeth fell out."

Cecilia lifted her head, shading her eyes to best see her friend. "Oh no. Not again."

"I don't know why, but this morning I told Mercedes about the dream. She said, After a dream like that, hay que tener cuidado. That frightened me."

Cecilia lay back down again. She placed a forearm over her eyes to block out the sun. She said nothing. She simply took in a long breath.

Elena looked upstream, at the way the water slipped quietly away from her. "I shouldn't have told you. These days, you have enough on your mind." She said this, but she wanted Cecilia to disregard the statement. She wanted Cecilia's full attention. She wanted the soothing comfort of Cecilia's understanding and common sense. In short, Elena wanted the old Cecilia back. The Cecilia who had existed before Armando's death.

Cecilia said, "Remember when we used to play interview?"

"Sí, me acuerdo," Elena said. They were young when they first played the game. Cecilia had made it up because her father owned the newspaper. Frequently the girls went down to La Tribuna and strolled around the newsroom, with its heady smell of raw paper and fresh ink and all its bustling industriousness. The girls regarded the reporters, how their quick index fingers punched out stories on the slender, cantilevered keys of their bulky Underwoods. When the girls played, Cecilia liked to ask the questions. "I'll be the reporter," she often said, "but you have to tell the truth, Elena Navarro. Papi says you can never lie to a reporter." Back then, Elena frequently acquiesced to Cecilia's demands. But always Elena had her own request: "Ask what you want," she would say, "but please don't make me cry." It was a futile plea, of course, for Cecilia always asked sad questions, as when she dug for details about Elena's little dog and how it was that the gardener had accidentally lopped off its back leg with the machete when he was pruning the jasmines in the patio.

"Let's play now. But I'll ask the questions," Cecilia said, here on the rock in the sun, her forearm still resting over her eyes.

Elena laughed softly. "I'm glad to see some things haven't changed."

For a moment or two there was silence, and then Cecilia said, "Tell me how you'll feel when I die, Nena."

The question startled Elena. "My God, Ceci, what a thing to say."

"That's not an answer," Cecilia said.

"I don't want to talk about things like that. You're not going to die."

"Someday I will, and you have to tell me what you'll feel. Come, Nena, you have to tell me. You said we could play interview."

"I'll be sad," Elena replied.

"Sad. That's nothing. Sad are the poor when they have nothing to eat."

"Okay. I'll cry when you die."

"Will you cry hard, Nena? Will you throw yourself on the ground? How many handkerchiefs will you need when I die?"

"I'll cry so loud all the world will hear. If you die, I'll never stop crying."

Cecilia lifted her forearm and gazed up at Elena. "I like that," she said.

"Stop it!" Elena said. "Why are you saying all this? Do you think my dream was about you dying?"

Cecilia covered her eyes again. "It can't be," she said. "That last bad dream you had was a dream about me."

▼   ▼   ▼

The two had almost reached home. They were under the ceiba when pain stabbed Elena's hand. She yelled out, holding her hand up, expecting to see a wasp or some such insect attached to her finger. But there was nothing like that. In all respects her hand looked normal, yet there was this pain gripping her finger, her ring finger at that. She clasped one hand with the other, but the pain worsened. "¡Ay Dios!" she exclaimed.

"Nena, ¿qué te pasa?" Cecilia said.

Elena bent over and placed her hand between her knees to ease the discomfort. "Ayayay," she wailed. The caporal who had accompanied the women had just walked off when Elena cried out. Now he ran back. Mercedes was at the water tank under the mango tree doing the laundry. When she heard Elena, she hastily dried her soapy hands against her apron and rushed toward her patrona. "Niña Elena, ¿qué fue?"

"My finger." Elena held up her hand as if for proof. She laid it against her heart, then down again, shaking it out.

Mercedes grasped Elena's hand and examined it. "It's your ring," she said. "Let's get it off. We'll use soap and water at the pila."

Magda, who had abandoned trying to fall back to sleep, and Isabel were sitting on the porch. The girls heard the commotion in the yard. They ran out through the back. Clara, the other servant, raced out, too.

At the water tank, Mercedes struggled with the ring. She rolled the yellow ball of soap over Elena's hand, lathering it up. Mercedes twisted the ring and eased it forward a little at a time. When at last the ring slipped off, Mercedes plunged Elena's hand into the cool water of the pila. She wiped the ring off on her apron before laying it on the scrubbing stand. The ring gleamed innocently in the sun.

"Virgen Santa," Clara said, taking a step back.

"My God, look at that!" Magda added. The ring was a wide gold band with diamonds encrusted along the top. Her father had given it to her mother on their wedding day. For twenty-two years, her mother had never taken it off. Now the underside of the ring was flattened into a line. It was as if someone had taken a hammer to the underside of the ring.

"The ring's deformed. How can that be?" Isabel said. She was in her robe, and she threw her arms around herself as if she were cold.

At the question, all the women went silent. They stared at the misshapen ring lying against smooth stone. Elena picked the ring up and tried replacing it on her finger, but the band was now so narrow it couldn't be done.

"Mami, ¡qué horror!" Magda said.

Cecilia said, "Tell me about your dream."

▼▼

CHAPTER THIRTEEN

Mercedes Prieto drew aside the curtain that served as a door to her daughter's room. "Jacinta," Mercedes said, but she saw the room was empty. It was early afternoon, and still the place was deep in shadow, for no windows graced the pickers' quarters, only the curtains hanging at the door frames.

The room was dingy and small. Four cots, each topped with a petate, lined up against the wall. The last one on the left belonged to Jacinta. On the wall above it, she had tacked the card of San Jacinto that Basilio Fermín had given her. The room contained no dresser, no chairs, no table, only the cots and the stifling heat. It smelled of the people living in it, of the people living up and down the gallery, of the rolled-up clothing and the meager belongings stashed under the cots, of the latrines only meters away down the ravine.

Mercedes let the curtain drop. She crossed the narrow gallery and stepped down into the road. It was payday; the notion that on days like these anything might happen hung over the finca like a thundercloud. Extra guardias patrolled the property, and this alone caused nerves to wear. Since early morning, a continuous stream of people had been snaking down the road in four lines that ultimately disappeared through the wide doors of the administration building.

Workers' names were called out alphabetically by the pagadores, the paymasters, who manned the four pay tables. Because Jacinta's last name was Prieto, it was always midafternoon before she stood in front of a pagador. Mercedes hastened around to the back to see if Jacinta might be there. Mercedes had left the day's laundry, scrubbed and soapy, spread over bushes and bleaching in the sun. She had little time before she must return to gather up the clothing and give it a final rinse before hanging it out to dry. Ernestina, one of the girls who shared Jacinta's room, walked up from the ravine. "Buenas, niña Mercedes," Ernestina said.

"Where's my daughter?" Mercedes asked.

"She's in line. She's with Chico Portales."

"Um," Mercedes said. The news did not surprise her. It was why she was here, away from the laundry. Chico Portales and Jacinta. Had Mercedes known what would spring up between the two, she would not have allowed Jacinta to pick coffee at La Abundancia. In El Congo, it was Luis Martínez, the young man who owned the fruit stand, who had turned Jacinta's head. In Santa Ana, Chico Portales had clearly displaced Luis. Since the start of picking season, Chico and Jacinta had taken to each other. Over the months, Mercedes had watched them. Coyly they began, but now there was a confidence about them, as if they had settled on a secret that pleased them both. A person didn't need much imagination to guess what that might be. Chico Portales came from Metapán, a city to the north that bordered on Guatemala. At seventeen, he stood muscular and tall, with a chocolate hue to his skin that made him quite attractive. Only a fool would be blind to what Jacinta saw in him. Still, Jacinta was fourteen, and though it was not lost on Mercedes that she herself had already given birth at that age, it was precisely this responsibility, this precipitous leap into adulthood, that she wanted to forestall in her daughter's life.

Mercedes headed toward the administration building. Shielding her eyes with a hand against the sun, she walked past the lines of pickers. An array of humanity was represented here, but all Mercedes noticed were the guardias. Ever at the ready, the men sauntered up and around the lines, their rifles slung on leather straps across their shoulders. Under the visors of their helmets, the guardias' eyes were indistinct. Although they were meters away, Mercedes felt the sear of their commanding gaze as if they were standing next to her.

Mercedes hurried into la administración. Inside, the temperature was only a little cooler than outside. Waiting for her eyes to adjust to the light, she noted the pickers inching their way down the hall. Some men in straw hats leaned silently against the walls as they waited. Others talked spiritedly. In the lines, old women wrapped in dull tapados, their arms crossed over their breasts, leaned toward each other as they quietly conversed. Young girls in tight dresses and strapping youths with dark mustaches shot furtive glances at one another up and down the line. The girls giggled behind spread hands, their eyes bright with expectation. Los machos cocked their narrow hips and guffawed out loud. Children of all ages, some dressed, most not, ran noisily about. Some mothers sprang periodically from lines to hurry after infants who had crawled away from reach. Because the line was moving, the dogs milling about moved along, too. At times, they plopped on their haunches, their tongues protruding at an angle from their mouths. In all this activity, there was not a sign of Jacinta.

Mercedes came to the place where the hall veered to the left and then ballooned into the large room that contained, at the back, the four payroll tables. A low gated railing was strung across the width of the room, passing in front of the tables and forming a barrier between authority and servitude.

The pagadores sat behind the tables. Stacks of bills rose in front of them, as well as large metal boxes with compartments holding coins of different denominations. Next to each pagador's hand was his own revolver. Don Samuel Vega and don Ernesto were present, too. So were Elena's sons. All were armed. They patrolled the space behind the tables, checking with one pagador and then with another.

Mercedes decided to give up her search. She retraced her steps and was about to head toward the laundry when Jacinta came through the door.

"What are you doing here?" Jacinta said, scratching an elbow, trying to keep reproof from surfacing on her tongue. It was tiresome to have her mother always checking on her. Why was she so meddlesome? So sure that she knew what was best in their lives.

Mercedes turned to the woman standing in line behind Jacinta.

"I'm not in line. I'm only here to talk to my daughter." Mercedes smiled and pointed to Jacinta before turning back to her.

Jacinta muttered hello and made perfunctory inquiries, softening her tone because Chico Portales stood just four pickers in front of her and it was obvious her mother had not seen him, which was very good. Jacinta lifted her hair off her neck. "It's so hot," she said. She did not braid her hair anymore, for she was too old for that. Now she wore her hair loose and flowing, the way Chico preferred it.

Mercedes narrowed her eyes, spying a pair of copper-colored hoops dangling from her daughter's earlobes. "Where did you get those earrings?"

I'm in for it now, Jacinta thought, letting her hair drop onto her shoulders. She looked away from her mother.

"That boy Chico gave them to you, didn't he?"

"Shush, Mamá, don't talk so loud," Jacinta said, laying a finger across her lips. Her hands were stained dark from stripping red berries. Little rag ribbons were tied around two abrasions on her fingers. She leaned in close to her mother. "It's true. Chico gave them to me," she whispered finally, deciding it was best to tell the truth and be done with it.

Mercedes lowered her voice. "I hope he gave them to you out of the kindness of his heart. I hope he's not expecting you to earn those earrings."

Jacinta stamped a foot. "¡Mamá! What a thing to say."

"Well," Mercedes said, "just so you know how I stand on these matters."

"That's something I never have to guess, Mamá: your feelings about anything." Jacinta sneaked a peek up the line. She could see Chico's hat with the distinct blue kerchief wound around the band. The line had made the turn down the hall, and now the railing and the pay tables were in view.

"Since you think that's the case," Mercedes said, "you should know one more thing. When picking is over, and after la niña Magda gets married, you'll be working for her. In the meantime, I'll see if you can work at the church with Basilio." Thanks to Elena, Basilio had left El Congo. Elena had helped him secure work at the cathedral of Santa Ana.

Not me, Jacinta thought. She and Chico had other plans. After the harvest, they would move to Metapán. They would live with Chico's tío Gaspar. Chico would work at a cattle ranch there and help his uncle with the union business. It's what Chico did besides picking. It was secret work, of course. Here, at la finca, Chico helped Alirio Pérez keep the pickers informed. Jacinta was proud of Chico, that he worked for justice. As had Antonio, may he rest in peace, and his father, el compadre Goyo, may he also rest in peace. They had worked for justice, and they had died for it.

"You heard me, didn't you?" Mercedes said, surprised Jacinta had not protested the news she brought.

"Sí, Mamá," Jacinta said, amazed at the coincidences that can spring up in life. She had just thought of Alirio Pérez and now there he was. He was in the line next to hers. He was at the railing gate, one person away from a pay table.

Mercedes repeated what she had said, in case it hadn't sunk in. She was about to go on when something in Jacinta's eyes silenced her. Mercedes turned her gaze to the line beside them.

"Alirio Pérez," the pagador called out.

A tall reedy man unsheathed his machete and placed the weapon on the ground beside the railing as all men had to do. With an insolent thrust of the knee, he pushed open the railing's low gate and stepped toward the table. When he reached the pagador, the paymaster did not look in his ledger as was the custom. Instead he kept his eyes on the man and counted out from a stack of bills, "Uno, dos." El pagador placed two bills on the table. He plucked two coins from the box and placed them on the bills. "Dos colones con diez centavos," he said, sliding the money across the table toward the man.

Alirio Pérez did not move. He did not pick up his pay. "I want to know why I was let go," he said, his voice loud and steady.

The room went quiet, and this sudden change was like the expectant moment between lightning and thunder. Mercedes took Jacinta's arm, tightening her grip on it.

The pagador pushed his hat back from his forehead. "We don't want your kind picking here," he said.

Alirio Pérez said nothing. He stood his ground. One of the guardias who had been at the edge of the room moved toward the table. Don Ernesto and don Samuel laid their hands on their revolvers.

"Go on," the pagador said. "Get out of here." He leaned back in his chair and waved his hand impatiently in the air. "Take your pay and get out of here."

Alirio Pérez reached across his waist. In one swift movement he pulled from his left pant leg a second machete concealed there. For an instant the weapon hung in the air, and then it whistled down over the table.

The blade cut through the pagador's wrist. The severed hand made a dull thud when it dropped on the table.

The guardia fired on Alirio, who spun crazily around before collapsing like a human drape over the railing. His machete went skittering under the pay table. Mercedes flung herself to the floor, pulling Jacinta down with her as the room erupted into chaos. People screamed. Dogs barked. The guardia continued firing. A second man went down. A woman toppled under the spray of bullets. When the shooting stopped moments later, others had also taken to the floor, but many started in all directions. Children wailed, searching wildly for their mothers. El pagador lay slumped over the money stacks. Blood spurted from the stump of his wrist, spilling, shiny and thick, over the edge of the pay table.

Mercedes thought she would be sick. The biting smell of gunpowder filled her nostrils; her arms were gray with floor dust that she could taste at the back of her throat.

Jacinta scrambled up. Keeping low to the ground, she went to the man sprawled on the floor, a hat, bright blue at the brim, lying beside him. "Chico," Jacinta said, dropping down next to him. She looked him over. His eyes were open. "My leg," he said hoarsely. He reached out and touched his thigh. Jacinta looked at his leg, at the red stain spreading through the trouser fabric. She glanced around the room, noting el patrón and la guardia, how their weapons were still drawn, how a semblance of order was returning to the room.

Jacinta threw back her head. "¡Auxilio!" she screamed, "¡Auxilio!" all the rage pent inside her loosening in the utterance of her cries for help.

▼   ▼   ▼

The Cadillac sedan pulled away from la casona and rolled across the big yard. Alberto was at the wheel. Next to him sat Cecilia, mute as stone, and Isabel, her daughter. Slumped down in the back between Magda and Elena was don Orlando. The Cadillac followed the pickup driven by Ernesto Contreras with Neto in the cab. In the bed of the truck, the clinic attendant ministered to el pagador and the two others who had been wounded. Traveling also in the pickup bed was Coffee. Ernesto's dog sat up by the cab's window. Occasionally he turned his head to test the wind, but mostly he kept his eyes on the back of his master's head. Both vehicles were traveling toward Santa Ana—one to the hospital, the other to the safety of Elena's house.

"Stop that, Papá," Elena said. She gave her father's hand a little slap as he pulled himself up and tried to reach the door handle again. Elena sighed deeply. Not thirty minutes had passed since she'd heard the sound of rifle shots. She had been resting in the comforting shadows of her room when the roar of the commotion came through the screens of the windows and over the babble of the brook. All the dogs in the world had begun to bark after that.

Now the family was rushing away. Elena had had barely enough time to gather up her valuables and collect those items she could not do without: her makeup, her correspondence, a few books, her down pillows. In the ensuing days, the servants left behind at la casona would take care of packing up and closing the house for the season. In Santa Ana, there would be peace again. Peace behind the cool walls of her house. Peace along the wide covered porch with the view of the patio and its charming tiled fountain that, day and night, brought her the soothing sound of cascading water.

Elena looked out the car window. Mercedes Prieto's daughter ran up beside the car, her brown graceful legs pumping swiftly. Because the car was moving slowly, she easily kept pace. Astonished, Elena watched Jacinta glide past without looking in the Cadillac. It was the pickup she ran after. When it went through the finca gates, Jacinta came to an abrupt halt. She stood and looked down the road in the direction the truck had taken. When the sedan passed, she paid it no heed. Her gaze remained fixed down the road, her arms stiff at her sides, her hands slowly opening and closing.

Elena leaned her head against the soft back of the seat. Her dream of just two nights ago had clearly augured this new violence. Despite the horror of what had transpired, she welcomed the relief from the dream's foreboding. None of her own had been touched today. Neto and Alberto. Her own beloved. They were all safe and driving away.

For perhaps the hundredth time, Elena felt the smooth flesh of her ring finger. She could not get used to not wearing Ernesto's ring. As soon as she could, tomorrow perhaps, she would take the ring to don Valdemar, the jeweler. Elena closed her eyes against the intruding thought of the paymaster's hand, wrapped round and round in lengths of gauze, and resting like a little package of gruesomeness somewhere in the pickup. Elena shook her head. "¿Cómo puede ocurrir esto en un país llamado El Salvador?" she whispered, mostly to herself she thought.

But this was not the case. Her father sat beside her, and he began to parrot what she had spoken. "How can this happen in a country named The Savior?" he said.

▼▼

CHAPTER FOURTEEN

Santa Ana
April 1933

La Pepa, don Orlando's speckled pet hen, squatted down in the bare spot she had scratched out for herself in Elena's patio. The hen fluffed her feathers and squirmed in the dust; then she gave a little squawk that propelled her into a barrel roll. She squawked again when she righted herself, producing a final shake before settling her feathers. This chore performed, la Pepa pecked the ground for the maíz that the gardener put out for her each day but which had long since disappeared. Clucking her dissatisfaction, she hopped onto the covered porch with its thick columns and quaint arches that ran along three sides of the patio. She strutted between two mossy clay pots spilling pink geraniums onto the terra-cotta tiles.

Elena and Cecilia were relaxing on the porch. They sat in the green wicker chairs that once had graced Elena's childhood porch. On the coffee table sat a tray with their afternoon snack: coffee and Galletas María, the shortbread cookies that were the women's favorite. Elena made a clucking sound to attract the hen and crumbled a corner of cookie onto the floor. La Pepa bustled over and pecked the crumbs up. Then she clucked and strutted off, her red crest bobbing, until she disappeared through the open door of don Orlando's room. Marking her passage along the tile lay the chalky

deposits that not only were la Pepa's signature, but that had everyone in the house looking down before they stepped.

"What a mess," Cecilia said.

"I know," Elena said. "But now that she's had her bath and an
evening snack, la Pepa's ready for bed." Over the rear wall of the
patio frothing over with bougainvillea, the setting sun painted the
sky the interior color of a conch shell.

"I can't believe you let her roost in there," Cecilia said, tipping
her head in the direction of don Orlando's room, one of many facing
the porch.

Elena shrugged. "She makes Papi happy. Every morning she lays
an egg for him." The gardener had constructed a laying box that sat
on her father's dresser. The box, lined with bits of straw, was strategically placed next to a lamp that helped warm it.

Elena fingered her wedding ring. She had picked the ring up
from don Valdemar's jewelry store more than a month ago, but still
she gave it a little twirl to assure herself it was truly on her finger.
When she had presented the ring to the jeweler and told him what
had happened, he had been as mystified as she about the ring's
condition. "My best gold went into that piece," he had said.

"I see you still can't leave your ring alone," Cecilia said, just to
make conversation. She was suddenly weary. The incident at the
finca had brought the old terrors back. These days she did not want
to do much of anything but sleep.

"What is it, Frijol?" Elena said. "You look so sad."

Cecilia gave a little laugh. "You called me Frijol. You haven't
called me that in years."

"I just thought of it." When they were girls and studying English
at school, Sister Teresa told the class they were all human beings.
"Repeat after me," Sister Teresa had said. "I am a human being."
For days after, Cecilia had wandered about glumly until she finally
confessed she didn't want to be a human bean. "No quiero ser frijol," she said, and for years the nickname stuck.

Jacinta Prieto emerged from the door at the far end of the porch
that led to the kitchen. "Ay, look at Pepa," she said, eyeing the hen's
droppings. "I'll be back for the tray after I get the mop." She hurried
down the porch again.

"That Jacinta is a miracle," Cecilia said when Jacinta was out of sight. "You don't have to repeat things to her. And she's only fourteen."

It was true that a servant who could think for herself, one who had a sense of responsibility, and a young one at that, was a rarity. Clearly Jacinta took after her mother. Never before had Elena employed a pair like them. Over the years, she had made a rule not to hire multiple members of a family. She had watched other households do it, heard of the disputes and the divisive cliques that inevitably had but one result: less work being done. In this case, however, Elena did not regret breaking her own rule. After they moved back to Santa Ana, Mercedes had implored her to give Jacinta a position in her house while they waited for Magda's wedding. It had been an opportune time, given that Clara, the inside girl, unnerved by what had happened at the finca, packed her things and returned to her home, seeking the safety and peace of her pueblo. So Jacinta had taken Clara's place. She caught on quickly to what needed to be done. At times, Elena thought, it's as if the girl can read my mind. "I'm going to miss her when she goes to work for Magda. But that's eight months away."

"Did you talk to Ernesto about the wedding?" Cecilia asked.

Elena nodded. "I talked to him. He said, given the times, we can't have a big wedding. Three hundred people at most, he said."

"Eso es ridículo," Cecilia said. "It'll be impossible not to invite at least double that amount. Lo mínimo, seiscientas personas."

Jacinta had returned to the porch and was mopping the tiles. She heard the women talk about the plans for la niña Magda's wedding. Magda was almost eighteen, a few years older than Jacinta. Despite the ocean of privilege between them, Jacinta was not envious. She had plans of her own. Thanks to don Ernesto, doctors had saved Chico's leg. Thanks also to el patrón, Chico was living in a mesón in Santa Ana. When she could, and over her mother's objections, over Basilio Fermín's wounded look when he heard of it, Jacinta visited Chico at the rooming house. She brought him steaming tortillas wrapped in a cloth, a pot of meaty soup redolent of chipilín, paper cornucopias filled with pineapple and papaya slices. Such good food was her portion from Elena's kitchen, and Jacinta was happy to share it with her man. Good food, rest, and fresh air would help him heal. When he fully recovered, the two would leave for Metapán.

Jacinta followed Pepa's trail into don Orlando's room. The old man was asleep. Beneath his blanket, he looked like a long bag of kindling. A special duty nurse sat in a chair by the window. She wore a starched uniform and was working on a square of embroidery. The nurse motioned for silence by laying a thimbled finger across her mouth. She pointed toward Pepa's droppings and made exasperated soft explosions with her mouth. "Under the bed, niña tonta," she whispered fiercely. "Over there. Over there." Jacinta turned her back on this overblown maid who called her "stupid girl." She mopped deep under the bed. She used the cleaning rag that hung from her waistband to swab the area under the foot of the bed where, above it, la Pepa was readying herself to roost on the crossbeam. Luckily the hen had not yet locked herself on for the night, so Jacinta picked her up as if she were a bundle. She sauntered over to the nurse and dropped la Pepa squarely on her lap.

In the corredor, Elena noticed Jacinta heading toward the kitchen just as Ernesto came in from the main hall with Coffee at his heels. "Buenas, amor," Elena said. The dog dropped down on the cool tiles, laid his head on his paws, and sighed.

Ernesto smiled a hello. He unbuckled his holster and set it on the coffee table. He kissed Elena's mouth and pecked Cecilia's cheek before dropping onto the wicker settee. "What a day," he said, raking a hand through his hair.

"Have a Scotch," Elena said. She motioned toward the side table with a tray of glasses and the cut-glass decanters necklaced with silver labels.

"Buena idea." Ernesto fixed himself a drink. He preferred it neat. "How about a sherry?" he asked the women. They both nodded and he poured three fingers of liquor into Baccarat glasses. "Salud," he said, passing the wine out.

The three sat on the porch for a time, sipping their drinks, watching the sun disappear behind the bougainvillea wall. The evening turned moist, accentuating the scent of the jasmines and the roses. The fountain spewed its musicality.

"A letter came from the boys today," Elena said, breaking the silence. Neto and Alberto were now living with relatives in San Salvador and attending the university.

"There couldn't be much news in it, given I saw them just yesterday," Ernesto said.

"By the way," Cecilia said, "thanks again for letting me and Isabel ride with you to San Salvador." The three had made the trip in the Cadillac. Cecilia had met with the officers at the bank. She had tried to cajole Elena into coming, too, but Elena had scheduled a meeting concerning the wedding reception, and Cecilia could not coax her into postponing.

"I'm happy I can help," Ernesto said.

"You help so much," Cecilia said. "Without Armando to take care of our financial matters . . ." She let the words trail off. Then she said, "I can't thank you enough for your concern and advice." Turning to Elena, she said, "Thanks for sharing him, Nena."

Elena laughed. "It's the least I could do."

Ernesto laughed, too. "You make it sound as if I'm property."

"Es verdad. Eres una comodidad," Elena said playfully.

"If I'm a commodity, then I'm not worth much," Ernesto said. "I'm like coffee. Prices are very low. I've been most of the day at the bank. Five years ago the country exported sixteen million dollars in coffee. Today we're down to a little over four. Finca workers are not happy. We've had to cut wages to twenty centavos a day."

"At La Merced we used to pay fifty centavos," Cecilia said. The sherry was warm in her throat and was revivifying.

"At La Abundancia, too," Ernesto said. "But now we do the best we can. Workers should understand that. They should understand we have to tighten our belts. Of course, the union leaders don't see things that way. It's only those comunistas who are getting ahead."

"We're not going to Europe this year," Elena said. "That's a savings right there." Usually they left in May and stayed two months. They traveled to Spain, Italy, and France, spending an especially long time in Paris.

"It's a good thing," Ernesto said.

"What we save not going to Europe, we can use for Magda's wedding," Elena said, deciding to strike now that the question of money had been raised, now that Cecilia was here to support her.

"We've already discussed that," Ernesto said.

"Nena says you can only invite three hundred," Cecilia said, leaping into the fray. "But you know as well as I do, Ernesto, that if you only invite that number, half the family will be missing."

"We should pay the kids to elope," Ernesto said.

Elena gave a soft snort. "That's a bad joke, amor."

"Before I forget," Ernesto said. "I went to the hospital to see el pagador. It doesn't look good. His arm is gangrenous. He needs to be transferred to San Salvador. They might have to amputate."

"What a shame," Elena said. "First his hand, now his arm. Will the violence never end?"

Ernesto replied, "I think, unfortunately, things are only just beginning."

▼▼▼

CHAPTER FIFTEEN

The bedroom closet in Elena's house resembled a small apartment. When she and Ernesto had first moved to the house, she had knocked down a wall between their bedroom and the adjoining room. In the space, Elena designed his-and-her dressing rooms with connecting private bathrooms. Elena's bathroom had a clawfoot tub and a high-tanked commode, a washstand with a porcelain bowl garlanded with dark blue irises. In the far corner, a bidet. Ernesto's bathroom featured, instead of a tub, a gleaming tiled shower with gold-plated faucets.

Today, Elena was puttering in Ernesto's dressing room, rearranging his clothing, something she did on a regular basis. From time to time, Mercedes Prieto brought in clean laundry. With the end of August approaching, and only three plus months remaining until Magda's wedding, Elena's mind churned with details: the never-ending wedding preparations, her uneasiness at the thought of Ernesto's fully realizing how she'd skirted his dictum and done what was right and proper for a wedding of an only daughter, her father's alarming decline in the past months, her weariness at long nights spent in vigil at his bedside. Thankfully, the doctor had prescribed a mild sedative, and so don Orlando took frequent naps, a blessing that allowed Elena time for household chores as well as for a few peaceful moments to herself. This afternoon she tossed cares aside, losing herself in reorganizing and handling fabrics, leathers, and accessories, a task she always enjoyed because it soothed her.

Elena used the edge of a shelf to pull herself up. Her legs were numb; she had been sitting on the floor, her legs tucked under herself. She stretched, rubbing a fist into the small of her back. She looked around at the shelving, the dresser drawers, the rods and the padded hangers. She had done a good job. Ernesto's shirts were folded and stacked neatly on the shelves. Trousers and jackets were arranged by weight and color. Most were made of lightweight fabrics in charcoal tones or black or navy. On the wall, Ernesto's ties hung from a rack of wooden pegs, each tie next to another of a complementary color. Shoes rested on sections of pitched shelving, each shoe buffed to a gloss by Macario who, in addition to the gardening, also polished shoes.

Mercedes appeared again with a new stack of laundry: white boxer shorts and silk undershirts still warm from the iron. Atop these, socks, smoothed and paired, toes poked into cuffs for ease in donning. A chest had been built in the dressing room for storing just these things. On the dresser rested a small silver tray, a repository for cuff links, tie tacks, loose change. These items rattled in the tray as Mercedes, her arms piled with clothing, made an awkward attempt to open one of the drawers.

"Here, let me," Elena said, pulling the drawer open. She stood next to Mercedes, who wore a loose dark dress and who was barefoot, as usual. Her salt-and-pepper hair was gathered with a string at the nape of her neck. Silently, she put the laundry away. Elena took a step back, noting the slump in Mercedes's shoulders. "Is something wrong?"

Mercedes held her hand against her eyes for a moment. "No, nada, niña Elenita."

"Something's wrong. What is it?"

Mercedes took a breath. She looked away. "I don't know how to tell you, but it's Jacinta. She's run away with Chico Portales."

"Chico? Is that the boy who was wounded at the finca? The one at the mesón?"

Mercedes nodded. "She left today. She took advantage of her day off." Mercedes allowed herself to collapse against the dresser.

"The worst is she didn't tell me herself she was leaving. She sent Basilio Fermín over. The boy from the church. She sent him over to tell me the news." But that really wasn't the worst of it. The worst was that her daughter was pregnant, but this fact Mercedes would not tell Elena.

"Where did they go?"

"Metapán, Basilio said."

"Is she pregnant?" Elena asked.

Mercedes shrugged in answer.

"My God, she's only fourteen," Elena said, and the two, standing in the fresh laundered smell of Ernesto's clothing, went silent at this new turn of circumstance.

In mid-November, Elena had the dream again. This time all her teeth crumbled into a gritty gray dust that she spit into her hand. The following day, during dinner, she was helping herself to the petits pois when her wedding ring went flat for the second time. The pain of it, as intense as the first time, caused her to bolt up from her chair, upsetting it with a clatter, causing Ester, the new servant, to drop the vegetable dish, sending a spray of tender new peas over the white linen tablecloth and onto the floor. It was the stick of butter, softening in the evening heat and only an arm's length away in the butter dish, that had helped dislodge the ring from Elena's swollen finger.

A few days later, Elena and Magda headed down the street toward don Valdemar's shop to pick up Elena's ring once again. Next they would visit La Boutique Europe to select lingerie and linens to complete Magda's trousseau. Finally, as a reward for shopping in the heat, they would meet Cecilia and Isabel at the Casino Santaneco for afternoon refrescos in the main salón.

Since the dream, Elena had been anxious and full of misgivings, but she made an effort to hide this. Who needed the black crepe of foreboding thrown over the joy of such festive times? Magda and Isabel were home now that they both had graduated. Each morning, Magda bounded out of bed, blissfully captive in the flush of her impending marriage, her days filled with friends who celebrated its coming with showers and teas. Happily, Elena navigated the steady stream of wedding gifts from the front door and onto the linen-draped tables she'd set up in a spare room off the porch. Visitors came to call; they toured the gift room and exclaimed over the bounty. Bending over the gifts, they peered past satin bows and through clear cellophane. They lifted each little card propped up by a gift and read the engraved name of the giver. "That's very good," so many said before putting the card back.

The situation with her wedding ring was a very different matter. When Elena returned it to don Valdemar, the jeweler had opened the small velvet box that contained it, and stared at the ring for some time before lifting it out. Once he did, he turned it over and over in his hand before taking out his lupa to squint through the lens at the ring rising like a glittering halo between his two pinched fingers. As a final examination, he'd held the ring to the light as if the sun itself might reveal what had caused its distortion. "It's a mystery. This ring was made with my best gold, with my best diamonds," he said, repeating what he had pronounced on her last visit. He shook his head and slipped the ring back into the velvet-lined slit of the box. "I will fix it once more, doña Elena, gratis this time. But if this occurs again, heaven forbid, I wash my hands of it." To be fully understood, he had made washing motions with his hands, then held them up, clean and free.

The women crossed the street at Avenida Cuatro and went down la Cinco. They stayed on the shaded side of the street. They passed the barber shop, the tobacconist, a religious shop that sold medals and rosaries and missals and such. In the middle of the block was el Hotel Florída, with its big windows spanned by decorative iron bars that bellied out and formed scrolls at top and bottom. At the door of the hotel, a black lacquered carriage reposed between trips. The broad-backed horse that drew it tossed its big head to shoo away the flies. Horse-drawn carriages were still commonplace, but more and more one saw gasoline sedans—Chevrolets, Packards, Studebakers—bumping along the cobblestoned streets of Santa Ana.

Don Valdemar's shop was on the corner of la Cinco and Delgado. When the women entered, the little bell at the top of the door tinkled their arrival. The shop consisted of one large room, banked by vitrinas and overhung with glass shelves along all the walls. In the glass cases, necklaces and bracelets were displayed on widths of indigo velvet, rings encircled velvet cones, earrings dangled from velvet lobes. The gems dazzled the senses: diamonds and rubies and pearls, aquamarines and opals, sapphires and emeralds. Gold was plentiful, too: thick chunky creations as well as slender filigree. On the shelves glistened Baccarat and Lalique crystal. Wedgwood and Spode, Haviland and Limoges dinnerware was pitched for better viewing. Cedar chests resplendent with cutlery, trays and serving pieces, coffee and tea sets provided silver accents all about the room.

Standing in the middle of the store, Magda gave a little spin of delight. "I've been here a million times, but I never get tired of it. Don't you just want *everything*, Mamá!" Magda's eyes, dark and expressive like her father's, gleamed.

"I think you have as much at home," Elena said.

Don Valdemar hustled in through a door at the back. He was Danish. Ten years earlier, he had fled Denmark and its repressive socialist ways and had migrated to El Salvador, where entrepreneurs were welcomed. "I couldn't help overhearing; I must say that most of what you have *has* come from my shop." He was rangy in his white guayabera, the tuniclike shirt with deep pockets and tucks across the chest that was his customary wear. "Over the years, I have learned what you want. When people come searching for a gift for you, I say, 'Magda Contreras likes Baccarat and Limoges.' Isn't that right, mi joyita?" His pale blue eyes lit up when he called her his little jewel, pronouncing the word in that curious way he mixed his Spanish with the lilt of Danish that no amount of living in the tropics would ever replace. He had watched her grow up. Had come to see that, even at a tender age, she had exquisite taste and a keen eye for detail. He remembered once when she was ten, eleven maybe. She had come into the shop with her mother, and Magda had gone straight to the left vitrina. "Those pearls, don Valdemar," she said, "they should be over there, by the aquamarines." She had pointed to the other vitrina. "Over there, next to their sisters, the pearls would look more luminous." She had notions like that, used gemlike words, even when she was small: luminoso, brillante, marquesa, cabuchón.

"And you're here for your ring, of course," don Valdemar said to Elena. "A woman needs her diamonds at a time of so many festivities."

"Precisamente," Elena said.

Moments later, the jeweler set Elena's velvet box on the counter. He opened it, plucked the ring out, handed it to her. "It's as good as new," he proclaimed. And it was. The ring was a perfect circle of wide gold. Along the top of the band, three diamonds, each as large as a ripe coffee bean, caught the afternoon light. Elena slipped the ring on, feeling at once its comforting, familiar presence. "I've hated being without it," she said, lifting her hand to show it off.

Magda did the same, bringing her own hand alongside her mother's. Magda's ring featured a large square-cut diamond with baguettes at the sides. Alvaro Tobar had bought the ring here because if he hadn't, he would not have heard the end of it. Don Valdemar watched the women exhibiting their rings. "Such beautiful creations," he said. "But please, señora, remember what I said. This will be the last time your ring sits on my workbench. If the ring distorts again, heaven forbid, you might consider taking it to the priest." What he did not go on to say was that he thought the ring was somehow bewitched, embrujado. He certainly didn't need a ring like that in the pristine haven of his shop.

Elena fingered her wedding ring all the way out of the shop and down the street and over the three blocks to Madame Yvette's boutique. Don Valdemar's words had been disturbing. Naturally, Elena had thought the ring's deformities had been caused by some metallurgic reaction, that they were scientific occurrences that, though they baffled her, were based in logic. But now the jeweler had mentioned the priest, and this aroused a disturbing implication. Was there some kind of evil at work here? Maybe she *should* see the priest. Take the ring in for el padre to bless.

Elena said nothing of this to Magda, who was chattering about the house she and Alvaro would move into. It was in San Salvador and it was being refurbished. Magda, in addition to the activities whirling about her in Santa Ana, was making frequent trips to the capital to keep tabs on the house's progress. The two arrived at La Boutique Europe, a shop redolent of verbena and a visual feast of linens and lingerie. When they walked in, Madame Yvette herself greeted them.

"Chérie," she exclaimed, "your peignoir. C'est arrivé!" Madame was a woman of indeterminate age. She had a classic French air: dark tinted hair pulled severely back into a chignon, translucent skin, pencil lines for eyebrows, a red bow of a mouth. She had lived in Santa Ana for as many years as don Valdemar. Her Spanish was spiced generously with the rolling and guttural sound of her mother tongue. She led them into one of the dressing rooms. "Voilà!" she said, pointing out Magda's negligee and its matching robe draped stylishly over a fainting couch. The peignoir was fashioned from snowy sarcenet. It featured ribbon straps, a smocked bodice, a bell-shaped ankle-length skirt. The robe was of the same soft silk, with a mandarin collar and pearly buttons along the edge.

"It's divine," Magda said, holding the gown up to herself. This was not the usual satin peignoir with the lace gussets most brides selected. Magda's peignoir was as distinct as Magda herself, and it had taken a concerted effort by Madame to find what Magda adamantly had demanded. The same held true for Magda's wedding dress, which had been shipped from the rue de Rivoli hanging up full length in a wooden crate.

"You look beautiful," Elena said, smiling. Magda's olive skin was striking against the creamy fabric of the negligee. Her hair was a mass of dark unruly curls. Contrary to fashion, she resisted taming it, as her hairdresser often suggested.

"No bride will be as lovely, no wedding as bright," Madame said, standing at the mirror, her age-spotted hands spread against her hips.

Elena and Cecilia, Magda and Isabel had refreshments at a table in the salón of the casino, a place that, over the years, had witnessed the coming-of-age of both sets of women. The room resonated with conversation and laughter, with the tinkling of spoons against china, ice against glass. This was the most frequented spot in town for capping a day of shopping. Gossipy stories floated up from every table: Did you hear that el fulano left la mengana? And what about la zutana? Did you see what she was wearing? And ay, the help these days, isn't it abominable the things they demand? At Elena's table, talk of the wedding dominated the conversation.

"So, did you tell him?" Cecilia asked Elena. She was referring to Ernesto and those certain costly elements of the wedding that were being kept from him.

Elena had sent out seven hundred engraved invitations, each envelope hand addressed by las carmelitas living in the convent on the hill. She had reserved this very salón and its three verandas for the reception. Guests would be seated at sixty tables draped with white linen and scalloped with satin ribbons and knots of pink roses. When they conversed, their glances would have to vault the tops of the rosebud topiaries placed at the center of each table. To whet the appetite, the guests would nibble on French cheeses and pâtés. Caviar, beluga, of course. Discerning palates would be well pleased by lomos de aguja—beef tenderloins—and lobster, by fresh asparagus flown in from Los Angeles, by tender lettuce greens in a classic vinaigrette. Throughout the day, champagne would be served unstintingly. So much Dom Perignon that after the wedding, Magda would use the empty bottles to fashion a "bottoms-up" path in the patio of her new house. And the wedding cake. Designed by doña Amparo, the only baker worthy of the task, the work of art would repose on a mirrored surface and consist of seven tiers of rich butter cake with white cherry filling. It would be iced with pleated fondant and adorned with roses fashioned from sugar dough. Music would underscore the celebration: a string quartet for the wedding at the cathedral, strolling violins during dinner, and a full orchestra for dancing afterward. In all, Elena de Contreras had seen to it that her daughter Madga's wedding would be on the lips of Santa Anans for years to come. That it would cost Ernesto a large portion of the profits of this year's harvest was something she could not help.

Magda answered Cecilia's question. "Mamá doesn't need to tell Papá. He'll find out soon enough." She gave a little laugh.

"Don't laugh," Elena said. "It's your duty to be so lovely your father won't mind all the expense."

"That'll be easy," Isabel said. "Magda will be so beautiful, tío Ernesto won't notice anything else." Isabel was Magda's primera madrina, her maid of honor, just as Elena and Cecilia had been primera madrinas for each other.

"One thing I've learned about men," Elena said. "Men are oblivious to most things but their business."

"Thank you for the lesson, Mamá," Magda said. "I'll be sure to keep that in mind with Alvaro."

"¡Ha!" Isabel exclaimed. "I think Alvaro Tobar has more on his mind these days than just his business."

"Niña, how suggestive," Cecilia jokingly admonished.

"Well, he isn't the only one," Magda said, and at that, all the women laughed.

Elena laid a hand on Cecilia's arm. "Don't our girls remind you of us, Ceci?"

"Even our own girls can't compare," Cecilia said. She smiled and patted Elena's hand. "Oh!" she added. "Don Valdemar fixed your ring."

Elena settled back in her chair. She wiggled her fingers at Cecilia. "I have it back."

"What did he say?" Cecilia asked.

"He said that if the ring was damaged again, I should take it to be blessed."

"Forget that," Cecilia said. "I have a better idea."

"What's that?" Elena asked.

"Take it to la Verídica."

Elena said, "La Verídica?"

"Who's that, Mamá?" Isabel asked.

Cecilia leaned in to the table conspiratorially. She looked around the room before confessing. "La Verídica's a curandera. She's part healer, part witch. I didn't want to say, but since Armando died, I've gone to see her twice."

▼▼▼

CHAPTER SIXTEEN

Cecilia was still in her nightgown, sitting up on the chaise longue in her bedroom when Elena came in. There were down pillows on the chaise, a bunched-up cashmere throw. Often Cecilia passed the night on the wide sturdy chaise with the view of the patio. Since Armando's death, their soft vaporous bed went most nights undisturbed.

Elena took a chair. "I just got back from early mass. After the service, I talked to el padre Lorenzo. I asked him to exorcise my ring, but he wouldn't do it. He prayed over it and sprinkled it with holy water, which was very nice. Still, the priest infuriates me. He's so patronizing, Ceci. It's like I'm a little lamb, and he's the shepherd who knows what I should do."

Cecilia rolled her sleepy eyes. "Didn't I tell you not to go? That ring's a puzzlement. If I were you, I'd stop wearing it."

"Por el amor de Dios, Ceci, it's my wedding ring you're talking about."

"I know. I know. A wedding ring's the symbol of a marriage, of the bond between a man and wife. I know all that. I myself would die if something happened to mine. Although Armando's gone, I'll never take mine off." Cecilia paused and then she added, "But what's happening to you, Nena, is eerie."

Elena rested a hand over her mouth. Call her naive, but she hadn't thought of that. About the ring, and how it symbolized her marriage. Was that what this was about? Did the ring's distortions mirror her marriage? It wasn't possible. She and Ernesto had a solid and secure marriage. "Maybe you're right," Elena said at length. "Maybe it's time to drop in on la Verídica."

"I'll take you there myself," Cecilia said.

La Verídica padded barefoot across the room to a table and chairs. She was a fleshy woman, perhaps in her mid-forties. She wore a loose, wraparound dress, and her large breasts were clearly unfettered inside it. The simplicity of the room surprised Elena. She had expected a roomful of frightening objects—black candles, masks, skulls and bones perhaps, but none were in evidence. There *was* a candle in the center of the table, an ordinary tall votive, one with the image of la Virgen de Guadalupe on the glass. The candle was lit, and it flickered like those in the cathedral.

La Verídica motioned them to take a seat. "La niña Cecilia says you've had a problem with your ring. Let's see."

Elena slipped the ring off her finger and handed it over. She watched la Verídica inspect it, then rub it between her palms as if to warm it. "Let me tell you what's happened with the ring," Elena said.

La Verídica held up a hand. "I don't want to know. I don't need to know. The ring itself is telling me its story." The story was one of betrayal, but she would not voice this until she had to.

Elena looked at Cecilia, who was sitting on the edge of the chair, hands bunched under her chin. With eyes alone, Elena asked Cecilia, What do you think?

Cecilia widened her eyes in answer. She had been here twice. Twice she had stood in the middle of the room while la Verídica made a circle around her before pronouncing Cecilia's own story: "You must prepare yourself for loneliness. Years and years of loneliness lie ahead." When Cecilia had confessed these words to Elena, Elena had held her close. Yes, with Armando gone, what else but this could be true? And Elena had said, "But you have me, Ceci. You have Ernesto. We will help you with the loneliness."

La Verídica spoke again. "When the moon is full, and it will be so in three days, you'll wait until dark. After dark, you'll place the ring in a glass jar. You'll seal the jar and bury it under a tree."

"There's a vanilla at my house," Cecilia said. Because she'd loved the vanilla tree in her parents' patio, when she had married, she had planted one of her own.

"Perfecto," la Verídica said. "When it's dark, bury the jar under the vanilla. Unearth the jar at dawn the next morning."

Elena and Cecilia looked at each other and nodded in agreement.

La Verídica went on: "In the morning, if the ring is unmarred, you may wear it freely and without worry."

"And if it isn't?" Elena and Cecilia said, almost in unison.

"Then be rid of it," la Verídica said.

The moon was bright above them. Its light illuminated Cecilia's patio, which, while not as lush as Elena's, held an imaginative collection of shrubs and flowers. The patio's glory was the vanilla tree with its curved, congenial trunk and its heart-shaped leaves. The two stood under the tree. In Elena's hand was a scrubbed glass jar that only this morning had contained honey. Tonight it held her wedding ring wrapped in a piece of swabbing cotton. "Hold the jar while I dig the hole." Elena spoke in whispers lest the servants catch them at this strange activity.

Elena used a small spade she had taken from the garden shed and carved a square of grass from the foot of the tree. She laid the square aside and began to dig.

Cecilia crouched beside her. "Want some help?"

"No. It's my ring. I have to do this myself." The earth was cool and surprisingly workable. It was grainy and moist under her fingertips. As she turned the dirt over, the earth released its sweet smell; the spade made dull crunching sounds in the dirt. After a bit, Elena said, "I think it's deep enough. Give me the jar." Elena nestled it gently into its little tomb. She mounded fresh earth around it, then covered it. To finish, she laid the divot of grass over the earth's wound and tamped it down with her foot. She combed the grass with her fingers until it blended in. "I hope no one's seen us," Elena said.

From the shadow of the vanilla, they checked the house for signs of spying eyes. The porch that formed a U around the patio was in darkness. Isabel's room was dark, too, for as luck would have it, she was in San Salvador with Magda. Light came from the main hall that led to the front door. Another spot of light shone from Cecilia's bedroom. At the end of the porch, beyond the dining room, was the kitchen. A wedge of light outlined its ill-fitting door. From behind it lilted the soft sounds of the servants' radio.

Elena started to giggle.

"Are you crying, Nena?" Cecilia asked, laying a hand on Elena's arm. "Don't cry. Your ring will be all right."

The tenderness in Cecilia's voice fed Elena's giggles. "I'm not crying," she said.

"You're not?"

"No," Elena said, dropping the spade. When Cecilia bent to retrieve it, the two bumped heads. Elena teetered back and rubbed her head. "Oh my God, I think we're crazy. I know I'm crazy. I just buried my ring." The whole idea of the burial struck her as hilarious, and her giggles turned into laughter.

"You're laughing," Cecilia said.

"Yes, I know. I just buried my ring, and that seems very funny."

Cecilia also began to laugh. She rushed out from under the tree and did a little spin in the moonlight.

"If Ernesto could only see us," Elena said.

"Come and dance in the moonlight," Cecilia said, and Elena joined her. The two lifted their arms. They spun lazily around.

"Look at the moon," Elena said. The moon hung like a bright ball above them.

"Let's be lobas and bay at the moon." Cecilia kicked off her shoes and twirled in a crazy circle. Elena kicked off her shoes, too. They began to howl, very softly at first, and then with more ardor as they spun. Elena closed her eyes. In two weeks her only daughter would be married. She felt dizzyingly free.

The kitchen door opened and the inside girl poked her head out. "¿Niña Cecilia? Is that you?" the girl called, but not very loud because it might have been a burglar she was alerting. She looked down the porch and out into the patio. La niña Cecilia y la niña Elena were dancing in the moonlight. The girl watched them for a time, then quietly closed the door and sat back down at the kitchen table.

"What is it?" the cook asked.

"It's the misses," the girl said. With a finger, she made circles near her temple. "The misses are crazy."

When morning laid its first pinks along the window ledge, Elena was waiting. She slipped out of bed, leaving the warmth of Ernesto's side, and went into her dressing room. She did not turn on the light but groped for a skirt, a soft shirt. A vase of cut roses rested on the dresser, and though she could not see them, their scent was strong and intoxicating. She splashed cool water on her face and stole out of the room, stepping over Coffee, who was stretched beside the door. The dog grunted a good morning, but he did not follow.

Cecilia's gardener stood at her front gate. His face showed surprise at this early arrival, but he only nodded and let her in. Elena hurried down Cecilia's hall. She turned left when she got to the porch, stopping for a moment to contemplate the patio, dewy and fresh with dawn. The vanilla tree was a silent sentinel; under it, the spade lay on the grass. Elena went down the porch to Cecilia's bedroom door. She let herself in.

Cecilia lay asleep on the chaise longue. Elena gently shook her friend's shoulder. "Wake up, Ceci," she said softly. "It's time."

Cecilia opened her eyes and squinted up at Elena. "What are you doing here?" She pulled the cashmere throw more tightly around her.

"It's time to get my ring. Look. It's already morning."

Cecilia yawned and glanced over her shoulder. "So it is."

"Come on. Hurry up. Dawn is slipping away."

"Okay, okay," Cecilia said. She lifted herself up into a sitting position and stretched. "God, my back is killing me."

"What's killing you is that chaise. It's as hard as stone. You should go back to sleeping in your bed."

"One of these days," Cecilia said. She stood up and fished under the chaise with her bare feet for her slippers.

The grass was wet under the vanilla. Cecilia was still in her nightgown because Elena insisted there was no time to spare for dressing.

Elena fingered the grass to find the edges of the divot. When she found it, she lifted it carefully with the spade. The loose earth was cooler than it had been the night before, and it yielded easily. When the tip of the spade struck glass, Elena put the spade aside and used her hands to continue digging. Moist dirt clung to the sides of the jar, and Elena brushed it off. She unscrewed its top and laid it on the grass. She pulled out the cotton, the dirt on her hands soiling its whiteness. "Here goes," she said.

Cecilia tucked her nightgown snugly around her legs. "It'll be all right. You'll see."

Elena unwound the length of cotton until the ring was revealed. Huddling shoulder to shoulder under the tree, the two stared down. Lying in Elena's hand was a ring so misshapen there was little hope it could be worn again.

▼▼

CHAPTER SEVENTEEN

Metapán, El Salvador
November 25, 1933

The train pulled into the Metapán station, crowded with travelers and noisy with vendors. Mercedes and Basilio walked briskly down the wooden platform, past the high loading docks and around food stands set under tin-roofed shelters. They ignored the inviting smell of hot tortillas and coffee. They had no time to eat. They marched directly out onto the sunny street and, according to plan, to the nearest tiendita. At the little store, they asked for directions to el mesón San Vito, the place where Jacinta had sent word that she lived.

Mercedes and Basilio had taken the train to Metapán very early in the morning, neither of them having asked permission at Elena's or at the church to leave on this trip. Given that Jacinta might be in danger, they had simply taken off, deciding to face any repercussions their absence might produce.

It was Basilio who informed Mercedes that Chico Portales, Jacinta's compañero, was involved with the unions in Metapán. Working at the cathedral in Santa Ana, Basilio had plenty of opportunities to learn about unionists and insurrectionists, about the Guardia and the National Police. All he had to do was remain quiet and not call attention to himself as he went about his business.

The day he learned that Metapán was a hub of unionist activities, that one of the union's organizers there was one Gaspar Díaz, that Díaz had recently disappeared with a sum of union money, and that unionists were out in search of him, Basilio had informed Mercedes of this news. He had also confessed what Jacinta had made him swear never to divulge: that Gaspar Díaz was Chico's uncle; that Chico, in addition to working as a field hand in Metapán, was working with his uncle as well.

Mercedes knocked on the door of room number 9, which appeared to have been blue at one time but was now weatherbeaten, with peeling paint. A stranger opened up, and Mercedes was surprised by the sight of the man. "I'm looking for Jacinta Prieto," she said, overriding her alarm. She must be cautious in making inquiries. If Jacinta was in danger, they had not come to make things worse for her.

"¿Quién?" The man had a beauty mark at one corner of his mouth, which gave his face a girlish appearance.

"Jacinta Prieto," Mercedes repeated.

"Jacinta Prieto?" he said, as if searching his mind for a woman with that name.

Mercedes checked the number on the door again. A green number nine was painted on the lintel. "Jacinta's my daughter. In a letter, she told me she lived here." Mercedes patted the letter, which she had folded and placed next to her bosom.

The man shrugged. "I've only been here since yesterday. Before I came, a man named Portales was staying here."

"¡Ah!" Mercedes said, shooting a glance Basilio's way. "That would be Chico Portales. He's my daughter's compañero. Chico works in the fields at la hacienda El Potosí."

"I tried to get work at El Potosí," the man said. "I was there yesterday, but they're not hiring."

"My daughter did laundry. In a letter, she said she worked for la niña Eugenia. Do you know this person?"

"That would be Eugenia Delgado," the man said. "She lives by the church. Maybe la niña Eugenia can tell you where your daughter is. If you want, I can take you there."

"That would be kind," Mercedes said. She smiled at the man. She smiled at Basilio. He did not smile back, and turned away.

"Let me get my hat," the man said, disappearing into the room.

"I don't like that man," Basilio said, taking advantage of the man's absence.

"Why? What's there not to like?" Mercedes asked, but the man came out of the room before Basilio could answer. He wore a yellow hat. "We can go now." He led the way through the streets of Metapán until they came to a wide wooden door built in the middle of a high adobe wall. "This is the place."

"Do you mind waiting?" Mercedes asked. "If I don't learn what I need here, maybe you can give us directions to El Potosí."

"Con mucho gusto," the man said. He leaned against the wall.

When Mercedes went into the house, the man pushed his hat back from his forehead. "Are you her son?" he asked Basilio.

"No," Basilio said. On the walk over, he'd tried to puzzle out what there was about the man that bothered him, but he could not put a finger on any one thing.

Mercedes appeared from inside the house. "She's at a ranchito outside of town. The woman inside said you go past the cantina La Chicha to get there."

The man flashed a big smile, and when he did, the beauty mark at the corner of his mouth moved close to his nose. "Well, there you are. The story has a happy ending."

Mercedes thanked the man for his help while Basilio hung back and said nothing. Before they started off, the man said, "La cantina is down the road, past the mercado." He pointed down the street. "Hasta luego."

"I don't like that man," Basilio repeated when he and Mercedes were on their way. "There's something about him I don't trust."

"He did us a favor."

"I don't like him even if he did."

"Think what you will," Mercedes said. She was impatient and eager to lay eyes on her daughter. Three months it had been. Five months left before the grandchild was born.

At the edge of town, the gravel road turned into an expanse of rocks and dirt that sloped at one side into a broad flat ditch. Up ahead and to the right, a path branched off the ditch and meandered through scrub. Stubby trees and teasel spilled across the trail. Mercedes kicked aside a clump of it, careful of the prickles on the stems. Walking this path is like going home again, she thought.

The two emerged into a clearing. Across it stood a hut. Mercedes had a surge of feeling for her daughter. She glanced back at Basilio trailing behind. "Are you coming?" Basilio plucked off his hat and ran a hand over his hair to smooth it. "I'm coming."

"Jacinta," Mercedes called when they reached the hut. She peered in through the opened door to note a table, a chair, two petates. Mercedes called out again. She had imagined a different sort of place. In her mind she had seen a cook fire burning and the comforting presence of animals. A long hedge of poinsettias perhaps, like the one she'd had at home. But none of this was here. Only a gloomy eerieness.

"Here she is," Basilio said.

Jacinta appeared at the edge of the yard. She wore a purple dress that hung like a sack from her shoulders. Her hair was matted, unruly. "¡Mamá! What are you doing here? Basilio? How did you find me?" She glanced from one to the other.

Basilio answered, "La niña Eugenia told us. I heard about Gaspar Díaz back in Santa Ana. I know I said I wouldn't, but I had to tell your mother." He drew off his hat and held it at his side.

Mercedes hastened over and took her daughter in her arms. "You're so thin," she said. Under her dress, Jacinta's shoulders were sharp. You could feel the bones in her back.

Chico Portales stepped out from a place in the scrub behind Jacinta. He wore a pair of trousers, but he was naked to the waist. He had drawn his machete. "Were you followed?"

"No," Mercedes said, "we're alone." She gave a soft snort and turned away from the sight of Chico's bare chest.

Chico Portales crossed the yard toward the hut. "I just hope you weren't followed." He went inside and emerged almost immediately with a green shirt. He set his machete by the door while he slipped into the shirt. "I hope you two didn't go around Metapán asking a lot of questions."

Mercedes strode purposefully over to Chico. "What kind of fools do you think we are? Like Basilio said, we asked la niña Eugenia. The only other person we talked to was the man at the mesón."

"What man at the mesón?" Chico had been buttoning his shirt. He stopped when he heard this.

"He was in room number nine," Mercedes replied. "He said he knew you."

"Dios Santo," Jacinta said. "Now they're after us, too."

"Who's after you?" Mercedes said.

"I knew there was something about that man," Basilio said. He had remained at Jacinta's side. He put his hat back on his head.

"Describe him," Chico said.

The man from number 9 popped off the path and into the yard. "See for yourself," he said. He had a pistol that he aimed in a slow arc across all of them.

The four stood there for a moment without saying a thing. It was curious, because one of them might have screamed or another might have run, but it didn't happen that way. The calmness of the group surprised the gunman. He had expected and was ready for action. Ready for Gaspar Díaz. For Gaspar Díaz's machete.

"Who are you? What do you want?" Out of the corner of an eye, Chico saw his machete propped beside the door.

"Never mind that," the man said. "Where's Gaspar Díaz?"

"He left," Jacinta yelled to him. "We don't know where he went."

The man snickered and the beauty mark on his face twitched a little. He spoke to Chico. "Díaz is your uncle, ¿verdad? Seems a man would know where his uncle is."

"He's not here," Mercedes said. "Can't you see that?" She shot a look toward Jacinta that said, Don't move. Another look toward Basilio that said, Keep her back.

"No. I can't see that," the man said. "He might be in the hut. I can't see in the hut."

"Then look inside yourself," Chico said.

"Maybe I will. But maybe Díaz is waiting there with his machete." The man now held his gun steady on Chico. "Move away from the door."

"Hij'ueputa, he's not here," Jacinta shouted, running over.

Stung by the insult, the man pointed the pistol toward her and she stopped in her tracks. Taking advantage of the diversion, Chico lunged for his machete, grabbed it, and all in one motion, rolled toward the door.

The gunman turned swiftly and fired as Chico disappeared through the doorway. The women screamed.

"Stay back," the man shouted to the others, pointing the gun at them. "Get down on the ground."

Across the yard, Basilio hesitated.

The man fired a shot his way. "Get down, or I'll put you down forever."

Basilio did as he was told.

The man aimed at Mercedes and Jacinta and they lay down, too. He said, "Suppose it's true Díaz is gone. Still, one of you is going to tell me where he went." He reached down for Mercedes, who was lying nearest him. "Get up," he said, giving her arm a quick yank.

Jacinta rose up. "Leave my mother out of this."

The man whacked Jacinta's head with the side of his pistol.

"Stay down, daughter," Mercedes said, just before the gunman circled her neck with the crook of an elbow. He pulled her tightly to him. Pressed the gun barrel into her back. Propelled her toward the hut.

The two, closely interlocked, stopped at the entrance. "Hola, Chico," the man called inside. "Did I get you with my gun? Are you hurt? Come out and we can talk."

Inside, Chico Portales was half lying at the edge of the door. He'd clamped a hand over his bleeding thigh. Clutched with the other his machete. He rose into a crouch. He would not go out. He'd make the man come in. When he did, he'd cut the man in two.

When no answer came from inside the hut, the man abruptly released Mercedes. He pushed her hard through the door. Ducked in low behind her.

Chico's blade flashed through the murk. A sound like rushing air filled Mercedes's ears. It's happening again. This her one last thought before the knife struck her squarely at the neck.

Before he could realize what he'd done, Chico took two blasts in the chest that spun him crazily into the yard.

"¡Ay no! ¡Ay no!" Jacinta shrieked, scrambling over to Chico and hurling herself upon him. Basilio knelt beside her, careful not to touch her.

The gunman stood over them.

Jacinta looked up into the muzzle of his gun. "Gaspar's in Guatemala. In Agua Blanca."

"You should have told me that before," the man said. "Saved yourself some trouble." He poked his gun into his waistband, turned, walked across the clearing, and disappeared down the path.

Basilio stood. Jacinta was draped across Chico's body. She sobbed wildly. Basilio looked toward the hut. "¿Niña Meches?" he said.

He went in after her.

▼▼▼

CHAPTER EIGHTEEN

El Congo
November 26, 1933

Elena had been at Cecilia's when the inside girl came rushing over to say that Jacinta Prieto was in hysterics on the telephone from Metapán. Elena and Cecilia dashed across the street. "Me la mataron, niña Elenita," Jacinta wailed into the phone. "Mataron a mi Chico, también. They killed her. They killed my Chico, too."

Standing beside her friend, her ear near the phone, Cecilia pieced together the details of Mercedes's death. It brought back her own vivid horror story. She turned away and went into Elena's sitting room. She lay on the fainting couch set under a massive pastoral painting with its own tiny lamp at the top of the frame.

Elena made arrangements for the funerals. Chico Portales's body would stay in Metapán; he had family there. But Mercedes's body, accompanied by Jacinta and Basilio Fermín, would go by train to El Congo, to Chenta Gómez's mesón for the wake. After quieting and reassuring Jacinta, Elena phoned a bank in Metapán and provided a sum of cash to be delivered to the girl.

All that had happened yesterday. Today, Cecilia had taken to her bed while Elena rode in the back of Ernesto's Cadillac. Angel, Ernesto's chauffeur, drove the sedan that bumped slowly down the potholed road. It took more than two hours for Angel to navigate the sixteen kilometers from Santa Ana to El Congo. At midmorning the Cadillac pulled up to Chenta Gómez's mesón. As Elena stepped out, a band of dirty-faced children yelled out her arrival. The children beckoned her to follow through the main door of the mesón, down the gallery lined with chairs on which neighbors and friends watched Elena go by. When she approached room number 5, a small girl with thick black hair called into the doorway, "Ya vino la señora." Moments later, Jacinta came out. Basilio Fermín was at her side.

"Ay, niña Elena," Jacinta said, her hands fluttering up for a moment before she dropped them at her side.

"I'm here with you," Elena said, pulling Jacinta close. The girl whimpered. She smelled of smoke and tortillas.

Jacinta wiped her eyes with the back of a hand. "Thank you for being here. I know you're busy. The wedding's next week."

"Magda would have come, but she's in San Salvador."

"These are mother's friends," Jacinta said, motioning toward the people who had formed a line to greet Elena: Chenta, who had a food stand and who owned the room; Luis Martínez, a fruit vendor; and old Josefa, who had no teeth. Joaquín Maldonado puffed himself up when Elena extended her hand to him. "I place myself at your service, señora," he said.

Basilio Fermín waited at the end of the line. "Thank you for taking care of Jacinta," Elena said. Basilio lowered his head and spoke toward the ground, "La niña Meches was like my mother."

Jacinta led Elena into Chenta's room, serving now as a viewing room. A few old women wrapped in dark tapados scurried out when Jacinta and Elena stepped in. Except for a table in the middle of the floor, the room had been cleared of furniture. Mercedes's white casket rested on the table. Around it flickered votive candles imprinted with images of saints. Copal burned in pottery shards, little spirals of pungent smoke allaying the smell of death. On the floor, under the table, lay a cross made of salt and lime, two elements for frightening evil spirits away.

Elena stepped up to the casket. Only the oval of Mercedes's face shone. Her body was hidden under puffs of cream satin. Like a nun, her head was swathed in her black tapado. Her eyes were closed. No marks or wounds showed on her face. No expression on it betrayed what she'd endured. Elena cocked her head, the better to read a line of text written in pencil directly on the coffin. The text read: "Mamá, te llevaré siempre conmigo. Cuando vengan mis niños, sabrán quien fuiste."

Elena made the sign of the cross. She laid a finger on the edge of the coffin.

"Don Joaquín wrote it down for me," Jacinta said.

"Your mother was a remarkable woman."

"I have no one now," Jacinta said. "Except for Chenta, all my family's gone."

"You'll have a child soon."

Jacinta shook her head. "No, niña Elena. I lost the child in a gush of blood."

"Oh no," Elena said.

"All the ones I've loved, I've lost in a gush of blood." She wept quietly, thinking of Antonio, her father, her little brother, Tino. Chico now. Her mother, too.

Elena pulled a handkerchief from her purse and pressed it into the girl's hand. "Don't worry, Jacinta. After this, you'll come with me. In my family's house, there's a place for you."

Out the window of the car, Elena observed the countryside: the long stretches of coffee trees interspersed with scrubby land, a lone papaya in a clearing, a lemon tree bejeweled with bright green fruit. It was midafternoon and the ride would deliver Elena back to her life: to the last-minute details of Magda's wedding, to her father's numbing illness, to Cecilia's backslide into depression. But for now, for this brief time, Elena focused on the barefoot woman with the salt-and-pepper hair, on the simple, good woman who had served her briefly but had served her well. Elena focused on the cramped viewing room with its smell of copal, on the glint of candlelight, on a daughter's words a scribe had scribbled over wood: "Mother, I'll carry you with me always. When my babies come, they will learn who you were."

▼▼

CHAPTER NINETEEN

Angel drove into Elena's porte cochere and halted next to the short pathway leading to the front door. He turned the ignition off and got out and opened the door for Elena. She untied her silk head scarf, a buffer against the roadway dust that during the trip had billowed interminably through the car window, and let the scarf drop around her shoulders. She was home and glad of it. She would have time for a long soak in the tub; then she would sit out by the patio with a good cup of coffee before Ernesto came home. Elena glanced past the opened gate toward Cecilia's gate across the street. On an impulse, Elena decided to pay her a quick visit. She would dash over to see how Cecilia had fared that day, ask her over for coffee and something sweet.

Elena rang the gate buzzer. The gardener let her in. The front door of the house was open, and in the hall, Elena called Cecilia's name. The inside girl came out from the kitchen.

"La niña Cecilia no está," the girl said.

Elena stopped short. This was strange. "Where did she go?"

"I don't know. She left in a hurry."

"¿Y la niña Isabel?" Maybe Ceci's daughter would know her mother's whereabouts.

The girl shook her head. "No está."

"Are they together?" Elena asked.

"I don't think so." She knew who la niña Cecilia was with, but she would never say.

Elena strode down the hall to the porch, avoiding the sight of the vanilla tree in the patio. The tree was a betrayer, and thanks to it she would never wear her ring again. She opened Cecilia's bedroom door. Lying in a heap over the petit point–covered bench at the end of the bed were her nightgown, a few underthings. Even this slight untidiness was unusual for Cecilia. Elena sat on a side chair by the door. She took a quick breath against the realization that crashed in her mind like waves against rock. That verbal game she and Cecilia had played at the finca. What will you do when I die, Nena? How will you feel when I'm dead? Cecilia had asked. It simply had been too much. All these months without Armando had been too much for Ceci. All the comfort and companionship Elena herself had provided, all the aid and support Ernesto had extended, none of this had been enough to assuage the loss.

But something more revealing burst into Elena's mind: When they were very young, when they were foolish and dramatic girls, Cecilia had said, If I was going to kill myself, Nena, I'd walk into the lake.

Elena ran down the porch and out of the house. She rushed across the street to the chauffeur, who was still in the driveway buffing the car. "Angel, take me to Coatepeque, to la niña Cecilia's lake house."

She couldn't get there fast enough. When they pulled up to the iron gate, it was already dusk. Elena did not wait for Angel to open the door. She jumped out of the car and ran up to the gate, but it was locked. Down the long cobbled drive, Cecilia's lake house looked empty and desolate. Elena jiggled the gate, hoping it might unlatch, but it did not, and for a moment, this inaccessibility sparked a change of heart. Perhaps she'd been too quick to guess at Cecilia's intentions.

Elena peered down the drive again to get one last, better look. Around a far corner of the house, at the place where the driveway made a turn, she thought she saw something. In the semidarkness, she could not be sure. It looked like the back end of a car. It merited investigation. This lake house had once belonged to Cecilia's parents, and when Cecilia and Elena were children, they had come here frequently during lake seasons. A short way up the road was a narrow opening in the wall that they sometimes would wiggle through when the gate was locked.

"I'll be back in a minute," Elena said to Angel, who was standing next to the car looking perplexed. She followed the wall, going parallel to the road until she found the old opening. She managed to wedge herself through it, and then she doubled back toward the driveway. At the end of the drive, the house was a boxy stuccoed building with a red-tiled roof. Overhead, a band of parrots squawked noisily. In unison, they banked over the roof and flew off over the turquoise waters of the lake.

No light came from inside the house. Tall pines and willows grew in the garden, and they created majestic reflections in the windows. Elena rounded the corner to where she thought she saw the vehicle. A vehicle was parked there, all right, and it wasn't Cecilia's. It was Ernesto's pickup, the black Ford he sometimes drove around the finca or when Elena used the Cadillac.

The sight of the pickup disconcerted her. What was Cecilia doing driving Ernesto's Ford? And where was Cecilia's chauffeur? Cecilia would never drive a car herself. Then another question supplanted the first ones: What was Ernesto doing here?

In years to come, when she thought of this moment, Elena would know that it was here, at this time—standing around the bend of Cecilia's lake house, the dying sun pouring itself into the blue bowl of the lake—that her life was forever divided into its own before and after.

Over the years, she would ask herself if she should have turned back. Turned back up the driveway and squirmed back through the gap in the wall, climbed back into the car and back into her life— her smooth and tranquil life. But she had not done so.

She had gone around the Ford, up the three steps that led to the unlatched door that opened into the kitchen. She had strode through the quaint kitchen with its wood-burning stove and with the charming pottery jugs and serving platters. She had walked silently over the cool tiles of the spacious living room, down the hall, toward the light beckoning her from the door of Cecilia's bedroom, the light illuminating the scene she would spend the rest of her life trying to forget: la cama. Cecilia y Ernesto. Ernesto y Cecilia en la cama.

▼▼▼

CHAPTER TWENTY

Don Orlando lay in his customary stupor, the light from the bedside lamp sending a golden circle past his chest but not to the end of the bed where la Pepa was roosting. Elena had sent the private duty nurse to the kitchen for her supper while she herself sat in the shadows across the room, her back to the window. The attar of roses in the garden slipped past the porch and nudged through the fleur-de-lis design of the lace curtains hanging from the window rod. A little breeze puffed the curtains out, and though Elena could not see this, she could sense, now and again, the curtain's edge lifting past her shoulder like someone whispering. There was a big moon to-night; she had watched it follow the car all the way back from the lake. She thought this was true, but then it could have been other-wise. Of one thing she was certain: Something huge had trailed her home tonight, and it had taken residence in her heart.

Ernesto and Cecilia. The two spun lazily in the eye of the storm in Elena's head. The two spun, enjoined: Cecilia's arms, her legs, wrapped around Ernesto. Elena stood and moved the chair next to her father's bed. She sat down again and watched him. He was a shrunken little man, his flesh translucently stretched over the elegant bones of his nose and cheeks, his arms and fingers. He lay eerily still under a gauzy blanket. Only his mouth moved: His lips molded themselves around each breath he took.

Elena placed a hand over his. "Papi," she murmured. "Something's happened." If it were possible, she would shake him awake, shake him until he was again the hale and courtly father he had been. If she possessed the magic word, could work the magic that would make him well again, she would do it for the sole purpose of exposing what Ernesto and Cecilia had done. This is what she wanted most: for her father to avenge this terrible betrayal, for her father to summon his sons, and for the three of them to strike out on her behalf. A simple wish. Punishment and retaliation dealt in her name.

Elena heard a sound at the door. She turned her face toward it and saw Ernesto standing in the doorway. The patio with its lush vegetation, the merry spill of the fountain, formed the backdrop behind him. At his side was Coffee, eager and innocent. "Elena," Ernesto said, his voice atremor, his eyes wide and wild with remorse. He came no closer than the door.

Elena inclined herself so that her forehead lay against her father's blanket. "Papi," she said.

"Elena, por favor." Ernesto's hand was on her shoulder, and at his touch, she gave a start and stood, toppling the chair. "Don't touch me."

Ernesto caught the chair before it hit the floor. "Please, Elena, listen."

Elena left the room. Out on the porch, the scent of roses, the way the milky moonlight washed over the patio, the sudden realization that she was dressed in funereal black, that her head scarf was still draped around her shoulders and that it had witnessed everything, all combined to assail her. She pulled the scarf off and tossed it aside. She threw out an arm, steadying herself against the green wicker chair. "I don't need to listen. I have seen enough," she said, her voice like bones snapping.

"I would give anything, I would give everything I have to take this afternoon back."

You don't have that luxury, she thought. You'll never have that luxury.

Heartened by her silence, he took a step closer and went on, the tone of his voice desperate. "This afternoon. It was the only time. Something irrational came over us, Elena. Please believe me. Cecilia's in her house. She's too ashamed to face you. She's out of her mind with shame and regret."

At the sound of Cecilia's name, the thinnest of blades pierced Elena's heart. "You listen to me. I want you to get out. I want you to go across the street. I want you to tell her I'm wearing black today. Tell her I'm wearing black because my best friend has died. Tell her she is never to come into this house. Tell her that in my life there will never again be room for her."

Ernesto pressed the back of his neck. "Surely, you don't mean this, Elena."

For the first time since standing in the lake-house hallway, Elena raised her voice. "Get out! Get out of this house!" She turned her face and closed her eyes, hearing Ernesto's ragged breathing behind her. After a moment, she heard his footsteps go down the hall. She heard the clickclickclick of Coffee's nails against the floor tiles. She heard the slight catch the front door made when it closed.

Not half an hour later, Magda Contreras arrived home from a late tea with Isabel and other friends to the sight of her mother's frenzied assault on the roses. Silhouetted in the moonlight, Elena was next to the hedge, in her hand the gardener's long pruning knife. With each strike of the cuma, she gave a little grunt and her loosened hair lifted and then dropped against her shoulders like a mantilla. Magda watched in stupefied horror. She watched the cuma cleave through plump blossoms and bright leaves. She watched rose petals showering down like ivory rain. In the air, the scent of roses was as strong as blood.

Magda rushed over to her mother. "¡Mami, por Dios!"

Elena turned and let go of the cuma, her breasts rising and falling under the black linen dress.

"Oh my God, look at your arms. Your hands. Look what the thorns did," Magda said.

Elena lifted her arms. Cuts welted and bled along her forearms and hands. Blood spotted the creamy petals scattered around her feet. She dropped her arms to her sides and trudged into the house.

Magda threw an arm around Elena's waist. "Here. Lean on me. What in God's name's happened?" Magda was frantic to know. At one end of the porch, the servants were huddled. "Please, Mamá. Please tell me what's happened."

"Ask your father," Elena said.

▼▼▼

CHAPTER TWENTY-ONE

In Santa Ana, most of the homes of the affluent were only a short distance from the cathedral, and long ago, this fortunate proximity gave birth to the custom of the wedding walk. Brides, having awakened at first light and having spent the morning in personal preparations, presented themselves minutes before the ceremony at the gateways of their houses and, accompanied by their attendants and immediate families, marched in grand procession over the cobblestoned streets strewn specially for the occasion with bright green lemon sprays to the commanding Gothic church, where the bridegroom and his entourage and the balance of the wedding guests, all alerted by the strident chords of Mendelssohn's Wedding March, rose in a great rustle of taffeta and gabardine to receive and honor the bride.

And so it was that Magda Contreras appeared at the gate of her house, three blocks from the cathedral and six days after the scandal that would forever divide all Contrerases' lives into the then and the now.

Magda made a stunning bride. The French couture gown, a luminous peau-de-soie paneled with alençon lace, set off her creamy shoulders and the fullness of her breasts. Her veil, a vaporous cascade crowned with seed pearls, fell to her waist, narrow as the span of a single hand.

Now, for perhaps the fourth time, Elena fluffed Magda's veil—the back, the sides, the front. This responsibility, as well as all duties that involved keeping the bride both lovely and serene, fell by tradition to la primera madrina, who, until a week ago, had been Isabel Aragón. Given that Cecilia had fled to the United States with Isabel in tow, Elena, for her daughter's sake, sought to calm the roiling waters of disgrace that swirled around them by promoting another girl to Isabel's role. But Magda had insisted that Isabel's honored place go unsupplanted, a demand not easy for Elena to accept. After all, an absent maid of honor was yet another red flag, sure to keep tongues wagging.

"There," Elena said, giving the impressive train of Magda's dress one final tug. Through the diaphanous fabric of her veil, Magda's face was soft and hazy. Not her eyes. Magda's dark eyes glowered through the gossamer and asked: Why? Why? Why?

"Don't look at me like that," Elena said, keeping her voice down, lest the five attendants, all decorously giddy with expectation, overhear. Elena pulled on the tops of the white silk gloves that reached past her elbows and concealed her wounded and healing flesh.

"I can't help it. It's my wedding day."

"I can't help it either."

Magda took a deep breath and squared her shoulders. "I'm sorry, Mamá. It's just that . . ."

"I know," Elena said, laying a gloved hand on Magda's arm. "Let's do the best we can."

Magda tried on a bright smile. She lifted her wedding skirt and stepped onto the sidewalk. In terms of the weather, it was a glorious day, and the cut sprays blanketing the cobbles filled the sunny morning with the scent of lemons. Already, the route to the church was lined with the curious. Behind her, the house's driveway was knotted with family—brothers, cousins, aunts and uncles. Next to the door, on the raised step that led to it, stood her father, elegant and somber in his black morning frac. Magda turned away from the sight of him. She choked back the questions hounding her: How could he? How could tía Ceci? It made her ill to imagine them together. What they had done had ruined her wedding. It had ruined her mother's

life. And what of Isabel? What would become of their own friendship?

Elena clapped her hands to get everyone's attention. Because of
the gloves, the sounds she made were muffled but effective. "It's
time," she called, and the members of the wedding aligned themselves behind Magda, behind the five madrinas all in matching daf-
fodil gowns. The florist was standing by, and she presented Magda
with the wedding bouquet: a lavish cluster of white magnolias trailing ivory ribbons, each delicately knotted at the end.

Elena took her place in line. Ernesto came up and stood beside
her. They did not speak. All week he had been meek and concilia-
tory. He had asked for forgiveness, for absolution. Through it all,
she had kept a stony silence, turning away from him whenever he
approached. One morning, he came into her dressing room while
she sat at her vanity brushing her hair. He laid an envelope in front
of her, propping it up against a bottle of Lanvin's My Sin before
turning silently on his heels again. Elena stared at the envelope, a
square of pale blue parchment. In royal blue ink, Cecilia's broad
familiar scrawl: Sra. Elena Navarro de Contreras. Presente. Elena
laid the hair brush down. She reached for the envelope but pulled
her hand away before she touched it. The muskiness of Ernesto's
cologne still perfumed the air, and it brought her to her senses:
Before Cecilia left for New York, she and Ernesto must have been
together again. How else could he have gotten the envelope? She felt
her skin flush. In the mirror, her green eyes smoldered. She picked
up the brush and pulled it through her hair. The envelope had called
to her, but she had not heeded its cry. Cecilia's missive, whatever it
contained, remained unopened. It was tucked, out of sight, along
with her misshapen wedding ring, in the back of a dresser drawer.

The procession began. It meandered down the fragrant streets,
past storefronts and house fronts bleached and aged by the weather,
past the people lined along the sidewalks—some who soberly raised
fingers to their hat brims, some who shyly scratched their elbows—
around the treed plaza, out from under the dazzling sun, and into
sudden coolness and the momentary shadows of the cathedral.

The string quartet played Brahms as Elena, arm in arm with her
older son, walked solemnly down the center aisle toward the first
pew and the places reserved for her and Ernesto. Throughout the

interminable trip, Elena smiled at the congregation. A tremor tugged at the corner of one lip, threatening to give her away, but she tamed it by smiling more broadly and, when it was appropriate, by lifting an arm and wiggling her fingers in a little wave to someone special. The church blazed with candles; the melodic strains of violins and cellos were at once a rhapsody and a lament. Stepping down the aisle, Elena noted sly looks and wry, quick smiles. Comments, rumors, questions—these were almost palpable. Curses on you, Cecilia de Aragón, Elena thought, and fresh anger stiffened her spine and gave her foot a firmer step.

Alvaro Tobar, tall and broad shouldered, curly haired and good-natured, stood with his back to the altar, his hands clasped together at the waist. Elena slipped into the pew as Brahms gave way to the majestic chords of Mendhelsson, the music resonating against the high vault of the church. Months ago she had had a dream. Months ago, she had spoken of the dream and set something on its course. Today, she turned and looked back down the aisle as her daughter and Ernesto began their procession. Elena bit the inside of her lip, feeling a sadness so pure it took her breath away. Blotting an imminent tear with a glove, she watched her future coming toward her.

PART TWO
▼

JACINTA
AND
MAGDA

▼▼

CHAPTER TWENTY-TWO

San Salvador
August 6, 1945

Jacinta Prieto stepped out of Magda's bedroom as Rosalba, the inside girl, came rushing down the hall. "It's time. The story's about to start," Rosalba said, darting around Jacinta. Rosalba was referring to the radio novela *Las dos,* which was broadcast at noon. Each day, the servants gathered in the kitchen for a half hour of lunch and the newest installment of the never-ending tale of two sisters, one wicked, one good, and of the entanglements resulting from such contrary natures. Today's episode promised to be particularly spicy: Inocencia Sinfín, the essence of goodness, was about to learn that her sister, Bárbara Parasiempre, was having an affair with Inocencia's husband.

Jacinta turned the lock of Magda's bedroom door and then gave the handle a yank to assure herself it was secured. She lowered the key ring attached to her belt so that the keys rested against her gray uniform once more. The keys were her passport to all the treasures in Magda's house. The slender bronze key admitted her to the room where the extra silver and the china and crystal were kept; the long plain key opened up the pantry, with its chocolates and biscuits, rich jams and preserves; another key, quite like the last, unlocked the fresh aroma of laundered linen: tablecloths and napkins, crisp white sheets and pillowcases, all embroidered with the interlocking silk initials of *C* for Contreras and *T* for Tobar. Also on the ring were the keys to Magda's and don Alvaro's private closets—it was Magda's closet that Jacinta had just straightened up. But the key with the heart at the top was Jacinta's favorite because it exposed a wide room lined with shelves replete with the merchandise that, over the years and despite the times, Magda had painstakingly accumulated. Merchandise that someday soon, and with la Virgen's intercession, as Magda was fond of saying, would be whisked out of the house and into the gift shop that for the nine years of Jacinta's employment had been the singular dream of her employer.

Jacinta started toward the kitchen. Like Elena's house, Magda's was a colonial structure whose main attraction was an interior patio and fountain and the broad corredor bordering them. Both houses had thick plaster walls that held the morning's coolness well into the afternoon. Both featured high ceilings encircled with decorative moldings, burnished oak floors, and many-paned windows set with wavy glass. The similarities ended there, however.

Elena's taste in furnishings and decoration lent her house a subdued, even staid, air. Elena preferred the popular dark and heavy woods: ungainly carved pieces in walnut, cherry, or rosewood. This glum palette was bolstered by the rococo framed paintings that were her predilection: in the living room and bedrooms, French panoramas or Italian madonnas and cavaliers; in the dining room, fruit and vegetable still lifes. In Elena's house, the wooden floors lay bare, and footsteps sounding in any one place echoed throughout. Since the trouble with Cecilia, and after don Orlando's passing, a melancholy mood prevailed in the house. Hardly a soul who visited escaped the contagious gloom. Each day, about four, the servants' spirits languished, and no evening cafecitos or nights of sound sleep kept the next afternoon's doldrums from striking them listless again. Even la Pepa, don Orlando's pet hen, succumbed. For weeks after her owner's demise, she put up a front and clucked and bobbed through every room of the house, earnestly in search of him. It was Jacinta who discovered the hen. Her garish yellow legs pointing up at the ceiling, she was wedged between don Orlando's rolled-up mattress and the foot of his bed.

Though business kept Ernesto Contreras away from the house during the day, he nevertheless carried with him a dark cloud of his own making, and so he, too, was much affected. It was only in Elena's patio that a semblance of gaiety endured; impassively, nature itself and the pretty tiled fountain imposed it.

The mood of Magda's house, on the other hand, was cheerful and lively. It was a showcase of the ease with which she had transformed the ordinary into the exceptional. While her patio fountain was but a simple stone affair, she had enhanced its commonness by surrounding it with a necklace of champagne-bottle bottoms. Not just any bottles buried neck down, of course, but those from the very Dom Perignon enjoyed at her wedding. In the patio, trees and flowering bushes turned leaves and even branches toward the interior sunniness of pimiento-, saffron-, and blush-painted walls. Mish the cat and Bruno the dog, when he could get away with it, napped on floral chintzes or under the new Mexican Chippendale furniture that, because it was light in weight and honey toned, was highly unconventional and had visitors prattling. The pets awakened from their naps to framed expanses of naïf art, lighted wall niches containing ancient santos, or narrow glass shelving displaying Magda's collection of paperweights by Baccarat, Saint Louis, and Clichy.

Jacinta crossed the speckled terrazzo corredor, the only place in the house besides the kitchen not covered by Persian carpets. The cluster of keys jingling at her side was the symbol of her power, and as she walked, the sound was a proclamation of her importance in Magda's household.

The August fiestas commemorating the Transfiguration of the Divine Savior of the world, the patron of El Salvador, were in full swing. Magda and don Alvaro, their three young sons, Tea, their nursemaid, and old Delfina, the cook, were at Lake Coatepeque for a short holiday. Each year at this time, the family and their entourage fled the capital's crowds and the boisterous vendors at street-corner braziers. At the lake, the family took refuge from the cacophony of dueling radios, the intermittent blasts of fireworks, and the accompanying howl of protesting dogs. At the lake, the days were free of the crush of humanity and of the smelly insolence of certain men who, feeling the weight of full bladders, turned toward street walls and, unzipping themselves with quick, arrogant moves, tinted the adobe with their steamy streams.

When Jacinta came into the kitchen, Rosalba was tuning in the radio. Basilio Fermín gazed between the iron bars of the window at the people milling in the street. Magda's house, one of many gracing the downtown area, was blocks from the cathedral, the permanent home of the statue of el Salvador del Mundo. On this day annually, the statue was carried in procession through the streets amid the faithful and honoring throng. Early this morning, Basilio and Rosalba had shouldered their way through the crowds and found a good spot in the square across from the church, where they had viewed the imposing figure of el Salvador, head crowned by rays of light, arms held high in benediction, breaking through and rising up past the crust of the enormous blue-and-white globe representing the world.

Rosalba adjusted the radio's volume because the cook, who was only a few decibels from deafness, kept the dial set on blaring even when she was away. "There," Rosalba said, "that's better." She went to the stove—it was a new gas appliance—and lifted the dancing lid off the soup pot, filling the kitchen with the hearty odor of chicken stock and potatoes and chipilín. "¡Ay! I burned myself," Rosalba cried, dropping the lid, which clattered against the stove top. She had taken advantage of Magda's absence to paint her lips bright red, and now she pouted them and sucked on her fingertips, shooting a glance Basilio's way. She was seventeen, and during the months she had worked at the house, whenever Basilio was in sight, she tossed her generous hips and thrust out the fullness of her chest so that her white uniform stood out, but Basilio paid no attention. All he ever noticed was Jacinta.

Basilio turned from the window. "You should have come with us this morning," he said to Jacinta.

Rosalba had ladled soup into bowls and was setting them around the table. "Someone had to stay in the house. La niña Magda's orders," she said, rubbing off the lipstick now smudging her fingers. She pursed her mouth, hoping her lips were not smudged as well. How embarrassing if they were.

"I didn't need to come. I watched the procession from the roof of your shed," Jacinta said. She and Bruno, the guard dog, had scampered up the rustic ramp Basilio had made for quick access to his roof. As the parade came down the street, Bruno barked excitedly down at the people and Jacinta batted a hand at him, but to no avail. She turned her attention to the dark, bearded Christ bobbing above the throng. The sight of him had stirred up old sorrows: Where was that girl she once had been? That pigtailed and brash ingenuous girl, secure always in the company of her people? People who formed their own parades and followed behind the feathered grandeur of el cacique's headdress.

"You climbed up on Basilio's roof?" Rosalba said, wrapping hot tortillas in a cloth and placing them next to Basilio's plate. "My goodness, Jacinta, aren't you too old for that?" Rosalba turned back to the radio and fiddled with the tuner. "Where's our story? It's time for it already."

"Jacinta's not old," Basilio said, blowing across his soup. When they had met—it was thirteen years before, but it seemed a life-time—she was just thirteen, he almost twelve. Though there was only a year and a half between them, back then it might as well have been a century. Now that they were both in their mid-twenties, the time that separated them hardly seemed to matter.

"Where's our story?" Rosalba repeated. She spun the dial and snippets of music and commentary floated up from the box.

"Here, let me," Jacinta said, "and wipe your mouth. It's smeared red with lipstick." She adjusted the dial to YSU, the sta-tion that carried *Las dos*. The familiar patter of The Two did not come from the radio. Instead, there was the somber voice of a ra-dio announcer: "We repeat for those now tuning in: The atomic bomb, the first of its kind and the most powerful weapon on earth, was dropped today by airships of the United States of America on Hiroshima, Japan."

"What?" Rosalba said, dabbing her lips with the back of a hand. "Does that mean we can't hear our story?"

"Be quiet, silly girl," Jacinta said, turning up the volume to hear the news: bombs, conflagration, death. She looked across the table at Basilio, and when their eyes met, a stubbled Izalco field glistening with dew rose up between them. Basilio palmed his dead father's hat, his eyes dull, his mouth slack. In the distance, fireworks ex-ploded.

▼   ▼   ▼

Later that evening, after the fiesta had ended and the streets were tranquil again, Jacinta had changed out of her uniform and into street clothes. She walked from the house to the number 2 bus and rode it for five minutes up Avenida España to Colonia La Rábida, the barrio where her best friend, Pilar Lazos, lived. Jacinta would spend the night at Pilar's house and return to Magda's in the morning. Over Jacinta's protests, Basilio had accompanied Jacinta and then watched her disappear through Pilar's door before turning away. He did not take the bus again but walked back, the trip taking half an hour or so, a blessed time to have to himself and to ponder that which he spent most of his days pondering: how to make Jacinta love him.

Jacinta and Pilar were in Pilar's kitchen. Rinsed dishes were stacked in the sink. Calendars for the years 1943, 1944, and 1945 hung in an uneven line on the wall. Each featured a religious figure, the reason Pilar had left them up. This year's calendar showed Nuestra Señora de los Dolores, Our Lady of Sorrows, with her rapier-pierced heart and the star-tipped thunderbolts circling her head.

At the table, Pilar poured a finger of liquor into a glass. She set the bottle down and slid it toward Jacinta. "Have a little," Pilar said. "Don't be such a saint." Jacinta shook her head. The bottle had a red label. On it was a long-legged man in black boots and tight white pants. He wore a red coat with flapping tails. On his head sat a high-top hat; in his hand, a black cane. Jacinta wondered if it was possible for such a man to exist. She couldn't read the label, for it was in English—she supposed it was English. She traced the words on the bottle with her forefinger. "Yo-nee Wal-quer." She looked up at Pilar. "Where did you get this?"

"From la niña Julia in Escalón." Pilar left the table and stashed the bottle in the back of the cupboard and away, she hoped, from the eyes and hands of her children. "I worked there for a week. Yesterday was my last day."

Pilar was a seamstress. She was twenty-nine, three years older than Jacinta. Years ago, before the depression and when she first started sewing, Pilar had set up shop in her living room. Back then, neighbors were her main source of income, and at all hours the house resounded with the whir of the Singer and the comings and goings of women who stepped through the door clutching the fashion clippings that, when copied by Pilar, would launch them, they hoped, on the road to transformation. When bad times came and the war followed, the need for Pilar's services might have declined were it not for the rich. Before the war, the rich had always preferred to buy their fashions abroad, but the downward shift in their fortunes forced them to economize. When they got wind of Pilar's magic, they vied among themselves for her work. Each household set aside room for Pilar. Each provided her with all she needed to create: a Singer (a few, as inducement, offered an electric machine, but she preferred the standard kind with the wide treadle she could rock back and forth with her feet), a broad cutting table, good sharp scissors, bolts of fabric, spools of thread, long and short zippers, and a variety of novelties, such as cards wrapped with lace and rickrack or slender glass tubes shimmering with sequins and beads.

Pilar returned to the table and gulped down her drink. She wrinkled her face and gave a little shudder.

"How can you drink that?" Jacinta said. She had met Pilar six years before when Pilar first came to sew for Magda. In six years, Pilar always shuddered when she took a drink of alcohol.

"*Las dos* didn't come on today," Pilar said, running a quick hand through the thick chestnut hair cascading to her shoulders. "Today was the day Inocencia would learn about Bárbara and Raúl."

"You sound just like Rosalba."

"That Bárbara is so bad," Pilar said. "Can you imagine? Your sister luring your own husband into an affair. ¡Uy!" Pilar rolled her brown almond-shaped eyes at the thought.

Jacinta could imagine very well. For three years after her mother's death, she had lived in Elena's household, and thus she had witnessed the consequence of a sisterlike betrayal: Cecilia had done what she had done, and Elena's heart had tightened with bitterness, a fact evident in the hard, determined line of her mouth, in the stiff manner in which she navigated through her days, and, curiously enough, in the way she absentmindedly chewed on her nails till they were ragged and so short they seemed to disappear into the fleshy pillows of her fingertips.

"We'll have to wait until tomorrow to hear what Inocencia thinks," Jacinta said. "Today the gringos dropped a bomb, and who knows what will happen next."

"Maybe the war will end," Pilar said.

"We can only hope," Jacinta replied. For all her life, there had been a war of some kind. Her girlhood was blighted by the interminable bloody warfare that wrenched all loved ones from her. Although the years she had spent with Elena and then Magda placed some distance between her and the horror of her past, she still lived in a world that held plenty of reminders. Just last year, at Eastertime, a military rebellion against the dictatorship in power transformed the city into a battlefield. For two days gunfights erupted in the streets. During the siege, telephones went dead, electricity was cut. Fighter planes circling overhead dropped bombs off target, setting two city blocks on fire. The Colón Theater went up in smoke, as did a major department store and many small businesses. In the end, bodies littered the street and the ancient stink of war was everywhere.

"Such a sad face," Pilar said.

"Who, me?"

"Who else?" Pilar reached across the table and patted her friend's hand. "What's troubling you?"

Jacinta shrugged. How to say that the war she battled now was not an outward but an inner one? A conflict made real, paradoxically, by her mother, who seemed still alive inside her. Sometimes, late at night or, most often, very early in the morning, when Jacinta lay on her cot in the little room she shared with Rosalba, her mother stirred within her. This was not a craziness but a consolation. To feel her mother's flesh, her bulk, shored up along the banks of her own bones and flesh. To hear her mother's voice rustling inside her head like a breeze through green leaves was eerily comforting. Don't forget what we left behind, Mercedes whispered, and Jacinta recalled the smoky smell of their hut, the cheerful line of their poinsettia hedge, the solid certainty of their rock wall. When dawn came and its wan light pointed out the room anew, Jacinta stared at the ceiling, at the crack in the plaster directly over her head. Depending on her disposition, she imagined the crack to be a river, and she was back in Izalco fording the creek and setting off confidently toward ironwoods and the shadows under them. Sometimes the crack in the ceiling was the deep cleft in the fuzzy skins of the perfect peaches

Magda imported by the crateful. Sometimes this image prompted another: her lost brother's little brown rump. When she thought of Tino, she remembered his grave dark eyes, the splotchy stain covering his ear. But always, despite what she imagined the ceiling crack to be, in the end she saw it as a divider. It was how she lived her life. Caught in the middle, remembering what she had come from and knowing what she had become. She was an Indian girl, now seemingly content to live her life with people like the very ones who had stolen her past from her.

"Come on. You can tell me," Pilar said. "What's wrong?"

"I don't know. I think I think too much. I wish I could be like Rosalba. The girl's all blabbering blissfulness."

"You know what you need? You need a man, that's what you need." Pilar knew Jacinta's past, of course. About her family. About Chico and how he was slaughtered along with her mother. About Chico and Jacinta's child. How the child never had had a chance to live.

Jacinta laughed. "I can't believe it. You think having a man is the solution to everything."

Pilar twirled an index finger around the inside rim of her glass. "You don't see a man hanging around me, do you?" She herself had fallen for three men: hard-living, sweetly cruel men. To prove it, she'd had a child by each one. For the time being, she was through with men. Pilar popped the finger into her mouth and talked around it. "But getting back to you. Mark my words, what you need is a man."

"No I don't."

Pilar raised a quick hand in protest. "Oh yes, you do. And you know who loves you? Basilio Fermín. That man worships the ground you walk on. That's all the man you need."

"He might be what I need, but to me, he's like a brother. Basilio knows that about us. He knows how it has to be. I can't help how I feel, Pilar."

"I guess you can't. In the end, we can't help who we fall in love with."

"It's also true," Jacinta said, "that we can't help who we can't love."

"Perhaps. Life is complicated, isn't it?" Pilar stood and stretched, kneading the small of her back with a hand. "Let's go sit outside and wait for the children. They should be home soon."

The two went to sit on the low concrete wall separating the houses and the sidewalk. After the heat of the day, the night was balmy and a thousand stars pricked the indigo above them. At the corner, a streetlamp threw a coin of light onto the middle of the road. It was a little after eight. Pilar's children were at the movie house a few blocks away. Because it was a holiday, they had been allowed to see the Cantinflas film that had been playing for a week. Cantinflas was the new Mexican comedy sensation.

"Smell it out here," Pilar said, breathing deeply. The air was scented with flowering San Carlos vine and with the moist haziness that rose off the cooling earth as night descended. Like Jacinta's, Pilar's legs dangled against the wall and the concrete was rough to her calves, but the alcohol she had drunk was warm in her belly and she didn't mind the roughness against her skin. Other neighbors sat along the wall talking quietly. Some strolled up and down the sidewalk before turning back toward their houses and beds. A plaintive guitar drifted from a radio someplace near. Two dark shapes came toward them, and soon the shapes materialized into a woman and a man.

"Buenas, Pilar," the woman said, pausing for a moment. The man hung back at the edge of the sidewalk, near the street. He was of medium height and solid; a lit cigarette glowed in the shadows obscuring his face. Jacinta could not clearly see his features, but she had the impression that if the lamplight could reach him, his face would please her. The man poked one hand into his trouser pocket, and he stood there like that, until the woman turned back to him.

"Who was that?" Jacinta said after the pair had gone by.

"Olivia and Miguel Acevedo. They live a few blocks over. I used to sew for her. In two years, she went up four sizes. Why do you ask?"

"No reason," Jacinta said, and then, "I think he has an interesting face. What I could see of it, that is."

"Ha!" Pilar said, throwing her head back. "Listen to you. We talk about men, about how you need one, and you quickly deny it. Now a man comes by, and you think he's interesting."

"I said I thought he had an interesting face. I didn't say I thought he was interesting."

"Same thing," Pilar said. "Anyway, Olivia's always tired. I'm surprised she's out tonight. I'm surprised she's not in bed."

"Oh," Jacinta muttered, wondering what a man did about a tired woman. Wasn't it always men who tired women out?

Very early the next morning, Jacinta left Pilar's to catch the bus home. Despite the hour, there was much activity on the street and along the sidewalks bordering the squat houses of the barrio. Some women swept their doorways with furious strokes, while others hurried along to a day of work outside the neighborhood. There were men about, too, of course. One man strode up the street a few meters from Jacinta. At first, she paid him no particular attention, but after trailing him for two blocks, she was taken by his confident, determined stride. He carried a folded newspaper in one hand; it brushed back and forth against his leg as he walked. Observing him further, she noted his broad shoulders and the starched white shirt stretched taut against them. She noted how neatly his shirt was tucked into his trousers and how the backs of his shoes gleamed as he walked along. Here was a man, she thought, who knew where he was going. A man who seemed not to regret where he had been.

The bus stop was up ahead, and the man slipped the newspaper under his arm and went to stand next to other people waiting at the curb. Something about the man seemed familiar.

"Buenos días, Miguel," an old woman said.

"Doña Faustina," the man said, inclining his head.

Miguel. The man from last night. Jacinta wanted to study him, but the bus rolled up and there was a small commotion as some tried to push their way ahead of others. Miguel waited for his time to board, and when it came, he seemed to sense Jacinta behind him. He turned and said to her, "After you." He made a little sweeping motion with his hand.

She got a good look at him then. His skin was lighter than hers. His eyes were dark and deeply set. His mouth was full and kind looking. A blackened matchstick was poked between his lips, and this lent him a playful air. He wore a dark tie tacked to his shirt by

a silver bar. All of this Jacinta observed in the mere seconds it took
to thank Miguel for his courtesy. She went up the steps of the bus
and down the aisle to a free bench. She scooted in against the window and watched him come toward her. The matchstick was no
longer between his lips. He stopped two rows in front of her and
took the opposite bench. From where she sat, if she looked past the
heads of others quickly filling up the bus, she had a good view of
him. He sat, his head bent over his newspaper, and this sight was
heartening. He was a man who could read. Not a common thing.
She herself could read, thanks to the schooling Elena had insisted
upon. Something else not commonplace.

"Your money, please," a voice said. Jacinta turned her attention
to the bus conductor who had reached her row; he stood in the aisle,
his arm extended. Jacinta dug into her pocket and handed the man
a five-centavo piece. She looked Miguel's way. Miguel was no longer
reading but sat very straight, as if at any moment he would spring
up. The bus came to a stop with a loud squeal of the brakes. Miguel
stood and came down the aisle, toward the back exit. Jacinta looked
out the window. The bus had stopped in front of the post office, a
massive wooden structure with a number of wide entrances. Miguel
walked directly under Jacinta's window, and then, before the bus
pulled away from the curb, she saw him stride into the post office.
Of course, she thought. Miguel was a postal clerk.

Jacinta sat very still as the bus traveled two more blocks to her
stop. She got off at the corner, only steps from Magda's door. Maybe
Pilar is right, she said to herself. Maybe I *do* need a man. For the
twelve years since Chico's murder, she had not given another man
a single consideration. This morning, she had given one a second
thought. A married man, at that.

▼▼▼

CHAPTER TWENTY-THREE

In the cavernous main room of the post office, Jacinta stood patiently in Miguel Acevedo's line. The line was long, so she had the time to note how voices melded with echoing footsteps and shuffling papers. The building's din had a hollow sound that rose from polished dark surfaces, past banks of letterboxes to resound against the ceiling and its wide carved beams. Around her, the rich odor of mahogany emanated from counters and walls and floors. In the air swirled the stories sealed in scores of envelopes entering and leaving the locale.

Jacinta shifted her weight from one foot to the other. She had checked the Tobar box for incoming mail and placed the correspondence in her string bag. Today there were three letters to post. She fanned them out in her hand: one from Magda to Elena; a second she'd transcribed for Delfina, who could not read or write; and a third from herself to Chenta in El Congo. Over the years, when she had the weekend off, an occasion that came only every three months, Jacinta periodically visited Chenta. But it was letters, not visits, they relied upon to keep in touch. Jacinta looked up the line again. Five people stood between her and Miguel. Since encountering him three weeks before at Pilar's and later on the bus, Jacinta had visited the post office twice. Each time she had usurped the duty from Basilio Fermín, who this morning had been in the patio pruning the gardenias when she approached him with the news. "Don't bother with the mail today. I'll be going after lunch." Basilio had laid his corvo down and pulled out a rag from his rear pocket and mopped his face with it. "This is the third time," he said, stuffing the rag back into his pocket. "So?" Jacinta had replied, hurrying off to change out of her uniform before any more could be said.

The line inched forward. If she craned her head, she could see Miguel clearly. He worked briskly. Deftly he tore stamps from large panes; he impressed envelopes and papers with quick blows of a rubber seal. And he answered questions put to him, tilting his head a bit, responding in a manner that showed he was neither engaged by a patron nor unconcerned. Both times before, they had not spoken. The first time, Jacinta had stood in the line next to his, not wishing to make contact. She had not known why she had come. Why, since that morning at the bus stop, the thought of this man was like a burr in her head. The second time, she had been bolder. She approached his window and slid the letters she had brought toward him over the hand-worn counter top. She looked at him wide-eyed and guileless, but he did not react any differently to her than he had to others, and so she simply reached for the stamps he handed her and then, in silence, turned away. That night she had lain in bed listening to Rosalba's soft snores across the room and to the whistle of el sereno who patrolled the block, announcing his presence periodically during his watch. El sereno's whistle was a signal in the night, and it brought home her own alarming questions: What has come over me? Why, after so many years, is my heart filling up with the thought of a man? Alone in her bed, she pictured Miguel, his fierce eyes, his light-skinned hands, sure and quick at work.

Jacinta was one person away from reaching the head of the line when Miguel drew shut the little door that closed him off from his customers. A sign spelling "Cerrado" was now where Miguel had been. Jacinta stared at the Closed sign for a moment, her disappointment keen. She stepped to a neighboring line and waited again to post her correspondence. Outside, she raised a hand to shield her eyes from the afternoon glare. She looked up the street and, miraculously, she saw Miguel. He was at the lottery stand. Jacinta walked over.

"I'll take four tickets," Miguel was saying to the vendor. Miguel peered at the large page printed with long columns of numbers tacked to the side of the ramshackle stand.

The vendor's face broke into a wide smile. He had blackened teeth that looked like tiny stumps. "Buy a whole sheet, señor," he said. "A sheet of twenty tickets will bring you luck. With it you can win one hundred thousand colones."

"No," Miguel said, "four vigésimos will be enough. But which four to choose? That's the eternal question."

"Buy these, señor," Jacinta said, deciding at once to act. She pointed to a random number on the sheet. "I'm buying four of these myself. I have a good feeling about this number." Was she crazy? She didn't believe in wasting money on the lottery.

"You think this one's good?"

"It's number one-nine-eight-three-five, isn't it?" Jacinta said, reading the figure off the page. "That's a very good number."

"You seem so sure. You must have won many times." Miguel looked at her, his face seriously earnest.

"I've won enough." What was she saying? She hardly recognized herself.

The vendor winked at Jacinta and spoke to Miguel: "La señorita has the lucky touch. Buy that number, señor. It plays five days from now."

Miguel studied Jacinta. "Is it true? Do you have the lucky touch?"

Jacinta tossed her head because her best feature was her thick black hair. "I do."

"Then it's decided. I'll have four of those numbers," Miguel said to the vendor.

"I'll take the same myself."

"A very good choice," the vendor said, detaching the eight tickets from a sheet of twenty. Jacinta opened her coin purse and plucked out the change. They paid for their tickets and started down the street with them.

"It seems I've placed my fortune in your hands," Miguel said, slipping his purchase into a trouser pocket. He paused abruptly in the middle of the sidewalk, a quizzical expression coming over his face. "Tell me, don't I know you? You look familiar."

Jacinta motioned toward the post office looming behind them. "I come frequently for the mail. Perhaps you come here, too. I'm Jacinta Prieto." No need to mention Pilar's barrio and the night he had strolled by.

"Ah, that's it. I work in the post office. Maybe you've come to my window. I'm Miguel Acevedo, civil servant." He tipped his head at her.

Jacinta laughed. "Civil servant. I like the sound of that." She tossed her head again and felt her hair brushing her shoulders. "Well, I should be going."

"Will I see you again? In five days our fortune will be decided."

"That would be on Monday."

"If our number wins, we'll have something to celebrate, don't you think?"

"We might at that," Jacinta said. She bid him farewell and walked away, feeling his eyes on her all the way down the street.

On Monday, Jacinta stood by as Magda had breakfast. The daily newspaper was lying on the table next to her linen place mat. Somewhere in the paper was the list of winning lottery numbers, and Jacinta itched to study them, but she could not get at the paper until the señores were through with it. Magda sipped on her coffee as she went over the week's menus. Jacinta responded to each of Magda's suggestions; she made a mental note of the ingredients each dish required so she could provide the cook with a market list. To divert herself, Jacinta studied the enormous painting over the sideboard portraying coffee pickers during harvest time. In the painting, the pickers looked uniformly joyous, a visual pretense that obviously made the harsh realities of picking more palatable to the rich.

Earlier, don Alvaro had come into the room, and as was his morning ritual, he ceremoniously unfolded the paper (God help the person who opened it before he) and read it during breakfast. As luck would have it, this morning he had pored over every word. When he finally finished, he pushed back his chair and grabbed his hat off the wall peg before going out the door. Jacinta was about to reach for the newspaper when Magda had appeared and sat down to her café con leche and toast. Magda flipped immediately to the Society section, laying the paper down when the children had bounced in dressed in their school uniforms. The boys—Alvaro (he was named after his father, so they called him Júnior) was eleven, Carlos was ten, and Orlando was eight—bolted down their breakfasts and in a flurry of hugs and kisses took leave of their mother. They left with Basilio for the short walk to el Liceo Centroamericano. A year ago, it was Tea, their nursemaid, who walked the boys to and from school, but Júnior had complained that he looked like a sissy with la nana trailing behind. Basilio's presence he had conceded to because it was manly. "It's like we have a bodyguard," the boy had said.

Magda had gone back to the newspaper. Now she pointed to a photograph appearing in the middle of the page. "Look at this," Magda said, gesturing toward other photographs and stories. "It's one party after another. Here's a baptism, here are three weddings, here's a tea. And look at all these showers. You know what this means, don't you, Jacinta? It means presents. Lots and lots of presents."

"It means Tesoros," Jacinta said.

"Yes! It means Tesoros. It means the time is getting ripe for starting up the store. All I'm waiting for is the perfect location to materialize." Magda pushed the paper aside and yawned and stretched, throwing her slender arms up. She took a sip from her coffee cup that three times before Jacinta herself had filled in an effort to speed the morning up. Magda dabbed her mouth with a napkin. "You know, when Tesoros opens, you'll be the one in charge of the house and the boys. You really don't mind, do you, Jacinta? It'll mean everything to me."

"The question still is, niña Magda, do you think I can do it?"

"Of course you can." Magda stood and laid a hand on Jacinta's arm. "You've *been* doing it. Nothing much would change." Magda leaned closer to Jacinta and pinned her with a conspiratorial gaze. "What we have to do is reassure don Alvaro that nothing will change when I open my store." Magda rolled her dark eyes. "You know how men are. Deep down, all men are babies."

"Yes," Jacinta said. The two men she had known, Antonio and

Chico, they *had* been babies. Young boys, in any case. She thought of her father. She couldn't even imagine Ignacio Prieto as a baby.

"By the way, there's mail to go out," Magda called over her shoulder, heading for her bedroom and the shower. She wrote her mother twice a week, receiving letters in return. A few days ago, there had been a letter from her father, too, a rare occurrence. The news in her father's letter was disturbing: Your mother refuses to eat very much. Isn't there something you can do?

Jacinta rushed the newspaper into the kitchen. "You can clear the table now," she said to Rosalba, who was at the servants' table drinking coffee from a saucer instead of a cup. Rosalba hauled herself up and went muttering out of the room. Tea was at the table, too. She was middle-aged and as slender and dry as a tree branch. She was the only one of the servants who could take or leave *Las dos*. Now that her three charges were in school, Tea had more time on her hands, though there was plenty for her to do, given that she was responsible for keeping the boys' rooms and closets in order, and tidying up the big dayroom where the train sets and model cars were displayed.

At the table, Jacinta opened the paper to the list of winning lottery numbers, which filled an entire page. She studied the list, first the large number at the top of the page, then the short list of medium-size numbers printed under it. One-nine-eight-three-five was not among them. She dropped into a chair, laid the paper on the table, and began searching the columns of numerals appearing on the better part of the page. She worked slowly, underscoring each tiny number with a finger. Across the room, Delfina rinsed out a pot at the sink. "You played the lottery." The cook shuffled across the room and took a chair next to Jacinta. "You never play the lottery." Because she was very deaf, she spoke very loudly.

Rosalba came in with a tray piled with breakfast dishes. "Who played the lottery?" She set the tray down at the sink.

"My number didn't win," Jacinta said, truly surprised at the development. She had been so certain of winning. She slipped a finger between the buttons of her uniform and extracted the tickets she'd tucked away in her bra. She laid the tickets on the table. Perhaps she'd remembered the number wrong. No. There it was: 19835.

Rosalba came over. "You never play the lottery."

"I can't believe I didn't win."

Tea gave a little snort. "Only the rich win the lottery. Don't you know that?"

Rosalba repositioned the big comb she had used to gather her hair up. She had seen the hairdo in one of Magda's magazines. It was in a photograph depicting a woman being kissed by a sailor. The gringo had bent the woman back, and he was kissing her right in the middle of the street. Rosalba saw herself being kissed in the same manner by Basilio. Under the tree in the far corner of the patio, he would place his arms around her. Bend her back like that. "Let me see the list."

Jacinta flicked the tickets aside. "It won't do any good. One-nine-eight-three-five. The number's a losing one." She went over and took a cup out of the cupboard and poured herself some coffee at the stove.

"See. Didn't I tell you?" Tea said. She was finishing a tortilla, taking quick little bites, as was her way of eating.

"You're wrong," Rosalba said. "Part of the number won something."

Delfina cupped a hand around an ear. "What did she say?"

"Part of Jacinta's number won something," Rosalba repeated, raising her voice to match the cook's.

"You're joking." Jacinta took a step back because she'd just come close to dribbling coffee on herself. She set the cup down and went over to the table.

"No, I'm not. Look. Number eight-three-five won something." Rosalba's head was bent over the paper. Strands of hair had escaped the comb and fell around her face.

"¿Qué pasó?" Delfina repeated.

"Jacinta's ticket won," Rosalba said.

"What did she win?" Delfina asked, her chin whiskers obvious in the light from the window.

"Five colones. Number eight-three-five won five colones."

"Let me see." Jacinta peered at the number Rosalba indicated. The girl was right. Under the five-colón win column the last three digits of her number appeared. "I can't believe it." She dropped into the chair again. "That's twenty colones." Her monthly pay was thirty colones, ten colones more than Tea and Delfina, the oldest members of the staff, fifteen colones more than the rest of them. "I won twenty colones."

Basilio came in from walking the children to school. "Did someone win money?" He hooked his hat over one of the back spindles of a kitchen chair.

"Jacinta won twenty colones," Delfina said.

"You never play the lottery," Basilio added.

"It was me who found the number," Rosalba pointed out.

A loud annoying buzzer sounded outside the kitchen, down a short interior hallway that led to the garage and to the back service entrance. "It's Juana," Basilio said. "I'll let her in." Juana was the laundress, the only member of the staff who didn't live at Magda's.

Jacinta picked up her winning tickets and tucked them back into her bra. "I'll be taking the mail to the post office today," she yelled, just as Basilio went out the kitchen door.

It was almost three o'clock when she got to the post office. She stood in Miguel's line, and when she finally reached him, she waited for him to look up and notice her.

"Ah, señorita Prieto." He smiled broadly when he saw her. "You're the face of lady luck." He lowered his voice and continued: "I'm sure you know our tickets brought us a return. I've played for many years, and never won but a few colones."

"We won twenty. Twenty each." Jacinta slid Magda's letter to Elena across the counter toward Miguel. "I was just now going to the lottery office to collect. I expect you did that already."

"As a matter of fact, no." He selected the proper stamp for Jacinta and handed it to her. He looked at his wristwatch. "Look, it's almost my lunch hour. I could take the time to cash in my ticket. Would you mind the company?"

Jacinta moistened the stamp with the tip of her tongue, then smoothed the stamp on the letter. "If you wish."

"Very well, then. I'll meet you at the lottery stand." Miguel pulled down his Cerrado sign, closing off his station, and Jacinta walked over to the Tobars' post office box to collect their mail before joining him. She distracted herself from the way her heart galloped by studying the return name on each letter she extracted from the box. Some of the mail was addressed to don Alvaro, but three letters were for Magda. The one from Elena was no surprise, nor was the second one from Leonor, her brother Neto's wife. The third letter was a very different matter, and it would have sent Jacinta hurrying home had she not made plans with Miguel. The third letter was a square, pale blue envelope with the name "Cecilia de Aragón" scrawled in dark blue ink on the upper left-hand side.

The main lottery office was located up Paseo Independencia near the Teatro Nacional. Jacinta and Miguel decided to walk there and ride the bus back. In the interest of time, they cut across neighborhood parks and then went down Calle Arce, a street bustling with shops and people. Jacinta's pulse had settled down, but now her mind churned furiously. In her string bag lay news of Cecilia; at her side strode a man in a resplendent white shirt, smelling faintly of something lemony. Walking along, Jacinta mulled over two questions: What kind of news was in the letter? and Why was Miguel Acevedo so accommodating? The fact that he had a wife made this last question troubling and thrilling at the same time.

Here and there, along the sides of buildings, enterprising women had set up small fruit stands. "A little fruit for you?" they asked as Jacinta went by. The comforting odor of hot tortillas wafted down the street, and soon they passed a comedor filled with patrons eating lunch. El Congo came rushing back. Her mother. Chenta. Luis's fruit stand. Oddly, toothless old Josefa and even cagey Joaquín Maldonado came to mind. Maybe it was Cecilia's letter that had triggered the flood of memory. When you least expected it, at the oddest hour, the past could reach its long arm out and touch your life again.

"Why so serious, señorita, when we're only blocks from new bills in our pockets?"

"I'm sorry. The street's so noisy. And please call me Jacinta. Jacinta Prieto."

They came to Paseo Independencia, a broad alameda lined with palms and shade trees. A grassy parkway ran down the middle. They waited for traffic to thin before they walked across to the lottery office. "My goodness," Jacinta said. "Look at the line." A queue snaked out the building. "Maybe this wasn't a good time."

Miguel checked his watch again. "There's still forty minutes." He had rolled his sleeves to his elbows, and Jacinta could see the hair growing thick on his well-turned arms. They took their place in line, the afternoon sun pressing down on them. Surprisingly, the line moved fast, and soon they were out on the street again, each richer by twenty colones. At the bus stand, Miguel lit a cigarette and poked the matchstick between his teeth before taking a puff.

"I feel indebted to you, you know." Miguel patted the pocket containing his winnings. "I hope you'll permit me to show my gratitude. Someday, after work, I'd like to buy you a cafecito."

She pictured herself sitting with Miguel in a café in one of the dresses Pilar had made for her. "Maybe. Maybe on my day off." In addition to a free weekend every three months, she had a day off every two weeks.

"And when is that?"

"Soon," she said, shying away from being too direct. So many years with no man in her life, and now this man with his pleated trousers and pressed shirt, with his deep-set eyes and the charming little matchstick bobbing between his lips when he spoke. She looked up the street and then back at him. "Tell me, señor, what will you do with your money?"

Miguel raised a hand. "Por favor, call me Miguel. After all, we are partners in good fortune, are we not?"

Jacinta laughed. "I suppose we are."

"As to the money, I have exact plans for it. I'll divide it between my children. They're planning a trip with their mother to their grandmother's house in San Vicente. The money will come in handy."

"Oh, you have children?" He had a wife *and* he had children. Madre de Dios. What was she doing?

"I have three. A boy and two girls."

"And how old are they?"

"The boy is ten; the girls, fifteen and seventeen. They're women now, really."

"You must be proud of them."

"Sometimes they make me proud. But tell me, what about yourself? Do you have children?"

"No, I don't."

"Are you a married woman, Jacinta?"

"No, I'm not married."

"You must have many suitors, then."

She didn't answer but looked down because she felt a blush starting at her neck.

"It is a good combination," he said after a moment. "You are a serious woman and a modest one as well."

▼▼

CHAPTER TWENTY-FOUR

Alvaro Tobar gripped the wheel of his convertible roadster and leaned into the approaching curve. He glanced down at the speedometer. The needle hovered at 130 kilometers per hour. He took the turn, fighting back the impulse to step harder on the gas pedal. Alvaro loved his car. He loved the sense of power he experienced when he was in the driver's seat. He'd owned the Ford since before the war, and maybe now that the war had ended and as soon as Ford began to manufacture again, he would buy a newer model. This roadster he would not sell, however. He patted the wheel as if reassuring the vehicle of his loyalty.

Alvaro glanced at the sky. It was a late afternoon in early November. A north wind swirled dark clouds above him. The air was heavy with coming rain, surely one of the last downpours before the dry season. He would wait for the first drops to fall before he stopped to raise the car's top. Maybe, if he was lucky, he would beat the rain. He was only a few kilometers from San Salvador and, once inside the city limits, only minutes from home.

Alvaro's thoughts turned to his cotton harvest. For the past week, he'd been on the eastern coast, at El Porvenir, his plantation outside Usulután. On this trip, he had helped ready the hacienda for the harvest, which would start at month's end. Much was riding on his cotton. He always referred to it as "mi algodón." My cotton, a venture that he, and not his mother, controlled. He pictured his mother's strong, handsome face. Eugenia Herrera de Tobar. At seventy-three, doña Eugenia was still the undisputed ruler of the Tobar family. As the doyenne, she controlled her business and private affairs with as much vigor as she had since her husband's death. Alvaro had been five when the finca administrador clattered up the farmhouse steps. "There's been an accident," the man called into the opened door of the big house. "It was the horse. It tossed el señor down the ravine." With time, these words had turned into heirlooms. As he grew older, Alvaro began to see their impact on his life.

He checked the sky again. It was growing even darker. His thoughts returned to his father, who had lain in a coma for three days before he died. It was only during this time that his mother allowed herself to grieve. After the funeral, and because she had Alvaro and his four older sisters to raise, she took over the reins of her husband's cattle-ranching operation and his vast property holdings and never relinquished them. Under her control, her husband's enterprises prospered. Oh, there were moments when she cried out against the quirk of fate that had sent her down a path strewn with so much responsibility. "It's a heavy burden life has handed me," she liked to say. "A burden I long to have lifted from my shoulders." When people heard this, they would nod their heads solemnly and they would make little clucking sounds that meant, My, what a courageous woman you are. How you sacrifice for your children. Even as a youngster, however, when Alvaro heard his mother's lamentations, he had glimpsed into her heart as if her chest were made of glass. In her heart, he had seen the pleasure the burden gave her.

It was power that obsessed her. And could he blame her? He had had a whiff of the heady scent of power himself. He smelled it in his cotton. He'd been in the business for four years. The first three years were hopeful ones. There was a world war, and unlike coffee, cotton prices rose steadily, thanks to the growth of the local textile industry. Though the harvest season coincided with that of coffee and both crops relied almost exclusively on migrant workers for the reaping, the labor force in the country was so plentiful it provided hands for both. Better yet, pickers were efficient and cheap—a boon especially to cotton, which, because it was an annual crop, needed yearly replanting.

From the start, his mother had not encouraged him to strike out on his own. "Only fools go into cotton when there's cattle to be raised or coffee to be grown," she said, compelling him to work all the harder to prove her wrong. He had spent months scouting for the right land among the family's properties on the flat coastal plain. When he found it, he had lovingly sown the best seed himself. And he had kept a vigil on the growing plants. Lying in a hut next to the field, he was present at the moment the buds broke into flower: first the pale white blossoms as delicate as hibiscus, then, wondrously only a day later, the blooms turning a soft shade of pink.

Alvaro entered the southern edge of town, reducing his speed as he passed the sprawling fort, El Zapote, with its imposing bastions still exhibiting bullet holes and mortar blows from last year's two coups. He kept his speed down for the time it took to make it beyond the Presidential Palace. After the takeover by General Castañeda, both these sites were garrisoned extra-heavily. Alvaro drove past soldiers standing guard, their bayoneted rifles held at port arms across their chests. Castañeda's regime was only a year old, and while he had not gone to the repressive extremes of Martínez, his predecessor, Castañeda had yet to make any real economic concessions. Yet it was too early to tell what he might do for middle-size cotton planters.

Once Alvaro reached Avenida Cuscatlán, he accelerated, weaving in and out of traffic. Cotton. A man took a risk growing it, for cotton might never make the money coffee would, but Alvaro did not allow this thought to perturb him. He had various means of making a living: There was real estate to be bought and sold, a seat on the bank board, the shrimping business on the coast. He had disbanded his law practice years ago, although, at times, he took a case or two on a consulting basis. But it was in the cotton business that he'd placed his heart and money. Last year, so sure was he of a better-than-ever yield, that he'd invested Magda's money in it as well. It was the inheritance from her grandfather, bequeathed to her twelve years before. Magda had entrusted it to Alvaro, and he had carefully managed the money, seeing to its growth. When the time was right, she would use her inheritance for her own business scheme: a gift shop named Tesoros. When they were first married, it was all she talked about. But then the children came, and there was a depression and the war. Circumstances and the times had worked in his favor. In spite of stocking a big closet with samples of merchandise she would offer in the store, she had remained at home, the place where she belonged. Alvaro believed the old adage A woman's place is in the home. Who better than he to know? A man who had been a child with a mother like his own.

The rain began as he was crossing Avenida Roosevelt. Alvaro made it through the intersection, then pulled the car up at the curb and jumped out. He worked quickly, tugging and pulling and then rolling the canvas across the top of the car. The rain stung his back and shoulders as he snapped the edge of the tarp into the metal rivets along the rim of the frame. Soon he was soaked through; the back of his shirt and khaki trousers clung to him. He hopped behind the wheel again as the heavens opened up. The downpour fell at an angle against the car, thrumming a rhythm against the top canvas and steel hood. The car's interior fogged up. The air turned close and humid. Alvaro rubbed a circle in the window with a fist. Other cars had pulled over. The gutters were filling, and soon the rain rushed down the center of the avenue.

The disaster of last year's harvest flooded his mind. He sank back against the seat, remembering his cotton, the bolls swollen and soon to burst into a cloud of white, infested malevolently with weevils.

But this year would be different. He had taken measures. He had spent the better part of the week stockpiling DDT, dieldrin, and malathion, insecticides that would insure this crop against failure. He had modeled for his caporales the way the cotton was to be patiently dusted, a procedure the overseers would then pass on to their pickers.

Alvaro ran a hand through his damp hair. He had not told Magda any of this, of course. Why cause her concern? It was all a matter of cash flow, of money transferred from one account to the other, of bank loans and promissory notes. This year, he would ride out the harvest. This year, because of insecticides, would bring his first bumper crop.

▼   ▼   ▼

Alvaro and Magda in the sanctuary of their bedroom, where Magda herself was the supreme illusionist: at center stage, a wide pillowed bed spanned by a canopy spilling from its corners an egg-shell voile that puddled onto a cinnamon carpet. As in a Rubens painting, walls gleamed coppery in the soft light of sconces and votive candles flickering on shelves and tables. The pale light extended along the carpet and up the side of the bed, so that the two figures lying against the pillows, their bodies musky and moist from lovemaking, shone in it.

Alvaro inhaled deeply and closed his eyes. He sank deeper into the pillows, a hand along Magda's thigh, his fingers resting on the thick cushion over her pubis. She was his, and he would never have enough of her. For twelve years, most nights that they were together, in this sorcerous room or in whatever room their travels took them to, they explored and scaled each other's bodies as if it were the first time. She was inexhaustible and inventive, a combination of qualities rare in a woman. Before his marriage, he had had a few others: a first love, a sweet shy girl who twice allowed him to straddle her but who both times kept her eyes shut and legs clamped so tightly together that he had come, despite the obstacle and no doubt because of his excitement, along the bony ridge of her thighs. And then there were the putas, gaudy, fleshy women who did not hesitate to open wide but who, when he came in muffled groans, rolled immediately away, their eyes as lackluster as when he peeled a colón from his wallet and laid it in their palms.

Since Magda, there had been no others. What man, having her, would need another? He possessed an enchantress and was possessed by her spells, by the spread of her legs, by the warm, salty place between them. He was possessed by her mouth, her tongue, her fingers.

Under his fingers, Magda moved. He turned his face to her and watched her watching him. Her eyes were bright, her hair dampened into ringlets. Perspiration sheened her cheeks, her breasts, and the thin brown line having babies had painted down her belly. Magda thrust her hips against his hand. "Do it with your fingers now," she said, and he shifted to his side and slid a finger into her. "Put more in," she said, reaching for his hand, arching her back to him. He did as she asked, and soon felt her wet inner flesh twitch around his touch. She gave out a long audible exhalation. "Yes," she said. "Exactly like that."

▼▼▼

CHAPTER TWENTY-FIVE

Magda transferred a chicken breast to her plate from the platter Rosalba held for her. "Qué rico," Magda said. The chicken looked appetizingly golden and it smelled rich and garlicky. Rosalba served Alvaro at the head of the table and then the boys, who, with the exception of Júnior, were fidgeting in their chairs and looked ready to bolt. "Be still, you monkeys," Magda said, "or you'll eat in the pantry as usual with Tea and not with me and Papá."

"We'll be good," Carlos and Orlando said, almost in unison. They sat on the same side of the table. Orlando had poked a napkin into the neckline of his shirt so that it appeared he was wearing a big white tie.

"That would be rare," Júnior said in his big-brother tone. He had one side of the table to himself, and he relished this distinction. He held his hands in his lap like his mother had taught him, and knew to raise them to fork and knife only when she began to eat.

Rosalba went on to serve cauliflower in butter sauce (all the boys wrinkled their noses at it), saffron rice jeweled with petits pois, and a fragrant dish of black beans seasoned with chorizo. She placed in the middle of the table, and next to a centerpiece of purple and white morning glories, a glass bowl filled with leaf lettuce and a small pitcher of freshly squeezed lemon juice. Magda believed greens dressed simply with lemon were an intestinal purifier. Each lunch-time, she insisted the family have a serving after the main course.

"When we go to the hacienda, can I ride the horses, Papá?" Orlando asked. In a few weeks, when Alvaro moved in to El Porvenir for the cotton harvest, he was taking the boys with him for a time. The school term had just ended, and the children were on vacation until February. Besides Tea, whose duty it was to see to their meals, keep them relatively clean, and get them to bed on time, Basilio Fermín would go along, too. At the hacienda, he would shadow the boys as they rode the horses, fished in the creek, or explored around the property.

"You can ride Brisa," Alvaro said. Brisa was the swaybacked mare who, because of her age, was capable only of plodding.

Orlando stuck out a lip. He had thick curly hair like his father. The same amiable open face. "Brisa's too old. I want to ride Sultán." With his fork, he poked around his rice and rolled a few peas toward the rim of his plate.

"Sultán's my horse," Júnior said. "Isn't he, Papá?"

"Niños, don't argue," Magda admonished. "Orlando, eat your petits pois." When all her men went off, she would turn her full attention to the store. Yesterday, when Alvaro returned from El Porvenir, she had not bothered him with details of her own news. After a week away, he had been eager to talk about the hacienda, about the preparations he had made for his harvest. And he was hungering, he had said, for a good home meal. For an early bed and the spells those bedtimes brought. Heartily, Magda had indulged his desires, in particular, the last one, because when Alvaro was away, she hungered for those moments herself. But that was yesterday. Today, relying on the knowledge that her husband was a satisfied man and thus, where it concerned his opinions and pronounce-ments, a softened one as well, she would give him her news.

"Amor," she said, looking over the morning glories at him so placidly enjoying his meal, "you won't believe what happened."

"What's that?" Alvaro took a sip of water.

"I found the perfect place for Tesoros. The absolute perfect place."

Alvaro set his water glass next to his plate. "Oh. And where is that?"

"Two doors down from the Gran Hotel. Only five blocks from the house. Can you believe it?"

Alvaro frowned. "Isn't that Quique Aguiluz's news shop?"

"Exactly. But Quique's decided to expand from newspapers and magazines into books. He needs a larger place. He's moving in February. When he does, I can have his present space. It's all decided. I made the deal while you were gone."

"You made a deal?"

"Well, yes. I signed a lease. I had to move fast. There's a list of others wanting the space. It's prime, you have to agree. Quique wants a down payment amounting to three months' rent and a security deposit. I thought that was fair. I even got him to agree to wait a week for the money." Magda took a drink of water herself. She dabbed her mouth with the napkin before going on. "Needless to say, I'll need some of my money."

Alvaro placed a quick hand on his knife and then his spoon as if he were protecting them. "You can't have your money."

"What do you mean, I can't have my money?"

"Your money's all invested. It's tied up. It's not liquid."

"How can that be?" Magda asked.

"It can be, because times have been difficult, need I remind you. It can be, because in order to get the best possible return, the safest possible return, I had to tie the money up. Who knew the war would end? It might have gone on forever. Had I known the war would end, I might have done things differently."

Magda was silent for a moment. Then she said, "And when do you think my money will be available?"

"Months from now. A year. I don't know offhand. I'd have to look at your portfolio."

"All right then, I'll borrow from you. *You* give me the money. And by the way, there's not only rent to consider, but between now and February, I'll have to make at least two buying trips abroad. One to New York, the other to London. Maybe a third trip to Germany. You knew this, Alvaro. I've been talking about it for years."

Carlos, the middle son, who had inherited the long countenance of don Orlando, his grandfather, scrunched up his face. "Papis, don't argue, please."

"We're not arguing, darling," Magda said, "Mamá and Papá are simply discussing."

"Qué discusión," Júnior said, leaning a cheek against a fist.

"No elbows on the table, please," Magda said.

"I can't lend you money," Alvaro said. "My money's tied up, too."

"All your money? All your money's tied up?"

"It's tied up in this year's harvest. After February, cash flow will improve. After February, I can lend you money."

"By then it'll be too late."

"It's all I can do."

"No, it isn't."

"What do you mean?"

"You're on the bank board. I'll go to your bank for a loan."

What Alvaro loved about the way Magda managed the house, the children, the staff, what he loved about her in bed, he hated when applied to her scheme of going into business. A woman had no place in business. Certainly not a woman who was a mother and a wife. "I tell you what: You don't have to go to the bank. Leave it to me. I'll talk to the loan committee."

"You mean it?" Magda said. "You'll sway them in my direction?"

Alvaro smiled across the table at Magda. "I'll do what I can," he said.

Magda rearranged her napkin on her lap. "Gracias, amor. I know you'll do your best."

He had done his best. He had done what was best for Magda. What was best for his children. What was best for him, though he put himself last.

He had requested a special meeting of the loan committee. When it convened, he had set before this panel of men, some his peers, most not, a few more venerable than he, the facts of Magda's situation: Here is an exemplary woman, he had said. A dedicated mother. A loving and faithful wife. Here is a dutiful citizen who wishes to leave the safety of her home for dangerous trips abroad, for long hours of work apart from her family. Make no mistake, gentlemen, he had said. Though this woman has no experience whatsoever in the retail field, though at present she is undercapitalized, this woman is capable, efficient, and discerning. She embodies the spirit of the Salvadoran woman, hardworking, clever. A woman dedicated to getting ahead. Under this woman's creative hand, under her watchful eye, under her skilled management, a new enterprise will flourish in our capital. This enterprise, which your wives, your daughters, your mothers will surely aid in making prosperous, deserves not only your keen consideration but your votes in providing the funds to launch it.

He, of course, abstained from the vote, for it was clear where he stood, given his impassioned discourse. It had taken them only minutes to come to a decision. Before they voiced it, all eyes had turned to him, and he allowed his shoulders to slump, but only for an instant, before he straighened up to hear that they were obliged to turn her down. That he had not said a single word against her helped take the sting from the defeat.

▼▼▼

CHAPTER TWENTY-SIX

T hough it was mid-November and the rains had ceased and the hot days and warm nights of summer were clearly entrenched for the season, to the north of the capital, in the mountainous, piney department of Chalatenago, summer was so cool that during the day people usually kept their arms covered. During the night, the air turned chilly so that sleepers made themselves small in their beds and, toward dawn, pulled covers up from the moorings of their mattresses and wrapped themselves like mummies. Nestled along the ridge of the cordillera Alotepeque was El Recreo, the ranch that belonged to Elena de Contreras. The place measured some ten thousand hectares and included broad valleys, sudden upsweeps of regal pines, jagged mountain crags, and the clear and bracing creeks that were actually fingers of both the río Lempa and the río Sumpul at the Honduran border a mere ten kilometers away.

When he was a young man, Orlando Navarro, Elena's father, had discovered the property on a deer hunting trip. Stepping out from under a stand of pines, his Remington slung across a shoulder, he had come to a clearing so green that he had to blink away the sting so much lushness brought to his eyes. "¡Virgen Santa!" he exclaimed, turning full circle on the heel of a boot, his vision struck not only by the verdant glen surrounding him but by the majestic sweep of the trees he'd just left, by the breeze murmuring between them, by the mountain ridge looming imperially above. The property lay in a valley called el Llano de la Virgen, and when he learned it was fortuitously for sale, he bought the land at once. A few years later, he built a house on the very spot where he first had stood.

When Orlando Navarro died, he bequeathed El Recreo to Elena. Of all her father's properties, she loved it best. Her two brothers, because they were the heads of families, inherited the coffee finca, the coffee mill, the real estate along the coast and in the capital. In a palliative move toward equality, Elena was also left a modest yearly income—not more, the will stated, because she had a husband to provide for her. Elena had no quarrel with the disparity of the bequests. El Recreo was hers, and that alone was enough to satisfy her. Since her father's death in 1934, she had not set foot on the property, at first because she had no heart or energy to confront the ghosts populating the place, and later, simply because of long-standing habit. It was Magda who, only yesterday, had nudged her mother into a visit. It would do them both good to get away, Magda had said. She herself needed a little time to adjust to the blow of the bank's loan refusal. She would talk to her mother about a new plan of action.

On this early morning, the two were curled up on chaise longues set before the fire that the caretaker had built in the fieldstone fireplace. The smell of the fire had awakened Elena, and she'd risen and quickly changed into trousers (they were Magda's, and it was she who insisted her mother wear them) and a cashmere sweater set. Elena had walked out to the back porch to the water pail, not surprised by the thin crust of ice she had to chip away before reaching the water she splashed on her face. Before going back in, she'd stood for a moment on the porch gazing out toward the stable and corral at the wash of mist rising up from field and creek and trees.

Inside, the room smelled of crackling pine resin. Mountain air seeped in through the window ledges and around the door. The caretaker's wife had placed an enameled coffeepot and a basket of pan dulce on a little table between the women. Elena and Magda held mugs against themselves, the mugs serving both as containers and hand warmers.

Magda was still in her bathrobe, and she kicked back the coverlet she'd brought from the bedroom and stretched her legs toward the fire. She was wearing slippers and a pair of Alvaro's tennis socks. "I'm finally not so cold."

"Wait till you rinse your face," Elena said. "There was ice in the water pail."

"No, gracias. I prefer to use the hot tap in the bathroom."

"When I was a girl there was no bathroom here. We had the big water barrels at the side of the house. And the toilet shack Papá built out by the creek. Back then, I was always the first one up. I'd rush to the barrels, eager to crack the ice." She took a sip of coffee before continuing. "I used to think the ice was a miracle. It made no difference what the sun did during the day; when evening came, night sealed the water up again. Each morning there was ice in the barrel, ice so smooth and undisturbed that I sometimes thought I could see my face in it." And Cecilia's face always next to mine, Elena went on to think, but she did not speak this.

"It sounds very romantic, Mamá, but I much prefer modern conveniences."

"How can I forget? It was you who demanded we build the bathroom."

"And why not? It was my honeymoon. Bad enough we couldn't go to Europe. I was not about to tote water and use the shed and wash in the creek on my honeymoon." She had taken full advantage of the creek, of course. Midafternoons, after the sun had lain for hours on the fields, after it had warmed down an inch or two into creek water, after the caretakers had hastily come and gone, Magda and Alvaro had run from the house and crossed the clearing, dropping clothing as they went, to slip, nude and sleek as otters, into the water hole. "Anyway, I'm sorry I even mentioned my honeymoon. I'm furious with Alvaro."

"Is that why we're here? Is that why you came storming into Santa Ana yesterday and whisked me off for the weekend? Because you're furious with Alvaro?"

Magda tucked her legs under herself as the fire sparked yellow and then green. "Well, yes. Partly that. But I also did it because it's time you got out of the house. You can't stay in the house forever."

"And who says I can't?"

"I say it. My brothers say it." Magda looked over at her mother, who was staring into the fire. Elena's right hand was cupped around the coffee mug. Around her wrist were the gold bracelets that were her signature. Her left hand, long-fingered and elegant once again since she'd stopped the manic biting of her nails, rested alongside her thigh. No wedding ring encircled her third finger. The ring, narrowed and deformed during the time of the bad dreams, still was so. Years ago, Elena had deposited it on the now tarnished silver tray atop Ernesto's dresser.

"Papá says you should get out more often, too," Magda added.

"That's interesting."

"Papá also says you haven't been eating."

"Why should he care whether I eat or not?"

Magda ignored the comment. "I care whether you eat or not, Mamá. Look at you. You're down to the bone. Nothing you wear fits you properly anymore."

Elena shrugged. She kept her gaze on the fire.

For a moment, Magda said nothing. Were she in her mother's shoes, she might not do things any differently. Who was she to say how it should be between her parents? It was clear that over the years, they had made a sort of peace. They spoke. They were cordial. They still shared the same bed, and whether they turned to each other in it was their secret. Magda swung her legs to the floor and poured herself more coffee. "¿Más café, Mamá?"

In answer, Elena spread a hand over the top of the mug. She rested her head against the back of the chaise. She had not tied her hair up as yet, and it lay golden around her face. Under the alabaster skin of her temples were thin blue veins.

"A few days ago, there was a letter in the mail." Magda had made up her mind to keep this to herself, but now she decided to take the risk. "The letter was from tía Ceci."

The hand Elena had spread over her coffee, she slowly curled into a fist. She spoke, not looking Magda's way, "Tell me, dear, just why are you furious with Alvaro?"

"Did you hear me, Mamá? I said . . ."

Elena raised her hand so quickly, her bracelets rose and fell in unison and hardly made a sound. "Don't say it. You know perfectly well I prohibit that name spoken in my house." Elena's green eyes were as bright as pine resin popping in the fire.

"Forgive me, Mamá." Magda lay back against the chair, relieved at having been silenced. How close she'd come to stirring up a new disaster between her parents. If she had told her mother of the contents of Cecilia's letter, that it was filled with Cecilia's deep concern with Elena's physical decline, would her mother not then ask who had informed Cecilia of the news? Though it was Isabel who'd first learned the news from Ernesto (they had bumped into each other at the bank, Cecilia's letter said), would her mother really believe the truth of it? Of course she would not. What else would she believe but that Cecilia and her father had been together again? Magda bristled at the thought of it. Those two. What damage they had caused! Because of them, her mother had sequestered herself in Santa Ana. In San Salvador, at Isabel's house, Cecilia's own actions had compelled her to do the same. As for Magda's friendship with Isabel, that, unhappily, was a thing of the past. Not that for years they hadn't tried to stay in touch. But meetings had been awkward, however eager both had been in planning them. When Isabel married Abraham Salah, the rich grandson of a Palestinian immigrant, she committed an overt act of self-banishment, stepping away, as she had, from the bosom of mainstream society and into the welcoming arms of a fringe community that, except where business was concerned, was both discriminated against and subtly reviled.

"Sometimes husbands are hard to love," Magda said at length.

"Why are you angry at Alvaro?"

"I'm angry because I'm sure he had something to do with the bank turning down my loan request."

"Well, of course he did," Elena said. "That's how men are. They don't want women to succeed. It threatens them. It's in their nature."

"That sounds so accepting. I'm afraid I can't be as understanding."

Elena shrugged again. "Men can't help their natures. In a way, they should be pitied." Sometimes, when she could not sleep, she lay in bed and pitied herself. She had tried to picture an image to illustrate this feeling she had of herself. This morning, coming back into the house after she'd been on the porch, the perfect image came to her: She pitied herself because over her heart was spread an icy crust that no light of day would ever crack, no warmth could ever dissolve.

"Well, I don't pity Alvaro. I don't pity any man. Men have everything. It angers me. And I'm angry with myself for allowing Alvaro to speak for me. I don't know what I was thinking. I should have gone to the bank myself. But no, I foolishly let Alvaro present my proposal for me." Magda stared at the fire for a moment before continuing. "But then I can't be discouraged by one loan refusal. Thank goodness there are other banks I can take my business to."

"Let's talk about Tesoros," Elena said. "Tell me again all your plans for the store."

Magda spared her mother no details. She went over the location that had opened up, her plans for decorating the store, the buying trips she would take to stock it. And she described her innovative shop-at-home plan to serve customers who weren't up to going out. These customers could call the store with their needs and Magda would provide a list of options that she would then deliver to their door. In this way, women could make selections at home, sending their choices back to the store for gift wrapping and for later delivery.

"To do that, you'll have to hire a driver," Elena said. She had been nibbling on a pan dulce, and now she took the last bite of sweet roll.

"Basilio can do it. He's a good worker. I trust him. I'll have someone teach him to drive."

Elena brushed a crumb from the corner of her mouth and from the front of her sweater, causing her bracelets to jangle. She stood and went to the fireplace. The logs had burned down so that they were a bed of rubies. She turned and faced her daughter. "Forget going to another bank."

Magda pulled herself up from the chaise. "But Mamá, it's the only way. All my money's tied up and . . ."

"Wait," Elena said. "I don't want you to go, because I'll lend you the money."

"My God, do you think that's why I insisted we get away? So I could ask you for the money? Believe me, Mamá, that isn't the case. You know I have Abuelo's money. I can do this myself. I really can."

"Will you listen to yourself? Of course you want to do this on your own. But for now you need help. Well, that's what a mother's for. I'll lend you the money." Elena smiled, feeling blessedly of use again.

Magda hurried over to her mother's side. "I can't let you do this."

"Of course you can. Whatever you need, you can have."

Magda placed her arms around her mother. "Oh, Mamá, I never thought of asking. I truly wanted to do this on my own."

"I know you did. And you will. With a little help from me."

Magda drew back her head so that she could look into Elena's eyes. "Gracias, Mamá, gracias. You've taught me so much. Thanks to you, I've learned we women have to stick together."

"No," Elena replied, "not that. It's mothers and daughters who never let each other down."

▼▼▼

CHAPTER TWENTY-SEVEN

February 1946

"Turn around," Pilar mumbled through a row of straight pins protruding from her mouth. She knelt at Jacinta's side and was pinning up the hem of Jacinta's new dress. The two were in Pilar's front room, which, since the arrival of better times, she'd transformed again into a workroom. The holidays had brought a rash of business. In addition to Christmas bonuses, aguinaldos, employers were also fond of bestowing cortes, that is, lengths of fabric sufficient and suitable for dresses or blouses and skirts. Since the holidays, half the neighborhood women had rapped on Pilar's door. As proof, folded cuts of fabric in a riot of colors and designs spilled from shelves and tabletops and awaited Pilar's deft hand.

"You think it's too short?" Jacinta asked, speaking over the rattle of the big metal fan sitting on the floor in the corner. To ease the summer heat, Pilar had opened both the front door and the back, and the fan helped draw a bit of air through one place and drive it, albeit unchanged, out the other. Jacinta twisted her shoulders and looked back at her image reflected in Pilar's swivel-stand mirror. The sight of herself so shapely in the glass pleased her.

"Stand still," Pilar said, giving Jacinta's leg a poke, "or the hem'll come out crooked."

Jacinta straightened up. She tucked her chin into her chest and looked down at her dress. It was made of a slippery sort of fabric imprinted with tiny crescent moons against a dark blue background. It featured capped sleeves and shoulder pads. A line of alabaster buttons traveled down the front of the dress. Jacinta raised a leg, the better to see them. "I love these little buttons. I love how they match the moons on the dress." Magda had purchased the corte and the buttons on the buying trip she'd made with her mother to New York.

"Be still, I said." After a moment, Pilar added, "You can turn a little now. I'm almost finished."

Jacinta turned a quarter circle; then she stood ramrod straight. "This is the best dress I ever had. I had another best dress once. When I was a girl, my mother, que en paz descanse, bought me one for my saint's day. It was lavender, and it had puffy sleeves. I wore that dress till the fabric was so thin you could almost see through it." With the memory of the dress came also the sound of church bells. Basilio Fermín ringing the bells of the church thirteen times. "Do you think this one's too short?"

"It's not too short. Besides, you have pretty legs. You should show off your legs more often. There. It's done." Pilar stood up and pointed to the mirror.

Jacinta cocked her head and observed herself in the glass. She was not tall, but she was slender, and this gave the illusion that she was taller than she was. The dress created another illusion, she thought. In the dress, she looked elegant. "I need new shoes with this."

Pilar went to sit at the Singer next to the open window. She had left a glass of lemonade on the counter of the machine, and she took a long drink from it. "You can borrow my red heels. Red looks good with blue." Pilar slipped a hand into her neckline and adjusted her bra strap. "This brassiere is driving me crazy. The strap never stays up."

"Maybe I will," Jacinta said, though she didn't care at all for the shoes Pilar had offered. They had open toes and very high heels. In short, they were not elegant.

"It looks to me like you have plans for that dress," Pilar said.

"Maybe I do." Jacinta went over to her own glass of lemonade and drank the last of it.

"Do they include Miguel Acevedo?" Pilar wiggled her eyebrows.

"Sush," Jacinta said, laying a finger across her lips and looking around as though Pilar's children were home from school, which they were not. "You promised never to say his name. You never know who can be listening." Jacinta dropped onto the cleared end of the settee, which was piled with magazines and cortes and sewing paraphernalia. "I don't know why I tell you anything." She gave a sudden yelp because some of the pins Pilar had set around the hem jabbed her legs when she sat back.

"And have you told me everything?" Pilar wiggled her eyebrows again.

Jacinta batted a hand desultorily at Pilar. She had told her friend everything. That since the day Miguel and she had cashed in their lottery tickets, they had met almost every week. On Jacinta's afternoon off or when she went for the mail, coinciding with the end of Miguel's shift. Their first meeting had been purely celebratory. Miguel had bought her a coffee and a slice of semita to thank her, he said, for picking out their winning numbers.

From the start, they found much to talk about and discovered they were compatible. They were both serious individuals and not inclined to much frivolity. At first their meetings were quick get-togethers, but as the weeks passed, their ordinary chitchat gave way to more personal disclosures. They both liked to read, and found a commonality in Corín Tellado stories. Miguel was shy about admitting this, given the sweet romantic nature of Corín Tellado's work, but Jacinta was touched by the confession, for it was like Miguel had opened the door to his heart so she could glimpse in. What he showed her had surprised her. Here was a man unlike any she'd been close to. A man living his own destiny and not down-trodden and therefore not beholden. A man not forced by circumstances to live his life driven by hard stances and radical philosophies. A man with a softness to his character and content with the middle ground.

All this Jacinta had told Pilar. What she had not revealed was that in a few weeks, Miguel's wife was planning a trip with their children to San Vicente. "Listen, I have to tell you something," Jacinta blurted, because the weight of the news was bearing down on her head. "Miguel's family is going away. They'll be gone for a week."

Pilar raised her eyebrows. "Miguel is staying home?"

"He's staying home. He has to work."

"He'll be alone for a week?"

Jacinta nodded. "Por una semana entera."

"My God, this is just like on *Las dos*. Remember the episode when la Bárbara goes off with Raúl?"

"Stop it. How can you say that? My life's not a radio novela." Jacinta propped an elbow on the arm of the settee. She dropped her cheek against a fist.

"I'm sorry. I didn't mean to make fun."

"Umph," Jacinta muttered.

"What are you going to do?"

"Miguel wants me to go away with him. It's my weekend off, so I can do it."

"Where would you go?"

"I don't know. Somewhere. I don't know." Jacinta twisted one of her dress's moon buttons.

"You've never been with him before, have you?"

"I've never been with him," Jacinta said, her voice a lament. "I'm frightened, Pilar. He's a married man. He has children."

"That has nothing to do with it."

"Every time I've given my heart, someone has died."

"You say that, my friend, but it wasn't your love that got Antonio and Chico killed. They died because they believed in dangerous notions. Answer this: Do you want to be with Miguel?"

"Yes. I want to be with him."

"Well, then. That does it," Pilar said. "If you go away with him, I expect you'll protect yourself."

"Protect myself?"

"You know," Pilar said, pointing out her own belly and making rounding motions with a hand. "Babies."

"Oh, you," Jacinta said. "The things that come out of your mouth." She didn't have to worry. Early on she had lost Chico's baby in a rush of scarlet tissue. She needed no protection. Her fate was clearly cast. In her future there would be no babies.

• • •

Fernanda, Pilar's eight-year-old daughter, bounded through the door from school an hour later. She held on haphazardly to her knapsack, and its leather straps dragged the ground as she came in.

"¡Nanda, niña!" Pilar said. "Look what you're doing."

Nanda dumped the knapsack by the door, next to the fan. She stood directly in front of the blades, and very soon her canary yellow skirt billowed out into a bell. "Ahhh," she said. She had clean brown legs, and they disappeared, straight and thin as arrows, into her sturdy school shoes.

"Nanda, where's your manners? Can't you say hello?" Pilar admonished, and then, "There's lemonade in the kitchen."

Nanda kissed her mother hello, and then Jacinta, too. "Hola, Tía. I don't want lemonade. I want fresco de Quaker."

"I didn't make fresco. I made lemonade." Pilar was at the Singer again, whipping the last stitches into the hem of Jacinta's dress. "I have a million things to do, and you want something other than what there is. Where are your brothers? And where's Harold?" She pronounced the name "Hah-rol."

"He's coming," Nanda said.

"I'll make you a fresco," Jacinta said. In the kitchen, she took the Quaker Oats down from the cupboard and spooned oat flakes into a strainer she set over a pan. She poured water over the oats and then mashed the wet oats down with the back of the spoon. When the pan was filled with milky liquid, she sprinkled in sugar and stirred the mixture up. "Here you are," she said, handing Nanda a glass.

"What do you say?" Pilar said from the front room.

"Gracias, Tía." Nanda drank the refreshment in one long swallow. She set the glass down and wiped her mouth with the back of a hand. "The teacher told us a story. It was about la Ciguanaba."

Eduardo, who was eleven, walked in the door. "La Ciguanaba. That's all Nanda can talk about." Emilio traipsed in behind Eduardo. He was seven and because this was his first year at school and away from his mother, he went directly over to Pilar and closed the circle of her embrace. "I don't like la Ciguanaba," Emilio said, his lower lip turned down. He laid his head on his mother's shoulder. The children all looked different and, consequently, appeared not related: Nanda was tall and dark and thin; Eduardo was as tall, but he had an olive complexion. Already, at his age, he was all muscle. Emilio, on the other hand, had light eyes and a pudgy face on which he wore a permanently woeful expression.

"La Ciguanaba is a witch," Nanda said to Jacinta. "She has long stringy hair and long sharp fingernails."

"La Ciguanaba is hiding by the river," Eduardo said, coming into the kitchen. He raised his arms and spread his fingers, making a deep moaning sound to scare his sister. "If Nanda isn't good, la Ciguanaba will leave the riverbank and come snatch her up."

Nanda stomped her foot. "Stop it, mono feo." She called her brother "ugly monkey" because it irritated him.

Pilar spoke out from the other room. "You're all monkeys. Have some lemonade and cool down."

"I'm not a monkey," Emilio said, his voice wavering.

"No, you're not. You're Mamá's treasure," Pilar said. There was the sound of a very loud kiss. "Look, here comes Harold up the street."

Jacinta joined Pilar while the three children disappeared into their room that was off the kitchen. "Harold! There's lemonade," Pilar yelled, leaning her head out the opened window beside her.

Harold Parada sauntered in. He was the son of Pilar's dead sister, and had lived with Pilar since his mother's death when he was six. Harold's shirtsleeves were rolled up to his elbows. Around one wrist he wore a loose-fitting name bracelet. Because he was fourteen and edgy, he shook his hand affectedly so that the bracelet danced along his arm.

"One of these days that lucky charm of yours is going to jump right off your arm," Pilar said. "Come and have something to drink." She stood up from the Singer and went into the kitchen.

Harold sat at the table and drank his lemonade. He had a gangly build and the dark stain of a coming mustache over his upper lip. "I'm going to the park."

Pilar rolled her eyes, as if saying "So what else is new?" She took a seat at the table, too.

"What park is that?" Jacinta asked, joining them.

"El Campo Marte. The soldiers take the flag down at five." Each afternoon, Harold stood under the plane trees, thrilled to watch such mighty, splendid men. He watched them march with soldierly aplomb to the reverberating cadence of a drum around the circumference of the playing field to the leveled-off rise where the flagpole stood. When he was much younger and ignorant of a man's duty to affect cool reserve, Harold had marched openly alongside the men, his plain-shod feet attempting to reproduce the same resounding steps his booted heroes made. Now that he was a man, Harold kept under the trees, following the soldiers nevertheless around the field to the flagpole for the exacting solemnity of lowering the flag. A few weeks ago, during the flag ceremony, Harold had met Victor Morales, a boy a year older and as obsessed with the soldiers as Harold was.

"Victor Morales says my name means 'commander of arms,' " Harold pointed out.

"When are you going to ask this Victor Morales home so we can meet him?" Pilar said.

Harold shrugged his shoulders. He raised a finger to his ear. "Victor has a birthmark. It's like a big stain on his ear."

"Goodness," Jacinta said. "I had a baby brother with a birthmark like that. It was the eclipse of the sun that caused it."

"El sol pone, la luna quita," Pilar said. "The sun adds, the moon subtracts."

"Where's your brother now?" Harold asked.

"He died."

"Oh," Harold said, and then, "Victor's going to military school. His father is a subteniente in the Guardia. When it's time, his father is going to get him in."

"I wouldn't count on it," Pilar said. "Getting into military school is very difficult. You have to be appointed." She knew this because for a very short time she'd had a boyfriend who was a military man. She cut the affair off the night he brought his gun to bed.

"I'm going to military school, too." Harold shook his wrist so that his lucky bracelet danced again.

"I hope you believe in miracles," Pilar said. "It'll take a miracle to get you in."

"I'm going. You'll see."

"Why would you want to be a soldier?" Jacinta asked, her mind filled with her baby brother and all that soldiers do. "Soldiers kill."

Harold took the last swallow of his lemonade. He scraped back his chair. "No, Tía, you're wrong," he said. "Soldiers defend."

The sharp sound of a Ford sedan's horn floated in to them.

"It's Basilio," Jacinta said, looking through the open front door, toward the road. "He said he'd pick me up after his last delivery."

They all went outside because it was a novelty to see a car stopping at a house in the neighborhood.

▼▼▼

CHAPTER TWENTY-EIGHT

Basilio Fermín stood in the yawning doorway of the Parque Bolívar bus station. In his big hands, he turned, again and again, his father's hat, the wide inner brim burnished with wear against his fingertips. While around him ricocheted the raucous sounds and assorted smells attendant to transportation, these did not distract him. Not the stink and squeal of buses pulling in and pulling out, not the incomprehensible strident voice reverberating on the loud-speaker, not the continuous stir of humanity, all travelers, all grimy, intent, and road weary. Jacinta had lied to him, and he thought his heart would break. Over and through the crowd, Basilio kept his eyes on bus number 9. She was going to El Congo to visit Chenta, she had said, but now she was on the bus that would soon head off to La Libertad.

It was not by mistake that she was on it. He had brought her to the station, though she had tried to talk him out of it. She wore her pretty new dress with the little creamy moons. When they arrived, some fifteen minutes before, Basilio himself deposited her in the El Congo bus line. "Go, go," she said with a little wave of the hand, "you've done enough." He had stayed only moments more to wish her a safe trip and to reach into his pocket for the little carved lamb he'd whittled for Chenta. He'd wrapped the gift in a square of bright

190

tissue paper that Rosalba had obligingly provided. As Jacinta took the package from him, her shoulders sagged a bit before she placed the gift into the big open-topped bag that was all of her luggage. Basilio noticed the small shift in Jacinta's posture. He attributed it to her being moved by his thoughtfulness, and he was happy he had touched her. The warm feeling of pleasing her propelled him away and through the throng and almost out the door to the street, but then he turned around. To catch a last glimpse of her, he turned at the door. He saw her then as she sprang from the line he had left her in and hurried over to another bus and a very different destination.

Basilio Fermín remained at the station door until the bus pulled away. He could not see Jacinta through the windows of the bus, but he pictured her inside nonetheless. He saw her back straight against the seat; he saw her hands cupped one against the other and resting over the bag she held on her lap. And he felt, too, the wild beat of her heart; he clearly saw, though the bus had only just departed, that already she was a long distance down the road from here.

Basilio placed his hat back on his head and left the station, his footsteps heavy with knowing that all he had feared in the last three months about Jacinta was on the way to coming true.

▼▼

CHAPTER TWENTY-NINE

La Libertad

Miguel Acevedo was waiting at the station when the bus pulled in. Through the open windows Jacinta caught sight of him leaning against a pillar. He was smoking a cigarette, and he wore the short-sleeved guayabera he'd had on the night she first saw him strolling up the street at Pilar's. When the bus shuddered to a stop, he flicked the cigarette to the ground and mashed it under a heel. He ran a quick hand through his hair and walked out from under the platform overhang. Jacinta did not join the others who leaped en masse into the aisle and jostled their way down it, yelling hola, hola out windows and perdone, perdone to fellow passengers in their way. When the commotion abated, she went slowly toward the exit, pressed between a woman with a fussing baby slung over her shoulder and a man smelling alarmingly of garlic. All the while, she watched Miguel out the window. He stood at the curb, one hand thrust into a pocket of his trousers, a look of anticipation and then disappointment crossing his face when each passenger descended. When her turn came, she wiped off the line of perspiration collecting over her lip and stepped down from the bus into summer light and the thick salty smell of a port town.

"There you are," Miguel said. "You were almost the last one

off." Characteristically, a little spent matchstick poked out the side of his mouth.

"Here I am," Jacinta said, and for a moment they stood uneasily and not touching before he took her arm and guided her into the shade of the overhang. "There's a place for us at the beach," he said. "It's much cooler there and it's only a short walk. Can I take your bag?" he added, and she pressed it more tightly against herself, saying, "It's fine. I have it."

They started off, each allowing the sights and sounds of the town to fill the clumsy silence between them. They went down cobbled streets, past faded adobe houses, around dogs sprawled here and there in the sidewalk shade. From time to time, Jacinta looked Miguel's way, and when she did, he caught her eye and smiled at her. This eased the roiling of emotions that filled her head with both self-reproach and expectation.

"Look," Miguel said, pointing at the sea that, when they turned a corner, was a turquoise slash before them. Along the shore, piers jutted. Fishermen lifted their catches from small boats toward clamorously bidding merchants standing along the landings. Shrill insistent gulls made their demands known, too.

"Virgen Santa," Jacinta said. The smell of salt and fish filled the air, and this brought back the one time before that she had experienced it. "When I was a girl, I went to the sea once with my parents." The three had trudged from Izalco to Acajutla to behold for themselves the vast shifting sea they had only heard about. "My mother was so surprised. She kept running toward the waves and then backing away from them. Before coming home, she filled a little bottle with seawater. Sealed it tightly with a cork. For a long time, she kept this treasure on the dresser. But then, though she never allowed the bottle to be opened, the seawater slowly disappeared. I always told Mamá I'd refill her little bottle, but I never got the chance to go back to the sea." Jacinta looked down at her sandals, at her brown toes and her pearly-button nails. "Ay Dios, that was probably more than you wanted to know."

"No, please. It was touching. But wait until you see the spot I found today. I think it'll mark a fitting return for you." He plucked the matchstick from his lips and tossed it aside.

The spot he had found was off the main road and through a grove of coconut palms. A well-traveled path meandered under the palms toward the pounding ocean. When they came out from under the trees, Jacinta set her bag down and threw a hand up to her mouth. She shook her head in disbelief at the panorama. The shore was a wide ribbon of glittering black volcanic sand, the sea flashing a deep blue beside it. Up the beach, a substantial grass hut rose under more palm trees. "Come," Miguel said, taking Jacinta's bag and starting off toward the hut. She unfastened her sandals and stepped out of them, hooking a finger through the straps before following him. The sand was firm and very hot, and though her tender soles protested, she did not relieve them by seeking patches of shade to walk in. After so long a time, she welcomed this unmistakable evidence of earth under her feet.

A very large woman wearing a very loose dress greeted them under the hut. "I see you've returned with la señora," the woman observed. "This is Ofelia; she's the owner," Miguel said, not looking Jacinta's way. Jacinta nodded a hello and stepped up onto a tiled floor. Aquamarine-painted tables and chairs, all sun bleached and timeworn, took up space around the hut that was opened to the elements. A long counter was set off to the side next to a loudly humming cooler painted with scarlet letters spelling out "Coca-Cola." Ofelia lifted the top of the cooler with one hand and swiftly extracted two bottles with the other. She popped off the bottle caps using the cooler's cap remover. "Sit, sit," she said, padding barefoot across the floor and setting the bottles down on a table.

"I'm sorry," Miguel said after the owner left. "When I went to meet the bus, I told her I was going to get my wife." Miguel rolled the sides of his bottle slowly between his hands.

Jacinta nodded. "I understand." She looked out across the beach. Gulls dipped and darted, and their shrieks sounded like a reprimand. She took a long swallow of her drink, the liquid an icy explosion in her mouth. She surveyed the surroundings, now noticing another hut and what appeared to be a cook's lean-to adjacent to this one. Beyond them, there seemed to be a clearing. She could see fence posts and a gate. A flock of chickens pecked around the fence. Up the beach were other, smaller huts tucked under the palm trees. Brightly colored hammocks were strung between some of the trees.

"In case you're wondering," Miguel said, "we're staying over there. In the last hut. See it under the palm trees?"

"Are many people staying here?" Jacinta asked, looking up the beach and preoccupied with how many others might witness their transgression.

"A few," Miguel said. He laid a hand on her arm, and she turned her face toward him and the look of concern clouding his eyes. "Please, Jacinta, don't worry."

She held his gaze for a moment, each of them somberly silent. Then she gave him a little smile and said, "Bueno," because they had come a long way in bright summer heat and because, for this brief time they had, they both deserved no gloominess.

They had strolled along the beach, Jacinta in her moon-sprinkled dress, Miguel in rolled-up trousers and a sleeveless undershirt. They skirted the waves, their fingers enlaced, their footsteps leaving craters in the sand, a momentary record of their togetherness. When the sun began to set, they had been eating in the main hut, and they turned their gaze from each other and from their meal to watch in amazement as two mottled cows ambled out from the back of the property and headed for the beach. The beasts plopped down on the sand and serenely watched the yellow sun drop below the horizon. As twilight spread over the water, the cows heaved themselves up in a graceful unfolding of legs and unperturbedly retraced their steps. Jacinta and Miguel, as well as the couples at other tables, laughed and commented on the sight before getting back to their meals, all platefuls of camarones del río, each shrimp the size of a tiny lobster and as sweetly succulent.

After dinner, Jacinta and Miguel nestled in a double hammock stretched between two palms near their hut. The kerosene lamps glowing here and there among the trees painted circles of soft light. From the main hut and floating over the beach, a thread of melody from the radio was periodically interrupted by the rhythmic rush of incoming waves. After the intensity of the day's heat, the night had turned balmy. Jacinta was in the loose-fitting slip that was all the clothing she'd brought besides her dress and a tapado. In the hammock, they were eating oranges Jacinta had carried from home. She thrust a finger through the rind of one and misted them with fragrant zest. She skinned the fruit, tossing the peels out the hammock. A dog, who had followed them back to the hut after dinner, hauled itself up and came over to investigate. "¡Chucho!" Miguel exclaimed, calling the dog "mutt" when the animal poked his head under them. He kicked out at the dog, and with the movement they almost toppled. Jacinta laughed and set her weight to steady them. "When you're in a hammock, there can be no sudden moves," she said. "Don't you know that?"

"I knew that," he said, laughing, too.

"Once, I had my own hammock. I used to sleep in it." She spread apart the orange sections. "But that was in another time. In another life." How far away that lifetime seemed.

"And what of your life now? Is your life good now?" He opened his mouth to the orange section Jacinta offered him.

"I have everything I want," she said, and she fed him the rest of the orange, watching him eat each section, brushing the juice from his mouth with her lips when he was done. "You taste like oranges."

"Mmm. And you have the magic touch. Remember? That's what the ticket seller said."

"The lucky touch. He said I had the lucky touch."

"You have that, too, Jacinta."

She kissed his hand and held it, taking in the golden aroma of tobacco on his fingers. "What do you want from me, Miguel?" she suddenly asked, alarming herself by the nature of her question.

He was obviously alarmed, too, for he gave a little start, and the languid look in his eyes changed to puzzlement.

She laid a hand over his lips. "Don't answer that. I'm sorry I said it."

Miguel kissed her fingertips. "I can't answer your question, Jacinta. All I can say is that I'm falling in love with you."

Jacinta closed her eyes and rested her head against his chest. In this close little world they had fashioned in the hammock, she was near enough to him to hear the beat of his heart, to taste the saltiness of his flesh. "Yo te quiero también, Miguel," she said at length.

For a time they lay entwined in the hammock feeling each other's heat, listening to the movement of the sea underscoring the enormity of their declarations. Soon, Miguel struggled out of the hammock and pulled Jacinta up and into his arms. He carried her, her arms draped around his neck, into the hut and set her down gently on the wide mat lying against a sandy floor. They slowly undressed, Jacinta revealing her full breasts with their brown berry nipples, Miguel his solid chest and the thickened evidence of his passion. Slowly, they lay down together, their only response to life's imponderables.

It was all so familiar: herself wrapped in a tapado lying on a petate set directly on the ground. From such a place, the looming shadow that was the thrust of the hut's roof smelled of dust and old palm fronds. A rectangle of colorless light outlined the door. The jarring salute of a rooster sounded nearby. In her slip and tapado, Jacinta rose from Miguel's side and stole out the hut and into the faint pink of morning. The sea moved majestically, unrushed. She strode to the water's edge and squatted down beside it. The sand was moist and cool and, in the unsubstantial light, richly black. Last night she had startled them both with the question What do you want from me, Miguel? She asked herself the same question now. What is it you want, Jacinta? ¿Qué es lo que quieres? Happiness. I want happiness, her instantaneous reply. Then a final question came: Was it bad to want so much?

Wrapped and warm in the tapado, Jacinta did not move back from the water. She allowed it to pool around her feet, and then sat directly on the beach, spreading her legs against the sand in front of her. "You have company," a voice behind her said, and she turned her head just as Miguel sat down beside her. He laid an arm along her shoulder, and they watched the morning pinks give way to yellow, purple, and blue.

Miguel took a final puff of the cigarette he'd lit when he awakened. The matchstick he'd used to do it was clamped between his teeth, and Jacinta plucked it from him, using it to write her name in the sand. Miguel took the cue and used the matchstick to write his own name beneath hers. He enclosed their names in a big heart with an arrow poking through.

"We have to leave after breakfast," Miguel said.

Jacinta leaned against him. "I know."

A wave rolled up. When it retreated, it took their names with it.

It was just after noon when their bus pulled into the Parque Bolívar station. During the two-hour ride, they had not sat together because they had hurried too slowly from the beach and had barely made the bus. Only Jacinta got a seat. Miguel had to stand in the aisle, at first directly next to Jacinta, but then, pushed and prodded by other standing passengers, he ended up in the back.

Their feet on the ground again, they stood in the station, the commotion of real life bursting around them. "I have something for you," Miguel said, and he reached into his trouser pocket and extracted a little bottle and handed it to Jacinta. "I got the bottle from Ofelia," he said. "I filled it with seawater."

"Oh," she said, the sweetness of what he'd done causing a knot in her throat. She laid the little bottle against her breast.

"Go," he said. "Or you'll be late."

She turned from him and started off, her life feeling different from yesterday when she'd come through the station door. When she stepped outside, she slipped Miguel's memento into her bag, wedging it in a corner, against the tissue-wrapped bundle that was Basilio Fermín's gift to Chenta.

▼▼

CHAPTER THIRTY

Basilio Fermín sat on his haunches, his back against the garden shed that was also his room. The day had ended and supper was over. He was blowing on the small wooden flute that he had carved himself a few years before. The melody he played, a plaintive tune that expressed what his heart contained, he had also created. Basilio was not alone; as on every night, he had Bruno for company. The dog was lying next to the bundles of shrub trimmings stacked neatly nearby. Each time Basilio played a high note, the dog pricked his ears and looked around the garden toward Magda's house, where the lighted lamps along the corredor and those turned on in back rooms produced a glow that grew stronger as night advanced. A door opened and shut and Bruno sprang up, his legs instantly aquiver. "Chucho, chucho," Basilio said to quiet the mutt, because once darkness fell, Bruno took his guarding duties seriously.

"Basilio," a voice called from the darkness at the side of the house. "It's me. Tell Bruno it's only me."

Basilio stood up as Rosalba stepped cautiously into the halo of light cast by the kerosene lamp resting on a shelf inside the shed. "Vaya, chucho," Basilio said, and the dog plopped down again once he recognized who was there.

"Keep playing," Rosalba said. "I like it when you play." She had

199

plaited her hair and crisscrossed the braids atop her head. A jaunty pink ribbon adorned them like a fabric crown. "What were you playing? It sounded so sad."

Basilio slipped the flute into his trouser pocket.

"Do you mind if I sit down?" Rosalba pointed to the crate near the shed door. She sat on it before Basilio could respond. "Hasn't it been hot? It's been so hot I wouldn't mind taking off a few clothes and jumping in the fountain. Not that I'd fit in the fountain, eh, Basilio." She tittered coyly and then poked a finger past the neckline of her uniform, giving it a few tugs as if to air herself out. "So tell me. What was that song you were playing? It made me want to cry."

"It was just a little tune."

"Let me see your flute." Rosalba wiggled her fingers toward him. "Come on. Let me see it."

Basilio handed her the instrument. If he humored her, maybe she'd go away. The night before, with Jacinta gone, and not to Chenta's but to who knew where, Rosalba had come visiting, and he'd had to feign needing something in the kitchen to extricate himself from her. That tactic he would not use tonight, for Jacinta was in the kitchen, and since her return this afternoon, a stiff silence had come between them that was, for him, a new kind of loneliness.

"You don't mind if I play, do you, Basilio?" Rosalba brought the flute to her lips and blew hard through the holes up and down its length, emitting a series of short discordant sounds. "Will you listen to me!"

"To play the flute you have to blow softly."

"I can blow softly." Rosalba tried again, this time with more pleasing results. "That's better, don't you think?"

"Sí."

Rosalba laid the flute on her lap, and it made a slender bridge between her ample thighs clearly outlined under her uniform. "You don't like me, do you, Basilio?"

The question was so dumbfounding that Basilio could not offer a reply.

"I know you don't like me, but I don't care." Rosalba picked up the flute and rose. Before he could stop her, she stole into the shed.

He stood there, feeling foolish because he didn't know what to do about this vexing girl. Bruno sauntered over to the shed and poked his head inside. He looked back at Basilio as if to say "She's in there, all right." Basilio kicked up a divot of grass and went to the door himself.

She was sitting on his cot and she was smiling. The kerosene lamp in the shed was positioned in such a way that it threw a giant shadow of her against a wall of shelves holding cans and jars and on the wooden animals he'd carved himself and lined up in a row. "It's like a little cave in here," she said. She was right about that. Besides the cot, there was a chair and these were his only furnishings. Bags of loam and fertilizer were bunched along another wall, and they, as well as the dirt floor, gave off a sweet earthy aroma. "I put your flute on the chair," she said, pointing to it. The space was so small that when she gestured, she knocked down his hat hanging low on a nail on the wall. "¡Ay Dios!" she exclaimed, and plucked up the hat and impetuously plopped it on her head. "Look at me."

"Give me that!" In an instant, he was beside her, and they were in a little skirmish for the only keepsake he possessed of his father. She giggled and with both hands held tight to the brim of the hat so that soon she was leaning back against the cot and he was straddling her. He reached for his hat, the length of his body against hers. Beneath him, she was soft and rounded and warm. She had stopped laughing and he could feel the hot bursts of her breath on his cheek and then at the side of his neck. He gave in to the press and feel of her under him. It was a visceral response he could not control, and his heart pumped something thick and burning down his chest and toward his thighs. Rosalba gave a sharp little cry that might have contained his name. She raised her legs and pressed her thighs around his hips and it was then Bruno growled. The dog was at the cot; his lips were peeled back so that his teeth were exposed. The rumbling in his throat was terrifying.

Basilio's chest tightened against his ribs. "Don't move," he said to the girl, who turned to stone under him. "Vaya, chucho," he said softly to the dog. "Vaya, vaya," he repeated like a mantra that soon relaxed the line of raised fur along the dog's spine. Basilio pulled himself up slowly; he continued murmuring until the dog relaxed a

bit and allowed him to get near. "Go," he said to the girl, "I'll hold
the dog," and then he heard Rosalba scrambling up behind him and
rushing out the door.

The next morning Basilio was pruning the jasmine growing next
to the water pila. He had bared his torso to the sun, and the searing
heat against the bend of his back was an atonement for last night's
close transgression. Rosalba. He did not want to think about the
girl, so he gave in to the mesmerizing sound of the fountain, to the
dull hacking rhythm of his corvo. So lulled was he by these, he did
not notice Jacinta's presence until she spoke to him. Basilio drew
himself straight, the corvo stilled and at his side.

"I brought your clothing." She pressed a bundle of laundry
against herself as if holding something in. Usually it was the laundress who delivered his wash, so it surprised him to see Jacinta
standing there with it.

"Actually, I want to talk to you." Jacinta went to sit on the tiled
edge of the fountain, in a square of shade offered by the trees.
"There's something I need to tell you." She dropped one arm from
around the laundry and trailed a hand in the water before continuing. "On Saturday, I didn't go to Chenta's. I wanted you to know
that."

He nodded from under the brim of his hat, feeling the sweat
slipping down his chest and over his sunburned back.

She raised her hand from the water and dried it on her skirt
before lowering the laundry to her lap. Lying atop the bundle was
a tissue-wrapped packet. "Here's the lamb you carved for Chenta. I
didn't feel right keeping it. Next time I go see her, when I *really* go
see her, I'll take it for you."

He stared at the turquoise packet that was proof of her rejection,
and jealousy lashed against his heart, but then he thought of Rosalba
and what they'd been about to do only meters away in the shed and
he was ashamed of it.

"I'm sorry, Basilio. I'm sorry I lied to you."

"Where did you go on Saturday?"

"It doesn't matter where I went."

"Did you go with the man from the post office?"

"¡Virgen Santa! How did you know about him?"

"I've seen you with him. I've seen you both together."

She stood. In two steps, she closed the space between them. "Where? Where have you seen us?"

"It doesn't matter where."

She stared at him, so close he could see the astonishing black-ness of her eyes, the small discoloration at one corner of her mouth. For a moment she made no response, and then the light shifted behind her eyes and she returned to the edge of the pila, the laundry clutched so tightly to her breast that it now seemed she was using it to keep herself erect. The heat Basilio had soaked up while working in the sun drained away from him, and he took a spot beside her because it was all he knew to do. For a time they remained like that, mute, water spilling over melodiously behind them.

It was Jacinta who broke their silence. "After my mother died, I always wished I'd died with her."

"I wouldn't want you to die." I couldn't live if you were dead, he thought, but this he could not say.

"Since that day in Metapán I've been living a different life. *We've* been living different lives." Jacinta lowered the laundry to her lap. "Look at us here, Basilio." She pointed toward the house, and then, in a sweeping gesture, she indicated the garden and the sky and beyond even these two things. "I can't forget where we came from. Our people. Our ways. Our blessed little parcels of land. I won't forget all that, but it's gone. What we were no longer exists."

He pressed the back of his neck, remembering the time when he was still a boy and how he had trudged away from El Congo and up the mountain on his way toward home. What she said was true. High on the mountaintop he had seen it for himself. In one sweeping glance, he had seen the barren emptiness of his past.

Jacinta looked away from his sharp profile, from his mouth twisted in thought. "So now we're in Magda's house. To get here, we've had to make adjustments. My mother made adjustments to survive. Your mother was cut down before she could. The two of us, we've made adjustments to keep safe. We live a sheltered life working for the rich." She turned to him again. "But it's a small price we pay for safety, don't you think, Basilio?"

He nodded in agreement, wishing he were man enough to lift his hand and lay his finger along the full curve of her cheek.

"So you see. Years pass, and I'm a different person now. Now I'm happy I'm alive."

Basilio made a choking sound that he disguised into a cough because he saw the sudden joy that filled Jacinta's face, and because he knew it was not he who caused it, but a man in a crisp white shirt who stamped letters for a living. "That man in the post office. Tell me his name?" This request was foolish, for it made the man more real than even the sight of him sitting under the trees in the park with Jacinta, or the sight of both of them in the café, their heads inclined toward each other over their coffee cups.

"What does it matter what his name is?"

"It matters," Basilio said because he could not help himself from wanting to know.

"His name is Miguel," Jacinta said at length. She stood and went toward the shed. "I'll put the wash on your cot," she added over a shoulder.

She was back before he knew it. She held a square of white fabric out before him. "Where did you get this?"

"What is it?"

"I found it in the shed. It was on the floor by your cot."

He stood up, alarmed by the sternness in her voice. "What is it?" he repeated.

"It's one of Magda's handkerchiefs. How did Magda's handkerchief end up in your shed?"

"Rosalba," Basilio said, the name escaping before he could contain it.

Jacinta found Rosalba in the living room. The girl had rolled up the Persian carpet and was sweeping the floor under it. Mish was bunched beneath an end table, stalking the broom. When the broom swept past its nose, Mish pounced. "¡Gato condenado!" Rosalba cried. She used the broom to jettison the cat away and then slapped the floor a few times with the end of the broom to drive the cat through the corredor and out into the garden. Rosalba turned and gave a little start when she saw Jacinta standing there. "My goodness, where did you come from?" she said.

Jacinta held Magda's handkerchief out as if it were a mouse she was holding by the tail. "See this?"

Rosalba drew the broom handle close to herself before responding. "What is it?"

"You know what it is. It's Magda's handkerchief. And you left it in Basilio's shed."

"What?"

"You heard me. Where did you get it?"

"I don't know what you're talking about."

"Don't lie, Rosalba. You dropped la señora's handkerchief in the shed."

"I wasn't in Basilio's shed. Did he say I was in his shed? If he said I was, then it's Basilio who's lying."

Jacinta folded the handkerchief and slipped it in her pocket. "Listen to me, Rosalba. Basilio Fermín is a decent man. A decent, hardworking man. I will not stand by and watch you get him into trouble."

Rosalba held the broom handle out at arm's length again. She cocked a broad hip in Jacinta's direction. "I'm sure Basilio can take care of himself, don't you think?"

"Listen to me. It's you who better watch herself. Going into a man's room is foolish and can only lead to trouble. Didn't your mother teach you anything?"

Rosalba jutted out her chin. "And who do you think you are, talking to me like that?"

"I'm the one in charge, that's who I am. And here's something else, you silly girl." Jacinta patted the pocket containing the handkerchief. "You and I know this came from la señora. How you got it I can only guess. In the future, you better watch yourself, girl. From now on, I'll be keeping an eye on you like that cat did that broom."

They couldn't see him, but out in the garden Basilio had heard everything. He turned back to the jasmines, dizzy with knowing Jacinta thought him a decent man.

▼▼

CHAPTER THIRTY-ONE

Magda's store, Tesoros, was aptly named. It was, indeed, a treasure trove. Tesoros turned the annoying and never-ending duty of finding the perfect gift for baptisms, first Holy Communions, birthdays, saint's days, engagements, showers, and weddings into an adventure. The store, unlike other gift shops with their gleaming showcases and shelving and their staid conventional elegance, was more a stage set, an event, a Magda de Tobar performance.

Tesoros occupied a strategic corner on the same block as the Gran Hotel San Salvador. It had two spacious rooms with high, broad windows. One room looked out on Avenida España; the other, on Calle Poniente. In addition to being steps from the country's best hotel and connected to it by way of an interior hallway, the store was within walking distance of el Teatro Nacional, el mercado central, and la catedral. In short, the store's location was unsurpassed.

But while all that was significant—necessary, really, were the business truly to prosper—it was what met the eye when one stepped into the store that counted most. In Tesoros, it was color and texture and scent that first greeted one. Blue añil shelves against pomegranate walls. Tobacco-colored floors. Bent-twig window cornices cascading coffee-stained netting. Mosquito netting soaked in pure Salvadoran coffee, if one cared to ask. Marveling at Magda's dash, clients went on to run quick hands over the pine and cedar tables laden with merchandise bunched or stacked provocatively and not arranged on crushed dark velvet in long cases under glass. ¡Ay, qué rústico! was a frequent comment, as was ¡Ay, que divino!

Although Magda was avant-garde, she was not so foolish as to deny the Salvadoran woman the comfort of her habitual selections. So in addition to gifts of cut glass, porcelain, crystal, linen, batiste, lace, teak, mahogany, gold, and silver, Tesoros offered punched tin retablos and clay figurines, old and new carved santos, hand-thrown pottery for a variety of purposes, plainly framed photos of very common things: a wooden door, an eggplant, raindrops gleaming on an iron bench. There were folk paintings on tin or pressed board, as well as pillows, napkins, and place mats in chintz and tapestry. And always for selection, a line of paperweights and decorative boxes, which had become Magda's trademark. In one corner, on a large round table and flanked by vases spewing sunflowers, was a collection of candles: tall votives in oxblood and carnelian glass, beeswax pillars and tapers.

In the six weeks since Tesoros opened, it had captured the attention of both clientele and press. Magda's innovative vision had people talking and buying. In all, it was a good beginning. Still, it was not lost on her that she owed much to the new postwar spirit that had loosened purse strings and induced people to spend on luxuries and frivolities. If she weathered this novelty stage (it was very promising, but not to be relied upon), if her business caught and held and grew, she would host a gala opening celebration. But not until then.

Home life was not as smooth: Alvaro, when he was not on the coast seeing to his cotton, was acting like a child. At the table, more often than not, he pushed away his favorite foods, demanding dishes the cook was not familiar with. He fussed over his shirts, running a finger along their blindingly white collars to point out smudges he insisted were there. On a few occasions, he made love to Magda in an intense, quick way, turning his back before going on to satisfy her. As she was with the store, at home Magda bided her time, determined to be patient. She talked some of the situation over with Jacinta, who was eager to enlist the staff's help to pacify el señor.

To herself, Magda said, Let the man have his little tantrums. Soon, when he grows used to reality, he'll once again become himself.

On this morning in April, Magda was at the back of the room, at the long hacienda table that served as a counter, rearranging a vase of tiger lilies and lemongrass before the day turned busy. Teresita, her assistant, was at the counter, too, answering a phone call. "Yes, we do have a nice choice of candleholders, niña Isabel," Teresita was saying.

Magda caught Teresita's eye. "Who is it?" she whispered, pointing to the phone.

Teresita held a hand over the mouthpiece. "La niña Isabel de Salah. She wants delivery service to her house."

"Oh, my God!" Magda exclaimed. "Let me talk to her." Magda took the phone and greeted her old childhood friend. The women chatted for a moment and soon they agreed that Magda herself would deliver a selection of merchandise for Isabel to peruse at home. It had been years since the two had seen each other, and Magda was happy for the opportunity to catch up.

At four o'clock, Basilio Fermín arrived in the sedan to pick up Magda and the merchandise. They drove up Avenida Roosevelt toward San José de la Montaña, the colonia where Isabel lived. At the monument to El Salvador del Mundo, Basilio turned right and went up the hill, past the church of San José for which the neighborhood was named. This part of the suburbs had been terraced into the side of the mountain. Unlike the one-story houses in the city that abutted one another on downtown blocks, the houses in San José de la Montaña were two-storied and set back from the street and from each other by stone walls and lawns and driveways. Unfamiliar with the neighborhood, Magda and Basilio crept along in the car, peering out the windows to find number 152.

"There it is," Basilio said. He pulled into the driveway of a white stucco house with dark wood trim and an arched wooden balcony extending halfway along the second floor. The front lawn, while not deep, featured in one corner a leafy mango tree, and in the middle, a circular flower bed of red and yellow margaritas. Magda stepped out of the car and surveyed the neighborhood, its still houses and quiet streets with hardly a car or person in view. How interesting, she thought, that Isabel lives here. Here, at the edge of town, banished for all purposes from society.

The wide door of the house was abruptly flung open, and Isabel herself bounded toward the car, her arms flung wide in welcome. "Magda! I can't believe you're here." The women embraced warmly, exclaiming one over the other. They said, "How long has it been?" and, "An eternity, I know that." Arm in arm, they walked through the door and into a small front room that smelled heavily of cedar. The room had a tiled floor and ponderous leather furniture. Magda and Isabel sat together on the sofa, the soft leather of the cushion puffing up around Isabel's bottom because she'd become heavy. "Really, how long has it been?" Magda asked.

"Since before baby Enrique was born." Isabel generously filled out a loose cotton dress. Unconventionally, she wore no hosiery, no high heels, no makeup. She was fair, like her father had been. Freckles sprinkled the bridge of her nose and made her arms golden. "As you can see, I've turned into a simple woman. Having babies has agreed with me. I have four now. One more than you, I think."

"I see you're working on number five," Magda said, pointing to the fullness of Isabel's dress.

Isabel threw her head back and laughed. "No, I'm not. I look like this because I'm fat!"

Magda felt herself redden. "Oh, my God, I'm sorry. Please forgive me, Isa."

"There's nothing to forgive. But look at you." Isabel drew back as if to gain a better view. "You're as beautiful as ever. Mamá and I have been reading about Tesoros in the paper, and we're so proud of you, Magda, so happy you followed your dreams." Isabel took Magda's hands, pulling her closer. "Remember when we used to lie in bed planning our lives? You would marry Alvaro Tobar. You always said that. And you would have the best gift shop in the world. Me? I never knew what I wanted to be. Until I met Abraham, then everything fell into place."

Magda smiled and squeezed her friend's hands, but she felt confused by Isabel's visible contentment. All these years Magda had imagined her living the sad and repentant life of a daughter making up for a mother's grave transgression. But here Isa was, clearly untroubled by the past. She had married a Salah, a wealthy member of the Arab community, essentially turning her back on the establishment. The Salahs were turcos, a derisive, ugly term used to indicate all Arab and Palestinian immigrants and their descendants. Turcos. The word did not fit well in the mouth, so weighted was it with contempt and exclusion and bigotry. In Salvadoran society, only the Chinese suffered as much discrimination. Discrimination in all but business, that is. In business, los chinos y los turcos were invited to the table. Because they were wise in business and honest and shrewd, they had remained in El Salvador, multiplying and prospering over the decades.

"Tell me, how's tía Ceci?" Magda asked, thinking that surely it was Isabel's mother who carried the burden of the past. It had been thirteen years since she had seen Cecilia. Two weeks before her marriage to Alvaro, it had been.

"She's out in the garden. Why don't I send a servant out to your car for the merchandise you brought. While I look it over, you can say hello to Mamá. Seeing you will please her very much."

When Magda stepped out the back of Isabel's house, it became obvious why her friend chose to live here. Out here there was room to sprawl, and Isabel's garden sprawled in all directions. If walls bordered it, they were not evident. An abundance of fruit trees flourished in the sun. Gentle grassy rises pleased the eye, as did lush flower beds ringed prettily with stones. Magda went off across the lawn, her high heels sinking into the spongy grass ("Don't worry, you're aerating," Isabel had assured her). Magda passed a glittering swimming pool, a few small benches positioned in the shade. Soon she came upon Cecilia wearing a big straw hat and a loose dress that, from the back, looked very much like Isabel's. Cecilia was kneeling beside a flower bed, working the rich black earth with a trowel.

"Hola, tía Ceci," Magda said, drawing up to her and feeling suddenly awkward and unsure of herself. What would her mother say if she knew she was here? If she learned that she had sought Cecilia out?

Cecilia glanced over her shoulder, raising a hand to shield her eyes against the sun. "Querida Magda," she said, springing up and causing her hat to flutter to the ground. "Isa said you might be coming. Here. Let me look at you." She took Magda's hands, giving her a quick turn. "Oh, but you're so pretty. Ay Dios, I'm getting you dirty." Cecilia brushed off Magda's hands and then her own. She seemed smaller than Magda remembered her. Cecilia's glorious raven hair was now white ringlets, but all in all, she was the same Cecilia of long ago. The same olive skin. The same dark luminous eyes. The same expression of impish amusement playing at the corners of her mouth. "Oh, leave the hat there," Cecilia said. "Come, let's sit.

"This is paradise," Cecilia said when they were on a bench under a tree. "I spend a lot of time here." She held her hands out, fingers spread. "Look at me. Look at the dirt." Her nails were short. Little black crescents outlined them. "When we first moved here, Isa and Abraham had a gardener. But after a year, I was doing more work than the man was doing. So I asked Isa to let him go."

"You do the garden? You do it all yourself?"

"I do. And it makes me very happy."

"Amazing," Magda said. Amazing, too, because all that she'd believed about Isa and Cecilia was turning out to be not even remotely true.

"So tell me about the children. I know you have three. Isa keeps me up to date. And, of course, there are the papers and their newsy society columns." Cecilia rolled her eyes and gave a little laugh.

Magda spent a few minutes reciting the litany concerning her boys: how Júnior was very serious and how he adored cars and wanted to be a race driver; how Carlos, the middle one, wanted to grow cotton like his father; how Orlando, the little one, hated school but loved his dog Bruno. During the recitation, Magda's mind was two horses going down different tracks. The one trotted along, filling Cecilia in about the family; the other started and bucked with thoughts about Cecilia herself: the way she sat there, leaning forward attentively, so engrossed. The way her face shone out, unlined and alive. And her eyes. Her eyes were wide and innocent and unashamed. It was this part of Magda's mind that kept asking the questions: Can this be the woman who betrayed my mother? Is this the one who lay down with my father? Magda continued on about her children, her hands in her lap, one finger making little circles over her thumb. She did not want to think about her father and Cecilia. A thought both unsavory and bewildering.

"So now you need a little girl, don't you think?" Cecilia was saying.

"¡Ay, Virgen, no!" Magda exclaimed. "Three's plenty for me. And I *do* have a daughter. Her name is Tesoros."

"I hear what a successful start you've had. Everyone is talking about how exciting Tesoros is. How innovative. Of course, that doesn't surprise me at all. From the minute you were born, we knew that you were different."

When she said "we knew," a look of regret skittered behind her eyes. "Tell me, dear Magda, how is your mother?"

Had she not asked, Magda would have faulted her. Now that she had, the question unsettled her somehow. "My mother is well, gracias, tía Ceci," Magda said.

"We were concerned, of course, about your mother. When Isa ran into your father and he spoke about your mother's health, about how she wasn't eating, about how thin she was, well, naturally, we were alarmed. That's why I wrote to you. I trust you didn't mind."

"How could I mind a thing like that?" Magda said. "Actually, my mother's quite involved with seeing me succeed." Magda did not go into the details of Elena's resurrection: the buying trips she had made for the store, the weight she had gained, the new wardrobe she'd had Pilar create.

Two red dachshunds, their ears flapping, came scrambling over the lawn. Behind them, a pudgy baby came toddling after. Isabel brought up the rear.

The child went to Cecilia and wrapped his little arms around her lap. He giggled uncontrollably as the dogs yipped around him and licked his chubby legs. "This is my grandson, Enrique. He's almost two," Cecilia said, raising her voice above the commotion. Isabel came up and settled the dogs down. "It's always a circus at my house," she said.

Magda was about to comment when she saw a deer come around a tree. She took a step back in disbelief. "My goodness," she said, and Enrique lifted his dark curly head from his grandmother's lap and looked in the direction Magda pointed.

"He's mine," Enrique said, and he minced off toward the fawn, one arm extended as if in benediction.

"I can't believe it," Magda said. "There's a deer in your garden."

"Enrique's named him Bambi," Isabel said. "He also has a peacock, but the bird's too mean to be let out all the time."

"Amazing," Magda said.

Later, after they'd all had a cool glass of lemonade, after Isabel had selected her merchandise and given directions for its delivery, after Cecilia had gathered up a basketful of flowers and fruits for Magda to take home, Isabel and Magda were in the driveway again. Isabel poked her head through the open back window of the car. "I'm so glad you came," Isabel said, her eyes calm and deep. In the backseat, Magda borrowed the serenity she saw in Isa's face. "I'm glad I came, too."

Basilio started down the hill, the car's interior flush with late afternoon sun and with the ripe smell of mangoes and papayas, with the biting scent of geraniums. Magda settled herself against the seat again. She thought, How wrong I've been, how wrong. She did not know if it was Cecilia she was thinking about, or if it was her mother she had in mind.

▼▼

CHAPTER THIRTY-TWO

El Parque Cuscatlán was the ideal spot for a rendezvous; it was on the bus line, up Avenída Roosevelt, twelve blocks from the main post office. The park was small. It was less frequented than the more popular parks in the downtown area. Still, Cuscatlán was one of the loveliest, for it abounded with maquilishuats, broad leafy trees producing plentiful shade and, when they blossomed, bright pink flowers as fine as butterflies drying wings in the sun. Jacinta and Miguel had come here once before, a month back, when the trees were abloom. Today the paths and walkways of the park were strewn with faded flowers that provided a unique carpet but made the passing slippery. Jacinta hooked an arm through Miguel's as they strolled under the green canopies in which clarineros and dichosofuis perched to sing their melodies. They had the park almost to themselves. Since their trip to the beach two months before, they had met for coffee once a week, but these were rushed meetings in out-of-the-way cafés filled with people and abuzz with chattering. Today the two had a few hours; it was Jacinta's half day off, only a monthly occurrence, and one to make the most of.

"It's going to rain," Miguel said, swinging an umbrella back and forth as they walked. The rainy season was almost upon them. From May to November an afternoon shower would be a daily event.

"You're the only man I've ever known who has his own um-brella."

"Well, then, the men you've known must have gotten very wet."

Jacinta laughed. "Getting wet is not a bad thing, you know."

"Maybe not."

"For sure not. Getting wet is cleansing."

"I prefer my shower." Miguel stopped now and reached into his shirt pocket for a cigarette. Jacinta watched him light one and take a puff; soon the smell of tobacco mingled with the pungency of crushed blossoms underfoot. Miguel slipped the matchstick between his teeth.

"Why do you always do that?" Jacinta asked as they started off again.

"The matchstick? I don't know. It's just a habit. Olivia, she doesn't like it. . . ." He shrugged and didn't go on.

Jacinta said nothing. This was the way it was between them. Sometimes Miguel made cryptic remarks about his wife that Jacinta deciphered into a fuller meaning: Olivia had let herself go after the children began to come; Olivia was always tired and seldom liked to go out. In turn, Jacinta sometimes talked about Basilio, she being more expansive in her remarks than Miguel. She said she felt sorry for Basilio; she wished it were possible to make Basilio happy. Still, when the subject of Olivia or Basilio arose, each listened to the other and made cursory comments because, given the nature of their af-fair, of what use were comments? Comments had a way of becoming suggestions; suggestions could soon turn into accusations, accusa-tions into recriminations.

They reached a point where the walkway ended, and there was a grassy clearing bordered prettily by forget-me-nots and dainty margaritas. They crossed the space and went up a small knoll, land-scaped on this side by a grouping of decorative boulders, on the other by a thicket of shrubs and trees. It was a haven up here, so compact and secluded. They had discovered the spot on their last visit. It was here they had lain against the spongy grass, here that they made love for only the second time. Since stepping into the park today, it was their silent understanding that this was their des-tination and making love was their purpose.

On the knoll, they raked fallen blossoms aside with their fingers and settled themselves on the grass, in a broad wedge of shade provided by the boulders and trees. Jacinta sunk her fingers into the thick grass in an effort to wipe away the pink stains the blossoms left behind. "I think you're wrong. I don't think it's going to rain," she said. The last time here, a profusion of flowers had obscured the sky, but today the sky was a patchwork of blue between the leafy branches of the trees.

"It's going to rain," Miguel said. He stubbed his cigarette out in the grass. "It's not the season yet, but it'll rain. I can feel it in my bones."

Jacinta gave him a little push. "You can feel it in your bones? You sound like an old man."

"I'm old compared to you."

"Thirty-five isn't old." She pulled the matchstick from his mouth and rubbed the soot off its end, then slipped the matchstick into her pocket. She wiped the soot off her fingertips in the grass.

"Why do you always do that?" Miguel asked, his voice playfully mocking her own same question. "You must have dozens of matchsticks by now."

"And what if I do?" She had collected them all into a matchbox, for no other reason but that he'd held them each between his lips. This treasure, as well as the little bottle of seawater he'd given her after their trip, she'd hidden in a box that was tucked away at the bottom of her dresser drawer. Jacinta lay back against the springy cushion of grass. She gazed up at the sky, watching the clouds move lazily through the trees. "It's curious, but the older I get, the smaller the sky becomes."

Miguel lay alongside her, also looking up. "You grew up in el campo. In the country the sky is always big."

"And you grew up in la ciudad."

"In the city the sky is always small."

She turned on her side to see him better. "We're so different, you and I. . . ." She let the words trail off because there was so much that she could say and she was too full of feeling to say it.

He turned to her, propping himself on an elbow. "How? How are we different?"

She laid a hand along the side of his face, taking in the sober way he looked at her. A clot of images rose up, choking her with memory: coffee branches ripe with fruit; her stiff abraded fingers reaching up to them; precipitous barrancos smelling of filth and crowded humanity; a burning laurel tree, its leaves curling in the heat; Tzi, the faithful dog, his pitiful ribs poking out from yellow fur; her mother's long black skirt with its border of embroidered birds. What was in Miguel's life that could match all this? she asked herself. Sidewalks and concrete? Well-shod feet? A thick mattress resting on a frame? The odor of baking bread wafting down a crowded street? "We're different, that's all," she said at length, but what she meant was, There's a sea of difference between us. It's the difference between chaos and tranquillity. For half her life she had endured one, and now, having had a taste of the other, how could she let it go?

He laid his own hand over hers still along his face. "Te quiero, Jacinta," he said. "I see such pain in your eyes and it breaks my heart." He laid her back gently and kissed her eyelids, his hands cupping her face as if it were a rare and fragile thing. The sweetness of his touch moved her so deeply, she felt the sting of tears and a sudden mournful lust that caused her to reach up and fiercely press herself to him.

And so it happened for the third and final time. On an afternoon in the park when he thought it would rain and she did not. When the furthest thing from their minds was that what they did together under a blue sky and upon the green grass would never happen again.

There was a commotion at Pilar's. The children had been halfway home from school when it abruptly began to rain, sending them scurrying for shelter under eaves and in doorways along the way. In her haste, Nanda had slipped and scraped her knee, and now she was sprawled on a chair by the sink, her skinny leg propped up on the kitchen table as Pilar applied Mercurochrome to the wound. "¡Aiiii!" Nanda screamed.

"Stop screaming." Pilar said, fanning the abrasion with a hand. "The neighbors'll think I'm killing you."

"Blow on it! Blow on it!" Nanda wailed. Emilio puffed up his fat cheeks and did as his sister asked.

"You're spitting on me!" Nanda cried, pushing her brother away. Emilio's face fell and his lip turned under. He went over to lean against his big brother Eduardo, who was at another chair.

"I told her not to run," Eduardo said.

"You can't tell me what to do," Nanda yelled, furiously fanning her knee herself.

"Qué exagerada," Eduardo said, rolling his eyes at his sister while slipping an arm around his little brother's waist.

"You'll all be the death of me, I swear," Pilar said, smoothing a bandage over Nanda's knee. Pilar capped the Mercurochrome bottle and put it back in the cupboard.

"I didn't do anything," Emilio whimpered.

Eduardo said, "Nanda, you can put your leg down now. I'm tired of seeing your underpants."

Emilio giggled as Nanda hastily dropped her leg. She glowered at Eduardo, smoothing her skirt down over herself. "My uniform's all dirty from the sidewalk."

Harold, Pilar's nephew, walked in. He was not alone; with him was a boy with the full brown face of an Indian who hung back by the door.

"I heard Nanda screaming all the way down the street," Harold said, raking a hand through his hair that was damp from the un- expected rain. "What happened?"

"She fell down and scraped her knee," Emilio said.

"See? Didn't I tell you? I bet the neighbors think you're dead," Pilar said. "Hola, Victor," she added, addressing Harold's friend. "You boys take a chair. I'll get you all something to drink."

Soon there were five Coca-Cola bottles sitting around the table. Pilar leaned against the sink and drank from one herself.

"How are things, Victor?" she asked. A few months before, Vic- tor's mother had died. He was fifteen, and he worked hard at hiding how he truly felt about his mother's loss.

"Bien," Victor replied. He gave his soda bottle a half turn and then gathered his hands into his lap.

Harold, who himself had lost a mother, said, "Victor should come live with us."

"I'm sure Victor's father would have a lot to say about that," Pilar said. The boy's father was Rolando Morales. She knew he was a subteniente in the Guardia Nacional. She had not met the man, but she knew men like that. Weapons. Tactics. Soldiering. Camaraderie. That was what most interested men of his kind.

"My father wouldn't care," Victor said. He reached for his bottle again and gave it another turn before taking a long drink. They lived in Colonia El Refugio. Now it was just the two of them in the little pink house with its souring air that, since his mother's passing, seemed to be shrinking daily. When he was off duty, his father sat in the dark, prohibiting lamp or candle, allowing only the ambient light that came from outside. He sat in rumpled trousers, foul-smelling undershirt, no shoes, no socks, while against the wall, draped around a hanger and impressive even in the gloom, his uniform hung, starched and pressed, pointed like a ready arrow toward his spit-polished shoes. It was that disembodied specter hanging against the wall that Victor loved. That apparition was a somebody, and there was power in his step and in the grip of his hand. If that man cuffed him on the cheek or against the back of the head, if he said things that made his heart clutch and his knees jelly, well, then, so be it. That was how it was with men like Rolando Morales. It was the man slouched down in the dark, his shoulders to his neck, sucking cerveza after cerveza, that Victor did not love. With each pull from the beer bottle, that man could grow more cruel.

"We could put up another cot in my room," Harold said, jiggling his name bracelet around his wrist.

"It's my room, too," Eduardo said. "But I wouldn't mind if Victor came to stay."

"Me either," Emilio said, because it was also his room. The three boys shared a bedroom—Eduardo and Emilio in the double bed, Harold in his own cot; Pilar and Nanda shared the big bed in the second bedroom.

"Well," Pilar said, "we'll have to think about that," though it was clear the matter had gone from idle chitchat to something much more serious. The boy sat there, stiff as starch and just as plain. Without a mother to ease the way, a hard road stretched before him. He was a homely boy and a dark one at that. As if this cross were not enough, there was the matter of the birthmark.

"Everybody's talking and talking, but nobody's asked Victor what he thinks," Nanda said.

"Nanda's right," Pilar said, laying a hand on her daughter's shoulder. She was only eight, but sometimes Nanda said surprising things. "What do you want, Victor?"

Victor jiggled his own name bracelet in an effort to feign indifference. What did he want? He wanted his mother. She had died unexpectedly. One day she was hearty and whole, the next, she was felled by a hemorrhage so severe that a year would pass before the landlord gave in to the fact that only by replacing the floor tiles would the problem with the bloodstains be resolved.

"Say what you want, Victor," Nanda said.

I'll tell you what I want, Victor thought, but didn't say. I want my mother. When the man sits in the dark and sucks on a beer, he sometimes whispers things to me. Don't forget I found you, boy, the man says. Don't forget you'd be dead if it wasn't for me. Victor took another drink of soda to help wash memory away. He knew he'd survived some terrible thing because his dreams confirmed it. In his dreams, the sound of gunfire was loud, the smell of gunpowder strong. His dreams were sometimes populated by dead bodies and burning huts. What did he want? He wanted his mother. Without his mother, who would protect him against his dreams? Who would protect him against his father?

"Well," Pilar said, struck by Victor's silence. "You don't have to say what you want." She went to the table and made a show of gathering up the soda bottles, and soon the tension that had collected in the room eased. The children, feeling the change, went off to their rooms to step out of their uniforms before tackling their homework. Harold and Victor remained in the kitchen for a moment, and Pilar was about to assure Victor that the subject of his moving in was not a closed one when Jacinta dropped by. The unexpected visit prompted a flurry of new activity: The children rushed out to say hello; Harold hastily introduced Victor and then excused both of them as they left.

"So that was the famous Victor," Jacinta said when only she and Pilar remained in the kitchen. Pilar had heated up some coffee and Jacinta was having some. "Pobrecito. Losing his mother. And that birthmark. I'm sure he's teased a lot." She thought of little Tino and his tiny stained ear.

"Harold wants him to move in," Pilar said. She wasn't drinking any coffee. The one Coca-Cola had been enough for her.

"Will you let him?"

"I don't know. There's his father to consider. His father is a guardia. A subteniente in the Guardia."

Jacinta lifted her shoulders and gave a little shudder. "That's reason enough for you to take the boy in."

"Maybe," Pilar said, and then she changed the subject because just the thought of the boy and his big sad eyes depressed her. "So, tell me. What brings you here today?"

"I had the afternoon off." Jacinta looked up at the clock. "I don't have much time. I have to be back at the house by five."

"If you don't have much time, what did you do all afternoon?"

"You don't want to know."

"Oh, I see." Pilar lifted a hand. "Stop. You don't have to say more."

"I won't."

"What's wrong? Aren't you happy?"

"I've never been happier."

"Then what's the problem?"

"That *is* the problem," Jacinta said.

▼▼

CHAPTER THIRTY-THREE

The truth was that no one looked more striking in green than Magda. The green of parrot wings to be exact. In green, Magda's white skin seemed whiter, her inky eyes and hair took on an even deeper hue. Flying in the face of tradition, which dictated that only black or navy should be worn after sunset, Magda wore green tonight. A strapless short evening dress in peau-de-soie that hugged her breasts and flared out around her waist. Emeralds circled her neck and wrist, a loan for the evening from Elena. And dangling from her earlobes, two emerald baguettes Alvaro had presented to celebrate his first successful cotton harvest. She had not worn the earrings before, knowing that it was at the gala opening of Tesoros that she must first show them off.

Magda leaned closer to the mirror of the vanity and applied an extra bit of kohl to the outside corners of her eyes. She wore her hair loose, pinning up the sides with small lacquered combs. She drew back to admire herself.

"In case there's any doubt, you look spectacular tonight," Alvaro said behind her. In the mirror, she caught him leaning against the frame of the dressing-room door. He wore his dark blue suit and the tie with the tiny red checks. The corner of a silk handkerchief peeked rakishly from his coat pocket.

"And how long have you been standing there?"

"Long enough to fall in love again." He walked over and pulled her up to him. He stroked the tops of her breasts, tracing the heart-shaped bustline of the dress. "You're very beautiful."

"Gracias, amor." She brought his hand against her cheek, taking in the spicy scent of his cologne. This is what she'd been waiting for. Her man of before.

Alvaro nuzzled her neck and she giggled softly, "Oh, that tickles." She closed her eyes, feeling the feathery flicker of his tongue on her skin. She pressed herself against him, and his excitement was evident even through the fabric of her dress.

He whispered in her ear, in that low, melodious way that was a caress in itself. "I want you, Magda. Right here in the dressing room."

"I want you, too, but I just began my fertile time."

"I'll use a condom. I'll slip it on. Here, feel me." He lowered her hand so that it covered him.

"Go get a condom, Alvaro. Quick. Get it. I want to feel you in me." She thought of her dress, her makeup. If she gave in to desire she'd muss these up, but it was only a passing thought.

He continued to entice her. "I'll sit on the bench. You'll lift your green dress. You'll step out of your panties."

"Yes, my love, yes." Between her legs, a whirl of electricity.

"And then you'll straddle me, won't you, Magda? In your high heels and your stockings and your garter belt. You'll straddle me very slowly, won't you?"

"Oh, yes." Between her legs, a dampness.

A furious rapping started at the bedroom door. Magda and Alvaro jumped apart. "What is it?" Magda called, her voice sounding as if it belonged to someone else. More rapping. "It's us, Mamá. Let us in. Let us in."

Alvaro shook out his shoulders, adjusting his trousers over his crotch. Magda's heart hammered and she took quick breaths to calm herself. "I'll get the door," Alvaro said. Before he turned away, Magda pressed her lips to his hand. "Remember this, my love. After the party. Here, on the bench, in my green dress, everything you want, I'll do."

▼   ▼   ▼

The party spilled out of Tesoros itself, down the short inner hallway of the hotel and into one of the great rooms off the lobby. Women milled about the store, which was radiant with candles and fragrant with flowers sent by well-wishers. Some women started a refined competition that soon had party-goers outbuying one another. Magda's assistant and a sales clerk, both dressed smartly in dark sheaths, worked the room in professional fashion, answering questions and taking orders, wrapping gifts and slipping them into the pomegranate paper bags that were to become Tesoros' signature.

The guests overflowed to the great room of the hotel, with its splendid Persian carpet and its ornamental paneling and friezes. Dwarf palms set in pots in the corners shivered in the slight currents produced by lazy ceiling fans. Waiters in crisp uniforms used the soft light of wall sconces to navigate around the room with salvers of hot hors d'oeuvres and glasses of chilled champagne. Male guests, having made the obligatory tour of the store, clumped around the massive carved bar and charged the air with cigarette smoke and with their vehement discussions about coffee and cotton, about cattle and sugar, about El Salvador's place in the new world order determined by the war.

Matrons, clad in black silk and sedately resplendent in pearls and gold, had gathered in cliques around linen-draped tables. The scent of their perfumes drifted up from their wrists, the sagging hollows at their throats, the backs of their pendulous earlobes, and emitted the distinct heady aroma of money and privilege.

Magda, an iridescent green butterfly, glided from group to group, buoyed by a host of compliments and congratulations and by the delicious expectation of what awaited in her dressing room with Alvaro. She was chatting at a table with her mother and mother-in-law when she spied Alvaro watching her from across the room. She smiled coquettishly and wiggled her fingers at him and then turned back to the conversation, the ardor in her husband's eyes heating her up again.

Also at the table was Margarita, the wife of Magda's brother. "I don't know how you do it," Margarita said. "I could never run a business and keep peace at home."

"I'm sure Magda bends over backward to keep my son happy," doña Eugenia, Alvaro's mother, said. "I'm sorry I didn't raise my son to be less demanding."

I'm sorry, too, Magda thought. For six months, she had gone out of her way to keep home waters calm. Now, by the look of things, the waters were parting.

"Don't fault yourself, Eugenia," Elena said. "All sons are demanding. That's what we mothers get for pampering them."

"Men deserve a little pampering," Margarita said. "After all, men work hard to provide."

Magda smiled sweetly at her sister-in-law. You're an obnoxious bitch, she thought.

Laura de Castillo, Margarita's best friend, sat at the table, too. "Some men provide hardly at all. Look at that Raúl on *Las dos.* Inocencia works her fingers to the bone, and what does it get her? A filandering, lazy, good-for-nothing husband." Laura scoffed and readjusted the thick gold choker circling her throat.

"He's a good-for-nothing, that's for sure," said doña Lydia de Campo, who was very old and who pursed the thin red line of her lips in such a way that for a moment it was like she'd swallowed them.

Magda smiled brightly. The women were on the subject of radio novelas now, so it was time to move on. "Well, ladies. I'm off to other guests. Don't forget that soon the priest will arrive to bless the store." She headed for Alvaro at the bar. She walked up behind him and laid a hand over his shoulder. He quickly covered her hand with his. She leaned close. "How did you know it was me?" He leaned even nearer, "You're the only woman with a hand so hot it burns right through my jacket."

"Don't you two know whispering's not polite in company?" Ernesto, Magda's father, asked jokingly.

Magda dropped her head in mock contrition. "You're right, Papá. We stand corrected." She lifted her head. "I was just telling Alvaro that el padre Adolfo will be here any minute." Magda shot her husband a glance. Alvaro rocked back on his heels and grinned at her.

"You think you need the priest's blessing for Tesoros to prosper?" Ernesto said.

"In business, people need all the help they can get. I remember when el padre Lorenzo blessed La Abundancia, Papi."

Ernesto took a deep breath. "El padre Lorenzo's dead now."

"But he was very old, don Ernesto," Alvaro said. "It's remarkable the priest lived long enough to marry both you *and* me. When he married you and doña Elena, he was old already."

"I suppose that's true," Ernesto said.

"What's this preoccupation you have with people dying, Papá? Lately, that's all I hear you talk about." Last week, at the family get-together, he had spent the better part of an hour listing all the people he knew who had died.

"People die, you know," Ernesto said.

"There's no denying that," Magda said. She craned her neck and caught padre Adolfo striding into the room. Given the turn of her father's conversation, the priest had not arrived a moment too soon.

Magda greeted the priest, who was not wearing his usual cassock but a black suit and a clerical collar. His hair was slicked fussily with brilliantine, his only visible affectation. Magda liked el padre Adolfo. He was in his late thirties, maybe even forty, and already he'd come far. He had spent thirteen years in Santa Ana at the cathedral, working with padre Lorenzo until he died, then moving up through the ranks until he filled the old priest's shoes. A year ago, el padre Adolfo had been transferred to San Salvador.

Magda and the priest and all of the women in the great room crossed the lobby and went down the hallway toward the store. The men, content to allow their wives to represent them, stayed behind at the bar. The women crowded into the store, standing there silently as el padre Adolfo ceremoniously draped an amice around his neck and extracted an aspergillum from its little traveling case. The priest raised a hand and intoned with sonorous voice the ancient Latin words of benediction. Soon he went dramatically about the room, shaking the perforated container, misting the women with holy water, blessing the merchandise that lay waiting all about them.

Alvaro dashed into the bathroom. He tripped the light switch, momentarily startled by the sight of himself in the mirror. He was nude. His cock rose stiffly against his belly. He yanked open the medicine cabinet, quickly pushing aside bottles and jars. Where were the condoms? Moments ago, he had been sitting on the bench in Magda's dressing room when she approached, her eyes wide and shining. The little light on the vanity was soft and diffused. Still he could see her green dress hiked around her waist, her long silky legs looking even longer in her high heels, the line of her garter belt rounded over the dark bushy vee of her crotch. She had been about to straddle him when she stopped herself. "My God, I almost forgot it's my fertile time."

Now he rummaged through the medicine chest, bumbled around in the counter drawers. Where in the hell were the fucking condoms!

"Did you find them?"

"I'm coming. I'm coming." My God, he *would* come if he didn't hurry. He'd come all over himself, right here in the bathroom.

"Hurry, my love. Hurry."

At the thought of her, moist and hot and waiting, he flipped off the light. Just this once, he said to himself. When they did it again, he'd go back into the bathroom. Take more time. Slip a condom on. He hurried back to her.

"Do you have it? Is it on?"

"Yes," he said, sitting on the bench again. As he usually did when he was protected, he circled a hand around himself, feeling his cock throb a crazy pulse as she stalked toward him.

▼▼

CHAPTER THIRTY-FOUR

*A*ll the servants were in the kitchen bunched around the radio. *Las dos* was on, and Bárbara had been wrapped in the arms of her sister's husband. Seconds ago, to close the episode, Bárbara confessed that she was pregnant.

Tea jumped up from her chair. "I knew it! I knew it!" A flurry of mellifluous music filled the room, and then the cheery jingle of the sponsor.

The cook, who had listened to the whole installment with squinted eyes as if this might aid her hearing, said, "What happened?"

Rosalba leaned toward the cook and shouted a response: "Bárbara is going to have a baby."

"Whose baby?" Delfina asked.

"Raúl's baby," Jacinta said under her breath. She left them all in the kitchen and proceeded to her room. She had eaten a full lunch, and something had not agreed with her. Her stomach felt queasy, and she needed to lie down for just a bit.

There wasn't much light coming in from the hall, but the room was peaceful in the dimness. Resting on her cot, Jacinta could make out the row of holy cards she'd tacked along the wall: San Jacinto, that relic Basilio had given her so long ago, la Virgen Dolorosa with her halo of lightning bolts. And here was the large print of el Divino Corazón, Jesus pointing to his exposed heart crowned by thorns and dripping blood. In Izalco, they'd had a card like that. The priest had brought it to them. Out of respect to him, her mother had tacked it up in the hut. It was yet another thing that had gone up in smoke.

The laundress came to stand in the doorway. Though she was backlit, Jacinta could tell it was Juana because she was the only one who was so tall. "What's wrong with you?" Juana asked. She was like that, an observant and considerate woman in her late fifties who reminded Jacinta of her mother.

"Something didn't agree with me." Jacinta rubbed her belly.

"Umm," Juana said. She went to sit on Rosalba's cot, which was across the room. After a minute or two, Jacinta said, "What is it?" because the sight of Juana sitting mutely by was disquieting.

"I know what ails you. And it isn't what you ate."

"What do you mean?"

"For two months your laundry has not needed special bleaching."

Jacinta raised herself. "So?"

"For two months there've been no feminine stains on your underthings."

Jacinta swung her legs to the floor. Two months of no bleeding? How could it be true? How could she be unaware of such a thing?

"You and la Bárbara," Juana said. "It looks like you're both in the same condition."

"Not me," Jacinta asserted, shaking her head emphatically. "I can't have a baby."

"And why not? All it takes to have a baby is being with a man, and judging from your behavior, it's pretty clear to me you're mixed up with some man."

"What behavior? What are you talking about?"

"Estás en la luna, niña. For months, you've been on the moon."

"I have not. And I'm not going to have a baby. I can't have a baby."

"Why would you think such a thing?"

"Because years ago, I lost a baby."

"So what? I've had five babies. I also lost another two."

"But it's different with me. Before I lost mine, I visited a curandero. The healer told me it would never happen again."

"He told you *what* would never happen again?"

"That I'd never have another baby." He *had* said that, hadn't he? She had not forgotten him, a kind, pudgy man with very long fingernails, smelling of copal incense. She had been spotting for a week when she went to him. She had stood in the middle of his hut, and he had circled her, taking swigs from a long-necked bottle, spraying her with quick bursts of water to clear away the negative, he had said. He had offered up chants and prayers while candles flickered and copal smoke spiraled in the room. He had laid her on a petate. Smoothing her dress and poking it under her, he had passed a laurel branch back and forth over her body. In a final act, he had broken an egg on her belly, gathering the whole mess up in a deft swipe of the hand. "Go, my child," he then had said, helping her up and escorting her out the door. "Your condition. It won't happen again." A week later, her baby was lost in a steady stream of blood, and the curandero's words were etched forever on her heart.

Juana said, "Maybe what el curandero meant was that you'd never *lose* another one again." The laundress stood up, her knees creaking when she did. "But whatever he meant, believe me, girl, you're going to have a baby." Juana went over and patted Jacinta's shoulder. "It's true. And you're not the only one. I've been doing laundry for thirty years and I know underwear. Underwear never lies."

"I hope it can keep its mouth shut," Jacinta said, feeling the room spin a bit. She *had* been on the moon. Two months of no bleeding, and she hadn't even noticed it.

Juana gave a laugh. "Don't worry. Your secret is safe with me."

The light came on and Rosalba strode in. "My goodness, you two are in the dark." She went over to her dresser and opened a drawer. "Can you believe our story? Don't you hate how they always leave us in suspense? Now we have to wait till Monday to find out what Raúl thinks."

For Jacinta, the weekend was interminable. At no time had she needed her mother more. One night she awoke shivering, her head filled with Mercedes's face. There, in the darkened room, a hand over her mouth to keep the sobs inside herself, Jacinta nestled up to her mother's memory, drawing what comfort she could from the ephemeral nature of recollection. Out in the night, the sereno passed by, the sound of the watchman's whistle a frail lament that echoed her own sorrow that, no matter how intensely she tried to conjure them, Mercedes's touch, her mother's voice, her counsel were as unsubstantial as dust.

Pilar she could count on, of course, and while this was a potential blessing, Jacinta had no time off soon, so an immediate visit to her friend's was out of the question. Juana, now her only other confidante, lived at home and did not work on weekends. Further reassurance from her would have to wait until later. And Miguel? What would she tell Miguel? As the hours crept by and she went about her chores, Jacinta relived the details of that third time with him: the mutual ardor that overtook them, the needy, trembling way they had been gratified. Afterward, it began to rain, just as he said it would, and they had huddled under his umbrella, their backs against the solid face of a boulder in the park. Stunned into silence by both fulfillment and depth of feeling, they had waited out the rain. Two months ago that had been. Since then, they'd enjoyed but a handful of hasty meetings. Since then, there had been no talks with Pilar about the state of her heart.

But it was only for two days that Jacinta would wrestle with her news alone. Pilar arrived at Magda's on Monday for a full week of work. At nine, Jacinta herself opened the side entrance to her friend. "We have to talk," Jacinta said, hurrying Pilar down the service hall and through the kitchen. As they swooshed past the cook at the stove and Rosalba lolling at the table, Jacinta handed out quick orders: "Pilar needs her coffee and lots of pan dulce. Black coffee, and very hot. Rosalba, get up off that chair. Bring Pilar's breakfast to the sewing room."

"Aren't you the little commander today," Pilar said after Rosalba had brusquely deposited the breakfast tray on the arm of the Singer and clomped out of the room. "What's the matter with you? I've never seen you so bossy." Pilar sat at the sewing machine; she used a scrap of fabric to mop up the coffee Rosalba had slopped over the rim of the cup.

"Something terrible's happened."

"What?" Pilar said, her eyes widening in alarm.

"I think I'm going to have a baby." It was the first time she'd said the words aloud.

Pilar gave a little shriek, causing her coffee to slosh over again. "Oooo, a baby!" She swept across the room and gave Jacinta a twirl. "When did you find out?"

Jacinta waved her hands frantically. "Niña, please. I don't want anyone to know." Basilio was in the garden. She could see him out the window standing by the shed. Rosalba? Who knew where that girl was lurking.

Pilar rolled her eyes. "That's a secret that won't keep for very long. When are you due?"

"I don't know."

"Haven't you seen a doctor?"

"No."

"Then how do you know you're pregnant?"

"I haven't bled for two months." She couldn't admit that it was Juana who'd had to point this out.

"You're pregnant," Pilar said, settling herself at the Singer. She bunched her hands under her chin. "Oooo, a baby. Such a wonderful thing."

Jacinta dropped into a chair. "I don't think it's so wonderful. I think it's terrible."

"What's so terrible about it?"

"For the love of God, Pilar, Miguel Acevedo is a married man."

"What does that have to do with it? Need I remind you that I have three children and that all of their fathers are married men?" Pilar pitched the scrap she'd used to mop up the coffee into the wastebasket.

"Did they know you were pregnant? Did you tell them?" She had known Pilar for six years; Emilio had just started to crawl when they met. In the time since, Jacinta had not asked these delicate questions because the answers hardly concerned her. That is, not until today.

"One of them knew. Fernanda's father. He wanted to set up a house for me." Pilar looked out the window, her face gone soft as if she were peering into the past. "I loved that man . . . ," she said. After a moment, she tossed her head and looked back at Jacinta.

"Being a kept woman wasn't something that appealed to me. The other two?" Pilar made a puffing sound with her lips to dismiss them. "They didn't need to know."

"But how could you not tell? What did you do, break it off with them?" There was so much to know, and she would not have dreamed that something could happen in her life to make the answers so important.

Pilar leaned into the Singer so that it was only her face and the chestnut halo of her hair that showed above it. "But you know how it is. For people like you and me, it's a very simple thing. A man loves a woman. A woman loves a man. Things happen between them, and children come. When children come, women stay, men go. It's the price we pay. Men get fleeting pleasure. Women get tangible rewards." Pilar gave a little laugh at this last thing she'd said.

Jacinta did not laugh herself because she did not see the humor in Pilar's statement. All she could see was the calamity of it.

Pilar was about to go on about woman-and-man relationships, but she did not because across the room she saw the corner of Jacinta's lip quiver and her shoulders crumple. She saw her tears begin. Pilar stepped over and laid her arms around her friend. "Don't cry, Jacinta. We'll go to the doctor and find out for sure. It's not the end of the world." Pilar brushed Jacinta's tears away. "Don't worry. You have me. I'll help you."

Jacinta smiled weakly. "Oh, Pilar. Look at me. What in God's name was I thinking?"

"You weren't thinking, mi corazón. You were in love."

"Yes. I was on the moon."

▼▼

CHAPTER THIRTY-FIVE

"Tell me that again," Magda said to Mario Ruiz. She was in her doctor's clinic, standing before his desk while he sat comfortably behind it. The doctor, a general practitioner, was in his early forties. His long face was set in the smug and fatherly expression that represented the bulk of his facial repertoire.

"Very well. You're going to have a baby." Mario Ruiz flashed an absurd smile that said "Congratulations" and "Aren't you the fortunate one."

Magda dropped into the chair he'd offered only moments before. The room seemed suddenly atilt, the way things looked after she'd had too much wine with dinner. "I can't believe it."

Mario Ruiz came around his desk and drew up a chair beside her. "Come now. The news can't be that much of a surprise. You yourself said you'd missed two of your cycles."

She raised a hand and then, in submission, let it drop to her lap. "I know. But I was hoping, praying really, that it might be something else. *Anything* but this." She leaned close to him. "Are you absolutely sure, Mario? Maybe it's a tumor or something like that." Tumors could be excised. Babies could not.

Mario Ruiz drew himself up. "Heaven forbid it! Of course it's a pregnancy. I just finished a thorough examination, and there's no question about it. I'm surprised at you, Magda. How can you prefer a tumor over a baby?" He ran a hand through his hair, his expression clearly reproving.

Magda fell back against the chair. "I know. I'm sorry. Having a baby is a gift, but believe me, Mario, this gift comes at an inopportune time."

"We don't plan these things, my dear. You should know that by now. A baby is God's will, God's plan." He sat back behind his desk as if putting distance between himself and nonsense.

Magda looked past his shoulder at his diplomas, all Latinate declarations with their golden seals, hanging on the wall behind him. God did not plan this, she thought. And *she* certainly had not. She and Alvaro had completed their family. They'd had their three boys, and it was understood that this chapter of their lives had closed. It was also understood that, no matter fertile time or not, when desire overtook them, they gave in to it. This lust between them was their strongest bond. After the children came, they tossed church rules aside, agreeing to use a condom or to try circumventive ways of lovemaking as a means of prevention. For eight years, give or take a few worrisome moments, their plan had succeeded. Until now, that is. And she knew exactly when she'd conceived. It was the night of the Tesoros celebration. They'd made love twice that night. In the morning, once again. She'd been fertile then, but each time Alvaro had used protection. She was sure of it. No matter how ardent their lovemaking, this detail she never overlooked.

"Four children in a family is not excessive," Mario Ruiz was saying. "Look at it this way—you'll be thirty in November. You're a healthy woman. An excellent mother. Another baby will do you good."

"Thank you for bringing up my age. All year I've been trying to forget this next birthday of mine."

Mario Ruiz laughed. "You women and your vanity."

"So when am I due?" Magda asked, preferring to ignore his comment.

Mario Ruiz made some quick calculations on a small paper tablet. "February tenth, 1947."

So there it was. A proclamation. She was pregnant, and there was nothing to be done about it. She had an overwhelming desire to be with her mother, but Elena was in Santa Ana. It was late afternoon and there was no time left in the day to make the trip. Magda rose and forced a smile. "Well, Mario. What will be, will be."

"That's my girl," Mario Ruiz said. He came around the desk and placed an arm around her shoulder. "Mark my words. In a few days, when you get used to the fact, you'll give thanks for this new blessing."

"I'm sure that's true," Magda said. She left the office, deciding in a flash of inspiration to visit Alvaro's mother. Now there was a woman who would understand her plight.

A half hour later, Magda sat in doña Eugenia's parlor, a light-filled and cozy room containing mementos and objets d'art. Wisteria branches and tuberoses jutted elegantly from two Chinese vases. The tuberoses imparted a subtle fragrance to the air. On a side table was a charming presentation of crystal paperweights, a collection that Magda herself had inspired. Over an ebony bombé table hung a brilliantly colored oil by Chagall. Silver frames throughout the room displayed family portraits and special events. On a table beside doña Eugenia was the large rococo frame surrounding Magda and Alvaro's wedding photograph.

"Are you sure the girl can't bring you some coffee?" doña Eugenia asked. She looked stately in a gray linen dress that featured a black lace collar. Her silver hair was gathered at the nape of her neck with a grosgrain bow, the loops of which seemed to sit on her shoulders like two small wings. Despite such reserve in her wardrobe, she had a penchant for the dramatic, evident in the impeccable way she kohled her eyelids and brightened her lips.

"No, gracias, niña Eugenia. I've had enough coffee for the day. I was on my way home and thought I'd drop by."

"I'm so glad you did. But knowing how busy you are these days with Tesoros, I'm surprised, frankly, to find you here." She lifted a hand. "Surprised, but very pleased."

"You're right. Any other day I'd be at the store. But today I had to see Mario Ruiz. I just left his clinic."

Doña Eugenia knit her brow. "Dios mío, I hope nothing's wrong."

"I'm going to have another baby," Magda said, going immediately to the heart of the matter.

"Oh my! This is news. I don't suppose this was planned."

Magda clapped her hands together. "I knew when I left Mario's clinic this was where I should come. I knew you'd understand. Right now, I don't need gushing congratulations and sentimentality. I'm pregnant, and you're right, this was not something I planned. As you might imagine, I'm a bit dismayed."

"Well, of course you are. News like this can hit like a bomb. No disrespect, you understand, to the institutions of family and motherhood. Does my son know? Well, how could he know, if you just now left Mario's clinic? Let me put it this way—does Alvaro suspect?"

"No, he doesn't suspect, but when I tell him, you can be sure his cry of joy will reach you even here."

Doña Eugenia took in a long breath. "Yes, I'm sure that's true. Of all my children, it was Alvaro who was the most attached to the family, to tradition, and to the tried-and-true way of doing things. Poor boy. What a trial for him to have me for a mother." She gave a rueful little laugh. "On the day Alvaro told me it was you he wished to marry, I lit a candle in thanks to Our Lady. I knew you'd make him happy, my dear. I knew it was a woman like you he needed. A woman who knows what she wants and demands the most of herself. It's refreshing to see that in a woman. *I* find it refreshing, in any event. Even my own daughters don't possess the qualities I see in you."

"You're too kind, niña Eugenia."

"Well, it's true. It's also true my son can be so foolish. All men are somewhat foolish when you stop and think of it. They want to be men, they *insist* on being men, but they never cease wanting to be mothered. This makes men children in my estimation." She stopped suddenly, her eyes as bright as a canary's. "But will you listen to me. Let's get back to you. I hope you're not thinking of giving up the store because of this pregnancy."

"It's going to be a battle." Magda's gaze swept over her wedding photograph that was across the coffee table, at doña Eugenia's elbow. There they were, she and Alvaro, arms linked and chins high, both joyous as they bounded down the aisle toward their life. Even then there was that energy between them—what they would do alone and when the night came. This secret life was her treasure. But so were her house and her sons and her work.

"A battle perhaps, my dear, but one you must fight."

"Oh yes, thank you, I will. Tesoros is thriving. In the months we've been open, the amount of business we're doing is astonishing. The place is always full of customers. And the women buy. Oh, how they buy! I won't give it up. Baby or no baby, I can't give it up."

"And you mustn't. In this world there's time and room for a woman to be all the things she wants to be. A wife, a mother, a businesswoman, too. I did it, though I'm getting on in years and slowing down. But you, my dear, you're in your prime and your life is before you. All you need to succeed is good planning and organization. Someone you can trust your home and children with. For that you have Jacinta. And I don't have to tell you a servant like Jacinta is as rare as March rain."

Magda was in her dressing room. She sat at the vanity with its charming disarray of perfume bottles bunched on small cut-glass trays, of footed silver bowls brimming over with jewelry, of little framed photogaphs, each a radiant smiling face. Magda fluffed her hair up with her fingers. She was rehearsing what she would say to Alvaro when Jacinta's image filled the mirror. "Niña Magda, can I talk to you?"

"Have the children settled down?" Magda asked. After visiting her mother-in-law's, Magda had come home instead of returning to the store. This early arrival had delighted her sons. They had been in the playroom racing miniature cars over tracks and ramps. Magda took command of the red Alfa Romeo. She made all the proper racing sounds when she played with her sons.

"The children are with Tea."

"What is it?" Magda asked, because in the mirror Jacinta's wrists were crisscrossed woodenly over her belly and her back was very straight, as if she were struggling to hold something in. Magda did not turn to hear Jacinta's answer. The vanity bench was not the swiveling kind, so she kept her eyes on Jacinta through the mirror.

"I'm having trouble with Rosalba again." Jacinta bit her lip. She had come resolved to confess that she had visited Pilar's doctor, that the doctor, after a humiliating and seemingly endless examination, had pronounced the words that would alter the direction of her life. She had come to Magda for that, yet somehow something very different had flown out of her mouth.

Magda tilted the bottle of L'air du Temps against a fingertip and daubed perfume behind each ear, imbuing the room with floral sweetness. "What now with that girl?" Rosalba was a headache. Too young, too moody, and a loafer at that. Magda sighed. Servants could be such a nuisance. A necessary nuisance, God knew.

"She's bothering Basilio."

"What do you mean, she's bothering Basilio?" Magda set the perfume back on the vanity, closing the bottle up with its glass-winged stopper.

"Well, she's always watching Basilio; she's always pestering him and interrupting his work." Jacinta turned her gaze away from Magda's because her disclosure sounded schoolgirlish. To make up for the inanity, she added, "I feel responsible for Basilio. I know he's a man, but somehow I see only the boy in him. He loved my mother and my mother loved him, so he's like a brother to me."

"I know," Magda said. "But it looks to me like Rosalba has a crush on Basilio and that's not good. That's the beginning of trouble."

Jacinta nodded and scratched an elbow. "There's also this: Rosalba's too busy flirting to be thorough with her work. I just wanted you to know, niña Magda, because one of these days the girl will try my patience one time too many." While she was on the subject of Rosalba, she would not bring up the matter with the handkerchief because that was certain to cast a shadow on her own work, and that's the last thing Jacinta needed. Not that it would make a difference in the end. When all the truth came out, her work here would be over.

"As you know, you're the one in charge of the house. Whatever you think you have to do, do it. I trust your judgment; I always do." After she said this, Magda scooted around on the bench because in the mirror Jacinta had dropped her arms and slumped against the doorjamb. "What is it?" Magda said, rising quickly. Two steps and she was at Jacinta's side. "Are you crying? Virgen Santa, you're crying. Here. Sit on the bench for a moment." Magda helped Jacinta over to the vanity. "What is it? Why are you crying?"

Jacinta's shoulders heaved as her predicament rose up like a brick wall she could not imagine scaling or going around. She was in love with a married man, and she was going to have his baby, and this fact would, by design, put an end to their affair. The blessed sheltered life she lived in Magda's house, that, too, would soon be over. "I don't know what to do," Jacinta blurted, her voice thin and pitiful.

"What are you talking about?"

"I'm going to have a baby." Jacinta's secret finally trailed out, the last word turning into a new wail.

"Oh, my God, I can't believe it," Magda said. If Jacinta had punched her in the stomach, she wouldn't have been more surprised.

"I know. I can't believe it either. I'm sorry, niña Magda. I'm so sorry." Jacinta set her mouth to stifle her cries, seeing, in her mind, the fortunate circumstances of her life fading swiftly away: no more keys jingling at her waist, no more awaking to this cheery house, to the assured company of those who now seemed very dear.

"How did this happen?"

Jacinta lifted her shoulders and then let them drop. About this she would not tell the truth. If pressed, she would mention El Congo. A reunion with an old friend who had a fruit stand. She would not name any names.

"Never mind that," Magda said. "Needless to say, we know how these things happen. Have you seen a doctor?"

Jacinta nodded.

"What did the doctor say?"

"He said I was going to have a baby."

"Yes, but when? When did he say the baby would come?"

"Next year. In February, the doctor said."

"It can't be." Was this some type of cosmic joke?

"Please, niña Magda, I know what you're thinking. But please don't fire me. I'll do anything for you." Fresh tears rolled down Jacinta's cheeks.

Magda sat on the bench. She placed an arm around Jacinta and drew her close. "Listen, listen to me. I'm not letting you go. Nothing

is going to change. You're staying here with us." Later, after she told
Alvaro and the children, after she told her mother and the rest of
the family, she would tell Jacinta the astonishing coincidence that
now bound them together.

Jacinta looked up. With a quick hand, she brushed tears away.
"Really?" How was this possible—that she'd been given this re-
prieve?

"Yes, really. I need you here, Jacinta." Magda gave the keys on
Jacinta's key ring a playful little flip. "I need you carrying these keys
and keeping my house in order. And I need you helping with the
menus and the shopping. I need you dealing with Delfina and Tea
and with the likes of Rosalba." Magda smiled. "And where would
Basilio Fermín be without Jacinta Prieto to look after him?"

Jacinta smiled feebly. "But what about the baby? Can the baby
stay here, too?"

Magda nodded. "Of course the baby can stay. Both you and
your baby have a home here with us." She looked into the future
and saw two girl babies playing together. Under Jacinta's watchful
eye, the girl babies would thrive.

"Gracias, niña Magda. You're so good to me."

Magda softly patted Jacinta's back. "I know. I know."

W here else but in bed would she tell him? They lay entwined and
she was snug and satisfied. She could feel the cooling dampness he
had left between her legs and on the top of one thigh. "Are you
happy?" she asked him.

"Mmmmm," he muttered. Her musky, intoxicating length was
against him, and it was all he needed of love. All he needed of joy.

She propped herself up and looked at him. Perspiration glistened
on his face. A damp curl fell over the middle of his forehead. "You
look like a little boy." She brushed back the curl with her fingers.

"Then I'm your little boy," he murmured. He lay there, eyes
closed, in that drowsy state that came over him after lovemaking.

"I have three boys already. What would I do with another one?"

"I don't know. But a mother can never have enough boys."

"Is that true? What about girls? How many girls should a mother
have?"

"At least one," he said. "One girl surrounded by boys. What could be better?" Dreamily, he thought of his own circumstances. How in his family it had been him amid the girls. He peered at her then through half-opened eyes. Candles burned in the room, and her face was a large shadow. "What did you say?" he asked.

"I didn't say anything."

He opened his eyes fully, and her face came into focus. Her dark radiant eyes. Her plump mouth. He lifted a finger and followed the bridge of her nose. "Funny. I thought you said something."

She shook her head. "Maybe you read my mind." She trapped his finger in her hand and nibbled on it. His flesh was firm and sweet. She loved his hands. His long, thick fingers. "Do you think you can read my mind?"

"Reading your mind might be very dangerous."

"Depends on what I'm thinking."

"And just what are you thinking?"

"I'm thinking about what you said about girls. How every mother should have one."

A light went on in his head and he pulled himself up on an elbow, suddenly alert. "And?"

"I went to see Mario Ruiz today, Alvaro. He said I'm going to have a baby. I think it's going to be a girl." She did not know how she knew this, but she knew it to be true just the same.

Alvaro dropped back onto the pillows. For two months he had been waiting for this news, and now he was speechless at hearing it.

Magda laid her head on his breast, his chest hair thick and springy against her cheek. She could hear his heart. Alvaro encircled her in his arms. He saw her ripe and filled with life. He saw normality and order returning to his family. "You are my love," he said.

"I know," she said. What she would slowly make him see was the reward she would extract for giving him a daughter. Carte blanche with her store seemed appropriate enough.

▼▼▼

ut toward the end of Paseo Independencia, near the railroad station and the main offices of la Lotería Nacional, was La Amapola, the café Jacinta and Miguel had settled on as a safe place to meet. They were there today: Jacinta had managed to slip out of the house—she could spare an hour at most; Miguel was on his lunch break. The café was filled with people, all, it seemed, abuzz with commentary about *Las dos*. The story had been on at noon.

"That program," Miguel said, shaking his head. "You'd think it was the only thing on the radio. When I get home, that's all Olivia talks about. Bárbara and Raúl. Raúl and Bárbara." They were sitting at the back of the room, and he had ordered a meal—arroz, frijoles, and carne sancochada; Jacinta sipped on a limonada. She'd had lunch already and was thankful Miguel could not witness how little she could eat without feeling sick.

"That man is a snake," Jacinta said.

Miguel shook his head. "From what I hear, snake or not, a man would have little chance with a woman like Bárbara."

"Still, don't you think Raúl owes Bárbara something?"

"It's not what he owes her. It's what he owes his baby. That's assuming the baby is his."

"Don't you think it is?"

243

"He says it isn't." Miguel speared a piece of meat, piling on around the fork tines some bean mash and rice. This loading-up method was his usual way of eating, and in the past, Jacinta had found it charming. Today she was beginning to find it irksome.

"Well of course he says it isn't. The man's a snake." Jacinta could hear the edge in her voice, and she took a long sip of lemonade to help dampen the little fire she'd lit in herself. If she told Miguel her secret, would he also deny his complicity? And suppose, if she did confess, he accepted responsibility—what then? He had a wife and a family. Didn't the path of his life forever lead to them?

Miguel looked up from his plate, his fork loaded and halfway to his mouth. "What's wrong? You sound angry. Are you angry?"

"What makes you think that?" Jacinta took another drink of lemonade. Pressed the back of a hand to her mouth.

Miguel frowned and lowered his fork to his plate again. "Is there something I should know?"

She could say it right then, in La Amapola, at two o'clock, on an afternoon in July: Miguel, remember when I told you I could never conceive? Well, it appears that I was wrong. She could say that. And she could add this: I'm going to have your baby, Miguel.

"Why do I have the feeling you're holding something back?" Miguel continued.

In the future, she would reexamine this moment again and again. She would revolve it to view it from another angle, to see how differently her life might have proceeded had she simply told the truth. Other weighty moments, already lived, she frequently revisited: that instant when she'd looked over the breakfast fire and, because of her mother's admonishing eyes, kept from her father the discovery of a headless guardia; that instant when she'd pulled her mother, little Tino in her arms, toward the arroyo and Pru's hut; that instant when she had kept Gaspar Díaz's whereabouts from the unionist until it was too late. Thus it was in every life. In an instant, you elected one thing over another. In an instant, the choice made all the difference.

"I'm not holding anything back," Jacinta said, because it came to her in a flash that if she told the truth, she did not know what she would want from Miguel once he knew her secret. Her future lay before her: her own path, leading to herself. She would stay with

Magda, who, in an astonishing coincidence, would have a child, too, in February. Two babies raised in Magda's house, one of them her own. How could Miguel offer her more?

"¿Estás segura?" he asked.

"Of course I'm sure," she replied.

Afterward, when she was home, Jacinta sought out Juana's company. The laundress was in the traspatio, laying soapy clothing over the bushes growing against the back wall. Juana came to sit at the edge of the hallway next to Jacinta. They both looked out across the patio. Jacinta jutted her chin in the direction of the bushes shrouded with laundry. "My mother used to bleach clothes like that," she said. After a moment, she dropped her chin into her chest. Before long, hot tears dripped into her lap. "I miss my mother," she whispered.

Jacinta began to go to church. Each morning, she arrived long before mass, just as the sky turned pink. She wasn't there for mass; she was there to sit on a burnished pew under the immense vault of the nave, taking in the lingering pungency of copal, looking up the broad aisle at the altar on which loomed the statue of Christ, dark faced and compassionate. Banks of candles glimmered in blue glass on the altar. Niches in the wall displayed virgins and saints with their exposed and wounded hearts. To the left of the main altar, a smaller one honored la Virgen Dolorosa, and it was here Jacinta ended her morning visits. Wrapped in Mercedes's old tapado, she dropped a one-centavo piece into the coin-box slot and heard its dull *ka-chunk* before lighting a tall votive candle with a reed of kindling. As the wick caught and held, she glanced at the yellowing slips of paper, the ragged-edged cardboard sections, the flat squares of tin, all tacked haphazardly on the wall beside the altar, each imploring heaven with its own singular plea: Through the intercession of your Blessed Mother, rescue me, O Lord, from this shame. Or, May my man live one hundred years more than me. Or, Little dolorous Mother, are we meant to be oxen in this life? Jacinta knelt at the severe prie-dieu, her head bowed before Our Lady. She willed her mind to picture nothingness, which is to say, she did not pray. She did not pray about her child, that it be allowed its life. She did not pray about Miguel, that she might find the words to tell him they must break it off. Though her time was running out (she had, at best, a month before she started showing), she did not pray for more time in which to utter this. She did not pray for strength. Or for peace of mind. Or for happiness. In short, she did not pray for anything. She was simply very still for five or ten minutes, after which she rose and stepped toward the main altar to genuflect before the Christ, signing herself and kissing her thumb. Hastening up the main aisle, she passed Basilio, who, hat in hand, was always waiting at the back.

This morning, having reached home, Basilio was about to press the service-entrance buzzer when Jacinta said, "Do me a favor, will you?" She had to speak over Bruno's ruckus. The dog was on the shed roof and barking down at them.

Basilio yelled up to quiet the dog. Then he said to Jacinta, "What do you want me to do?"

"When you go to the post office this afternoon, I want you to stand in Miguel's line. Tell him I can't meet him. Just tell him, 'Jacinta says she can't come today.' Just say that, will you?"

Basilio bobbed his head and then pressed the buzzer.

The day stretched out long, dividing itself into two distinct halves: the "he doesn't know yet" half, and the "now he does" one. Since the morning and most of the afternoon belonged to the former, Jacinta went about her chores, keeping an eye on Basilio when he was in the garden or out in the garage taking a slow chamois to don Alvaro's roadster, keeping herself from rushing up to Basilio to say, You know what I asked you to do today? Well, don't do it. I've changed my mind.

Sometime past three, when the first division of the day gave way inexorably to the second, Jacinta pictured Basilio inching down Miguel's line, nudging Magda's correspondence toward him when he reached the window, uttering the words she'd asked him to say. She pictured Miguel's face. She could see, as if she were standing at his window herself, the little look of surprise breaking over it, and then his frown that was a way of seeking explanations.

Jacinta was in the linen closet, the one unlocked by the long plain key, when all her imagining ran its course and dried up. She closed up the closet then and went in search of Basilio, who evidently was home from the post office and from picking up the children at school. She could hear the boys carousing in the patio with Tea, so she headed there and looked for him. He was not in the garden nor in his shed. And he was not in the garage. Instead, he was sweeping down the front sidewalk in such a way that pedestrians had to make a wide path around him before continuing.

"What are you doing?" Jacinta said. "You don't need to do that. It's going to rain soon." She pointed up at the sky, at the dark clouds that every day at this time collected there.

"I know," he said, and continued his furious sweeping.

She went to stand beside him, raising her voice above the rasping of his broom. "Did you go to the post office?"

He nodded. Scratch, scratch went the broom.

"Did you do what I said?"

He nodded again.

"What did he say when you told him?"

"He wanted to know if you were sick."

"What?"

"That's what he said. He said, 'Is Jacinta sick?' "

"What did you tell him?"

"I said I didn't know. I said, 'She just told me to say she couldn't come.' "

Jacinta went over to the front door with its big iron ring that served as a knocker. Basilio stopped sweeping and came to stand beside her. "So tell me, are you sick?"

"No, I'm not."

"Oh," he said, "because if you're sick . . ."

He did not finish the sentence because Jacinta interrupted him. "I'm not sick," she said. "I'm going to have a baby, and I don't want Miguel to know. He must never know, do you understand that?"

Basilio nodded, struck dumb by the revelation.

"Soon, it'll be over between us," Jacinta said. She looked toward the post office four blocks away, toward Miguel's line and his window with its little gate and the slender bars.

A week later, at midmorning, after the house was running smoothly, Jacinta stole out the back entrance and caught the bus to Pilar's. The bus was crowded and all the seats were taken, so she made the ten-minute trip standing in the aisle, holding on to the overhead bar. This vantage point suited her, given that from the aisle the post office went unnoticed when they passed it. For two weeks she had not seen Miguel. Twice Basilio had brought him her regrets, the last time only yesterday.

Today, she needed Pilar to help make sense of the clatter in her head that had caused her to vacillate between breaking up with Miguel and telling him the truth and taking her chances. Jacinta got off the bus and started down the street, feeling herself brighten at the mere sight of her friend's turquoise house. Pilar's door was ajar and Jacinta pushed it open. "I only have a minute," she called as she strode in, but then she stopped short because Pilar was in the middle of a fitting.

Pilar's client was a large woman with broad hips and her hair swept up atop her head. She was facing Pilar's floor mirror with her back to the door. Still Jacinta knew, in a jolt of recognition, who it was standing there in her slip, one plump arm thrown up into a graceful curve above her head.

"I'll wait in the kitchen," Jacinta said, gliding past Pilar, whose eyes widened when she saw her friend burst in. Jacinta pulled a chair out from the kitchen table, quietly so as not to call attention to herself, and dropped onto it. She looked down at her uniform, at the apron that thankfully covered her belly and imminent evidence. Pilar poked her head into the kitchen. She smiled brightly, her eyes still wild. "I'm almost through with Olivia. Make yourself at home," she said, then popped back out again. It might not have been so, but Jacinta was certain Pilar put special emphasis on the word "Olivia."

Jacinta sat in the kitchen as the two continued their conversation in the front room.

"Here. Slip this on," Pilar said.

There was a pause, and then Olivia said, "Oh, it's going to be so pretty!" And then, "So, like we were saying, if I was Inocencia I would never, in all my life, take Bárbara's baby. What a martyr she is. To agree to take her sister and her husband's love child."

"Turn back this way."

"Poor Inocencia. If you ask me, she's too good. And what does she get for being good? She gets a roving husband and a disgrace for a sister. There is no justice, I tell you. In all my life, I could never live through that."

"Stand still, Olivia. You're moving too much."

"Oh, sorry."

"Where do you want the hem? Is this too short?"

"Right here. Mark it right here." There was a pause, and then, "Yes, right there."

"I think that's too short."

"It's that I'm too fat, isn't it, Pilar?"

"I didn't say that, Olivia."

"I know you didn't, but look at me. I'm just too fat."

"You've had three babies, Olivia; don't forget that."

"Yes, but so have you, and look at you; you're not fat. Miguel hates that I'm fat. He doesn't say it, but he does. I know he does."

"I'm sure he understands."

"He's too good to me. He is. It's true. I'm going to go on a diet. No more pupusas and curtido. No more tamales and queso Petacones. No more semita. You'll see. I can do it. And it'll make him happy. Do you think this dress will make him happy, Pilar? It's his favorite color. It's blue."

Jacinta pushed back the chair and went through the door that led outside from the kitchen. She rounded the house and soon she boarded the bus. When it stopped at the post office, she got off and went inside and stood in Miguel's line. When she reached his window, he looked at her, the smile on his face almost enough to topple her intent.

"Tomorrow. At three. En La Amapola," she said, turning on a heel and heading for home before he could answer.

In the future, when Jacinta and Basilio reminisced, and they would reminisce about this because it was the nature of longing to offer both the bitter and the sweet for nostalgic review, Basilio would say that she was a coiled spring that day before her last meeting with Miguel. No, he would say, correcting himself, you were like a caged animal being poked at through bars. This, of course, was his way of reminding her how much snapping and snarling and pacing she had done. All of which I needed, she would say. I needed an angry hot energy to help me get through that thing I had to do.

Per her dictum, they met at La Amapola at three. She did not change out of her uniform, relying on the shielding nature of her apron, but more than that, wanting to present herself as she was: a woman whose mission it was to serve. And she meant that in the noblest sense, for to serve was to aid, to assist, to care for. He took pride, she knew, in such a mission himself, for he, too, was a man of service. "I'm a civil servant," he had said on more than one occasion.

La Amapola was busy when she came in, though not as crowded as it usually was at lunchtime. Still, there were plenty of people. Miguel was at a back table, and he rose when she approached him. Nervously, he twice reached to center his tie even before she finished sitting down.

"Have you been sick?" he asked, leaning over his coffee and so far toward her that the end of his tie slipped into his cup. "Look at you. You look so thin."

She lifted his tie out of the coffee and used the napkin to dry it. "No, I haven't been sick."

"Oh, look at the mess," he said, taking the tie from her, completing the job she had begun.

She decided right then that she must charge ahead, say what she had to say, get up, and get out. There was danger everywhere, and it threatened to ruin everything. There was danger in the sweet boyishness that came over him as he mopped up his tie. Danger in the fullness of his arms. Danger in his big capable hands, lighting now a cigarette, poking the little matchstick between his lips.

"I don't have much time," she said. "I can only stay a minute."

The waitress came up and asked for her order. "No, gracias," she said. "I don't want anything."

"But you should have something," he said when the waitress moved on. "Look at you. You're much too thin." He plucked the matchstick from his lips and, smiling conspiratorially, pushed it toward her across the table.

Ignoring his offering, she plunged in: "Miguel, there is no other way to say this. We can't go on."

He sat back in his chair, as if pushed against it by an invisible force. "What do you mean, we can't go on?"

"I mean just that. You and me. We can't go on."

He looked around him. Lowered his voice. "But why? What have I done? Have I done something? Tell me what I've done." He mashed the cigarette out.

"I don't want to discuss it. We can't go on; that's all I have to say." That wounded look that clouded his eyes was danger, as was the little tremor that tugged at the corner of his mouth. She took in a long breath for reinforcement, seeing in her mind's eye a woman in a slip, seeing the curve of one plump arm thrown up in an elegant gesture of surrender. And she saw the woman's long neck, the up-sweep of thick shining hair, the tendrils, their lazy swirls, lying along the top of her shoulders.

He leaned toward her again, moving his cup aside, so he could get even closer. "You don't love me, is that what this is about?"

"Miguel . . . ," she began.

"Tell me you don't love me," he interrupted, whispering this, his words fierce and very clear. "Look me in the eyes and tell me you don't love me."

For this she needed her greatest medicine. Since yesterday, she had clutched it to her, hoarded it, said it to herself again and again. The woman in the slip: *In all my life, I could never live through that.*

"Say it. Look me in the eye, and tell me you don't love me."

She looked into his face. His eyes were moist. They were the color of dark honey. "No te quiero, Miguel."

He held her gaze. "Say it again. I don't believe you."

"I don't love you, Miguel."

He leaned back away from her then. Centered his black tie against the whiteness of his shirt. "Very well," he said.

She stood up, laid a finger on the little matchstick, but then walked away from it and from him.

The next morning, at church, her eyes puffy from weeping, her limbs leaden from a sleepless night, Jacinta lit a candle in a ruby glass and knelt before the Holy Mother. She bowed her head. Very softly, she said, "Sweet Mother of God, like yours, my heart is bleeding." She stopped there. What more was there to say? It might have been comforting to think about her baby, but her baby was like the end of a pin, too small to see, too unsubstantial yet to imagine. So she knelt there, and soon the tears began again, hot and fat, sliding down her cheeks, collecting in the folds of her mother's tapado that was a shroud around shoulders and head.

The grief she felt was a pain between her breasts and in her belly. It was black butterfly wings spread over these soft tender places. It was the weight of all her torments pressing down, pressing down. "Ay, Madrecita," she kept repeating in a whisper. O, little Mother.

After a time, she pulled herself up, drying her eyes with an end of Mercedes's tapado. She went over to the wall of petitions. She tacked one up herself. On a slip of new white paper, the question ¿Por qué? Why?

▼▼

CHAPTER THIRTY-SEVEN

W hen tossing and turning became his nightly rest, when hardly anything his wife prepared could rouse his appetite, when his children's most frequent lament became "pobrecito Papá," when no book, no magazine, no newspaper interested him, no conversation stimulated him, no event motivated him, when on the radio the tangos of Carlos Gardel sent him out to pace along the sidewalk, a cigarette hanging from his lip, smoke curling up into his face, the smoke and memories turning his eyes to water, when standing behind his postal window was torture because every patron approaching might be her, Miguel Acevedo walked out of the post office one day after work and headed for Magda de Tobar's house at Tercera Avenida Norte y Septima Calle Poniente. The place was only blocks away and as he neared it, he felt suddenly alive after four months of living among the dead.

When he reached the house, he used the big iron knocker to announce himself. The rapping started a dog barking somewhere behind the door. Miguel waited patiently, surprised at how calm he was. Out on the street, cars and buses rolled past; on the sidewalk, people strolled by; birds perched and chittered on a leafed-out branch that curved over the wall of the house; and the sun, though its light was slanting down, still warmed his back and the iron ring of the door. All things purposefully employed, he thought. And now he, too, was occupied with purpose.

The wide door of the house swung open. The young man who usually came for the mail stood there. If memory served, his name was Basilio. Behind him ran a small cobbled driveway, and beyond that, the main door of the house.

"¿Sí?" the young man said.

"Do you remember me?" Miguel said. "You're Basilio, correct?"

A quick nod that did not jostle the wide-brimmed hat he wore.

"I want to talk to Jacinta. Jacinta Prieto. I believe she works here."

"How did you know to come here?"

"I work at the post office, don't I? Addresses are my business."

There was a pause and then Basilio said, "Come around the back." He looped a finger in the air to indicate the path to be taken. "To the service entrance. There's a buzzer there." He pushed the door closed.

Miguel stood there for a moment, a current of feeling charging through him because very soon, it seemed, he would lay eyes on Jacinta, and now he realized how rash he'd been to come without giving a thought to what he might say to her, to how he might say it. He hastened down the sidewalk and turned the corner—the house took up most of the block—and the back entrance was there, a regular-size door next to what was clearly a garage. He pressed the little black button and the dog started up again. Miguel thrust his hands deep into his pockets, reaching down that way to steady himself.

The service door opened and Basilio reappeared. He pulled the door so it remained ajar behind him.

"Where's Jacinta?" Miguel asked.

"She can't come." Basilio pushed his hat back with a thumb so that it sat farther back on his head.

"What do you mean? I thought you went to get her."

"She doesn't want to see you."

"Is that what she said? Did she say that?"

"She doesn't want to see you." Basilio kept his gaze steady and expressionless.

"Where is she? I want to talk to her."

"She's not here." Basilio stepped up on the sill, his back to the door.

"But you said she didn't want to see me. If she's not here, how could she say that?"

"She's not here. And she doesn't want to see you." Basilio thrust the door open with a shoulder and stepped back into the traspatio. Before closing the door, he said, "She never wants to see you."

The buzzer went off once more. Again and again in short, insistent bursts. Eventually, they stopped.

Basilio went into the kitchen. The cook was at the stove stirring diced onions and big chunks of tomatoes around in a large iron frying pan. Jacinta was at the kitchen table. She was seven months pregnant and her legs tended to swell, so she sat on one chair with both legs propped up on another. "Those tomatoes smell good," she said to the cook. To Basilio, she said, "Who was that out there ringing the door down?"

Basilio hooked his hat on the rung of the chair. "Nobody important," he said, "just a man begging."

▼▼

CHAPTER THIRTY-EIGHT

February 3, 1947

The telephone call announcing the birth of Magda's child came in to Elena's house while she was out. Lent had just begun, and she liked to rise early and walk to the cathedral to attend mass. This morning, the big clock in Santa Ana's plaza was striking eight when she rounded her street corner and almost collided with the inside girl, hurrying toward her. "¡Niña Elenita!" the servant exclaimed. "They called! They called!"

"Who called?" Elena said, feeling a rush of foreboding. It was coffee-picking season, and Ernesto had left at daybreak for the finca. Today was payday and, God knew, paydays had ways of erupting into disquiet.

"Don Alvaro from San Salvador," the servant said, her dark round face intent and ebullient. "He said to tell you la niña Magda had a little girl."

Elena clapped her hands together. "¡A Dios gracias!" She had two other granddaughters—her sons each had one, but this glad news, that her only daughter now had an only daughter herself, placed this baby in a category of her own. "But, my God, she's a week early," Elena said, realizing it. She went off toward the house and the telephone.

Elena made three calls. One was to the hospital, where she

learned that, despite the early birth, her daughter and Florencia Elena (only this name had been chosen, for there was never a doubt in Magda's mind that she was carrying a girl) were healthy and well. Her second call was to the finca, where Ernesto promised to leave as soon as the payroll was completed. Next, Elena rang the hospital back to advise Magda that she and Ernesto would arrive late in the day.

After breakfast, Elena had the servant bring suitcases out of storage and into the bedroom. The two began to pack. Magda would be confined for forty days, the first few of these spent in the hospital. During Magda's convalescence, Elena would occupy a spare bedroom and help see to the house and to the boys. She would serve as hostess to the many visitors. And she would help plan the baby's baptism and all its attendant festivities: the church ceremony, the elegant tea to be offered afterward at home. Such an at-home schedule made packing easy, calling, as it did, only for day dresses and a single party dress, an afternoon dress at that. At Elena's direction, the inside girl brought clothing in from the dressing room, laying it on the bed for Elena's selection.

"This was in your dresser, niña Elenita," she said now, extending an envelope while attempting not to spill a stack of slippery underwear she was balancing on a forearm.

"Let's see," Elena said, taking the envelope and then almost dropping it when she saw it was Cecilia's old letter the servant had offered. "Put the underwear there," Elena went on to say, pointing to a cleared spot on the bed. "I'll need the shoes I picked out next." Elena placed the envelope on the night table, turning quickly away from the dark blue scrawl of Cecilia's handwriting. Fourteen years had passed, and the letter had not been opened. For the first few months after Ernesto had carried it across the street from Cecilia's house, the letter had remained where he had placed it: propped on the vanity against a bottle of Lanvin. For months, Elena had not laid a hand on the perfume or on the letter. When she sat before her mirror and her gaze swept over the table, she squinted to blur her vision lest the sight of Cecilia's handwriting break her down. Eventually, she had buried the letter at the bottom of the dresser, slipping it into one of the silk bags she owned for storing handkerchiefs and hosiery. Over the years, she had moved the letter from one dresser drawer to another. Where exactly it had been when the servant happened upon it today, Elena could not say. Enough that it was on the night table now, filling the room with its presence.

Elena continued to pack and, despite her efforts, to remember: Cecilia and she, two small children swinging giddily on the columpios hanging from the big oak in Elena's childhood patio. Cecilia and she swaying back and forth in perfect lazy rhythm, their chubby legs pointing up together toward a blue cloudless sky. Elena shook her head to clear it. Of all the scenes to be recalled, why that one radiant remembrance?

"Here are the shoes," the girl said, coming back into the room. She clutched a number of pairs awkwardly to her chest.

Elena took the shoes from her; one of them escaped both their grasps and fell to the floor. The servant bent to reach it. "No, don't worry about that," Elena said. "Just put that letter back in the dresser where you found it. I'll take care of the rest of it."

"Very well," the girl said. She did as Elena asked and then went off to other household chores.

Elena turned back to her packing. Her hands smoothed and folded linen and sarcenet dresses, silky underthings, batiste nightgowns, a jaconet dressing gown. Contrastingly, her heart went over coarser matters: betrayal, fury, misery. Elena squeezed her eyes shut against the sting of coming tears. Your absence, Cecilia, she thought. Your absence is the greatest presence in my life.

Elena and Ernesto rode in the new Buick Roadmaster made affordable by rising coffee prices. Between them, on the broad leather seat of the sedan, lay Ernesto's revolver, its dull grip poking out of a weathered holster. During the trip, they spoke of little Florencia, asking themselves whom she might resemble and making lists about how they would spoil her. As they drove, Elena felt the ice re-form over the gentle, thawing memories of Cecilia. She had allowed her resolve to waver. In the future, she must guard against this. Succumbing to maudlin remembrances would bring a whirlwind into their lives again. Perhaps even awaken dreams of crumbling teeth.

They entered into the little town of El Congo. The car bumped over the cobblestone streets as they went around the town square, a cheerless spot devoid of trees. They turned off the square and passed the mesón where, years before, Mercedes's wake had taken place. How sad, Elena thought, that any day now Jacinta will give birth and her mother will not be there to pamper her. "Pobrecita la Mercedes," Elena said, her eyes sweeping over the long line of mesón doors. "Poor Mercedes."

On the opposite corner of the street, a knot of men, some inebriated by the looks of them, all with machetes dangling at their sides, were clumped around a cantina door. One man stepped off the sidewalk, and Ernesto stepped on the brakes. He laid a hand on his revolver, all the time watching the man lurch and weave across the street. Ernesto started off again. He shook his head. "Another picker wastes his pay," he said. "Pobrecito El Salvador."

As they drove on, Elena turned her attention to her husband. She fixed her eyes on his profile, on the curve of his cheek, the long line of his nose, the fullness of his mouth. She watched his sure hands, how they grasped the shiny black wheel, how he laid a quick hand over the round knob of the floor shift. She looked out the window, certain of one thing. Tonight, she would love her husband long and hard. It was always like that. When Cecilia's live ghost rose up to haunt her, it drove her directly into Ernesto's arms.

At the hospital, a celebration was in full swing. Alvaro Tobar had set aside the room next to Magda's for visitors. He had stocked it with a full bar. The room was bustling with men, both family and friends. The air was blue with cigarette smoke and with off-color stories of amorous conquests and vigorous copulation. Next door, in Magda's room, the women to whom the men belonged had congregated. They lined the wall, sitting stalwartly on straight-backed chairs, their legs crossed demurely at the ankles, their stylish pocketbooks resting like small battlements on their laps. Occasionally, one of the older women hooked an arm through her purse handle and poked her head into the adjoining room in a futile attempt to quiet things down. "Boys, boys, what a racket," the woman would say, raising her voice above the merriment.

Magda had long given in to the commotion. She had birthed

her sons in her own bed at home, used the same bed to recuperate upon. But now hospital deliveries were the modern thing to do. Yet, clearly, it was not in the hospital that a woman could rest. This room was abuzz with birthing tales and boastful comparisons: lengths and severities of labor, alarming circumferences of certain babies' heads, various perilous deliveries, be they breech or traverse, and always Clara Fermina droning on with the age-old account of how her little Sebastián (who was now fifty-two and in the very next room) first reached out into this world with a tiny hand and a tiny foot.

Magda lay against the downy pillows that her sister-in-law jumped up periodically to fluff. Bed and bath linens had been brought from home: pillows, sheets, towels, all white, all emblazoned with Magda's personal monogram. The bedspread extending over the bed was handmade for the occasion, fashioned from fine linen, intercut with lace. Leonor smoothed the spread. She was refolding it over Magda's legs yet again when Elena and Ernesto popped into the room. Alvaro followed close behind. The arrival precipitated a new fuss of greetings and congratulations that died away when the others stepped into the hall to give the family privacy.

Elena leaned over the bed and embraced Magda. Ernesto did the same. "We peeked in the nursery," Elena said. "What a precious baby Florencia is! She has the biggest eyes and such a head of curly hair."

"She looks just like her father," Magda said.

Alvaro stood at the foot of the bed. "Magda did good work, don't you think?"

"She did very good work," Elena said.

"It wasn't *all* my doing," Magda said, casting a smile in her husband's direction.

Alvaro rocked back on his heels and grinned. He was on top of the world. His beautiful wife had given birth to a beautiful daughter. His family was complete. Was there any doubt that now his wife would stay at home?

Ernesto Contreras sat on one of the chairs and crossed his legs. He motioned toward the adjoining room. "What a party in there. I expect you can't wait for the peace you'll find at home."

"She'll have the rest of her life at home," Alvaro said.

"She'll have forty days," Elena added, plumping up Magda's pillows.

"That's right," Magda said, agreeing with her mother but being purposefully vague for her husband's sake.

▼▼▼

CHAPTER THIRTY-NINE

February 5, 1947

Jacinta, one week overdue and her belly like a balloon ready to burst, fussed with little Florencia's moisés, the willow cradle that had always been the focal point of Magda's nurseries. For three babies, the cradle and its canopy had been lined with blue satin, but thanks to Pilar's expertise, it now featured pleated pink bunting and clusters of silk rosettes spewing tendrils of ribbon. Jacinta squatted to fluff the tiers of pink voile that obscured the cradle's pedestal. Magda and the baby would be home from the hospital in a few days; Tea and the boys had been staying at their aunt's house, and they, too, would be coming home.

Jacinta used the rim of the cradle to pull herself up, grunting a little because it seemed her baby would never arrive and she felt awkward and torpid. Since dawn there had been a dull ache, low in her back. Between her legs, a heaviness. She looked around the room, pleased at what she saw. Months before, per Magda's instructions, Basilio had decorated the nursery in shades of pink and persimmon. Also at Magda's direction, he had added a goodly amount of milk to the pigments to give them a tender cloudiness that would delight and soothe the baby, Magda said.

Jacinta ran a hand over the changing table with its padded top and its line of drawers beneath. This table had been Basilio's handiwork, too. He had used pine to make it, salvaging enough from the leftovers to make a box cradle for Jacinta's baby as well. Jacinta went around the rocking chair and rearranged the pillows on the narrow daybed that the registered nurse would be using during her stay. Dolores had tended all of Magda's babies for the first three months of their lives. She was a sturdy, middle-aged woman with a no-nonsense air that Jacinta much appreciated. Maybe while Dolores was here, she might talk some sense into Rosalba, who, since Magda had left for the hospital, had taken advantage of both the disruption in the household schedule and Jacinta's weary vulnerability. Just yesterday, Rosalba had gone off in the middle of the afternoon for who knows where. When she returned to face Jacinta's interroga-tion, Rosalba had laughed at her questions, scoffing, "I don't have to tell you anything."

At the thought of the girl's defiance, Jacinta bristled. She was angry with herself for allowing it, for being too tired to want to fool with dismissing her. Jacinta left the nursery, determined to make sure Rosalba was getting her work done. For the family's arrival, nothing but a house in perfect order would do. Jacinta went down the corredor, past the wicker settee on which the cat groomed itself in the bright sun. She looked out into the patio and then searched in the living room and the dining room as well. Where was that girl? Jacinta felt an added prick of irritation. Had the girl gone off again today? Jacinta stepped into the kitchen, but only the cook occupied the room. She walked out to the traspatio and questioned Juana, who was at the pila doing the never-ending laundry. "Allá está," Juana said, motioning toward the hall with her head. Because her hands were soapy, she scratched her nose with a forearm, then went back to her scrubbing.

When Jacinta reached her room, Rosalba was at Jacinta's dresser. She had pulled a drawer out. She had extracted from it the cigar box containing Jacinta's treasures. "What are you doing!" Jacinta cried out. Despite her cumbersome condition, she leaped across the room toward the open box resting on the dresser top, toward the bottle of seawater the girl held in her hand.

Rosalba jumped, turning to face Jacinta, her eyes wild with sur-prise.

"Give me that!" Jacinta yelled, and the girl started again and dropped the bottle. It hit the floor with a sharp crack and skitted under the dresser. Jacinta fell to her knees. She thrust an arm beneath the dresser, groping around blindly. Soon she felt the bottle lying against the wall. She felt, too, the wetness spreading along the floor tiles.

Behind her, Rosalba blubbered. "I'm sorry. I'm sorry. I didn't mean to drop it. You yelled and it scared me. I dropped it because you scared me."

Jacinta swabbed the seawater with a hand. She reached for the bottle again and pulled it out from under the dresser and looked at it. Miraculously the bottle was not broken, but not a drop of seawater remained in it.

Jacinta let out a moan; she held the bottle against herself, struggling up, her knees wet, the front hem of her uniform wet, too. On the dresser rested her treasure box. She raked a finger through its contents until her eyes fell on the matchbox with the red-and-yellow words "Fósforos La Chispa" (The Spark Matches). Jacinta gave the matchbox a shake. The contents rattled.

"There's nothing in there," Rosalba said. "Just some old blackened matches."

Basilio was sweeping the sidewalk when he heard Jacinta scream. It was a cry like the one he'd heard from her once before, years and years ago, after coming upon Mercedes's body in Chico Portales's hut. Basilio sprang through the service-entrance door and slammed it shut. He ran in the direction the screams were coming from. Juana came running, too.

They found Jacinta in her room. She had pulled out all the drawers of Rosalba's dresser. By handfuls, she was flinging drawer contents to the floor. Rosalba watched, cowering silently against the wall.

"Get out!" Jacinta yelled. "Pack your things, and get out of the house!" When she saw Basilio and Juana standing there, Jacinta yelled at them, too: "Tell her to get out! I'll kill her if she doesn't!"

Juana stretched both arms out toward Jacinta. "Easy. Easy now, girl."

▼   ▼   ▼

Jacinta allowed Basilio to walk her around the patio. While Juana saw to Rosalba's swift departure, Jacinta leaned on Basilio's arm as they went in circles around his shed and under the trees and then around the fountain. "I didn't know I could be so angry," Jacinta said.

Basilio nodded. He had never seen her in such a state. Her face so flushed. Her voice so harsh and terrifying.

"Here. Let me sit for a minute." Jacinta hobbled over to sit on the edge of the fountain because the dull ache in her back had been building and now it took a sudden sharp turn. "Ay," she said, a long breath escaping her. She kneaded her back with her fingers. The fountain tiles were very warm, and so it took a moment to realize that it was more than the sun's heat she felt under her. Jacinta bit down on her lip as a moist warmth gushed from between her legs and slipped down the fountain wall. "¡Dios mío!" she exclaimed, springing up reflexively. In an instant, pain turned her knees to rubber.

Basilio reached to steady her.

"The baby's coming," Jacinta said, each word distinct and strangulated. She cradled her belly with open hands as if with them she might stay her delivery.

Basilio led her into the shed because his cot was there. He laid her back against the scratchy blanket and the thin hard pillow that were the extent of his nightly consolations.

"Get Juana," Jacinta said, drawing her knees up and thankful for the wan light that rescued her from indecorous displays.

For a time it was like she was back in Izalco inside her mother's hut. There was the same loamy smell, the same soothing murkiness. And then it was her mother at her side, lighting the kerosene lamp, turning down the wick so that its glow was soft and comforting. It was her mother who drew the blanket out from under her. Her mother replacing it with sheets. Her mother bunching pillows up behind her. Caught in the ebb and flow of pain, Jacinta heard her mother's voice, strong and commanding: "Don't push. It's not time for that. Take deep breaths. Big deep ones."

Jacinta grasped the edges of the cot to keep from the overpowering desire she had to force her child into the world with one explosive grunt. "Very good," her mother said. "Breathe deep. Very good." For a time it went on like that.

At length a cool hand was laid on Jacinta s forehead. "Now it's time. Now you can push."

Jacinta gripped the cot sides again. She pulled herself up and pushed down with all her strength. "Push harder now." Jacinta took in another huge breath. She forced it down, down toward the bone-breaking pain, down toward the flesh-tearing pain, down toward the one moment of quick release that was like the world stopping just for her. She collapsed against the pillows, soaked through and trembling. Soon, this was said: "Look. You have a daughter." Then came the loud thin cry, the clearest sound Jacinta would ever hear.

PART THREE
▼

María
Mercedes
and
Florencia

▼▼▼

CHAPTER FORTY

San Salvador
May 1953

Socorro the cook was making tamales for Mother's Day, and Florencia and María Mercedes were helping. Unlike the old cook, who during her long tenure had considered such help as interference, Socorro welcomed the girls in the kitchen and creatively assigned them tasks. She was a large, unabashedly sunny woman of indeterminate age with a snub Indian face. She was fond of going barefoot and wore her hair in braids plaited tightly at the temples. Today Socorro had tied dish cloths around the girls' waists to serve as aprons. She had set them up at the table where the staff took their meals: Florencia, who everyone called Flor, on one end and María Mercedes on the other. The pair were stuffing the pillows of corn dough that Socorro would wrap in green husks and steam. Flor's duty was to fill the sweet tamales—tamales de azúcar—with raisins and prunes and chicken chunks; María Mercedes's, the salted ones—tamales de sal—with olives and capers and bits of ground pork and diced potatoes. The kitchen was replete with cooking odors: sweet spices and sharp seasonings, the earthy freshness of newly ground corn.

"Here, let me tie back your hair," Socorro said. María Mercedes had plunged her hands into a bowl and was bunching ground pork with her fingers. Like a dark curtain, the girl's hair swept past the sides of her face and almost fell into the bowl. Socorro split a corn husk into a long strip and used it to secure María Mercedes's hair into a ponytail.

"Do mine, too," Flor said. She was eating more raisins than she was stuffing dough with them. She had blond and curly hair, the former because she took after her grandmother Elena; the latter she had inherited from her father.

"Flor's hair's too short to tie back," María Mercedes said.

"Let's see," Socorro said, tying two husk strips together and circling Flor's head. She formed the ends of the strip into a bow and gave it a pat. When she did, her upper arms jiggled.

"Gracias, Nana," Flor said.

"Don't say that," María Mercedes said. "Tea's your nana, not Socorro." Flor called Jacinta "Nana," too, and María Mercedes didn't like it, though she could not tell you why.

Flor popped a prune into her mouth. She sucked on the meat and spit the pit into her palm. "All the servants are my nanas," Flor said. She deposited the pit carefully on the table.

María Mercedes frowned and thought of Basilio. "Basilio's not a nana," María Mercedes said. She had been born in his shed, on his cot, and this made him her father, though she did not call him that, because he discouraged it. María Mercedes frowned. "Flor, were you born on your papi's bed?" María Mercedes was six, and in that time she had not thought to ask this question.

Flor shook her head. "I was born in the hospital."

María Mercedes buried an olive in the center of a tamal. She watched the dough swallow the olive up. "Did they move your papi's bed to the hospital?"

"No, silly," Flor said. "Who ever heard of anything like that!"

María Mercedes rolled her eyes. It was obvious Flor had a small imagination. María Mercedes decided to pursue her line of questioning with the cook. "Were you born on your papi's bed, Socorro?" María Mercedes gave a giggle because she had a mental picture of the cook's big jolly body tumbling off a cot.

Socorro grunted a response. She was busy centering filled dough on corn leaves, folding and tucking them into bundles. On the stove behind her, a deep pot of boiling water bubbled out a tune. "What's all this talk about fathers and beds? It'll be Mother's Day tomorrow. It's your mamis you should be talking about."

Flor said, "I'm pinning a red rosebud on my blouse tomorrow." She poked her chin into her chest and looked down at her yellow blouse. "I'm going to wear my rose right there." Because her fingers were sticky, she only pointed to a buttonhole.

"Me, too. Only mine's going here." María Mercedes pointed her doughy fingers at her hair. The girls were referring to the tradition of honoring mothers by wearing a rose—either a red one or a white one—on Mother's Day.

"Do you have a mami, Socorro?" Flor asked.

"My mamá's in heaven. I'll have to wear a white rose to remember Mamá."

"Poor thing," Flor said, putting on a sad expression.

"It's not the dead who should be pitied," Socorro said. "It's the living. We're the poor ones in this world."

"I'm not poor," Flor said.

"That you are not, niña Flor." Socorro laid another completed tamal on the growing stack.

María Mercedes said, "I'm not either." She scraped up the last of the ground meat that was clinging to the bowl.

"Yes, you *are*," Flor said. "All servants are poor."

"I'm not a servant, am I Socorro?"

"Girls, girls," the cook said. "Today you're both servants. You're *my* servants today." Holy God, she thought.

Basilio strode in. He wore his new hat. The old one occupied a permanent place on a long nail in his shed. "Here's the mail." He laid a stack of envelopes beside the tamales.

"Look at us, Basilio. We're cooking." María Mercedes wiped her hands on her apron. "But now I'm done."

"Very good," Basilio said. "Tamales de azúcar are my favorite."

"That's what I made!" Flor said. "Now I'm finished, too." She held her hands out helplessly until Socorro wiped her fingers clean. Then she plopped down on a chair and stuck her thumb in her mouth. María Mercedes went to the sink and washed her hands and dried them off. She came over, and Flor scooted aside and the two sat together. Flor threw an arm around María Mercedes's neck.

Tea joined the others in the kitchen. "Niña, el dedo," she said, pulling Flor's thumb out of her mouth. "Did you behave for Socorro? What's that in your hair?" She removed the cornhusk bow and tossed it on the table.

"They both were good," Socorro said. "Look at all the tamales they made." She wiped her hands on her apron and began to clear the table. "It's almost time for *Las dos*. I'll get the coffee ready. There's pan dulce from yesterday."

A few years before, the radio novela had been switched from airing at noon to four o'clock. It was a less convenient time for a gathering. Still, Jacinta had not allowed the new time to keep them all from listening; she'd simply adjusted their work schedules. At four, they pulled up chairs around the table and for half an hour allowed themselves to be entranced. In this way, as was the case in all of El Salvador, it was story and coffee and, if fortune smiled, a bit of something sweet that fortified people for the work awaiting them well into evening, until the time they went to bed.

Rocío, the inside girl, walked in with Juana, who'd been at the ironing board all day. As was her habit, the laundress had rolled up her hands and arms, mummylike, in her apron. She did this because she was certain that, after hours of steamy work, if her arms took a sudden chill, she'd come down with rheumatism. "Where'd we leave off?" she said, plunking herself down on a chair and recapitulating the episode of the previous day. She always did this. That the others went about getting settled and seemingly ignored her did not dissuade her from the recitation. "Let's see. Yesterday la Bárbara came back from her six-year trip around the world. We left off when she decided to finally meet her little daughter."

Jacinta slipped into the room. She helped Socorro pass the rolls and coffee around. On the radio, the merry tune of the sponsor announced the program's opening.

For half an hour, the real world fell away. For half an hour it was Inocencia in her wheelchair (the good sister had lost both her filandering husband and the use of her legs after an emergency thirteen-hour operation for a rare disease of the spine) and Dulce Alegría (Sweet Happiness), her sister's daughter. Today mother met daughter in a tearful, moving reunion.

After the program ended, there was stunned silence for some

moments. Then Juana said, "Can you imagine? And just in time for Mother's Day." She rose as the others were doing, and started off toward the final stack of daily shirts dampening on the ironing board.

Basilio scraped back his chair. He reached for his hat and placed it on his head. "I got the mail," he said to Jacinta. Basilio jutted his chin in the mail's direction. "There's a letter there for you."

Jacinta glanced at the envelopes sitting on the table. For more than seven years she had not been to the post office. But each time Basilio brought the mail, it was as if he'd brought something of Miguel Acevedo with him. Hadn't they stood on the same planked floor? Hadn't the same burnished walls surrounded them? Though she ached for word of him, she'd prohibited Basilio from mentioning Miguel's name, from bringing her any news. This cutting herself off from her beloved she had done for her daughter's sake, and for Miguel's sake as well. Nor was Pilar any longer privy to information she might have been compelled to pass along. Five years ago, she had moved out of the colonia her family had shared with Miguel's.

It was María Mercedes who this time riffled through the mail. She handed her mother an envelope. "Here's yours, Mamá." María Mercedes could not read or write as yet, but she knew how to spell all the names of the people in the household.

The letter was from El Congo. When Jacinta noted the return address, she let out a quiet breath. Absurd as it was, each time a letter came for her, she was certain it was from Miguel. "Wait Basilio; don't go. There's news from Chenta."

Basilio remained in the kitchen doorway. He knew who the letter was from. Chenta was the only person who sent Jacinta letters, though over the years Miguel Acevedo had sent three. Two of them soon after Jacinta broke off with him. The third just last year. Basilio had intercepted them all, and following Jacinta's firm instructions, he had not mentioned them to her. He had not opened the letters either, of course, but he had saved them. He'd secured them with a rubber band, wrapping the bundle in a length of butcher paper for camouflage. He'd stashed the packet behind a can of nails set on a high shelf in his shed.

Jacinta read Chenta's letter aloud. It began in the customary way: "I hope that when you receive this, you and Basilio and María

Mercedes find yourselves in good health and fine spirits." The letter went on to describe Chenta's swollen feet. The long hours she put in at her eating place. The gossip emanating from it. Still, all was well in El Congo. The weather had been kind. The neighbors were solicitous and therefore a solace. But greater solace, she said, would come from seeing them at her door. "Do you think you and Basilio and María Mercedes could grant me a few days?" Chenta asked. "It would do me a world of good to see you all again."

"We should go," Basilio said. "Doña Chenta's not getting any younger."

"Maybe we could," Jacinta replied. "But I have no weekend free till the end of June. Maybe if I ask far in advance, la niña Magda will give us both the time off."

Basilio nodded and went out the door. Since moving to San Salvador, he had been in El Congo only once. It would please him to return. To return this time with both Jacinta and María Mercedes. The three of them. Like a little family going home again.

María Mercedes, her face lifted to the sun, stood next to the water basin. Jacinta used a pan to scoop water from the pila and rinse her. When the cool water slipped down her sleek naked body, María Mercedes bunched her hands under her chin and hunched her shoulders to her neck. She raised herself on tiptoe and gave a quick jump. "There," Jacinta said, "all clean." She wrapped a towel around her daughter and walked her across the traspatio and down the hall into their room. The two had the space all to themselves. This arrangement, convenient as it was, had not been orchestrated by Jacinta. Since Rosalba's departure, Rocío, her replacement, had lived in the room. But last year, Rocío had moved into the larger room next door with Tea and Socorro. Rocío, unlike her name, which meant "dew," was a wizened, childless woman who worked hard and whose patience with children ran out after four years of sharing quarters with one. Jacinta, who'd always felt awkwardly privileged given her advantages in Magda's house, went begging to get Rocío back. But Rocío was adamant. She would remain with Tea and Socorro, who preferred living three in a room to sharing with Jacinta and María Mercedes. It was an unpleasant situation, but not a hateful one. Socorro and Tea had children of their own. Children they'd left behind in home villages and in the care of relatives. They hoped Jacinta understood, they said, and no offense. Sharing a room with a child like their own was troubling.

Jacinta helped her daughter into a green dress with puffy sleeves and a wide sash. Thanks to Pilar, María Mercedes's wardrobe was plentiful. "Turn around. I'll make a bow." Jacinta fluffed the sash material until it stood out prettily. She went on to brush María Mercedes's thick hair, taming with vigorous strokes the unruly strands that sprung out around her face. She chose a pink ribbon to hold the hair in place. "You're all bows today," Jacinta said.

The service-door buzzer went off, and Bruno started his furious barking. María Mercedes sprung off the bed. "Nanda's here!" Pilar's daughter, who was now fifteen, dropped by every Sunday and took María Mercedes to mass. Jacinta herself did not attend. Since giving up Miguel, she felt God had given up on her.

▼▼

CHAPTER FORTY-ONE

Santa Ana

"And why citronella candles?" Ernesto Contreras asked Alvaro Tobar, his son-in-law.

"Because citronella repels insects, and God knows there are plenty of them in the country to be repelled. Because the candles being made at present are crude and of mercado quality. At our factory, we'll manufacture finer candles for all types of uses. For the house. The porch. The patio." Alvaro leaned back in his chair. He was full and felt pleasantly drowsy. He had just eaten a good meal— roast loin of pork run through with garlic, whipped potatoes with petits pois. He brought a hand to his mouth and burped softly behind it. He and Ernesto, as well as a number of other family members, were relaxing on the wide veranda of Ernesto and Elena's house. It was a Sunday afternoon in June. While it was hot, quick bursts of breeze rustled the leaves of the orange trees in the patio. After lunch, the men had grouped themselves at this end of the porch, close to the dining room where two servants circled the linen-draped table gathering up dirty plates and goblets, serving dishes and silverware. The family women, on the other hand, were clustered at the opposite end of the porch. Some had taken out embroidery hoops and thimbles, while a few worked at enhancing the breeze with slender Spanish fans. In contrast to the adults, the children—sisters, brothers, cousins—bounded gleefully around the patio and in and out of rooms. Their grandmother's meal, including a fig compote with clotted cream for dessert, had obviously energized them.

These family luncheons had become a monthly event at the Contreras house. Ernesto instituted them the year before Florencia, his last grandbaby, was born, and just after he dreamed his teeth had turned to dust in his mouth. This had been Elena's old nightmare, and when it visited him for the one and only time, he had awoken in a sweat, his mind swirling with the image of crumbling teeth and of a skeletal left hand, its bony finger ringed with a distorted, tarnished wedding band. That night, Ernesto had heaved himself out of bed, stumbled into the bathroom, and turned on the light to absurdly inspect both hand and mouth in the mirror. He went then into his dressing room and stared at the tiny silver tray on the dresser that still contained Elena's wedding ring. Both tray and ring were black with oxidation. In the morning, he had not shared the dream with Elena. Convinced that it had been meant for her, he was thankful for the miracle that had allowed him to intercept it.

For days after, his head swam with death thoughts. He pictured his father, a pasty giant in his casket, and don Orlando, Elena's father, a shrunken little man in his. He pictured other relatives and those unfortunate friends whom death had snatched up. To hie such thoughts away, Ernesto called his family home the very weekend after the dream. His entire family, which meant his children, their spouses, his grandchildren, his children's in-laws. As if it were Christmas, he had the house opened up, deriving such comfort from the family's presence that he'd announced, then and there, the start of a tradition: a get-together on the second Sunday of each month, at noon after mass.

On the porch, Neto, Ernesto's older son, now forty, took a long pull on his cigar. He allowed the smoke to escape lazily from his lips, casting around him the pungent smell of tobacco sweetened with rum. "Isn't citronella a type of lemongrass?"

"That's right," Alvaro said. "Both have aromatic oils used in perfume making and flavorings. Fortunately most insects are repelled by its smell."

"If citronella is a grass, it must grow like a weed," Alberto, Ernesto's other son, observed.

"Exactly!" Alvaro said. "A very valuable weed. I plan to set aside a good number of hectares on the coast. I'll cultivate it along with my cotton."

"That should help you with Article one-thirty-eight!" Neto said.

All the men laughed at the remark. Article 138 was a sticking point for the rich in El Salvador's new consititution enacted three years earlier. This recent ratification (since independence from Spain, El Salvador had ratified a number of constitutions) was brought about by Major Oscar Osorio, the sitting president. It provided, among other reforms, for a minimum wage (except for farm workers) and placed limits on working hours for labor. Article 138 declared that land could be expropriated if it was legally proven that a property owner failed in his civic duty to care for the land, or if he failed to have a "social conscience" regarding the people he employed to work on it. If, due to such failings, a property was expropriated, indemnification was to be paid in installments not to exceed twenty years.

Tío Fidel, who was such a close friend of the family's that all called him "uncle," and who in seven years hadn't missed a luncheon, asked, "How's your social conscience, Alvaro?" El tío sported a dapper mustache that looked like a stiff white brush. When he asked the question, he stroked it with a quick hand, then set his mouth into a grin.

"It's very well, thank you very much," Alvaro parried. "As evidence of it, I employ thousands of campesinos. I house them. I feed them. I pay them well. When I start growing citronella, that'll mean more work, more jobs for people."

El tío lifted both hands in surrender. "My goodness, boy, I was only joking. I didn't mean to rile you."

Alvaro's brother-in-law jumped in with a remark that dissipated any tension. "This candle venture should entitle you to tax exemptions." He was a coffee planter and financier. He relied upon the tax concessions that coffee growers had been enjoying for years.

Alvaro gave a rueful laugh. He shot a glance down the veranda at his mother sitting with the ladies. "My mother always chided me for being in cotton instead of coffee. You coffee growers get all the breaks. But now it appears my time's finally come. Osorio's industrial development law is my ticket to both a tax break and easy credit."

"The president's been on a seesaw of concessions and repression," the brother-in-law said. "Take revolutionaries. On the one hand he represses open demonstrations, which is good. But then he condones advocates of milder reforms, urging them to form opposition parties."

"And he's allowed trade unions," Ernesto said.

"As long as they behave themselves," Alberto added. "As long as the unions accept the fact their activities are being carefully monitored."

The brother-in-law shook his head. "Like I said, Osorio's government is one big seesaw."

Júnior Tobar said, "Papá and I plan to take advantage of Osorio's concessions." Júnior, who had recently graduated from Rutgers with a degree in business, had a head full of ideas and was eager to make his mark.

"How's that?" tío Fidel asked.

"We'll manufacture here for all of Central America," Alvaro said, speaking for his son.

Júnior was sitting with one leg crossed wide over his knee, a hand around his ankle. He was wearing blue denim trousers, white sport socks, and moccasins, a habit he'd acquired in New Jersey but one that was not popular with the older members of his family. "And we'll take in a foreign partner." He tugged the hem of his trouser down over his sock.

Alvaro went on, "The law says that if a foreign investor contributes fifty percent of the capital, the business qualifies for tax and tariff exemptions."

"Have you found a partner yet?" Alberto asked.

"Actually, we've found two," Alvaro said.

"Abraham Salah is one," Júnior said.

"Ramón Salah, Abraham's cousin, is the other," Alvaro added.

"Abraham Salah?" tío Fidel remarked. "That's Benjamin's son. The Salahs are in textiles."

"The cousin Ramón is in textiles, too," Júnior said. "But in the States. In North Carolina actually. So he's our foreign investor. He can use the tax break there. We can use our own here. And, needless to say, the Salahs' know-how in factory setup and operations will be invaluable."

"Not to mention our being able to take advantage of their extensive markets," Alvaro said.

"That's all very clever," Alberto observed.

Ernesto Contreras repositioned himself in the chair. Abraham Salah. That was Cecilia's son-in-law. Ernesto looked toward the women gossiping animatedly at the other end of the veranda. From where he sat, he could see Elena's back rising over the top of the wicker settee. He could see her hair gathered in a knot against her slender neck. What would she say when she learned that the Tobars and the Salahs would soon form a partnership? Should he, Ernesto, do anything about it?

The men continued talking, but Ernesto did not follow the track of their conversation. In the patio, there were seven children, only one his grandchild, the others Alvaro's nieces and nephews. The teenagers of the family were getting hard to corral on these Sunday afternoons. Either they slept late, or they went off with their friends. Ernesto kept his eyes on Flor, who was crouched next to the spot where Elena's roses had once flourished. Flor was with her cousin. The two girls were playing with the big land turtle that made her home in the patio. Ernesto caught Flor's attention and waved her over. She straightened up and hurried over, leaving her cousin and the turtle behind.

"How's my darling?" Ernesto spoke softly so as not to interrupt the men around him. Flor stood next to his chair. She leaned against him and draped an arm around his neck. She wore a yellow dress with raised fuzzy dots, and her little body was lithe and warm. "I want you to do your old grandfather a favor." He whispered this in her ear.

"¿Qué, Tata?" she said, whispering, too, using the word that was a sweet name for "Daddy."

"I want you to go over to your grandmother and give her a kiss. Give her a kiss and say, 'This is from Tata.' "

Flor drew her head back, a quizzical look on her face. "¿De verdad?"

"Yes, really."

"Do I kiss her on the mouth like you do, Tata?"

"No. You kiss her on the cheek. Go on. Say, 'This kiss is from Tata.' " Ernesto gave his granddaughter a nudge to start her off.

Flor skipped over the length of the veranda to her grandmother. "Perdón, perdón," Flor said, because she was interrupting the ladies and because, in order to reach Elena, she had to scoot between the coffee table and around the legs of those sitting on the settee. Flor bent over Elena and kissed her cheek resonantly. "Tata sends you this."

"What?" Elena said, giving Flor a quick hug.

"Tata. He said, 'Give your grandmother a kiss for me.' "

"¡Ay, que lindo!" said doña Lydia, who had come with doña Eugenia, Alvaro's mother. Doña Lydia was sitting beside a pot of crimson geraniums that matched exactly the colored slash that was her mouth.

Flor's cousin ran up to the edge of the veranda. She was holding the turtle with two hands and stiffly away from herself. The turtle was used to being handled. Her old wrinkled legs jutted from her shell, and she was scrambling them wildly. "Look, Flor, the turtle wants to play some more." The cousins went off together.

Elena turned to look behind her, but she was sitting between Eugenia and Magda, and catching her husband's eye was difficult. Elena shook her head instead. "Men are so surprising," she muttered, but Magda overheard and gave Elena a wink.

Margarita, Magda's sister-in-law, was holding a silk fan printed with cabbage roses. Margarita opened it with a graceful ruffle and began to fan herself. "I think you should reconsider sending that servant girl to school with Flor."

It was Magda whom Margarita addressed. She was talking about María Mercedes. About Magda's wanting to send both Flor and María Mercedes to La Asunción next year. The private school was close to home. It was run by the Sisters of the Assumption, the same order that ran the Santa Ana school that both Elena and Magda had attended.

"But the girls are like sisters," Magda said, taking a new stitch in her petit point design. Though it seemed out of character, she had recently taken up embroidery. Her life was filled with details, and she had found that sewing calmed her.

"But they're *not* sisters," Alvaro's mother said. "I think you've done a great thing, allowing those two girls so much time together. But the moment is soon coming when they'll be going out into the world . . ."

"And they come from different worlds," Margarita said. "Better to separate them now, while they're still young and resilient."

Alvaro's sister, who had been silent for a great part of the conversation, now said, "Where would you send María Mercedes if you didn't send her to La Asunción?"

Magda rested the embroidery hoop in her lap. She fingered the silkiness of the stitches she'd laid down. "There's a public school nearby. La Escuela Don Alberto Masferrer."

"Don't get me wrong," Margarita said. "The fact that you're willing to educate the girl at all is commendable." The wind she was creating with her fan was sizable enough to toss her thick black hair about.

"I promised her mother," Magda said. "I promised Jacinta I'd do it, and I will."

"Yes. But I'm certain you didn't promise to send the girl to La Asunción. After all, the girl's a servant." Margarita gave a snort. "To send a maid to La Asunción would be ridiculous."

"María Mercedes is not a maid." Magda heard the edge in her voice, and she took a quick breath and added in a softer tone, "She's just a little girl."

"She's a maid's little girl, which amounts to the same thing," Margarita said. "Anyway, the Masferrer school seems a much more appropriate choice." She closed her fan with a sharp decisive snap.

Laura de Castillo, Margarita's best friend and shadow, put on a bright smile and attempted, as she always did, to calm the waters her friend had once again roiled up. "Come on, girls. Let's talk about more pleasant things. What do you think about the latest with *Las dos*?"

Doña Lydia slapped herself softly on the cheek. "Can you believe it? La Bárbara stealing Dulce Alegría from Inocencia?"

Laura said, "She stole her away because she claims Inocencia's not a fit mother. Just because she's in a wheelchair."

Magda took up her embroidery once again. She allowed the talk about the radio novela to wash over her. A moment before, Elena had patted Magda's hand, the gesture seemingly saying, Don't let your sister-in-law's overbearingness disturb you. We're all aware of the type of person Margarita is. In response, Magda smiled weakly at her mother, but the fact was that most of what Margarita had said was true. It had been advantageous to allow the girls to grow up together. If she were truly honest with herself, she would have to admit that all the privileges she'd bestowed on both Jacinta and María Mercedes had been in her own best interest, and therefore a selfish thing.

Magda glanced up from her sewing. In the patio Flor and her cousins were hunkered down around the turtle. Flor wagged a limp leaf of lettuce in front of it, but it preferred its siesta to poking its head out for a nibble. Flor's ringlets looked shot with gold. Her happy precious face beamed with promise and innocence. Magda plunged her needle into the taut fabric of her embroidery project. A few more stitches and she finished the plume of smoke spiraling from the chimney of the cozy cabin in the woods. She asked herself, What, dear God, did Jacinta and I set in motion the day we gave birth to our daughters?

▼▼▼

CHAPTER FORTY-TWO

P ilar Lazos, her younger son, Emilio, and her daughter, Nanda, rode the bus up Avenida Roosevelt to la Academia Militar. María Mercedes had come along, too. It was the annual Day of the Soldier, and as was the custom, the academy had thrown open its gates for tours and a parade. The academy was located on the outskirts of San Salvador, near the village of La Ceiba, which took its name from the silk-cotton tree growing majestically near its heart. Though she'd visited only twice before with her mother, Nanda Lazos could have reached the school blindfolded. Frequently, after prayers and before she fell asleep, she imagined boarding the bus unaccompanied, riding up the avenue, past el Hospital Bloom, where she helped the crippled children, past el Parque Cuscatlán, where she played with those who still could walk, past the church at San José de la Montaña, where she attended Bible study.

She imagined stepping off the bus, her heart thumping wildly, hurrying past the impressive iron gates, going toward the quadrangle around which the cadets' barracks rose. In her imagination, Nanda Lazos stood before barracks number 3 and soon Victor Morales, splendid in his uniform, strode purposefully toward her and gathered her up into his powerful arms. This was Nanda's dream, awake or asleep. An uncomplicated, innocent dream that quickened her pulse but contained no occasion for sin. She was sixteen. She had loved Victor Morales, six years her elder and her cousin Harold's friend and fellow cadet, since that day, two years before, when for a brief tender moment Victor had shown her that, despite his love of soldiering and its attendant need for combativeness, there was inside him a vulnerable softness that, Nanda was certain, she alone could coax into full bloom.

A late September sun had warmed the tin-roofed viewing stand, and Nanda demurely pulled her skirt away from her thighs and rearranged herself on the wooden bench. María Mercedes sat beside her; Pilar, beside María Mercedes. Nanda's brother had found a spot for himself four tiers down, in the first row, behind the military officers inspecting the troop.

"Is that Harold over there?" María Mercedes asked, pointing across the field. She spoke rather loudly, her voice having to hurdle the thunderous beat of drums and the blare of trumpets and cornets. A battalion of cadets bedecked in stiffly pressed uniforms, their boots gleaming, their rifles carried smartly on their shoulders, marched past the reviewing stand. As they tramped by, their heads snapped sharply right toward the school superintendent.

"Where?" Nanda asked, but only to appease. She herself was searching for Victor among the rows and rows of men who—she would not have believed this—looked one very much like the other.

"There he is!" María Mercedes cried, rising up in a sudden burst of recognition before Pilar pulled her down onto the bench again.

"¡Niña, shhh!" Pilar admonished, laying a gloved finger up to her lips but not across them, lest she stain the glove with Paint the Town Red lip color. Pilar wore a chic blue suit that, naturally, she had made herself. The hat that sat on her head she had not made. It featured a long pointy feather that once had belonged to a very large grouse. To complete the ensemble, she sported white gloves and matching high heels. Gloves, because all the magazines featured gloved ladies these days, and when Pilar had remarked about this, it was Magda who provided a pair.

Although these military occasions were rare, Pilar took them quite seriously, being that Harold, her nephew who was really like a son, and Victor, his friend, had been a part of this setting going on the second year. The two had done the impossible. They had finished the whole of their schooling, thirteen years in all, received their bachilleratos, all for the chance—just the chance—of being appointed to the academy.

"Where is he?" Nanda asked in earnest now, craning her neck to see the soldier María Mercedes pointed out.

"There," said María Mercedes. "There's Harold."

"Oh," Nanda said. "Yes, that's Harold, all right."

After the parade, the academy hosted a reception of a sort in the mess hall, which, though it had plenty of open windows, had heated up to such an extent that the liquid refreshments—fresco de tamarindo and horchata—were being consumed hastily. The room brimmed with noisy chitchat, back-slapping, and congratulatory abrazos. The permeating odor of marching was in the air, but somehow it did not offend, for it spoke of vigorous men who toiled and sweated so as to defend a country and its people.

Harold and Victor were a set of bookends: each had long-waisted tunics with spacious pockets at breast and hip; each was sashed at the waist by a wide ribbed belt with metal studs; each wore blousy-legged trousers that disappeared into ankle-high boots, spit-polished and resplendent. The men's headgear, however, was a disappointment, consisting as it did of plain visored caps with the Salvadoran coat of arms—Dios, Unión, Libertad—stitched on cloth medallions over the bill.

Emilio, Nanda's brother, shook his wrist so that his name bracelet—Harold's name bracelet, actually—danced a bit, an old habit of his cousin's.

"I see you're still wearing that thing," Harold said. He had given the bracelet to Emilio two years before, on the day he learned he'd been admitted to the academy, thanks to Victor Morales's father. Rolando Morales, it seemed, had greatly distinguished himself in the coup led by Oscar Osorio in 1948. Exactly what the major had done for the new president was unknown. Morales himself did not say. He was not a boastful man. But neither, evidently, was he so shy that he could not ask for a couple of appointments.

"Since you gave him that bracelet, it has never left his wrist," Pilar said. She poked a strand of hair back into her hatband, keeping one eye on María Mercedes, who was at the refreshment table, helping herself to sugar cookies made in the shape of guns.

"You should have my name removed," Harold said, pointing to the bracelet. "Have your own engraved on it."

Emilio shrugged, for his mother had already said too much. He lifted his wrist and made the bracelet dance again.

"And what happend to *your* bracelet, Victor?" Nanda asked. "You used to wear one just like Harold's." If she had Victor's bracelet, in all her life she would never take it off.

"It's at home, Fernanda. Here at the academy, we can't wear things like that."

Only Victor Morales used her full name, and Nanda found this so touching, she felt a blush creeping up her neck and hoped it would not give her away. "Can you wear your medals?" she added, meaning religious medals, like the oval one of the Holy Family she had given him on a chain for moral strength and protection. She had given a similar medal to Harold as well.

"We can't wear jewelry of any kind here," Victor said. "My bracelet and medal are in a little box at home."

Nanda smiled. "I see." What she saw in her head was a dresser of some kind. A drawer. Under a stack of clothing, perhaps, a metal box with a lock. In the box, mementos: his bracelet, *her* medal, a necklace of ixtle fiber strung with three agate nuggets, tiny as corn kernels. Nanda had not seen the necklace, but Victor had described it, explaining that his mother had made it when he was an infant. To make clear its circumference, Victor had taken Nanda's hand, circling her slender wrist with his fingers. As he spoke, his eyes glistened, and the stain that splotched his ear deepened in color. Was it any wonder she had fallen in love?

At the refreshment table, María Mercedes filled a pocket with cookies; then she joined Pilar and the others. "Look, Pilar," María Mercedes said, patting her pocket. "I have lots of cookies. I'm taking some to tía Chenta when Mamá and I visit her tomorrow."

"Of course, you are," Pilar said, rolling her eyes, wishing she'd kept a better watch on María Mercedes. Truth was, she'd been concentrating on Victor, on how striking he was in his uniform: that sharp nose, that full, cruel-looking mouth. It was shameful, God knew, how the boy had piqued her interest. Boy? How old was he? Twenty-something? Some boy! For years, after he'd lost his mother and started coming to the house, he had held Pilar's gaze steadily when he spoke, his dark eyes smoldering. To be sure, his attention was alluring, not to mention flattering. She was, after all, thirty-eight, a woman clearly in decline. Still, this itch she would never scratch. It would kill Nanda if she did. It saddened Pilar seeing Nanda so painfully smitten. It was too bad, for Victor would have made a great catch. Instead, it was like something from a radio novela: Man ruins chances with daughter by flirting with her mother.

▼▼

CHAPTER FORTY-THREE

San Salvador
October 1955

María Mercedes attended la Escuela Alberto Masferrer, named after one of El Salvador's literary greats. This morning, on the walk to school, she hiked up her satchel, plump with books and notepads and pencil holders. In it also was a cloth bag Pilar had made for holding rubber bands and paper clips, for erasers and the sharpener. In the satchel, too, were a compass and protractor, as well as María Mercedes's dearest possession: a flat shiny tin of Venus colored pencils, the largest of the tins, holding eighteen creamy colors. Contrastingly, Flor attended La Asunción, and her satchel was always practically empty. Each afternoon, during their homework time in the pantry, Flor dumped her satchel contents and the same objects thumped against the table: a notebook, a pencil with a perennially blunt point, a book of some sort, most often not the one needed for her assignment.

María Mercedes reached the school, which took up most of a downtown block. It was across from the post office and was one of the modern school buildings, governmental and severe-looking. María Mercedes loved her school. She loved her teacher, la señora Ardón, who made a game of numbers and words, and who told stories that reverberated in María Mercedes's head even after school. Last week the teacher had told about los cadejos, folkloric beasts with long snouts and eyes that glowed red in the night. Teresita Novoa, who sat next to María Mercedes, had plugged her ears with her fingers, so she didn't hear the teacher tell about the good white cadejo and the evil black one. María Mercedes herself had not been frightened by the evil one. To prove it, she'd made up a rhyme on the spot: Aunque el cadejo negro es muy furtivo, no le tengo miedo, pues no soy su captivo. Though the black cadejo is very furtive, I do not fear it because I'm not its captive. She had recited the rhyme to the teacher, who pronounced it somewhat awkward, though profound in concept for an eight-year-old. María Mercedes beamed at the appraisal, not discouraged in the least by the critique. She had decided on the spot to become a poet.

School had been in session for only a few hours when the electric power failed. María Mercedes was at her desk, the tin of colored pencils opened prettily before her, when the lights blinked a few times and dimmed and then went out completely. The whir of the big ceiling fan shifted and the blades wound down. Because the classroom was an interior one and had no windows, they were plunged into the dark. Teresita Novoa gave a frightened yelp and clutched María Mercedes's arm. "It's only the lights," María Mercedes said, but she did not push Teresita's hand away. A quick commotion erupted, but the teacher, who not only had eyes in the back of her head but could see in the dark, put a stop to it at once. "Manolo," she commanded, "sit back down! Arturo, I'll have none of that. Emilia, help Leopoldo lay a hand on his crutches. Now, class, I'm sure all will be back to normal soon. In the meantime, I'll tell you a story."

The teacher's voice was low and soothing. Teresita lessened her grip on María Mercedes's arm but did not let go of it. After what seemed like a long time, a beam of light came down the hall and el director appeared at the door with a flashlight. With the aid of his beam, the class groped around for their belongings and then followed it as it bounced up the hall and down the stairwell. In el director's wake, the students were well behaved, even Manolo and Arturo, the rabble-rousers, who usually took advantage of even the slightest distraction to live up to their reputation. Because there was help, Leopoldo made it safely down the steps on his crutches. As for

Teresita, she did not let go of María Mercedes's arm until they had left the building and walked out into brightness and fresh air.

When the power failed, the radio on Pilar Lazos's bedside table went off. She and Victor Morales were in bed, and the room was steamy due to the shuttered windows and drawn curtains needed for privacy. For additional camouflage, Pilar had turned on the radio, because Victor was an athletic lover whose sexual gymnastics prompted her to moan and squeal with delight. Heaven knows, it was a disgrace, this frantic coupling of theirs. She was sixteen years his senior and a grandmother twice over as well. She had struggled to resist, for Nanda's sake, and for her own sake as well, but, God help her, she was not good at walking away from temptation. Especially temptation of the sexual kind. For months Victor Morales had pursued her with unspoken words and fervent looks. He was a graduate of the academy now, a lieutenant in a uniform that blared power and importance. A seductive lieutenant whose full savage lips and fiery eyes scorched hers. There was that touching birthmark that splotched his left ear. What was a woman to do when beguiled by a man-boy like that? A woman gave in, but not for romantic notions like her sweet daughter entertained. No. A woman like Pilar gave in because, for a few weeks, she lived the thrill of the chase and the delight of surrender. She did not fool herself. What mattered here was this brief time of delicious gratification, after which Victor would depart from National Police Headquarters, where he was now training (it was conveniently a few blocks away) and go off to command some police station in the countryside just as her nephew Harold was doing. And she? She would go on with the rest of her life, no one the wiser for their interlude.

When the radio went off, Pilar heard the silence at once. She lifted her head and looked over to the table. "¿Y la música?" she asked, but Victor pulled her down against himself again. "No importa," he said.

The students massed in front of the school building. They clumped in groups by grade, and the teachers patrolled around them, calling for order, warning the disobedient that severe punishment loomed. Across the street, the post office was dark. A number of workers had come outside, too. This led to hopeful chatter among the students that el apagón, the blackout, might be more than just momentary. Indeed, before long, school was dismissed for the day. The students cheered at the news and scampered off. Suddenly freed, María Mercedes looked around for Nanda Lazos, who attended the school, too. When she found her, she asked, "What do we do now?"

"It's early," Nanda said. "Come home with me. After lunch, I'll walk you back to Magda's." Today, Nanda was teaching catechism at five. María Mercedes could help her organize papers for the class. Today, Nanda would teach the parable of the prodigal son. The handouts she would use showed an illustration of a young man herding pigs into a sty. During the discussion, she would use examples from her own life: her older brother, Eduardo, off in Aguilares working in a slaughtering plant to help support his little family. Her younger brother, Emilio, running around the countryside with a pack of wild boys. Their stories were not quite the same as the one from the Bible, but she would tell them in such a way as to make them fit.

María Mercedes smiled at the prospect of an impromptu visit with Pilar. She fell into step with Nanda. "Why did the electricity go out?"

"There was a short in a transformer," Nanda said, repeating what she'd heard, not bothering to explain. She had a lot on her mind. She was only months away from graduation, and there was plenty of schoolwork to be done. She was a member of the Christian Student Catechists. At their meetings, the students discussed the Bible and were given a weekly poser. This week, the assignment was the first beatitude: Blessed are the poor in spirit, for theirs is the kingdom of heaven.

The girls walked on. They passed the cathedral (both making the sign of the cross as they went by the door), the Gran Hotel, and the central market. Soon they reached Colonia El Paraíso, and Nanda's house rose up ahead. Years before, because the landlord had sold their previous house out from under them, Pilar and her family had unhappily left Colonia La Rábida and the only home they'd known together. But now Nanda was content. In El Paraíso, because her brothers were away, she had a room of her own, and it was cozy with books and a rocker; it had a spiritual air lent by her altar that held the baby Jesus in his little cradle, her special saints, and the tall votive candles she was careful to keep burning.

Nanda left María Mercedes on the sidewalk petting the neighbor's dog. She stepped into the house. "¿Mamá?" Nanda called, because she was used to immediately seeing her mother bent over the Singer. Nanda frowned and went quickly through the front room. She turned left at the dining room, where the Kelvinator refrigerator towered in a corner for the very best showing. She stepped softly down the hall, toward the puzzling sounds coming from behind the door of her mother's room.

"¿Mamá?" she asked again, before reaching for the knob.

In November, as soon as she graduated, Nanda left home, a place where she could no longer breathe because the air was foul with betrayal. She went to Aguilares and moved in with her brother Eduardo. Until she found a steady job and then a place of her own, Nanda tended to his children as a way of repaying him for the cot in the corner.

In addition to clothing and her books, Nanda brought to Aguilares only the baby Jesus in his cradle. She made a shelf for him and tacked it over the cot. She kept a votive candle burning next to the baby, in an earnest effort to help her pray, to help her search for healing.

In time, she found solace in the impassioned homilies of the parish priest, in joining his brigade to work among the poor. In time, el padre Rutilio Grande helped Nanda see that there were more important things to do in this world than grieve over a worthless man and hate your mother.

▼▼

CHAPTER FORTY-FOUR

San Salvador
January 1962

Flor Tobar's feet were so dainty it made shopping for shoes a problem. She and Magda had scoured the downtown in search of just the right pair, sized four narrow. Flor needed the shoes for her party. Not just any party, but her fifteenth birthday party, la Fiesta Rosa, *the* birthday of her life.

"You know what?" Magda said. "We'll have shoes made at la Adoc." She shifted her clumsy shopping bag from one hand to the other. She hadn't planned these purchases—books, long-playing records, a bottle of Ma Griffe perfume. Had she planned on buying something other than shoes, she would have asked Basilio to wait with the car. As it was, he'd pick them up at the Gran Hotel at noon.

"What about Maison Blanche?" Flor said. They'd been trudging in and out of stores for two hours.

Magda stopped short in the middle of the sidewalk. "Are you crazy? Maison Blanche is in New Orleans!"

Flor shrugged. "So?"

Magda gave a puff of exasperation. "We just went to New Orleans, remember? It seems to me we found a pair then."

"But now I need another pair."

Magda shook her head. She started down the street again, her shopping bag feeling heavier by the step. The hotel was just around

294

the corner. While they waited for the car to arrive, they would collapse in a lobby chair and order something very cold.

Flor trailed after her mother. She remembered New Orleans, all right. As soon as school vacation started in November, her mother had cajoled her into coming along on a quick buying trip for Tesoros. In New Orleans, there had been numerous visits to the French Quarter, where Magda had wrangled interminably with an antiques dealer over his paperweight collection. And there had been the uncharacteristic cold and the mist, a perturbing mist that caused them to bundle up and tie scarves under their chins like Russian peasants. No matter. The dour weather had matched Flor's mood. Last June her mother had set events in motion that, when Christmas came, had been the ruination of Flor's life.

Last June, Magda had moved Tesoros up la Doble Vía to the crossroads formed by the outer reach of downtown and the new expanding suburbs, including the exclusive neighborhoods of San Benito and Escalón. To the new Tesoros, Magda added a coffee room, capitalizing on its adjacency to El Caribe, the much frequented cinema, and across the street from El Salvador del Mundo, the park with the cedars and the towering statue of the Savior of the world. These two attractions alone, movie and park, provided a plentiful supply of shoppers, and the fact that Tesoros was no longer in the increasingly tawdry center of the city made it a pleasure for women to drop in and relax over a coffee and a pastry. No question. Tesoros on Doble Vía was a chic and popular place, and Flor was proud of her mother's industriousness, happy with her much deserved success. What Flor protested, what struck her as totally unjust, was that her mother had moved them out of their beloved old house with its cozy confusion of thick walls and tiled corridors and into a glass-and-marble strongbox in San Benito that was supposedly the paragon of modernity. Not to mention the transfer in schools the move had provoked. Clearly this was the greatest calamity that had ever befallen Florencia Elena Tobar.

The hotel was not air-conditioned, but with fans spinning, the lobby was cool compared to the outdoors. Flor and Magda sat off to the side of the reception desk, on an unyielding banquette next to a potted palm. From this vantage point they could keep a lookout for Basilio.

"Let's get something to drink," Magda said. She wished propriety would allow her to lift her legs and prop them up.

"What are we going to do about the shoes?" Flor asked. A waiter in a white tunic came up and they ordered lemonades. Magda asked for hers with lots of ice.

"We bought shoes in New Orleans," Magda said. "If you hadn't changed your mind about your dress, you'd have shoes already. I've never heard of such a thing. It's like a bride buying one gown and then settling on another." Magda had found the perfect Fiesta Rosa dress in a small couture shop off Canal Street. The dress was pink, naturally. Cerise peau-de-soie and alençon lace.

"I didn't like the dress. It didn't have a waistline."

"It was princess style."

"I know it was princess style. I don't like princess style."

"Why didn't you say so? Why did you let me buy the dress if you didn't like it? Heaven knows it cost a fortune." They had been through this before, of course, but Magda passed up no opportunity to remind Flor she'd spent two hundred and twenty dollars.

"Because *you* liked the dress, Mamá. Because from the minute you saw it in the window, you couldn't stop talking about it."

Magda tossed her head. "Well, we still have to get shoes. Though I don't see why you can't wear the ones we bought in New Orleans."

Flor took in a quick breath. "Because they don't match my dress." Pilar Lazos had made the dress she truly wanted. It was soft blush, with a scalloped hem like tulip petals. She looked like a flower in it, an appropriate thing for a girl named as such.

The waiter set their drinks on a small walnut table. Magda paid, then took quick sips of the icy tart lemonade. She set the glass down again. "On the way home, we'll pick up the envelopes." The sisters at La Asunción had hand-addressed 150 invitation envelopes.

"You go in when we get there," Flor said. "I'm staying in the car." She couldn't bear going into her school knowing that, when classes resumed, she would no longer be part of it.

Magda took another sip, regretting having raised the subject. In a little over a month, Flor would enter the American School in San Benito. Admittedly, changing schools was a difficult thing for any young girl, but given time, her daughter would adjust. A day would come, Magda was certain, when Flor would thank her for the move.

On the way home, after they'd stopped at La Asunción, Basilio ran into the post office for the mail. In the car, Magda sorted through it. There was a letter from Alvaro, which she'd read later. As always, on the back of the envelope, their own number, "83." Magda smiled to herself. Alvaro's letters were always steamy, and she preferred to read them lingeringly. Alvaro was harvesting cotton in Usulután. He would be home at the end of the month, several days before Flor's big party. For Alvaro, business was very good. Cotton was productive, due in large part to the improvement in pest control and to the fact that the Litoral, the paved road winding along the coast, had made it possible to expand the plantation's acreage. La Luz, Alvaro's candle factory in Santa Tecla, was also thriving. The formation last year of the Central American Common Market had provided a free trade zone and, just as importantly, the political infrastructure for an influx of capital from the United States. Alvaro and his partner, Abraham Salah, had taken full advantage of this opportunity, opening a second factory on the road to La Libertad.

There was another letter. It was from Elena, and it was embossed on the upper left-hand corner with the emblem of L'Hotel Palais, her parents' favorite Parisian haunt. The letter contained sketchy but startling news. And from the way it was written, it indicated there had been an earlier letter, as yet not received. This one stated that Ernesto was much improved. It had been those French sauces and cheeses, Elena wrote. Still, because the doctor they had seen recommended less rich food and a more restful pace, the trip to the Loire Valley was canceled.

The news of her father's health was disturbing but not a surprise. In past years, Ernesto had suffered from a variety of gastric disturbances. So much so that Elena made sure there was always sal de frutas, Epsom salts, in the house. And her parents had not been to Europe in five years. Where French gastronomy was concerned, Magda could well see her father making up for lost time. "When we get home, we'll put in a call to them," Magda said, though it would take hours to get through to Europe. If they ever were connected, communication would be riddled with static and maddening abruptions.

"What if they miss the party?" Flor said.

"Goodness," Magda said, "they would never do that."

▼   ▼   ▼

As Flor's birthday neared, a pyrotechnist began to construct, at the back of Magda's garden, a fireworks frame as lacy as a spiderweb. Workmen balancing long boards lumbered in and hammered out two dozen tables to be set under the trees and draped into elegance on February third. The men built a dance floor next to the pool; they fashioned a charming footbridge, straight from a fairy tale, to span it. Gardenias were ordered to float on the water. Fifteen attendants, las damas, all dressed in shades of pink, would open the party, proceeding from house, over lawn, to footbridge in a ceremonious parade before Flor herself appeared. At midnight, the fireworks would be launched. In a spectacular finale, the name "Florencia" would pinwheel against the stars.

The selection of the damas, however, was proving to be troublesome. Flor had included María Mercedes in the group, but Jacinta was adamantly against it.

"But why?" María Mercedes asked, her voice sliding into an atypical whine, even though her feelings about being included were mixed. More and more, she fit in less and less.

"Because it's not right, that's all," Jacinta said. They were in the kitchen, and Tea had just switched off *Las dos*.

"That's not a good reason," María Mercedes said.

"Yes it is," Tea said. "It's not your place to be a dama."

"What do you think, Basilio?" María Mercedes asked. Basilio was in the kitchen, too. He was his usual silent self.

"Your place is here, with us," he said.

In the end, had peering into the future been possible, all debates might have been avoided. Had they a seer's ball, they would have seen this: A week after sailing from Le Havre, on a clear, starry night and after rash indulgence at the captain's table, Ernesto Contreras's gastric disturbances took a drastic turn. Before the ship reached shore, Flor's grandfather had passed on.

▼▼▼

CHAPTER FORTY-FIVE

For a day before his funeral, Ernesto Contreras's body lay in state, de cuerpo presente. He rested in a lustrous mahogany casket placed in the sitting room of Elena's house, the room sober with rigid furniture ordinarily forsaken for the cushioned wicker of the porch. Cavaliers and ladies framed in oil paintings decorating the walls gazed down at him benevolently. Directly across the street, the house that had belonged to Cecilia de Aragón was shuttered and still.

Ernesto Contreras was four years past seventy when he died, and there were those who said that as many years were enough for any man. Had he been alive, the deceased would have mightily disagreed. Were he able to rise up from the casket, lift his dark-suited torso off the satin tucked and gathered under him, Ernesto Contreras would have said, "Whatever years we are given, it's never years enough." What he'd not ever discussed was his fear of death, though each morning over breakfast he gave himself heart by turning to the obituaries before going on to plan the day.

Blessedly, the coronary infarct that killed him was so swift that when he died, he did not so much as cause a bobble on his side of the stateroom bed. Like a ship over calm water, his passage was silent and silky. Yet, were he able, he would confess he'd had an instant of clarity before the blackness overtook him. In that instant, he understood that death itself was not frightening; it was the finality of death that overwhelmed. Knowing this at last, he reached to touch Elena, to say he was sorry one more time again.

In tribute, family and friends, employees and servants were gathered in the Cementerio Santa Isabel at the edge of Santa Ana. Neto and Alberto Contreras flanked their mother, and she slumped against them so that they had to hold her up. Elena gazed dully through the fog of her grief and the black veil cascading from her still golden head. Magda, shrouded in black herself, was propped against Alvaro, who had laid his arm along Flor's narrow, heaving shoulders. Júnior, Carlos, and Orlando, Flor's brothers, stood woodenly behind their mother. All eyes were on the mason toiling waist deep in the trench the gravedigger had dug earlier. The mason worked at closing the marble tomb watched over by the stone archangel at whose alabaster feet trailed a granite ribbon. The words "Familia Contreras Rivas, Ni Tiempo Ni Distancia Podrán Separarnos" were etched in the granite. "Neither Time Nor Distance Can Separate Us."

The mason slapped mortar against the bricks he'd piled up to seal the vault. As he worked, his trowel chinked and rasped, the sound made more pitiful by the bright cloudless sky, by cheery chirping birds in the fragrant trees nearby.

Isabel and Abraham Salah stood arm in arm toward the back of the gathering. Their son Enrique, a young man turned handsome and tall, accompanied them. Isabel, large even in black, had come for Magda and Elena's sakes, not so much for Ernesto's, who had once been like a father. Days back, when Isabel opened the newspaper to the headline "Ilustre hacendado muere sobre el mar," "Illustrious Landowner Dies at Sea," she'd had to collect herself before pointing it out to her mother. After Cecilia read the news, she looked off for a long moment. "Poor Nena," she'd said at length.

At the very back of the cemetery, the servants, all of Elena's and a few of Magda's, clumped together in solidarity, arms folded stoically over waists. Jacinta, María Mercedes, and Basilio had come from Magda's, just the three of them in Magda's car, a rare thing resulting from the Tobars' needing two cars to get everyone to the funeral. The three were lined up side by side, all wearing their good going-out clothes. They listened to padre Adolfo, who'd come from San Salvador to officiate. After the tomb was sealed, the priest enjoined them all to be brave and to accept.

"Death is the beginning of true life," el padre said, his words harsh, like the sound of the trowel.

While the Contreras family assembled for a luncheon at Elena's, Jacinta's small family, with Magda's permission, slipped away to Izalco to pay respects to their own dead. The trip from Santa Ana, thirty kilometers over good road, was short and swift when traveled by car. Years back, when they lived in another world, Jacinta and Basilio had covered the way on foot in a journey of a different kind. Today, in the dry heat of the afternoon, he and Jacinta and María Mercedes entered a graveyard devoid of statues or ordered beauty. He and Jacinta brushed and plucked debris—dried twigs and leaves, pebbles and curiously small chunks of cement—off the grassless plot. Basilio was not wearing a hat, a relatively new development. Periodically, he pulled a handkerchief from his back pocket and mopped his brow with it. Despite turning him more reticent, the years had been kind. They had softened the sharp planes of his face and rounded his shoulders a bit, but he was the selfsame man, steadfast and a believer that, to be at peace, a man made connections where he could. What could not be changed, a man accepted. His dead did not rest here, of course (God knew what had become of them), but today he could pretend they did.

María Mercedes, who had not visited before, stood to the side for a time before she joined in. Together the three bent at the waist, heads inclined and silent, raking now with fingers, now with wrenched-off leafy branches, around weathered wooden crosses, each carved with a name: Apolonia Sandoval, Jacinta's grandmother; Cirilo Prieto, her brother; Segunda, Grata, Ursula, and Digna Prieto, her sisters.

A large stone cross provided by Elena marked Mercedes's grave. Etched on it was: "Mercedes Prieto Sandoval, Hija, Madre, Mártir," "Daughter, Mother, Martyr."

Satisfied they had done what they could to tidy up, Jacinta slipped off her shoes and hunkered down, her black dress pulled and tucked neatly over her knees and under her. She patted the soil over her mother's grave, and quick puffs of brown silt rose up around her palm. "Come," she said, and Basilio hunched down beside her, his legs bent and wide apart, his chocolate arms hanging down between them. Jacinta looked up at her daughter, who then dropped down, too.

"Listen to me, María Mercedes. Until now you haven't had to think of anything but your own good life. It is I who made sure of it. Perhaps I did wrong. Look around you. The dead are calling out. They cry, 'We are the bones of your bones.'

"Your grandmother died, a blade at her neck, but she was not a martyr, although la niña Elena set it in stone as if it were the truth. You're young, daughter. You're only just beginning. But listen to me: You must start to live your life by the light of what you yourself would want carved on your stone."

Jacinta dug into her pocket, leaning back a bit for easier access. She brought out a small packet, a bright pink square of tissue paper. "Here, I want you to have this."

María Mercedes unfolded the paper, one direction after the other. She opened the package to a coiled object she did not recognize: a short length of leather cord, knotted at the ends, stiff with age; three red nuggets, tiny as a child's fingernail, were threaded on the cord and fixed in place. "What is it?"

"It's an amulet. Your grandmother made it. Don Feliciano, the tribe cacique, blessed the stones. They're red agates for health and longevity." Jacinta placed a hand to her throat. "I wore it when I was a baby."

María Mercedes lifted the cord toward her mother. "You wore it around your neck?"

Jacinta nodded. "I wore it till it was too small for me."

"You've had it all these years?" María Mercedes was sure she'd laid a hand on all her mother's belongings, but this she'd never set eyes upon.

"When you were a baby, you wore it, too. But then I put it away." She'd kept it in her treasure box that was now in Magda's personal closet for safekeeping. Her treasure box with the sooty matches, with the little bottle empty of seawater, with a few other precious things.

Jacinta motioned to the crosses dotting the plot. "Mamá made an amulet for each of the babies. Each of them was buried with his own." The three went silent in acknowledgment of five tiny necklaces lying among the bones only meters below.

"What about Tino, Mamá? Did your baby brother have one, too?"

"He had one. We prayed that whoever buried him, buried him with it."

María Mercedes refolded the gift reverently. She held the bright pink package against her heart. "Gracias, Mamá."

Jacinta smiled and stood up. She knocked the dust off her feet and slipped into her shoes. She pointed out over the cemetery, toward town and beyond it, toward Izalco, the volcano, still towering but dormant in the distance. "Come, Basilio," she said. "Let's try to show this girl who she is."

The three headed off to the path leading up to a rock wall and a laurel tree growing alongside the place where once a hut had stood. It was María Mercedes's fifteenth birthday. She would write a poem to mark the occasion. Years later, when her mother went through her papers, she would find the poem. It would be titled "Empezando a comprender," "Beginning to Understand." On it, today's date would appear—2.5.62.

▼▼▼

CHAPTER FORTY-SIX

Flor was a fading flower after her grandfather died, and nothing her family did helped revive her. Alvaro planned diversionary outings to the beach and to the cool piney countryside. Magda, battling her own deep sorrow at her father's loss and at her mother's alarming decline, brought home baubles for her daughter as well as for herself: stacks of magazines, the latest phonograph records, photo albums and scrap books they could fill together. Socorro, the cook, prepared enticing dishes known for their power to blunt grief: herb-stuffed chicken, asparagus sprinkled with buttered bread crumbs, dark chocolate pudding molded into stars. María Mercedes volunteered to help Flor with homework or to read aloud the love stories by Corín Tellado in *Vanidades* magazine. But distracting Flor was more difficult for María Mercedes, given that months back, to be closer to school, she'd moved in with Pilar.

Jacinta made it her duty to second-guess the collective mind of the household, attempting, thereby, to satisfy the Contrerases' every whim. Basilio, in contrast to his nature, played cheerful tunes on his sad flute. And, because he'd long fixed both Flor and María Mercedes in his mind as the little girls they'd once been, instead of the young señoritas they had become, he carved a corral of horses for Flor, fashioning for each animal a miniature leather saddle and reins as slender as darning thread.

Not that Flor wasn't grateful for her family's solicitude. She smiled appreciatively at their thoughtfulness and gave profuse thanks, but her pale blue eyes did not light up for long. Not even the new Zenith television could breathe fresh life into her, though she occasionally laughed watching *I Love Lucy* and *Bewitched*.

So, for a year after Ernesto Contreras died, despite all attentions, Flor's happiness was elusive. Each morning, she awakened with a start and went doggedly through the day, the memory of her Tata, a pasty mannequin in his casket, an anchor that held her down.

But there was more to it than that, of course. True, her beloved Tata was dead, but it was also true that she was angry with him for dying. Because he died when he did, her Fiesta Rosa was a never-to-be event.

Flor knew this feeling was tantamount to a sin. Still, she could not bring herself to whisper it past the grille of the confession booth. She could not concede to padre Adolfo what a vile and hateful girl she was. Instead, the truth roiled in her heart, a silent torment that turned down the corners of her mouth and dulled the light in her eyes. Seeing her unhappy face, people shook their heads and murmured, "Poor Flor. Look how she misses her Tata." And Flor *did* miss her grandfather. She missed him fiercely. But she also missed wearing the petal-hemmed dress Pilar had made. She missed stepping elegantly over the footbridge spanning the pool. She missed beholding the fireworks hurling her name against the night.

It was Enrique Salah who put the spring in Flor's step again. Enrique with the thick curly hair and the beauty mark, like butterfly dust, at the corner of his mouth. Enrique, the grandson of Cecilia de Aragón.

Flor had seen him at school and in the candle factory on those rare occasions when she accompanied her father. The first time she'd truly noticed him, Enrique had been in the waxing room, blending tallow into a molten mass before feeding it into the molding machines.

"Who's that?" Flor asked her father, noting how the cloying, steamy air had turned Enrique's hair into ringlets.

"Enrique Salah, Abraham's son. Enrique's learning the business. He's a good boy. Why do you ask?" Alvaro's eyes narrowed as if suddenly understanding the nature of his daughter's question.

Flor shrugged. "Just asking. I hadn't seen him before."

"The boy's a Salah, you know."

Flor turned away from her father's gaze. Yes, she knew what being a Salah meant. Enrique was a turco. The word was unsettling, and even in her mind, she stumbled over it. The word spoke volumes and cautioned, When it comes to turcos, unless it's business, keep away.

As they drove home that day, Flor had broached the subject of Enrique again. He had reminded her of someone, and in the car, she realized who. Enrique looked like Warren Beatty, Natalie Wood's boyfriend in *Splendor in the Grass,* which next to *West Side Story*, was Flor's favorite movie. "Wasn't there some kind of disagreement between the Salahs and abuela Elena, Papá?" Over the years Flor had overheard the adults whispering about the matter. Always when her presence was detected, the adults grew silent or changed the subject. "I remember Abuela was never happy that you and don Abraham started the candle business."

Alvaro gave a quick roll of his shoulders, as if throwing off a memory. "Your grandmother and his grandmother had a falling out, but that was long ago."

"What was it about?"

Alvaro shook his head and answered the question with an observation: "Women are funny creatures. They have their own particular brand of complaints."

It was at la Escuela Americana, on one of those infrequent days when she had brought her lunch, that Flor and Enrique had their first conversation. At the American School the students sat directly on the tiled corridor for lunch, a wide breezy spot beside the grassy courtyard where one wing of the school intersected with the other. Flor had been with Gladis Díaz, who was also in the tenth grade. "Look," Flor said, opening her lunch bag and inspecting what was there. "It's a tomato sandwich. I hate tomato sandwiches."

"I like them," someone said.

Flor looked around, noting it was Enrique Salah who had spoken. He sat a few meters away, with his knees drawn up and his back against the wall.

"Does it have mayonnaise?" he asked.

Flor peeled the bread slices apart as if opening a book. She peered at the red wheels embedded in white sweeps of condiment. "Yes. It has plenty of that."

"I'll trade you for my chicken breast." Enrique pointed at the sandwich he held centered in a square of waxed paper.

Flor lifted her brows and glanced pointedly at Enrique's broad chest. She laughed, and he realized what he'd said and began to laugh, too. This exchange marked their beginning.

The progress of their relationship was gradual. Because he was in twelfth grade, and two years older, they shared no classes, but each morning their eyes lingered on each other at assembly. They occasionally had a chance to talk if Flor stayed for lunch, something she began to do more often. Gladis Díaz, in the way girls have of abetting one another, and who found an entanglement with a turco hopelessly romantic, offered her services as a go-between, were such services needed.

At home, the rise in Flor's spirits did not cause suspicions. "See. Time truly heals," the family observed, and they went on about their business, relieved and thankful that Flor's depression was finally lifting. Not that she wasn't still moody. There was much to think about. Her friendship with Enrique had moved her beyond anger at her Tata to thoughts of her grandmother Elena and Enrique's grandmother, Cecilia. Just what had happened long ago between the two of them? The secret was enticingly mysterious.

Someday, when Enrique and she were better acquainted, she would ask him what he knew about the rift. But in October, after school ended and with hardly a week between, Enrique Salah departed for New Orleans to study at Tulane.

During the Christmas holidays, Flor and Gladis were in Tazas, the Tesoros coffee shop, having a Coca-Cola. They had just seen Flor's favorite female movie star, Natalie Wood, in her latest movie, *Love With the Proper Stranger*. It was a movie about a girl in New York who worked at a department store and who gets pregnant by a musician played by Steve McQueen. The pair spends half the movie looking for a doctor to solve their problem. Usually Flor and Gladis went to a movie and stayed through the second showing, especially a Natalie Wood movie, but not today. This movie was disturbing.

"Can you believe that the doctor they found turned out to be a woman?" Flor said, sipping Coke through a straw.

"That wasn't a doctor," Gladis said. "And that apartment they went to was spooky." Gladis lifted her shoulders in a shudder.

Flor shuddered, too. The situation Natalie had been in, she did not want to imagine.

"Oh, my goodness. Look who's there," Gladis said, setting her Coke down on the little glass table. "It's Enrique Salah."

"Where?" Flor said nonchalantly. She used her fingers to lift her bangs. She wished she'd done a better job with the hair brush this morning. Since seeing *Splendor in the Grass*, she'd worn her hair like Natalie Wood, shoulder length and with swept-aside bangs.

"He's going into the bank," Gladis said. "Let's go talk to him."

"Absolutely not," Flor said, plunging her straw down into her glass. "Why would we want to do that?" She raised her head a bit in hopes the angle would allow for a surreptitious glance in the bank's direction.

Gladis leaned over the table and whispered, "Look at you. You're flushed."

"I am not," Flor said, but she did feel feverish. Months back, Enrique Salah had started a pool of wax melting around her heart. Over the weeks he'd been away, just the thought of him, of the beauty mark next to his mouth, left a soft impression.

Flor and Gladis were finishing their sodas when Enrique strode in. Gladis wiggled her fingers and waved him over.

"Hola, Pollo," Flor said, using the nickname she'd given him after the exchange of sandwiches they'd had that first day at lunch.

"Hola, Repollo," he said, his own pet name for her. The word meant "cabbage."

"How was the university?" Flor cast a quick glance over Enrique's shoulder, through the café door into Tesoros' main room, where her mother was working. She looked back at him. He wore a casual shirt, open at the neck. A tuft of dark chest hair curled in the hollow of his throat.

"It's good, but I don't like New Orleans."

"I've been there with Mamá," Flor said. "It was cold and rainy when we went."

"Since Kennedy was killed, the whole world's cold and rainy," Enrique said.

"Pobrecito el presidente," Gladis said. "Here, Enrique. Sit down." She pointed to the chair beside her.

"Such a terrible thing," Flor said. Though it had been weeks, the image of little John-John saluting his father's casket was still fresh in her head.

"Are you going to the movie?" Enrique asked.

"We saw it already," Gladis said.

Enrique said, "I was thinking of going. Maybe I will one night."

"Are you working at the factory?" Flor asked to deflect the direction of the conversation. She didn't want to discuss the movie and the unsavory subject it explored. Not with Enrique.

"You know what?" Enrique said to Flor. "I think you look like Natalie Wood."

Flor looked down at the floor and then quickly up again. It had always been her secret hope that she looked like Natalie Wood. In the mirror, she often squinted her eyes and imagined herself dark and beguiling like Natalie. "I don't think I look like her at all," Flor said.

Gladis said, "Flor's right, she doesn't. Natalie Wood's dark, Flor's not. Flor's a chele, just like her father." "Chele" was the word for "fair-skinned."

"You look like Natalie in the eyes," Enrique said. "Your eyes are two big moons set in white clouds."

Two big moons set in white clouds. Flor didn't exactly know what it meant, but she was sure it was the sweetest, the most charming thing she had ever heard.

▼▼

CHAPTER FORTY-SEVEN

María Mercedes and Pilar were at Pilar's kitchen table, listening to *Las dos*. In the episode just now ended, Dulce Alegría had had enough. Today, she nervously had declared her approaching independence to Bárbara, her real mother: Next year, when she turned eighteen and reached legal age, Dulce Alegría said, she would return to the loving home of Inocencia. Hearing the news, la Bárbara had swooned and dropped her coffee cup. Then she herself hit the floor, but carefully lest she raise a bruise.

"Finally!" María Mercedes said.

"It's about time the girl asserted herself," Pilar said, pushing back her chair. She poked a finger into her beehive hairdo and scratched her head. "Well, back to work. I have two dresses to finish by morning." She went through the kitchen door, her flip-flops sounding against the floor tile.

María Mercedes went into Nanda's room, which was next to Pilar's. Nanda had not been back since she had left nine years before. Though the relationship with her mother had improved over time, Nanda remained in Aguilares, giving herself entirely to the church and to the work of el padre Rutilio Grande. She traveled the countryside bringing the people el padre's word: the church is a living thing, she said, echoing Grande, and you, dear people, are the heart and the body of the church.

Since moving in, María Mercedes had not changed a thing in the room. The bed remained in the corner. The desk under the window. The dresser against the wall. Spanning the top of the dresser was a shelf with holy images, squares and rectangles yellowing against the wall. There was the rocking chair and the books María Mercedes had read once, some even twice: *The Lives of the Saints, Our Lady of Fátima, Padre Pio and the Stigmata.*

Now she settled down to homework at the desk. In history, they'd been studying the expansion of the Arabs after Muhammad, Prophet of Islam. Part of the assignment was to memorize the names of Muhammad's thirteen wives.

María Mercedes was fascinated by the subject, and given Flor and Enrique Salah's relationship, studying the Arabs was timely and thought provoking. Enrique was a "turco," implying his family had come from Turkey, a Muslim country. But they had not. While his ancestors had been Palestinian, his father and grandfather had been born in El Salvador. The family was not Muslim, but Catholic. All this she had learned from Flor. For further clarification, María Mercedes had questioned her teacher about the puzzling discrimination against "turcos." The teacher explained that when Arabs first arrived in El Salvador they had fought hard and, some believed, fought dirty, to carve out a place for themselves in society. Over the years, a few families, the Salahs being a prime example, were admitted into the world of business, but on a social level, their kind remained pariahs.

Was it any wonder, then, that Enrique Salah was Flor's big secret? María Mercedes, of course, was privy to the secret, as were Pilar and Basilio and Jacinta, all four because of circumstance and not by choice. It was to Pilar's house that Enrique's letters came, and he was a faithful correspondent, writing to Flor from New Orleans three, four, sometimes five times a week.

It was not surprising that today's letter lay atop two others that had arrived this week. All were addressed to Señorita Florencia Elena Tobar, c/d María Mercedes Prieto, Colonia El Paraíso, No. 56, San Salvador, El Salvador. On the point of the back flap, the number 83 was circled. This was Flor and Enrique's code, borrowed from Flor's parents, who, needless to say, knew nothing about the correspondence.

María Mercedes squared the envelopes up, securing the little bundle with a rubber band. She set the bundle down. Any moment now, the ritual would begin. Flor would drop by. She did twice a week. She would burst in the door, asking for her letters before saying anything else.

And now the door did burst open. But it was Pilar, not Flor who flew in through it. "The post office is burning! The news is on the radio!"

The two ran out of the house just as Basilio and Flor pulled up in the car. "What's wrong?" Flor asked. Other neighbors had rushed from their houses. They pointed up the street, toward the column of smoke rising up on the horizon.

"It's the post office. It's burning down." Pilar hopped up and down on the sidewalk because the cement was hot and she was barefoot. "I'll get my shoes and we'll go see."

"My letters!" Flor cried, sprinting off.

"No! Come back," María Mercedes called. "Your letters are on the desk."

Flor stopped short and turned back. "¡Ay! Gracias a Dios." She sped into the house, María Mercedes in her wake.

Basilio and Pilar got only as close as a block from the post office when the fire's heat and the commotion at the scene stopped them in their tracks. They had run six blocks, something not recommended for those wearing flip-flops. Twice the rubber soles of Pilar's thongs had bent back upon themselves, almost pitching her to the ground. Now she stood in a mass of people, gasping for breath and giving herself resuscitating pats on the chest. The whole world, it seemed, had rushed to see the spectacle. The people stood, mute and improbably still, chins lifted, mouths opened into Os. All eyes swept past the gridlock of police cars and fire trucks to rest on the awesome sight of their post office in flames. Yellow licks of fire leaped from doors and windows. Towers of smoke billowed and turned dark as they rose. The noise was deafening. The blaze had a sound all its own: a deep rustling and then resounding cracks and pops, and occasionally something like a long low moan. And there was the hiss of fire meeting water as it cascaded in arcs from the hoses. In the distance, approaching ambulances wailed sharp warnings and laments.

"My God," Pilar said, reaching for Basilio's hand. She felt it, rough, weathered, strong, and comforting. After a moment, she let go of it. By silent mutual agreement, they turned back. It was senseless to witness such destruction.

They walked slowly this time, the smell of scorched wood churning around them. Ash floated in the air.

"Do you think other buildings'll go up?" Pilar said. She was thinking of María Mercedes's school, which was directly across the street. The image of her godchild, of Nanda, who also had attended, of them both caught in a burning building frightened her into silence. The fear made her want to take Basilio's hand again, but she resisted.

Basilio shook his head and said nothing. On his mind was Jacinta. What would Jacinta make of all of this?

María Mercedes had propped the kitchen door open, and when they walked into the house, they saw Flor at the table, head bent over her letters. María Mercedes was in the front room talking earnestly on the telephone.

"Is it really burning?" Flor asked, looking up.

"It's really burning," Pilar said.

"I have letters for Enrique. How in the world am I going to mail them?" Flor asked.

María Mercedes called out to Pilar, her hand over the mouthpiece. "It's Mamá. She called because she heard the news on the radio." María Mercedes held the phone out to Pilar. "Here, you talk to her. She's very upset."

Pilar took the phone. "Jacinta?" she said, but all that greeted her on the other end of the line was a low moan like that which had come from the fire. "Jacinta?" Pilar said again.

Muffled sobs came over the phone, "Ay, Pilar. Mi Miguel. Mi Miguel, Pilar."

Pilar lowered the phone for an instant. Miguel Acevedo. She had not thought of him. She raised the phone to her ear again.

"Pilar," Jacinta was saying, "listen to me. You went over there.

María Mercedes said you and Basilio went. Tell me the fire isn't bad, Pilar."

"I can't do that."

Jacinta's voice turned demanding. "Put Basilio on. I want to talk to him."

Pilar handed the phone over.

"Pilar won't say. Is the fire bad?"

"It's bad."

There was a pause and then, "Listen to me. I'm going to ask you a favor. You have to do what I say. You hear me, Basilio?"

"I'm listening."

"I want you to go to La Rábida. Go to his house. You know who I'm talking about. You know where he lives. Leave Flor at Pilar's and drive over there right now. Find out if he's all right. You understand me, Basilio?"

"Yes."

"Will you do it? Tell me that you'll do it."

"Yes," Basilio said, and then he gave the phone to María Mercedes again.

"Mamá? Don't worry, Mamá. I'm all right. Can't you tell I'm all right? I'm talking to you, aren't I?"

Basilio stood at the front door. Dusk was coming on, but then it might have been flames causing the sky to turn so many colors. In the richly leafed tree at the edge of the sidewalk, black chiltotas gathered noisily. Pilar came to stand beside him.

"She's in agony about Miguel," Pilar said under her breath.

"I know."

"I pray to God he wasn't in there," Pilar said. She gave a swift, sweeping thought to her own list of lovers. The last one, that Victor Morales, could burn in hell for all the trouble he had caused.

"Tell the girl we have to go," Basilio said, jerking a thumb in the direction of Flor in the kitchen. "If we wait any longer, we won't get through." He stepped down onto the path leading to the sidewalk. He waited at the car. Soon María Mercedes came out and gave him a quick embrace. "Mamá's all right. She was just worried about me."

Flor climbed in the car and they went off. At the corner, he didn't turn and go toward La Rábida. There wasn't any point. Miguel Acevedo did not live there anymore. A year ago there had been another letter from him to Jacinta. It had joined the three other unopened letters hidden away in Basilio's shed. That last one had not been posted in San Salvador. From the looks of the return address, Miguel Acevedo lived in San Vicente now.

▼▼▼

CHAPTER FORTY-EIGHT

El Congo
November 1964

"I'm so happy you're here," Chenta said, as María Mercedes stood behind the chair and brushed her hair.

"Me too, Tía." María Mercedes had arrived in El Congo days back, after school let out for the year and to escape another of Magda's exuberantly planned parties, this one in celebration of Flor and her graduation. Extricating herself from the festivities had been awkward. It had annoyed her mother and disappointed Magda. As far as Flor was concerned, who knew what she really felt, her head was so full of Enrique these days. Why the quick getaway? María Mercedes was hard pressed to explain it, even to herself. She would readily admit she was a fortunate young woman. Thanks to Magda, she had an education, a bachillerato, and while Flor might dismiss its importance, María Mercedes would not. Simply put, having a diploma showed she had risen above her inherent limitations, and therein lay the rub. Now that she had bettered herself, why this deep, rumbling dissatisfaction with her life? Now that she had risen above, to what could she aspire? Not to the life Magda and Flor led, of course. And not to the life of service her mother and Basilio led, though their allegiance to the Tobars had been commendable. One station too high, the other too . . . She couldn't complete the thought. To do so seemed like a betrayal. Better to seek the middle ground. A life like Pilar's, perhaps.

No question, María Mercedes was at a crossroads. Because of it, she had fled having to attend a party where baffling questions were sure to be posed: So tell us, what will you do now? Tell us, what exactly are your plans? Because she was at a crossroads, she quit the city, seeking time away in the company of an old woman who might help reason out her quandary.

"Noventiocho, noventinueve, cien," María Mercedes said, counting out the strokes around a big hairpin she held between her teeth. "There, one hundred. Just like in the movies." She put the brush down on Chenta's dresser an arm's length away.

"There's no movies in El Congo, you know." Chenta's scalp felt tingly. She sat in her scrubbed little room, the door open to sunlight and to the sounds of neighbors bustling off to work. She wore a freshly laundered shift, her legs bare, the sores that plagued her ankles exposed to the air.

María Mercedes twisted Chenta's gray hair into a bun and pinned it in place. "Did you ever go to the movies?"

"A long time ago la Gorda Pérez and I, we took the bus to Coatepeque. We saw *Nosotros los pobres, ustedes los ricos.*" She gave the bun at the nape of her neck a reassuring pat.

"*We the Poor, You the Rich.* I never heard of it."

"It was a terrible movie. Terrible. There was a boy in it with legs so deformed, he used a little platform with wheels to get around on. One day, he was scooting across the street when a machine ran over him. Squashed him flat."

"Goodness. Run over by a car."

"No. It was a big rolling machine they use for smoothing pavement."

"My God. A steamroller. That was in the movie?"

"Yes. And there were other things in it like that. It was the only movie I ever saw. But that poor squashed boy didn't stop la Gorda." Chenta tossed her head back and laughed. "She's the one who wants to buy my food stand, you know."

"Will you sell it?"

"Maybe. La Gorda's been shouting at me across the mercado aisle for twenty years."

"And you always shout back. Before, when I came visiting and heard you both, I thought you were fighting."

"Not Gorda and me. We have a good time. If I sold my stand to anyone, it would be to her."

"If you do, you'll have time for movies."

"I don't need el cine. I have my stories on the radio. There's *Las dos*, *El derecho de nacer*, and *Las mujeres de Tiburcio*." She ticked her three favorite novelas off on her fingers.

The radio was on the dresser, resting beside a fan with blades that clickclickclicked as they revolved, pushing the heat around the room. At the moment, because the radio novelas came on in the afternoon, the set was tuned to a station that featured rancheras. Chenta liked rancheras because each song told a story. "La cama de piedra" was on now. "Listen to that. They're playing 'The Bed of Stone.' Well, thanks to you, hija, I'm sleeping softly now." When María Mercedes arrived from San Salvador, it was like a hurricane had touched down. She had aired out the room, scoured the walls and floor, gathered up and done the wash. Amazingly, she had even talked Chenta into buying a bed to replace the pitiful petate that had her sleeping directly on the floor.

"You deserve comfort, Tía. I don't know how you slept on that thin old mat all these years. Your poor bones."

"Ay, life's hard. What's the difference." Chenta hauled herself up from the chair. "Well, I'm off. Before we know it, it'll be noon. The girls need help for the lunchtime crowd." Three women worked at La Cucharona: la Tulia, la Amada, and la Beva. These days, it was they who opened up the stand, got the fires and meals started. In the evening, it was they who cleaned up and closed down.

"Sit, Tía. It's not even nine. The girls know very well what to do. Besides, you can't go without fresh bandages on your ankles."

"Ay, these stupid old legs," Chenta grumped. She settled herself on the chair again. While María Mercedes tended to the bandages, Chenta gazed at the shelf above the dresser where the dear child had created an altar. Prints of saints were propped against the wall. Next to them a candle flickered in a tall glass holder. A plug of copal chased night odors away. It was like the old days when Mercedes was alive and both she and Jacinta lived here. Chenta made three quick signs of the cross, one on her forehead, one over her lips, one against her heart, in loving memory of Mercedes, may she rest in peace.

A big red dog poked its head into the room.

María Mercedes had squatted down beside the chair, and the animal momentarily startled her. "Get!" she said, giving a little clap, but her efforts to drive the dog away were in vain. It came into the room and sniffed around.

"The mutt's pretty brazen," Chenta said, lifting her legs out of its way.

"It must belong to someone in the mesón."

"I don't think I've seen it before," Chenta said.

A voice out on the gallery called, "¡Colorado!"

The dog pricked up its ears and trotted out.

As the dog retreated through the doorway, he was replaced by a young man who appeared to be in his twenties. Medium height. Muscular. Dark hair clipped short. The shadow of a beard high-lighted his cheeks and set off his eyes. He wore a patterned shirt with long sleeves neatly folded to the elbows. Khaki pants. Tightly laced boots. "Sorry about my dog. I'm moving in and he's con-fused." The man pointed across the patio. "I'm Fernando Lira. I'll be in number ten." The dog—lean, sinewy, thick shiny coat—sat obediently at his side. Somehow, man and beast complemented one another. "This is Colorado. But then, you've met already."

"You have a fearless dog," Chenta said, standing. "I'm Chenta. This is María Mercedes. I own an eating place in the market. La Cucharona de Chenta. I'm just now heading there. If you're new in El Congo, it's the only place to eat."

"Gracias, señora. I'll keep it in mind. A person always needs to eat." He dipped his head to the two of them. "Pleased to meet you both." As quickly as he'd materialized in the doorway, he disap-peared from it.

Chenta went to the door and looked after him. "Did you see the boots? What does a man need boots for? It's summer. It's hot."

"I wondered that too."

That night, very late, María Mercedes brought a chair out onto the gallery and tried to catch a breeze. She sat in the dark, listening to the soft sounds of Chenta's snoring, watching the lights going out, one after another, in the rooms around the patio. She smoked a cigarette, a habit she'd taken up, much to Pilar's consternation. Not that Pilar had a right to complain. Each night, she pulled out a bottle and had a shot or two before going to sleep. Her mother? Jacinta was ignorant of both these habits, neither María Mercedes nor Pilar having told on the other.

Long ago, both the women who'd shaped her flesh had sat on this very spot. Chenta had spoken often of the past: "You're just like your mother and your grandmother. They used to sit outside like that. Staring out into the night. Thinking their thoughts." Had they asked themselves the questions now churning through her head: What's my purpose, dear God? How will I fit in? María Mercedes took a last pull of her cigarette and flipped the lit butt into the patio. She wiped her eyes with the flat of a hand. These days, imponderable questions seemed always to bring tears. Across the patio, on the opposite gallery, a glowing point of light caught her attention. She watched it for a moment thinking it was a firefly, but then she recognized the lit end of a cigarette. Someone else was sitting out there in the night. Someone smoking and watching her. Fernando Lira in number 10?

One day, while Chenta was at the market, María Mercedes decided to whitewash the room. True, she'd already scrubbed the walls, but that was only a beginning. Years of living and the soot thrown out by the kerosene stove had turned them an indelible dirty gray. Besides, she was restless, and laboring at something physical was satisfying and, strangely enough, relaxing. Chenta gladly approved of all the fussiness and provided the colones to pay for whatever María Mercedes dreamed up to do. Today she whitewashed. Tomorrow she'd purchase a length of fabric, in a cheery yellow print, perhaps, and stitch curtains by hand to decorate the room's only window.

Before painting, María Mercedes cleared the room of furniture. She lugged outside a table, three chairs, a cot, the new bed, a dresser, the wardrobe. The wardrobe was the only cumbersome piece, and she'd had an anxious moment when it had almost toppled as she edged it past the doorsill and down onto the gallery. To protect the floor, she'd collected newspapers from the little store across the street and laid pages down along the walls. While the door and windows were thrown open to air and light, she'd set Chenta's only lamp in the middle of the room for added illumination. She turned the radio on and sang along as she worked: "Por vivir en Quinto Patio, desprecias mis besos. Because I live in Quinto Patio, you scorn my caresses." She dipped one of the balled-up rags she was using into the whitewash container. Already her hand looked as if she were wearing a chalky glove. Her skin tingled from the whiting. She was perspiring heavily—she could feel the sweat lined up above her lip, feel the moisture slipping between her breasts. She ignored all that. She ignored the heat and how unattractive she must look: hair pulled back and secured haphazardly on her head, shirt pulled out and tails knotted at her waist, skirt skimming her knees, bare legs and feet dotted with flecks from the whitewash. Chenta's room was coming alive, and that was all that mattered. It had the sharp fresh smell of quicklime, and soon, were the lamp to be removed, the room would radiate a brightness of its own.

Up on a stool she'd borrowed from the neighbor, she was daubing a corner, the final spot that needed doing. "¡Vaya!" she exclaimed, over the music on the radio. "All done." She stepped from the stool and almost onto the red dog. "¡Ay, chucho!" she said, startled by the animal sitting calmly upon his haunches. "What in the world are you doing here?" The dog's tail made quick wide arcs against the floor. She dropped the painting rag into the bucket. Went to turn down the radio for, given an intruder had stolen in, the music had clearly been too loud.

"Nothing like whitewash to improve the look of things."

María Mercedes glanced up from the radio, and there stood the dog's owner in the doorway, just as he had the week before. "This is getting to be a habit," she said, an edge of irritation to her voice because she was a mess and she hated that he'd caught her looking as she did.

"You're quite a sight," he said. The dog went loping over to him.

"So? What do you expect? I've been busy." She switched the radio completely off.

"I didn't mean that like it sounded," he said. "What I meant was that you're a sight for sore eyes."

"Sure you did." She poked a long strand of hair back up on her head.

"No, I mean it. I've had quite a week. I've been gone. I just now got back."

"Oh, really? I hadn't noticed." She stood in the middle of the room for a moment and then resolutely stepped outside because the heat seemed to intensify, and besides, what else could she do? She'd left a Coca-Cola on the gallery next to the dresser. She picked up the bottle and took a swig. The soda was flat. Warm.

"I'll go over to the tiendita. I'll get us two fresh bottles. You could use something cold."

She shrugged and turned her back on him. She went across the patio to the water pila. She scrubbed her hands with the ball of yellow soap lying on the edge of the stand. She ran a clean fingernail under the others caked white with lime. Out on the gallery, Chenta's belongings stood pushed together beside her door. The man and the dog, had they really been there?

María Mercedes leaned her head over the stand and splashed water on her face. She moistened the back of her neck, dangled her arms in the basin. The water in the pila wasn't cold, but it was refreshing.

"Here's your Coke." The words drifted across the patio.

She unknotted her shirttails and used them to dry her face and arms. She thought about tucking the tails in, but decided against it, letting them hang over her skirt instead. She strode back to Chenta's. Took the soda he held out. "I owe you twenty cents."

He shook his head. "You buy the next ones."

She went to sit at the edge of the gallery. She was in the shade, but her toes and half her feet were in the sun. She took a long drink as he sat down beside her, the tops of his dusty boots in the sun, too. She swallowed down the small burp that rose up, laid a hand over her mouth lest it try to escape. "Why the boots?"

"It's my work."

"It's summer. It's too hot for boots."

"I know, but they're useful for work." The dog had lain down, and he tipped the bottle and dribbled liquid into its mouth. The dog lapped noisily. "Colorado likes Coke."

"What an animal." She couldn't help smiling. She'd never seen a dog drink soda before. "So, what do you do?"

He set his bottle down, and it made a hollow sound against the tile. "Have you ever heard of the Acción Católica Universitaria?"

She shook her head, though it sounded vaguely familiar. When Nanda lived at home, she'd belonged to la Juventud de Estudiantes Cristianos, or JEC. "Is it like the Christian Students Youth Group?"

"It's similar. We do social service. We work in the countryside."

In Aguilares, Nanda did the same. "What does the university have to do with it?" María Mercedes asked.

"I'm going to the university. It's the university that sends me out."

For the first time, what he said intrigued her. "You're at the university? In San Salvador?"

He nodded. "La Universidad Nacional. I'll be starting my second year."

"I just got my bachillerato. Last month, in San Salvador. I went to la Masferrer. I think I want to go to the university."

"You should. And you should join la ACUS. You'd be good. I can see that. What you've been doing here, that's the kind of work we do. Clean things up. Fix things that don't work. Do things people don't know how to do. Or don't have time to do, given they're always busy breaking their backs trying to make a living."

"I have a cousin. Well, she's like a cousin. Her name is Nanda. She works in Aguilares with el padre Rutilio Grande. They do work like you."

"I know about Grande. He's a good priest. Your cousin is lucky to work with him."

"So what did you do this week? You mentioned you'd had quite a week."

"I was in Coatepeque. Cleaned out a ravine. Not a deep one, but a ravine just the same. It was filled with garbage. All kinds of filth. There were rats. Rats bring disease."

"I've never heard of that."

"Rats and disease? That's common knowledge."

"No, not that. I've never heard of a person cleaning a ravine."

"Well, you're looking at one who did."

"How's it done?"

"You rake the stuff around. Take out what won't burn. Fortunately, there's not much of that. Set fire to all the rest." He hoisted his chin to point out his boots. "That's why I wear boots. Long sleeves, too." Like the time before, his sleeves were folded back neatly.

"You don't look like you've spent a week in a ravine."

"What you mean is, I don't smell like I've spent a week in a ravine."

She laughed because that's exactly what she'd thought.

"They do have laundries in Coatepeque, you know. Running water, too. Actually, there's a lake there. It's the deepest blue you've ever seen."

"They also have a movie. My auntie went there once."

"I thought she was your grandmother."

"No. She's my aunt. Actually, she's not really my aunt. She's like an aunt, only better."

"Speaking of that, can I help with your aunt's furniture? I'm very good at being helpful, you know."

"I'll be the judge of that." María Mercedes held out a hand. "By the way, I'm María Mercedes Prieto."

He shook her hand firmly. "And I'm Fernando Lira."

"Do you like to be called Nando?"

"No. Prefiero Fernando."

"Then Fernando it is," she said, withdrawing her hand from his and springing up. "Come on. We'll start with Tía's wardrobe."

A week before Christmas, María Mercedes and Fernando paused from their labor in a copse of trees just outside town. At María Mercedes's instigation, they had dug up a stunted evergreen—a pitch pine most probably, half again as tall as themselves—to lug to the mesón and set out in the patio.

"Good thing the mesón's close," Fernando said. "It'll take the two of us to haul this thing." He mopped his brow with a swipe of one hand, propping the shovel up with the other.

"Want a drink?" María Mercedes lifted the canteen—his canteen—filled with cool water. She'd carried it by the strap slung over her shoulder.

"Here. Let's sit for a minute. Colorado has the right idea." The dog had sprawled out under an ironwood, but they'd been laboring in a patch of clearing directly in the sun. When they sat down in the shade, Colorado lifted his big head in acknowledgment. They took long drinks from the canteen. The dog sauntered up for his share.

"The bugs are bad." María Mercedes slapped a gnat off her arm, moist with sweat. She widened an eye to rid herself of some tiny thing trapped annoyingly under the eyelid. "Tomorrow. Where will you be going?"

"Cantarrana. It's west. Not too far from here."

" 'Singing Frog.' That's pretty."

"Not 'singing frog,' it just sounds that way. This Cantarrana has two rs."

"Oh." She waved away another pest fluttering around her face. "So what's there to do in Cantarrana? Cantarrana with the two rs."

He laughed and batted the air himself. "We're rebuilding the market."

"What's wrong with the market that it has to be rebuilt?"

"It's falling down. Actually one section did fall down. Last winter, during one of the big rains. The roof caved in. Some people were killed."

"Goodness. Maybe they should have shut the place down."

"You can't shut a mercado down. The people won't let you. After the church, a market provides a town with its only other meeting place." In El Congo, laborers, both rural and urban, shop owners and shopkeepers, domestic servants and civil employees eagerly made their way once or twice a day down cramped streets, cobbled as yet with ancient stones, to el mercado and its converging aisles and colorful piles of produce and meat. People collected under the spans of corrugated iron to roam in search of a meal's ingredients, to sit on comedor benches to have a bite, a sip, to trade bits of gossip, the details and particulars of their lives. "Actually, a mercado's like a country," Fernando added. "It has a population, a topography. Its own economy. Even its own politics. It's all there in the market."

"Politics? How does it have that?"

"It has to do with power. With who has the power in the market. Can you guess who does?"

Tía Chenta came immediately to mind. "Stall owners. They have the power."

"No. What they have is position," Fernando said. "As you know, stall owners don't own their stalls. They're really stallkeepers. They rent space. Some of them turn around and rent out part of the space they rent."

"I didn't know that. Chenta's always called herself a stall owner. In fact, she's thinking about selling hers one day."

"What she'll do is sell her rights to the space she rents."

"Then why does she call herself a stall owner when she's not?" María Mercedes slapped at still another gnat.

"It's human nature to claim things for your own when you've put years and sweat and heaven knows how many colones into them. A campesino still talks about 'his' milpa, 'his' little plot of land, when in reality the people's communal lands were abolished almost a hundred years ago."

"I thought that when someone said they owned something, they owned it. Period."

"Oh no. Not in this country. In this country, only the very few own things outright. The people certainly don't. For the people, there are always strings attached."

"So who has the power in the market, then?"

"The market owners have it. They own the land. They own the stalls and take in rent. And if stallkeepers rent out their space, the market owners get a share of that."

"You mean they collect twice for the same space?"

"That's right. That's power. And that's politics."

"My God, what you're saying is that when Chenta sells her stall, she'll have to give part of her money to the market owners."

"That's right."

"But that's not fair. That's wrong."

Fernando nodded.

"I wonder if Chenta knows all this?"

"Your tía Chenta not only knows it, she's living it." Fernando paused. "Anyway, enough of the lecture. I could go on and on if you let me." He stood and brushed off the back of his trousers.

María Mercedes was amazed. In minutes, he'd provided an education. More and more she was intrigued by him. "Do you think you'll be finished in Cantarrana in time for Christmas?" Before he could answer, she added, "But then, you're probably going home for Christmas. To San Salvador, I mean." In the few weeks since they'd met, he had not divulged much personal information, and she had not pressed him for it.

"No. I'll be working for Christmas," he said cryptically.

It was like a little cloud had come over them. María Mercedes scrambled up to help dissipate it. "Well, let's get this tree to the mesón."

As they walked, they took turns holding the top and the bottom of the tree, the bottom being heavier because of the earth clumped around the roots. There was the shovel, too, so they had that to juggle, which made the going awkward. Colorado trotted up ahead of them, the marshal of their parade. Along the way, people stuck heads out of windows, stood in doorways calling out their admiration, but no one volunteered to lend a hand. Still, María Mercedes passed out oral invitations: Come to the mesón and help decorate the tree. On Christmas Eve we'll have a party: fireworks, music, a feast.

Half the town, it seemed, turned up at the mesón for the party. Tacked along the edge of the gallery were strings of lights and colorful paper chains. The neighbors had thrown their doors open to the celebration, brought chairs out from their rooms, tables on which to display contributions to the feast: tamalitos, pupusas, curtido, frijolitos, plátanos en miel, tortas, and dulces. Pilsners and Coca-Colas bobbed in tubs of chipped ice. A five-gallon container of agua de canela sat directly on the gallery floor, a ladle for dipping hooked on to the rim.

Radios were synchronized to the same station—YSU, "La más popular"—and turned up so loud that Lucho Gatica, the singer featured on the air and now crooning "El reloj," seemed to be doing it smack in the middle of the patio. In this spot, too, the lighted little tree groaned happily under its handmade decorations: paper twists and chains, painted tin stars, ribbons, bows, and corn-husk figurines.

For the party, María Mercedes had worn her green dress with the flattering neckline and the sandals her mother had sent as a Christmas gift. In the letter accompanying the package, there was this news from Jacinta: Basilio and she were sad because a daughter was not coming home, Pilar had gone off to Aguilares to visit Nanda and Eduardo and his family, Magda's house was in full holiday splendor, and Florencia was lovesick and would hardly come out of her room.

María Mercedes's package home contained a string bag for Jacinta and a straw hat for Basilio. Also, there was a letter with her own news: She was happy in El Congo. The little town was opening her eyes.

"Did I mention we once had a party for your mother in this very patio?" Joaquín Maldonado said to María Mercedes. They stood by the tree, the night sky showing off its own pretty lights. The heat of the day had vanished, and the air was a pleasure against bare flesh.

"I think you *have* mentioned that, don Joaquín."

"Well, it was her saint's day as I recall. She wore a lilac dress. A ribbon in her hair." With a fingertip, he gave a few perfunctory swipes to the trim mustache lining his upper lip. "I remember details like that. I pride myself on remembering things."

"I think it's a great talent, don Joaquín."

"Especially at my age. Did I mention I just turned seventy-five?"

He'd mentioned it before, but she said, "Seventy-five? Goodness. I wouldn't have guessed it."

"I know," he said, his expression birdlike and intense. "I'm a wonder. I remember everything. You have a question, you come ask me. I'm at the mercado. Stall thirteen. Me and my machine. We write letters for people."

"I'm aware of that. For years you've written letters for tía Chenta."

"When you write letters for people, you get to know many things."

A host of children cavorted along the gallery and in the patio around the tree. The little girl from number 8 poked María Mercedes's leg. "When are the fireworks?"

"Do you like fireworks?"

The girl shook her head and cupped her hands over her ears.

"How about sparklers? Sparklers don't make noise."

"Let me see."

María Mercedes excused herself from don Joaquín. She led the girl over to el Chato Arenas, who had a face as flat as a bulldog's, and who was in charge of the fireworks. "Light a sparkler for her, Chato. Show her they don't make noise."

Chato, proud to be entrusted on such a significant night with such an important task, touched a match to a stick and held it up, and soon star beams sprinkled over them.

"See?" María Mercedes said when the light shower died down. She looked around for the girl, but apparently she had darted off. In the spot where she had been, Colorado sat. María Mercedes spun around. Fernando Lira appeared behind her. "We came back," was what he said.

▼▼

CHAPTER FORTY-NINE

Magda was in the upstairs family room, a room spanned by a row of windows projecting over the garden and overlooking the pool. She sat at her desk, a wooden harvest table lacquered the color of marigolds. She'd risen early, had breakfast, dressed in a caftan of geometric designs, and settled in to a mountain of paperwork in the cheerful peacefulness of her favorite room with its splendid view and its apricot walls, with the nubby maize sofa and the overstuffed chairs. All alarmingly modern, her friends would say, by which they meant the furniture was armless, and when you sat on it, it could swallow you up.

The house was quiet, thanks to the early hour and to Alvaro's and Flor's absence. Alvaro was harvesting cotton—he now had three plantations at various locations on the coast. He would be home in time for the holidays. Flor, on the other hand, had been away for only a week at Lake Ilopango with Gladis Díaz, her best friend. The girls would be back later in the day. Since their graduation last month, the two were inseparable.

Flor's academic conversion had been a miracle. Throughout her school life she had been a reluctant, average student. It was prodding and gentle threats that got her through to the end. A few months before graduation, the subject of college came up. Gladis Díaz would be going to Maryknoll, and suddenly Flor was also eager to attend. The change in attitude both surprised and thrilled Magda. Looking back, she was wistful that she herself had settled for a simple bachillerato. But times were different then. Back then love and marriage and family were all a girl could envision as a future. The regrets about her schooling did not extend to her life with Alvaro Tobar. Far from it. He and the children, and now her grandchildren, were the glories of her life. But they were not her everything. This she would admit only to a precious few: Her everything was family and home, *plus* her career.

Thus when Flor confessed an earnest desire to forgo the planned debutante's ball and go off to college instead, Magda had been only mildly disappointed. Once the decision had been made, she threw herself into gaining Flor admittance to Maryknoll, the Catholic women's college, working with the determination and vigor that formed the hallmark of all projects she undertook. She wrote letters, placed phone calls, made endless to-do lists, and, with smug satisfaction, crossed out each accomplished step in her carefully planned crusade. Her labor paid off. Though it would be bittersweet to send her little girl away, come January, Flor and Gladis would head for New Orleans to be welcomed into the stern but loving community of the Maryknoll sisters.

Magda turned back to her desk. Christmas was ten days away, and her head overflowed with details: menus and decorations to plan, gift lists and cards to write. This year she'd settled on a tree theme for the holidays. Trees would be everywhere. In every principal room of the house, lavishly decorated and lighted. Even in the garden, Basilio would thread lights through the orange trees. Gifts, too, would come from trees; every one would be fashioned of wood.

Elena walked in and dropped heavily onto the sofa. She was visiting from Santa Ana, and her presence in the household was calming and a blessing. When she was about, she was helpful and unobtrusive as air. Not so this morning. Her face was pinched and pale this morning.

"Look at this," Elena said, handing Magda a packet of envelopes tied in a bunch with grosgrain ribbon.

"What is it?" Magda said.

"Letters. They were on Flor's dresser. I went in to open up the room and see what needed doing."

Magda untied the ribbon. She fanned the envelopes out. There were ten of them. Each had the name "Salah" written on the upper left-hand corner. Each envelope was addressed to Srta. Florencia Elena Tobar. She turned the envelopes over. On the back flaps was the number eighty-three. Magda looked up at her mother. "What do you suppose . . . ?" She let her voice trail off because there was no mistaking what this pointed to.

"Flor is getting letters from a Salah in New Orleans." It was distasteful to say the name. Saying the name led to thinking of Isabel; thinking of Isabel led directly to Cecilia. "Cecilia" was the one name she would never say. It had been thirty-some years, and she had not uttered it once.

"They're from Enrique Salah," Magda said. "We have to read these, Mamá. We have no choice." Magda counted out five letters. "Here. You read these; I'll read the rest."

The two sat together on the sofa. Shoulder to shoulder, heads bent over vellum, they discovered a hidden life.

Flor and Gladis returned from Lake Ilopango late in the afternoon. They rode in "la lancha," the maroon Oldsmobile as spacious as a boat belonging to Gladis's father and chauffeured by Mauricio, he of the stout arms and the mustache like a quick swipe from a dirty thumb. Cruising home, Flor and Gladis talked softly in the backseat. The topic of their conversation was that which had consumed most of their waking hours at the lake: True Love. Specifically, true love in the face of grave societal and family objections. Flor discussed the matter avidly because she was the one in love and Gladis was her sole confidante. Gladis discussed it because she had no true love of her own and because being near the ardor blazing in Flor's heart provided her a spark from which to warm her own. True love aside, the friends had talked about their many plans for Maryknoll, among them, the room they would share, the path Flor would forge between their room and Enrique Salah's at Tulane.

The Oldsmobile turned into the long graveled driveway that led to Flor's house. In anticipation of her arrival, Basilio had thrown open the iron gates and shut Alvaro's three German shepherds up in their pens. Basilio stood at the top of the drive watching the big car roll toward him. He glanced beyond it, beyond the steep walls enclosing the place, beyond the stone pillars heading the drive. The gathering twilight showing through the tops of the locaria trees on Avenida La Capilla dispirited him. All day disharmony had reigned in Magda's house. All day accusations and reprimands. Now here came the cause of it all.

At the front door, Flor stepped out of the car. Her skin was golden from the sun, her blond tousled hair blonder yet from it. Basilio gathered Flor's suitcase and her nécessaire, and set them on the gleaming tiles of the portico.

"Call me," Gladis said, poking her head through the open window before Mauricio started off.

Flor waved good-bye. She picked up the nécessaire while Basilio took up the suitcase. "How are things, Basilio?" she said. Then she turned toward the open door and toward Jacinta, standing there in her dove gray uniform with the perennial key ring at her waist.

"What's wrong?" Flor said, weakness surging down her legs at the sight of Jacinta's face. Flor hurried into the foyer.

"Your grandmother found your letters," Jacinta said.

"What are you talking about?" Flor raised her nécessaire up instinctively. It contained her makeup and toiletries. It contained the packet of Enrique's latest letters.

"Your letters from the boy. La niña Elena found them on your dresser." She did not go on to say that Magda had confronted her. That Magda had voiced keen disappointment at not being told from the beginning about Flor's letters going to Pilar's. "You let me down, Jacinta," Magda had said, and the accusation stung because all along she'd been caught in the middle. They all had. She, Pilar, Basilio, and María Mercedes.

"Are you saying Abuela showed the letters to Mamá?" Flor asked.

Jacinta nodded.

Flor reached for Jacinta to steady herself. When packing for the lake, she'd taken a number of letters out from hiding, sorted through them before stashing them back away. Unthinkingly, she must have left a packet out. How could she have done such a stupid thing? "Where's Mamá?"

"Upstairs. In the family room. She and your grandmother."

"Very well," Flor said. She squared her shoulders, crossed the foyer, and went up the wide curving staircase to the second floor. The nécessaire bumped against her thigh as she went, the small valise and its one beribboned content a reminder that the only thing that mattered in this world was true love.

When Flor came in the family room, her mother and grandmother turned their heads and the words they were speaking were suspended in the air. Flor made out the words. They were "liar," "deceiver," "disappointment," "disgrace." The words rose over the sofa. Flor saw them collide one off the other, saw them ricochet over the coffee table, a massive carved door covered cleverly with glass. On the table sat the silver coffee service, the demitasses, the silver teaspoons with tiny coffee berries on the end. From the elegant curve of the coffee spout, a trail of steam spelled its own accusation: "perfidy" the word.

Enrique's letters were strewn on the table. The ribbon used to lash them lay, without purpose, on the glass. Flor bent to kiss her mother; she kissed her grandmother as well. She took a seat on the lounge chair, pregnant with pillows. To fortify herself, she placed the nécessaire squarely on her lap. "I don't know what to say," she said finally.

"I know what to say," Magda retorted. "You're not going to New Orleans."

Flor raised her chin against the pronouncement, against the coldness creeping down her back. She glanced out the big window. In the time it took to walk upstairs, darkness had thickened outside. Lights along the inside of the pool had come on. In the room, the soft lighting recessed at the back of glass shelves lining one wall swam like a mirage before her eyes. The shelving held old wooden santos, some with a palm held up and three fingers raised in blessing. There was no solace in the sight. Flor turned her face her mother's way. "It's because he's a turco," she said.

"You lied to us," Magda said, deflecting Flor's remark.

"I never lied, Mamá."

"Deception. It's the same thing."

Elena said nothing. She sat on the sofa, her face looking like stone.

Tears slipped down Flor's cheeks. They fell on her hands bunched around the sturdy handle of the nécessaire. "Enrique and I, we've done nothing wrong. We love each other. That's all."

What do you know about love, Elena thought. You're a child; you know nothing about love.

"How long has this been going on?" Magda said.

Flor raised her shoulders, then dropped them again.

"Do you realize what you're doing?" Magda asked.

"Obviously you think I don't. So why don't you tell me, Mamá." In a dizzying rush of feeling, the words hurled out.

"Don't get insolent with me," Magda said, her voice clotted with anger.

"Perdóname, Mamá."

There was a moment of raw silence. Then Magda said, "You have to end this thing. Cut it off. I have nothing against the Salahs. God knows, Isabel is an old friend. Abraham Salah is your father's partner. But life with a Salah, well, it would be different than what you know."

"How could it be different? Tell me. How?"

"Look what happened to Isabel. She was one of us. Then she married a Salah . . ."

". . . and she became one of them," Flor said, holding her mother's gaze.

"Yes. She became a Salah and that was a banishment. Do you know what that means? It means friends will drop you, some as if you were plagued, others with slow insidious sureness. It means doors will close in your face. In your children's faces. In your children's children's faces. Think of that."

"I don't care."

Magda stood and began to pace. With stiff fingers, she stabbed at her hair. "Well, I care. And believe me, I'm not about to let that happen. Not to my daughter, I won't."

"You already let it happen," Flor said. "Isabel was your friend until you banished her."

"¡Niña insolente!" Elena exclaimed, finally speaking out. "You don't know what you're talking about."

Flor gripped the nécessaire's handle more fiercely. "Yes I do, Abuela. You and Mamá and Enrique's mother and his grandmother. For years and years, you've been feuding about something. Exactly what, I don't know. I don't care to know. Neither does Enrique. Enrique and I love each other. That's all we care about."

Elena crumpled against the soft cushions of the sofa.

"You're breaking my mother's heart," Magda said, her feet like they were bolted to the floor.

"You're both breaking mine," Flor said.

Before the showdown ended, admonitions were meted. Rules were set. It all boiled down to one thing: There was to be no further contact between Flor Tobar and Enrique Salah.

It was Gladis Díaz who acted on Flor's behalf. When Enrique came home for the holidays, she was the one sent to break the news.

CHAPTER FIFTY

▼▼

I n all of Flor's life, no Christmas had been as dismal. Not since her grandfather's death had her spirit been as broken. For virtually the whole holiday, she languished in her room, supine, stricken on the bed. She'd tucked Enrique's letters between the mattress and the box springs, and the endearments contained in them were a life raft keeping her afloat. She'd committed most of the letters to memory, and so she placed herself atop them, eyes gritty from little sleep and much sobbing, turning his words over and over in her mind: "Nothing I do, nothing I see, makes any sense without you near me," or "How can a man concentrate on studies when all that fills his head is Florencia Elena Tobar?" or "You are my queen and the whole of my sky. In short, you are my destiny." Because communication was prohibited and attempts to thwart the ban were impossible, Flor resorted to sending him short telepathic messages: I love you, my darling, and It wasn't my idea, and It isn't my fault.

All those in the house were touched by Flor's heartache. Jacinta and Basilio (putting the incident with Magda behind them), and Socorro, the cook, reached back into their own experience and said quick prayers for the healing balm of time. Tea, though sensitive to Flor's condition, was peeved nevertheless because she'd not been included in the letter-writing ruse. That Jacinta and Basilio had been admonished for it took the sting out of the slight.

Magda and Elena were practical about Flor's condition: Broken hearts always mend, they said, intending to comfort. For the greater good, painful situations have to be endured. Alvaro, on the other hand, was oblivious to the crisis. Either that, or he chose to act as if he were. In any case, the household buzzed with the festivities attendant to Christmas and the New Year. They had scant time for doling out consolation. Wrapped in the whirl of the holidays, they set the matter aside. Give Flor time, they thought, and her infatuation will pass.

Unfortunately, they all misjudged.

Not true of Gladis Díaz. Gladis who viewed life through the rosy lens of romance. Gladis who devoured love stories by Corín Tellado. Gladis who adored movies that made you cry and who, every weekday at four, tuned the radio to *Las dos*.

A few days after New Year's, Gladis and Flor were attending a matinee at the cine next to Tesoros. *Doctor Zhivago* with Omar Sharif was playing. Gladis had seen it twice during the holidays, and she thought Enrique looked like Yuri Zhivago, that Flor looked like Lara. She was happy that Magda had finally loosened her grip on Flor's movements so that Flor could come see the similarities for herself.

Gladis waited until the movie began before she sprang her surprise. After the credits rolled by, the Cyrillic-type letters scrolling past sweeping images of grimy Moscow and the lush Russian countryside, she nudged Flor in the arm. "Te tengo una sorpresa," Gladis whispered, leaning close. "Enrique's here."

"What!" Flor exclaimed a bit too loudly, so she lowered her voice and her head as well. "¿Enrique?" She felt the blood drain away from her head.

"I called to tell him we were coming." It was very dark, but even in the dark, Gladis's face beamed.

Flor craned her neck and peered around. It was a weekday afternoon. Despite the movie's fresh acclaim, not many were at the cine. Those attending were mere bundles in the gloom. Gladis tugged on Flor's sleeve. "No, niña. Not down here. I told him you'd meet him in the balcony."

El balcón. Where lovers met for assignations.

"You do want to see him, don't you?" Gladis whispered.

Flor shot a whisper back: "What a question."

"Come, then," Gladis said, springing up and leading the way. They climbed the stairs to the balcony. "Ta-da!" Gladis said, pointing with a flourish to the lone figure sitting at the top of the theater, in the back row and off to the side.

Flor slipped in beside Enrique. "Hola, Pollo."

"Hola, Repollo," he said, completing their ritual greeting.

For a long moment they stared at each other, both softly bathed in the grainy light streaming in a tunnel from the projection booth. The whir of the movie reel was her own quavering heart.

He took her hand and pulled her close, the armrest a barrier between them. "I missed you so much."

"Thank God for Gladis," Flor exclaimed breathlessly. She went on, the rush of murmured words keeping pace with the rapidity of her pulse. "My mother and my grandmother. They won't be budged. I thought I'd die through the holidays. I never went anywhere. All I did was think of you, crazed with what might happen to us because of them."

"I know. I know." He brought his face near and laid his mouth over hers, taking in the heady fullness of her lips, the eager way her mouth molded itself to his. He kissed her eyes, her cheeks, her mouth again. "Te quiero, Repollo," he murmured.

"Te quiero a ti." She clung to him, even over the broad paddle of the armrest.

After a moment, he tipped his head and looked into her eyes. "I have to go back in five days."

"They're sending me to Boston. To the Maryknolls there."

"Boston?"

"In April. It's too late to get in now."

"I have to stay at Tulane. For two and a half years."

"I know."

The reality of their situation stunned them. For a moment, they turned their faces toward the screen. Toward the story unfolding even as theirs was. On the screen, Yuri rushed after Lara as she fled the glittering ball, following her home to find Lara's keeper unconscious on the bed. "Please do something," Lara said to Yuri, her brow creased with apprehension.

The predicament on the screen prompted furious whisperings again. "We have to do something, Enrique. Mamá's less watchful. She thinks you've gone back to school."

"Let's meet tomorrow. At la Escuela Americana. We can talk freely there; school's still out."

"I'll slip away right after lunch."

"Promise?" He gathered her hands against his lips.

"Te lo prometo," she said.

The next day, he watched her come through the wide opening in the wall built at the back of the school. She hurried over the sports field, tanned legs flashing, her golden hair bouncing in the sun. He rushed to meet her, embracing her at midfield. Hand in hand, they walked back to the wooden bleachers, going up a few rows to sit in the shade. Enrique laid an arm along her shoulders, thinking it was a miracle they were at last alone. For this moment, it was only them in the world under this bright spacious sky. "Was it hard to get away?"

She shook her head. "In the house, everyone's drowsy after lunch. Also, they think you've gone back. They're not paying much attention." During lunch, she had eaten little, her appetite dulled by the thought of him only minutes away. At the table, she'd made conversation with her mother and her grandmother, keeping her emotions in check lest suspicions be raised. She'd been spared her father's further scrutiny: He was back on the coast and out of the way.

"I leave on Sunday." He squeezed her shoulder reassuringly. Then, as if it might help, he added, "The plane leaves at two."

"We have four days. Four and a half, if you count part of Sunday." Flor laid her head on his shoulder.

"What can we do?" He kissed the top of her head, her hair smelling of sunshine and something like lavender.

"Mamá says I have to make my debut. In March, after the cotton harvest and before I'm sent to school." What irony. Three years back, so many tears when her Fiesta Rosa was canceled. Now, a more significant celebration loomed, unimpeded, ahead. In her life, she could not have wanted anything less.

"It'll be at the Campestre, won't it?"

"Oh, God," she said, dumb with realization. She lifted her head and looked into his eyes. His dark, long-lashed eyes, filled with resignation. He was a Salah. Salahs were not allowed at the club. For the first time, the enormity of his burden crashed down upon her. She threw her arms around him, pressed her mouth hard against his, her arms tightening as if with a fervent embrace she might ease injustice and the past. "It's not fair," she said, muttering the words against his mouth. He pulled her finally away, holding her tenderly. "Forget about me, Repollo. Life's too complicated with someone like me."

"No, no." She buried her face against his chest. He smelled of leather and salt and the powdery fragrance of talc. Under his shirt, his chest hair was springy against her cheek. The bulk of him, sure and strong, filled her with such wild sweetness that her eyes misted. She could not live on this earth without him. She must never let him go.

"You and me," he said, "we're like Romeo y Julieta."

"No," she said, raising her face to his again. "Look what they had to do to be together."

"They got married," he said.

"No, they didn't; they died."

"We could get married," he said in a rush. Such a simple statement. Such a formidable challenge.

"My parents would never allow such a thing. Your parents wouldn't either." She did not have much experience with his parents, don Abraham and la niña Isabel. Over the years, she had seen don Abraham at the candle factory on several occasions when she accompanied her father. Flor had met Isabel only twice: once at Tesoros, another time when Basilio delivered some gifts to her house. And she'd seen the pair together only once, at her grandfather's funeral in Santa Ana. Doña Cecilia, Flor had never met. Enrique's grandmother was a puzzling mystery, a specter, in Flor's imagination.

"Would you do it?" Enrique said, his expression solemnly expectant. "Would you marry me?"

"Is that a question, Enrique?"

He nodded. "Will you marry me, Flor?"

She started to cry. All the heartache of the past weeks welled up behind her eyes and spilled over. "Ay, si, mí Pollo. I'll marry you." She lowered her head, bunching her hands over her mouth as if to dam herself up.

"Don't cry," he said, taking her in his arms.

"I can't help it." A storm had erupted inside her, and there was nothing left to do but ride it out.

He held her, running a hand slowly up and down her back until she quieted. "Here," he said, fishing a handkerchief out of a pocket.

"But how can we do it?" she asked, her voice still hiccuppy and strange. She blew her nose demurely, then dabbed her eyes. The handkerchief had the same fresh smell captured in his shirt. It was the smell she wanted with her for the rest of her days. The smell of him on her fingers, on her flesh, just under her nose.

"Like Romeo y Julieta, we'll have to run away."

She wiped her eyes again, and in an instant, the solution to their problem came to her, clear as crystal but equally fragile and vulnerable. She laid a fingertip on the dear beauty mark above his lip, then brought the finger to her lips. She drew in a deep bolstering breath before continuing. "We don't have to run away to get married. I know something better."

"What?" he said, a quizzical look spreading over his face.

"If I was going to have a baby, they'd make us get married."

It was like she'd thrown a punch to his stomach. "You're joking," he blurted.

"No."

"You're not joking?"

"No. I'm serious."

"But to have a baby, we'd have to . . ."

She laid a hand over his mouth. "I know," she said.

He kissed her fingers. "Could you do it? Would you do it?"

"Yes," she said.

"But why?" he asked because he could hardly believe what she was saying, that she truly meant what she said.

She looked him directly in the eye. "Because I want to," she replied. "Because I love you. Because it's the only way."

▼   ▼   ▼

Two months later, Flor was in Mario Ruiz's office, sitting in the same spot her mother had occupied when learning she was pregnant with Flor. Flor had come to the doctor's office alone. Basilio had driven her. She had not called ahead. She had simply walked in and asked the nurse to announce her arrival. "It's an emergency," Flor had said.

"It's a tragedy," Mario Ruiz said now, his long face looking even longer. "You're a child. You're only, what? seventeen?"

"Eighteen. Two weeks ago. And it's not a tragedy, Doctor."

"Please tell me who did this to you, my child. Tell me the truth. Allow me to bring the brute who abused you to justice."

"Believe me, Doctor, what happened was not abuse." It was heaven, she thought, those last three days before Enrique left, those stolen hours together, their meeting at the school, their going off in his car to Lake Ilopango. Flor stood and thanked the doctor for seeing her so promptly. "And please don't call my mother," Flor said. "Let me break the news myself."

Back in the car, she asked Basilio to drive her to Enrique's house. When a servant opened the door, she said, "I'm Florencia Tobar. I need to see la niña Isabel."

"Pase adelante," the servant said, leading Flor to the gallery that overlooked a lush, colorful garden. "I'll let la señora know you're here." The servant turned heel and disappeared.

Sets of wrought-iron furniture were grouped on the gallery, but Flor ignored the chairs and stood waiting. She was numbed yet strangely fortified by the knowledge that what she and Enrique had put in motion had succeeded as planned.

"¡Chula!" Isabel said, "Darling!" She came out of the house, all cheerfulness and vigor. She swept Flor up in a hearty embrace. "What a lovely surprise! Come, come sit." Isabel scraped back a chair and set both Flor and herself down. "So, tell me. What brings you to my door?" A pause, then her face collapsed. "What's wrong? Something's wrong?"

"I'm going to have a baby."

"You're going to have a baby?" Isabel repeated, her brow knit with puzzlement. She might as well have said, Why tell me this?

"Actually, Enrique and I are going to have a baby."

In an instant all manner of expressions skitted across Isabel's face: befuddlement, shock, disbelief. "My Enrique?" she said at length, stubby fingers pointing toward the shelf of her breasts.

"Yes. Enrique."

"Does he know about this? He's away at school, you know."

Flor nodded. "I called him last night. I told him I was going to the doctor today. I just came from there."

"What did he say?"

"He said I'm two months along."

"No, not the doctor. Enrique. What did Enrique say?"

"He said he loved me."

A wisp of a woman came out of the house. She crossed the gallery and approached the table. The woman's hair was a cap of white fluff. Her face was deeply tanned and crisscrossed with furrows. "This is my mother," Isabel said.

Flor stood up. "Buenas, doña Cecilia."

"This is Enrique's friend, Mamá."

"Soy Florencia Tobar." Flor gave a slight bow of the head.

"Flor is Magda and Alvaro's daughter," Isabel said. She pulled a chair out for her mother.

Cecilia dropped into the chair. She sat there, breathing laboriously for a moment. "It's my lungs," she said, almost in apology, pointing fleetingly to her chest. She nested her hands together on her lap. When it appeared she had regained her strength, she said, "So. This is Florencia."

"Excuse me a minute," Isabel said. "Let me see to some refreshments." She hurried out.

Cecilia and Flor sat in silence for a moment, the two keenly aware of each other. Then Cecilia said, "I see you're fair like your father, but determined like your mother."

Flor laughed. "You're right. My mother's very determined."

"Determination runs in your family," Cecilia said.

"Yes." What more determination than abuela Elena and her imperial silence of thirty-odd years?

"Enrique has told me much about you, Flor," Cecilia said.

"He did?" She heard her voice wobble, the first chink in the armor she'd built around herself.

"He did. I know all about you and Enrique."

Flor sat back and looked into Cecilia's rutted, open face. The dark penetrating gaze. The kind mouth. This was a woman who had not been defeated by isolation but had made it a staff to lean upon instead. This woman she could trust. Flor borrowed what she needed from Cecilia's presence and said, "I just came from the doctor."

"You're here, so you must have had good news."

"Yes. It was good news."

"I'm so pleased, my dear." Cecilia laid a veiny hand on Flor's arm. Flor covered Cecilia's hand with her own.

Isabel came out of the house again. "I called Enrique. He's on the phone. He wants to talk with you, Flor."

Flor stiffened and pressed the back of her neck. The afternoon was hot and humid, yet all the air seemed to go out of it.

"Come. The phone's in my bedroom."

Flor followed Isabel through the house: across the speckled tile of the living room, past the dining room and down the hall. The bedroom was thickly carpeted and cool. An air conditioner hummed from the wall. Shades were drawn and the light was dim. The telephone lay on a night table beside a marriage bed spread with pale blue satin. Flor lifted the receiver. "Pollo?" she said.

"I'm coming home," he said.

"When?"

"Tomorrow."

She dropped onto the bed. Her pulse throbbed like a drumbeat in her temples and her chest. "I was so afraid," she said, choking out the words.

Over the limitless cord connecting them, he said, "Don't cry, Repollo. I'm coming home. We'll get married; then you're coming back with me. It'll be just the way we planned."

"Oh, yes." She wiped tears away with a hand. On the dresser, family pictures framed in silver. Among them, Enrique with a chubby arm thrown around the neck of a spotted fawn. Enrique, broadly grinning, eyes shut tight against a dachshund's sloppy licks.

The bed bobbed as Cecilia sat down. She pressed a linen handkerchief into Flor's hand. "All is well," Cecilia said, circling an arm around Flor's slender waist.

▼   ▼   ▼

Flor and Enrique were married by el padre Adolfo in the small downstairs chapel at the Guadalupe Church. Given the circumstances, a white dress was inappropriate, so Flor wore the long abandoned pale-pink dress Pilar had made for her Fiesta Rosa. The dress was snug, but it still fit. For the whole of the wedding, Enrique, rakishly handsome in a dark three-piece suit, was solicitous of his bride and tender with her. Throughout the affair the pair never left each other's side. In attendance were parents, grandparents, siblings, cousins, uncles, and aunts. Some loyal servants also witnessed the union: Jacinta and Basilio, Tea and Pilar. María Mercedes came from El Congo. Gladis Díaz, the only school friend represented, flew in from New Orleans only weeks after enrolling at Maryknoll.

The mood of the wedding was subdued, all anger and accusations having been vented days before. Flor took rounds with both her parents and then with Elena, while Enrique went the distance with Alvaro. As such, by wedding time, the attendees were mannerly and tolerant. The damage was done. Flor was pregnant. Flor had married a turco, and Cecilia de Aragón's grandson at that. In the face of such immutable calamity, what use were remonstrations?

After the wedding, Magda held a small reception at her house. Cecilia de Aragón excused herself from it. At the church, she had withstood Elena's icy disregard. It was their first reunion, but enough was enough. Cecilia went home.

In all, it was the happiest day of Flor de Salah's life.

▼▼

CHAPTER FIFTY-ONE

El Congo
June 1965

I t was a growing awareness of disparities that opened María Mercedes's eyes. Magda's house, Chenta's room. Tesoros on the one hand, La Cucharona on the other. Flor's frivolous, self-absorbed nature, her own intractable weighty view of things. Fernando Lira, the work he did, and the lengthy discussions they had when work was over, helped also to peel the blinders off. When all is said and done, he'd once remarked, there are the few who have and the most who don't. Between the two, there's a chasm with no bridges to link them. Navigating in the light of this reality, María Mercedes saw El Congo as it truly was—not a simple, dusty town, charming and provincial, but a backpost of desolation awash in poverty and the ignorance that fed it. No longer was the market a winsome place of conviviality, but a teeming, bedraggled morass into which unseen and mighty hands reach perpetually to wrest rewards from those who had rightly earned them.

Despite her efforts to improve it, even the mesón lost its engaging homeyness, turning instead into a collection of airless, cramped rooms arranged around a dreary grassless patio with its reeking latrine, all unmercifully exposed to the sun. Seeing the bitter truth of her people's lives, María Mercedes clumped them into one pitiful, downtrodden group. As such, she began to love them. Because they were accursed by circumstance, the people became all the more deserving. Because they were deserving, she resolved to do what she could to help them. And so it was that, at eighteen, María Mercedes Prieto found what she had most prayed to be shown: her own purposeful place in the world.

Her enlightenment freed her. Invigorated by determination, she wrote home to say she'd be staying in El Congo for a time. There was work to be done at church, mercado, mesón, and school. And not to worry, she wrote. She had plenty of money left from the amount she'd received for graduation. As far as starting at the university, that would have to wait. She had not mentioned Fernando Lira, though had she done it, she would have said: I have a new friend. He's like Nanda, only different.

Interestingly, there had been a letter, just today, from Nanda Lazos. She wrote about padre Grande and the mandate of the recently concluded Second Vatican Council: "For years el padre Rutilio has assured us that the church is in the world and for the world, and not unearthly and out of touch. Now that the council's work has ended, el padre's message is confirmed. The council charges us to address the worldly needs of the people and not just the condition of their souls. What a blessing, dear María Mercedes, to get this reassurance. What a blessing to be working with a saintly man and with the awesome task of helping the people alter the course of their lives."

The news was providential. It focused a beacon of light on a path to be followed. María Mercedes lost no time. She headed for the church, a simple structure across from the square with two bell towers that, for the last decade, had no bells at all. She sought out el padre Hortensio, finding him at a cluttered desk in a tiny office off the sacristy. "Padre," she declared without fanfare, "this Second Vatican Council. Do you know of it?"

"The Vatican's in Rome," el padre said, looking up in surprise. He was an arrow of a man who sported a goatee and looked similar to the drawings María Mercedes had seen of don Quijote.

"Yes, I know. But do you know about the council? The council says the church must go beyond caring for people's souls. It must comfort and offer people hope in this world as well as trusting in the next." Her words rushed out in a foolish garble. To help clarify, she added, "I have a letter that explains what I mean. I should have brought the letter."

"My dear, the people's souls *are* their hope," el padre said.

"Well, yes, that's true to a certain point. But surely we're more than our souls, padre. There's our minds and our flesh to consider." Virgen Santa. Where was this coming from?

He puckered his lips. "It's not proper to talk about the flesh, my dear."

"My God, padre Hortensio, I didn't mean it the way you think. I was talking about . . ."

"You know what I suggest? I suggest you come to our Bible circle. We meet once a week, out in the sacristy. If it gets too hot, we go into the church, where it's always cool. Of course, when we're in the church, we have to keep our voices down." To make it clear, he laid a finger across his mouth.

"Actually, in San Salvador, I led my own circle." She hadn't. It was Nanda who had, but she'd helped Nanda so many times it was as if she'd had a group herself. "But getting back to the council, el padre Rutilio Grande in Aguilares says that—"

"Stop right there. That man's a rabble-rouser."

"¿Qué?"

"Rutilio Grande. In Aguilares. He's a Jesuit. Jesuits put ideas into people's heads."

"But the Vatican Council and padre Grande, it appears they've come to the same conclusion."

Padre Hortensio drew himself up into a straight edge of indignation. "Please. Don't mention our Holy Father and that freethinker in the same breath."

"But I wasn't talking about el papa. I was talking about the council."

"Same thing." The dull-black phone on the desk rang in shrill, quick bursts. The priest picked up the receiver. "¿Sí?" He listened for a moment, his head inclined, then looked up, a hand over the mouthpiece. "Un momentito." He measured out an inch of time with two fingers.

María Mercedes hastily pantomimed a good-bye. She slipped from the church, stepping into the glare of the afternoon sun. She took a few breaths to still her irritation. She must not allow one absurd exchange to color her resolve. She crossed the square, going under the trees, and headed for the mercado, thinking she'd clear her head with a cool refresco at Chenta's. She didn't get that far. Joaquín Maldonado was at his scrivener's stall and she stopped to say hello.

"Sit, sit. As you can see, I'm between clients." In greeting, Joaquín rose halfway up from the table that served as both a counter and a desk. He wore a white shirt that was on its last day, a bow tie with little checks on it. He pointed to the wooden chair beside his own, pulling a handkerchief from a pocket and making grand sweeping motions over the seat as if to free it of dust. "Here. Sit."

María Mercedes joined him behind the table, a wide unpainted piece with wood grain darkened and smoothed by time. His typewriter, the cornerstone of his enterprise, was a bulky mass under a lime green towel, and it took up one side of the table. Displayed beside it were a jar of ink, a few pens, numerous pencils, a manual sharpener screwed to the table but missing the shavings basket, a stack of paper and a pile of envelopes, a ledger with a dimpled cover containing lists of addresses. A desk pad, cottony and green and tattooed with ink blots, defined the space where he wrote things out by hand.

"How's the letter-writing business, don Joaquín?" María Mercedes asked, her usual question when she came visiting.

"Thank God for illiteracy."

She'd heard the reply before, but it was the first time it rankled. To hide her annoyance, she straightened the edge of a tray holding rubber bands, paper clips, an eraser, stamps. "I think it's a tragedy that people can't write."

"They also can't read."

"Well, that, too. I think it's a tragedy."

"It might be a tragedy, but that's the way it is. One person's failing is another person's gain. To survive in this world, you have to deal with reality."

"It's not right." The next stall offered cut flowers: red and white carnations, yellow and white daisies, spears of multicolored gladiolas, clusters of blue flowers she could not name. Neither the fresh smell of the flowers plunged in tubs of water nor their gaudy beauty improved the tone of their discussion.

Joaquín Maldonado frowned, his playfulness vanishing. "¿Qué te pasa, niña?"

"What's wrong, you ask? Everything in the world's wrong."

He shook his head confirmingly. "I know what's wrong. It's that young man of yours. He's filled your mind with nonsense."

"What young man?"

"Fernando Lira. Who else?"

"He's not 'my man.' He's a friend. That's all."

"Whatever. He's still filled up your head."

"I don't know what you mean."

Conspiratorially, Joaquín drew his face close. "The boy's an agitator. He likes to stir things up."

"Why do you say that?"

"He's attended the university, am I not right? Agitation and rebellion, the university's the place for teaching that." To nail down his point, he rapped the table with a ruler.

"But you're wrong about Fernando, don Joaquín. Fernando works with Acción Católica Universitaria. ACUS workers build things. They fix things. They teach the people what they need to know."

Joaquín Maldonado rolled his eyes. "That's what he might say. But mark my words, what he actually does could well be something else."

She had to wait a week before finding out for herself. She and Fernando were sitting outside Chenta's door again, having one of their late-night conversations. The moon, a day away from being full, threw a bluish light over the patio and along the edge of the gallery. They were enjoying Viceroy cigarettes. Colorado lay at Fernando's feet. The dog was dreaming. You could tell by the way his legs moved jerkily, by the way his eyelids jumped and his muzzle twitched. Fernando tapped gently on Colorado's side. "Hey boy, calm down."

"He's having a bad dream," María Mercedes said.

"Might be. We did a lot of traveling this past ten days. Some days were nightmarish."

"Why's that?"

Fernando took a drag of his Viceroy, allowing smoke to curl

slowly from his nose and mouth. "It's not easy being out there. It's dangerous sometimes."

Her opportunity had come. He'd opened a door, and she decided to walk in. "The other day, I was talking with don Joaquín at the mercado. You know, el escribiente? Don Joaquín says you're an agitator."

Fernando Lira laughed, almost ruefully, it seemed to María Mercedes. "I guess you could call me that."

"Don Joaquín said, 'Fernando Lira likes to stir things up.' "

"I can't deny that."

His response took her aback. "I thought you built things and fixed things. I thought you helped people, Fernando." She flicked her spent cigarette into the patio. "That's what I told don Joaquín, anyway."

Fernando tossed his own stub on the gallery floor and mashed it out with a foot. He stood. "Let's take a walk."

El Congo was a very small town. If you entered it on the south side, you could walk out the north end not more than fifteen minutes later. The same held true if you traveled east to west. Late at night the town was all the things it could not be by day. Under the sun, its buildings, one-storied most of them, adjoined one another haphazardly and at blunt, harsh angles, but in the moonlight, crooks and corners softened and the buildings melded sensibly into each other. Walls, sooty and smudged in the sun, were now moon-washed clean.

They strode down the street, Colorado trudging with forbearance beside them. It was past midnight. Naturally, house doors along the way were secured, windows shuttered, and not a sound came from behind them. They passed little shops—the bakery, the knife-sharpening place, the bottle depository, the store no larger than a closet and replete with religious prints and figurines. Only the cantina, El Brunswick Anniversary, name taken from the metal plaque on its pool table and scrawled in large, uneven letters in an arc above the door, showed any signs of life. María Mercedes and Fernando crossed the street to avoid passing a place where some came to nurse their grievances. When they reached the square, they took one of the two iron benches that, in a stab at beautification, the town gov-

ernment had installed. Thirty-two years back, when Jacinta and
Mercedes had lived here, the square was devoid of trees and had
only patches of sharp grass. But then the old priest, the one who'd
taken Basilio in when he was twelve, planted a few mango trees and
tended them with care until they flourished. Now the trees' trunks
were as big around as metal drums. Tonight María Mercedes and
Fernando sat under one of them.

"When my mother and Basilio lived here, he worked at the
church and rang the bell for mass. Now there's no bell for ringing."

"Basilio? Is he your father?"

"No, but he's like a father. He and my mother have worked for
the Tobars for almost thirty years. Basilio can do anything. Gardening, driving, fixing, building. You name it, Basilio can do it." She
paused abruptly, struck by the enormity of how much she missed
him. "I used to think Basilio was my father. He lived in the garden
shed at the end of the patio. I was born in that shed. On his cot.
For some reason I thought that made him my father." She gave a
laugh because she could feel her voice breaking. "Funny, the things
we think when we're little."

"And do you know your father?" Fernando asked, and as soon
as he said it, slapped a hand against his head. "I'm sorry. That's a
personal matter. I had no right to ask such a thing."

She made a vague gesture to excuse him. "Don't apologize. I
don't mind talking about it. I don't know who my father is, though,
heaven knows, I've asked. There was a time, when I was eight or
nine, when all I ever did was pester my mother about it. She opened
up just once. She told me my father was dead. She told me he'd
been a civil servant."

"I'm sorry."

"For a long time, the fact that he was dead was eclipsed by the
fact he'd been a civil servant. I didn't know what the term meant,
but I imagined it was a grand thing. My father had been a servant
who was civil. That meant he'd been polite and mannerly and cour-
teous." The sting of loss moistened her eyes. She blinked the tears
back, crossed her arms, and hugged herself because she was touched
by the way everything around her in the night appeared so lovely,
yet so sad.

354 ▼ SANDRA BENÍTEZ

"We started talking about something back there in the mesón," Fernando said, breaking at length the respectful silence that had come between them. "I want to tell you about what I do."

María Mercedes said nothing. It was as if he'd thrown a stone from a great height. She held her breath, waiting for it to land.

"The truth is I work for ACUS. As you know, I've cleaned up dumps. Fixed roofs. Built things that needed building. I don't do it by myself, of course. There's a group of us who do the work. We recruit labor from the towns to help us get it done."

"How large is your group?"

"There are six of us. Me and Olga, Diego, Elías, Berta, and Felipe."

"I see." Olga and Berta. Who were these women?

"The work we do is highly visible. It gets attention. Sometimes it gets attention we don't need."

"How's that?"

"Sometimes our work sites are watched by the guardia or the police. They're sent by the mayor or by an officer in charge of the military post to check up on us. These authorities can't readily object to the physical work we do. After all, the work needs doing. It's the talking we do while we work they're wary of." Fernando paused and fished in his pocket for his pack of Viceroys. He pulled one out and offered the pack to María Mercedes, but she declined. He lit a cigarette before continuing. "Naturally we're careful about what we say and how we say it. We're speaking the truth, you understand. Cloaked in whatever activity we're engaged in, we point out to the people how their lives could be better. You need an education, we say. You need three good meals a day. Meaningful work. Fitting wages. Your friend, old don Joaquín, called me an agitator. It's true. I'm an agitator because I'm agitated by our people's plight."

The stone he'd dropped had come to ground. María Mercedes looked at him but could not make out his expression because of the shadows. "My friend Nanda in Aguilares. She does the kind of work you do."

"The work is needed everywhere. Not just here, but in every department of the country."

"The work is hard," she said.

"It's dangerous, both for us and for the people."

"No matter. It's work that must be done," María Mercedes said.

He laid a hand on her shoulder. The first time he had touched her. "Would you consider joining us?" he said.

He gave her a week to think it over. A week while he and the dog went off to tend to business. Before he left he made sure she understood the road that lay ahead: She would be traveling from town to town with the group. Sometimes great distances by foot. Remuneration would be minimal. The group relied on private contributions. Church collections. Town funds. They relied on volunteers whom they'd recruit. On donated or discarded materials. Always there were the seeds of awareness to be sown. Always the danger that came with the sowing. From time to time, she could return to El Congo. But for the most part, she would depend on the kindness of the people themselves: share what food was offered, throw down a petate to sleep where she could.

Tomorrow he would return. Tonight she lay on her cot, sleep as remote as the life she'd led at Magda's. On the shelf, a candle flickered. Shadows danced along the wall that months ago she'd whitened. Across the room, Chenta had lain down, too. No snoring came from her direction. "Are you awake, Tía?" María Mercedes said.

"I was going to ask you that."

"I'm awake."

There was a long pause. Then Chenta said, "You're leaving, aren't you?"

"How did you know?"

"It's not so hard to see, dear girl. For months I've watched you wrestle with some giant inner storm. At times, I've been tempted to speak out, but then I thought it best to keep quiet. It does youngsters a world of good to tame their tempests on their own."

"You're a wise woman, Tía."

"Oh, I don't know about that. I'm an old woman; that's for certain. I remember when your mother left, after your grandmother died. Your mother acted the same as you. Like a horse kept in the barn too long. But then, your mother had different reasons for leaving."

"Sometimes I think about my mother being in this room when she was young. Abuela, too."

"I can see your mother so plainly in my head. She was a skinny girl with fat braids. Mercedes was skinny, too. But she was strong. She had fortitude, your grandmother."

"Fortaleza."

"When she first came, after that terrible time of la matanza, she lay on a petate, just about where you are now. Basilio, too. Curled up beside her like a newborn pup."

La matanza. María Mercedes knew its realities because both her mother and Basilio had spoken of it. The carnage. The senseless, tragic destruction. When she studied history in school, she'd searched for explanations in her books, but all she found were cryptic descriptions such as: "In January 1932, the first communist uprising in the Americas occurred in the southwest region of the country when campesinos rose up violently against patrones. In three days, the insurgency was completely put down." In no book had she seen the words "la matanza," the massacre.

"Sometimes I think of the little boy that was lost," María Mercedes said. She laid a hand on the amulet with the three red stones she'd slipped, cord and all, through a chain she now wore around her neck. "Justino, he was called. He would have been my uncle."

"Poor little thing," Chenta said. "He was taken from Pru's hut. Pru was my sister." A sigh came from across the room. "I remember when I left my sister, when I left Izalco. I was fourteen."

"Why did you leave?"

"My heart led me. My heart took notice of another. He left Izalco and moved here. I followed."

"Who was this person?"

"He was called Macario."

"What did your family say when you left?"

"My father never spoke to me again. He said I was not his daughter. No daughter of his would shamefacedly leave home and her people, my father said. No daughter of his would follow some muchacho who had no decency because he would not marry her."

"Why wouldn't Macario marry you?"

"Because he didn't know that I existed. He didn't even know I followed him."

"You followed someone you didn't even know?"

"I did. And I've never regretted it."

"What happened to Macario?"

"I forget. It's been so long ago. But one thing I'm sure of: sometimes a girl has to leap without knowing where she'll land."

"I know, Tía. I know."

▼▼

CHAPTER FIFTY-TWO

When María Mercedes joined Fernando's group, she plunged into the world in which her grandmother and mother had lived. A world unseen from main roads, where the people walked down meandering paths leading to paltry milpas so small that maíz and frijoles had to be sown side by side. A world of thatched huts smelling of old dust and stacked-up corn, of earth packed down so hard you could slip on it. In thirty-three years, not much had changed. True, los indios were not called indios anymore, unless it was to insult; except for the very old, most had never known their mother tongue, Nahuatl, the language that pleases the ear with its cha, che, chi, cho, chu sounds. Still, much had stayed the same: empty pockets, empty bellies, empty dreams.

In mid-October the skies had dried up, but the days had yet to turn blistery. Earlier in the week, Fernando's group had come together in Coatepeque. There they'd formed new pairs, drawn new assignments, and gone out again. This time, María Mercedes's partner was Elías, whom some boldly called Manco because he'd lost half an arm when he was child and a mortero, the most powerful of fireworks, exploded before he could toss it the hell away. Elías also went deaf as a consequence, but his mother, who believed one impediment was enough for anyone, dripped warmed romero oil into his ears for ten days until her boy could hear again. Elías, his left sleeve folded and always pinned up, was very dark. He had sharp cheekbones under birdy, darting eyes.

María Mercedes and Elías had crisscrossed the area between Las Cruces and Cantarrana, tramping from one hut and field to another, encouraging the people to meet with them, a delicate task given that the coffee harvest was less than a month away and that the guardia had tripled its presence in the countryside. With patience and re-assurance, they'd coaxed Juan Hernández (Juan had a wife, Otilia, and five children, only the baby a much needed boy) into allowing the people to gather at his place, a convenient central location. Elías's dog, a black mutt that, on command, chased its own tail, had had the most to do with Juan's acquiescence. Elías had set the dog upon himself while Juan watched for a time and then grinned, thinking he might make a wager with Santiago Peña, his neighbor, who was always keen to bet on anything.

Elías and the men (there were eight of them and as many dogs) went out to Juan's field. They squatted under a pepeto tree, a glance away from rows of carmel-colored cornstalks, doubled over by hand to allow the ears to dry better, and from frijol leaves, wide as a palm and as startling as green stars, twining up between the corn. The sight of coming bounty, even if a meager one, softened the men; it opened their ears to a gentle lecture on the perils of cantinas, of shots of aguardiente good for fueling tempers and for hastening hands toward machete hilts.

While the men met, the women congregated under the big amate in Otilia's yard. There were more women in María Mercedes's group than men in Elías's. Most of the women were young, but a few were old, including Otilia's mother, doña Pura. The old one's tapado wound around her head and shoulders as if the weather might turn chilly, although there was no chance of that. A dozen children milled about, some clinging to their mothers. The rest pelted Otilia's hens with pebbles, sending the fowl squawking before they turned back stupidly to peck at what to them was shucked corn. The children had soccer ball bellies, smudged faces, and noses caked with snot. María Mercedes had opened the meeting with a prayer asking for God's blessing and protection. She liked to do this, though Elías found it awkward to start the men off like that. She'd gone on

to talk about cleanliness, instructing the women to wash hands before food handling, entreating them to keep children's faces
scrubbed. "It's not extra work," she said. "It's just a matter of keeping a water bucket filled for that purpose." Earlier, in preparation
for the demonstration, María Mercedes had gone down the path to
the stream and filled up a bucket. It rested next to her chair. "Here.
Let me show you." She had brought squares of cotton manta for
the women, and she dipped a gourd ladle into the bucket, wet one
of the cloths, and squeezed it out. "Can I borrow your baby?" she
asked Otilia, holding her arms out to the child who had just nursed
and who was lying sleepily in the crook of his mother's arm.

Otilia handed the baby over, and María Mercedes cradled him
for a moment against herself. "Chichi," she said, soothingly using
the Nahuatl word for baby. She bounced him gently in her arms
before laying him on her lap. She wiped his face, working the end
of the cloth around his dirty nostrils. Spread out on her lap, he
looked up at her questioningly, and then his penis, small as half a
thumb, gave a jerk and he began to pee. A stream of urine shot
straight out, and María Mercedes gave a yelp. She dropped the cloth
and lifted the baby away from herself, holding him up under his
little arms. The women laughed, and for a moment María Mercedes
did not completely understand their merriment, but then she saw
it: while she was holding the baby, he was sending an arc of pee
directly into the water bucket. Otilia took the baby over, his urine
gone to dribble that left dark, then soon-fading spots on the earth
of the yard.

María Mercedes laughed and gave the bucket a playful kick.
"Well, so much for that water!" she said. "I planned to talk about
toilet habits, and I think Otilia's baby just provided the introduction.
Let me ask you, when nature calls, where do you go?"

"We don't go in water buckets," one of the women said, tittering
behind a hand raised to her mouth. She, too, nursed a baby. Her
breast was stretched from so much use.

Doña Pura unwound her tapado and spoke up for the first time.
"Leave it to a male to do something like that. When they make
water, los hombres go anywhere they want. Against a tree, in the
yard, out in the field. Some men make water against their huts."

"Not my man," Otilia said, shooting her mother a look.

"I'm just saying," doña Pura responded, setting her jaw and throwing up a hand.

"What about us women?" María Mercedes asked.

"Women are modest. We pee in the bushes," Blanca Peña said. She was young and large. When she said the word "pee," the rest of them giggled.

"Well, it's true," Blanca Peña said.

"And when we have to do the other, where is that done?" María Mercedes asked.

Almost in unison everyone said, "En el arroyo. That's done in the stream."

"Why the stream?"

"Because water carries shit away," Blanca Peña said, rolling her eyes as if María Mercedes were a dolt. At the word "caca" there was even more laughter.

María Mercedes picked up a stick and sketched a wavy line in the dirt. "Look," she said, and the women made a wide ring around her. Even doña Pura stood up to get a better view.

"Let's say this line is the stream. If people do their business in one place, it ends up in another. Like this." She marked a big X on the line, then another X down a ways from it.

Blanca Peña, who had appointed herself the group's mouthpiece, said, "Shit's not a stone or a pebble. It doesn't go from place to place. Shit disintegrates; everybody knows that."

"You're right, shit disintegrates, but it carries with it parasites and microbes. These things are too small for us to see, but parasites and microbes don't disintegrate. The truth is, señoras, if we use the stream both for drinking and for doing our business, then there'll be parasites and microbes in the water we drink." María Mercedes let it sink in before continuing. "Parásitos. That's why our children all have big bellies. That's why we all suffer from stomach complaints."

She went on like that, posing remedies to the problem: boil water before drinking it, dig a hole for a toilet, sprinkle a little lime over what you've deposited in the hole. She would have said more, but the woman nursing her child lifted him from her breast and hastily covered herself up. "La guardia," she said, pointing across the yard, toward the path that led to the road.

All heads turned to the pair in green khaki uniforms striding purposefully toward them. Fear, electric, tangible, stiffened their spines and sharpened their eyes. For a moment, the playing children went still; then they darted over to join siblings at their mothers' sides.

"I'll take care of this," María Mercedes said. Virgen Santa, she thought as the pair strolled into the yard, rifles on straps and slung behind their backs. She stepped up to intercept them. "Buenas tardes, mis capitanes," she said, promoting them instantly in rank. "¿Qué se les ofrece? What can we do for you?"

The guardias did not respond. Their eyes shifted, taking everything in: the women, the children, the hut, the row of gourds thriving in the sun. At length, one guardia asked, "Where are your men?"

"The men are working." María Mercedes shrugged. "You know how it is."

"What's this?" the other guardia asked. He pointed the tip of his boot toward the wavy line, drawn out thick, in the dirt.

"I made it with a stick," María Mercedes said. She lifted the stick as yet clasped in her hand, her mouth going dry at the thought that what she'd sketched could be misinterpreted. The sketch looked like some kind of plan: the line, the Xs. If she told the simple truth, that they'd been talking about shitting in the river, she would never be believed. It was the deepest of fears, that somehow the very truth would serve to sink you.

"So you made this with a stick," the guardia said, boot tip still pointing out the line. "What is it?"

"It's meant to be the stream." This much of the truth she would state. She set her own boot on the line. "Before you came up, I was talking about the stream."

"And who are you?" the first guardia asked.

One of the first directives she'd received when she joined Fernando's group was never to give her name to the authorities unless it was absolutely necessary. To distract the men from the question, she made up a story on the spot. "Do you know don Neto Contreras? He owns La Abundancia. The finca is up the road a few kilometers. All these women will be picking there. Don Neto's wife, la niña Margarita, she sent me to talk to the women. While the women pick, la niña Margarita wants their children in her school."

The guardias said nothing. Their eyes narrowed under the stiff bills of their caps.

María Mercedes went on because another group rule was When confronted by the authorities, try to confuse them with information. "La Abundancia has a school. It's very close to the beneficio. Up the path from la casona. Do you know the place?"

"I know where the school is," the one guardia said. "But what does the stream have to do with mocosos, snotty kids, getting to school?"

"It has everything to do with it. I drew the stream to show the children how far they'd have to go. This X is where we are today." María Mercedes pointed to the first X, then to the second. "This one marks the place they'll be at school. It's really very simple. When you draw things out for children, it helps them to see what you're trying to explain." She smiled and held her breath, thankful that her life with the Tobars had provided information she could use to her advantage.

The one guardia lifted his cap and mopped his forehead with the length of an arm before dropping the cap back on again.

"Would you care for a drink, mis capitanes?" María Mercedes said. "We just brought a fresh bucket up from the stream."

Blanca Peña hurried over to the bucket and dipped the gourd in. "Allow me to serve you," she said, holding the gourd out. The men drank greedily, one and then the other, their eyes pinned to Blanca's plentiful chest. The last to drink handed the gourd back. Blanca dropped it in the bucket, and it made a little splash. "Will there be anything else, mis capitanes?" she said.

The one guardia readjusted his rifle against his back.

The second one did the same. The first one walked over to the line María Mercedes had drawn. He rubbed it out with his boot. It took one step, two steps to do it. "No more figures in the dirt," he said.

"As you say, mi capitán," María Mercedes said. She had to resist the urge to throw a hand up in salute.

The guardias turned on their heels. María Mercedes watched them go, Blanca Peña beside her. For some time, there was no sound anywhere, only the guardias' footsteps falling along the path. When they reached the top of the path, they veered and abruptly vanished from view. María Mercedes threw an arm around Blanca Peña's shoulder, but Blanca remained stiff and still and did not budge. María Mercedes drew her arm away. She faced the rest of the women. The women were mute. There was no relief in their expressions, only resigned apprehension in their eyes.

Blanca Peña spit on the ground. "Hijos de la gran puta, sons of bitches," she said. Just beyond the hut, on this side of the field, a swarm of dogs came up over a hillock. Soon Elías and the men followed, their straw sombreros like targets you could aim at. When the men came into the yard, not one of the women said a word about what had just taken place.

Fernando Lira and the group—María Mercedes and Elías, Olga, Diego, Felipe, and Berta—were camping along the shores of el lago Coatepeque, a placid sapphire blue lake crowned at the west by the coffee-furred slopes of el volcán Santa Ana. At seven thousand feet it was the highest peak in the land.

The group had built a fire. They had cooked fish fresh from the catch and skewered on sticks. At the market, Berta had found tomatoes, skins bursting with juice, thick tortillas and guineos manzano, bananas as short as index fingers and apple sweet. Naturally, the animals joined in the meal, after which they snoozed in the fire's glow.

Wood smoke perfumed the night; firelight wavered over petates lashed with string into rolls, over boots, backpacks, and sombreros. Supper over, the group turned to discussion, going around the circle, each speaking when their turn arose. They'd made trips to various towns in the Department of Santa Ana: Rancheador, Cutumey Camones, El Porvenir, San Sebastián Saltrillo, Las Cruces, Cantarrana, Duraznillo, Ochupse Arriba.

"Coffee harvest starts tomorrow," Fernando said. He was sitting beside Olga. "Guardias are everywhere. Today, Olga and I had to skirt Duraznillo to avoid them."

"My feet are killing me," Olga said, kneading the instep of a foot.

Diego, who for the most part was the silent type, said, "The guardia's getting to be a problem."

"They think we're all a bunch of communists," Berta said.

María Mercedes recounted what had occurred at Juan Hernández's milpa. They all laughed when she described Blanca Peña offering the guardia tainted water. They congratulated her on the clever story she had fabricated about teaching at La Abundancia. The story was so good, in fact, they all decided to use it in case emergencies arose in the area. To this end, María Mercedes went over details of the finca and the names of personnel. She had no qualms about doing so. They were all teachers, were they not? Whether on the finca or in the countryside.

"I don't know," Olga said after a moment. "I sometimes wonder if what we do makes a difference."

"Of course it does," Berta said, her round face shining eagerly in firelight. "We teach people to write their names. We talk to women about fertile times and sex. These things alone make a difference. If campesinos were literate, if the birth rate declined, then they might begin to save themselves."

Felipe flicked his cigarette butt into the fire. "Watch what you say, girl. 'The people saving themselves,' that's the language of insurrection."

"Oh, yes. I forgot," Berta said. "It's the church that saves the people." She was small in stature, but she drew herself up in a priestly pose. "Come to me, my children," she declared. "True, your life is full of hardships, but oh! the rewards awaiting you in heaven."

Olga hugged her long slender legs against her chest. "What tripe. For ages the church has been dishing that out."

"And for ages the people have gobbled it up," Diego replied.

"The church says, Reject materialism! Draw on spiritual virtues instead!" Elías raised his half-arm to make the point, and his pinned-up sleeve flapped a bit.

"You sound like a Christian Democrat," Felipe said.

"They're for a new social order," Berta observed. "How do they put it? 'A new order, built, not on materialistic values, but on solidarity among human beings.'"

"That's Napoleon Duarte talk," Fernando said.

"That's all right," Berta retorted, "as long as I don't look like him. Duarte might be mayor, but he's not very pretty."

"We should talk to the campesinos about that," María Mercedes said.

"About Duarte not being pretty?" Olga said.

"No, niña. About a new social order. We should do like padre Grande does in Aguilares. He talks about class struggle. About capitalistic exploitation. He talks about unions and land reform." In her backpack was a letter from Nanda with all the details.

"I agree," Fernando said. "For months I've been saying if we want true reform, we have to turn radical."

"And for months I've been saying that spells a sea of trouble," Olga shot back.

"Of course it does," Fernando said. "Reform and trouble go hand in hand. Question is, if you want reform, are you willing to take the trouble?"

Felipe nodded. "Easy for us to be willing. What we have to do is help the people decide on the same."

Olga shook her head. "I don't know about that."

Elías said, "Here's something I *do* know. I'm tired. Let's plan our work, then call it a day."

They drew names for new teams, pairing up and deciding where each team would work for the next two days. That done, they bustled about, getting ready for bed. This stirred the dogs, who rose on creaky legs and went from spot to spot, sniffing petates, backpacks, and boots. María Mercedes unrolled her mat in the glow of the fire, now burned down to embers. She sat and peeled off her boots. One sock had slipped below her heel and rubbed a sore on her skin. She fished a tin of unguent from her backpack and applied it to the sore, grimacing against the sting. Colorado joined her, peering up in her face. Although the light was poor, she pulled her notebook from the backpack and worked on the poem Blanca Peña had inspired. Its title was "Allow Me to Serve You." When the light from the embers faded further, she replaced the notebook, extracted a thin blanket, and pummeled the pack into an acceptable pillow. She lay back and covered herself, squirming to make the ground more comfortable. The night was pleasant and sweet, and where Colorado's bulk touched her, there was a reassuring warmth.

She thought of Nanda's letter. Penning a reply in her head, she described her travels, the insights she'd had along the way. With

Nanda, she could spill her heart on the page. She could confess her distaste for who she once had been: a foolish girl, entrapped by feckless comforts. Yes. Corresponding with Nanda was one of her delights. Less so writing home. Unlike her candor with Nanda, she was circumspect with her mother and Basilio. How else to be? She loved them. She would not think of wounding them with the realities of her new life.

At present, she owed her mother a letter. Jacinta had written weeks before with general news about herself and Basilio. As far as the Tobars were concerned, a single piece of news surpassed all else: Flor had had a healthy baby girl. She was named Iris. With Flor and Enrique for parents, little Iris was sure to be a beauty. María Mercedes was happy for Flor. She was proud of the way Flor had flown in the face of convention to obtain what she most wanted.

María Mercedes tucked the blanket under her chin. She gazed up at the sky. Heaven and stars were pricked tin. Flor and she. When girls, the two had been like sisters. Though each was headstrong in her own way, how like strangers they were now. María Mercedes felt a pang of melancholy as a memory arose: La Abundancia. The soujourns to the finca with Flor. She remembered early mornings, when they skipped along the paths leading from the big house to the beneficio. When they sprawled, torpid with boredom in the late afternoons, on the chintz-cushioned settee of the side porch. She remembered how they giggled themselves to sleep lying side by side on the high iron bed in Flor's airy room.

Colorado lifted his head and started to rise, but María Mercedes threw a hand out and held him back. "Stay, boy," she whispered. She watched Fernando and Olga steal off toward the lake. Hand in hand, the pair disappeared beyond the edge of the dying fire's glow.

Colorado whimpered, wanting to follow, but María Mercedes held him firmly in place. "You stay here," she said, and he did. Tomorrow she would be working again with Fernando, something she'd done only twice since joining the group. It pleased her that she'd drawn his name tonight. She looked forward to clarifying the group's foggy future with him. Just a short time together, then Olga could have him back.

▼   ▼   ▼

Over the course of three days, bands of campesinos left their milpas and meager livestock in the care of uncles or grandfathers too old to pick, and journeyed in waves to the fincas rising up the skirts of el volcán. The majority of the pickers traveled by foot, for the plantations were less than a day's walk away. Others, not encumbered by large families and lucky enough to get rides, elbowed a spot for themselves aboard the flatbed trucks sent out by the fincas. In all, the migration unleashed a time of camaraderie and boisterous celebration of new work. In high spirits, the people sauntered up the roads, belongings lashed against their backs or balanced on their heads. Moving brightly, they told stories and joked, stepping off the road as the trucks rumbled by, kicking up what seemed like all the dust in El Salvador. Those on foot stopped periodically at streams to refresh themselves. They hunkered down under trees to catch a moment of shade, to share with fellow workers a little something from their knapsacks.

For two days, Fernando and María Mercedes plied the five kilometers between San Juan and La Majada. They worked separately during the day, moving from group to group, informing the workers about meetings they could attend once the picking began. They rendezvoused at dusk, at a place well off the road and under a canopy of trees, as safe a place as they could find.

On this second evening, María Mercedes had again arrived first at the rendezvous point. There was not much to do: no fire to build since it might give them away, no food to cook. Supper was cold. A stack of tortillas, a hunk of cheese, a few bananas, all bought from a vendor who had strategically stationed herself along the road for the duration of the migration. Fernando had promised to go into La Majada as he had the day before, to pick up Coca-Colas.

María Mercedes checked her watch. It was after six, and being that she was sheltered under trees, daylight was quickly fading. She leaned back against the trunk of the conacaste behind her. It felt good to be off her feet. Yesterday in La Majada, Fernando had found a small farmacia and bought some Curitas for the sore on her heel. After supper, she would refresh the ointment and apply a new bandage. For now, she lit a cigarette to bide the time. She relished the quiet after a long day of explaining and cajoling. After a day of watching for the guardia. She enjoyed the dimming nightfall. She caught the sound of squirrels skittering in the underbrush and along tree branches. She felt tired. Exhausted. She wanted to eat, spread out her petate, wrap herself up, and go to sleep. Tonight she could not contemplate a repeat of the night before, when she and Fernando talked well into morning.

In the span of a few minutes it had grown so dark her watch was no longer visible. Slowly, her eyes adjusted and she made out her backpack, her rolled-up petate. She stretched her legs out. She felt around for a bald spot on the ground and crushed her cigarette. As the minutes slipped by, she dampened her irritation with Fernando's tardiness by mentally going over lines of her poem about Blanca Peña. She thought that when it was finished, and the harvest over, she'd go back and find Blanca and read the poem to her.

María Mercedes lit another match to read the time. Almost a quarter to seven. Her irritation flipped over into alarm. She stood up and looked around, holding the burning match away for illumination. It hardly lit anything. When the flame got too close to her fingers, she blew it out and threw it down. Nothing out there but darkness. The same darkness of the night before, but now, because she was alone, the darkness seemed menacing. She sat back down. She lifted the matchbook cover and fingered the sticks, counted out the remaining match heads. Ten. If needed, she would rip a page from her notebook. Light the paper. Use it as a torch. She pocketed the matchbook. She must resist the urge to go out into the road. Safer to be here, cloaked by darkness, under the trees.

She willed herself to be patient and still. She did not want to imagine what might have happened to Fernando. A scenario came to mind nonetheless. Fernando running into Olga during the day and going off with her at night. Her alarm turned back into irritation. She endured its prickly barb for a time, then lit another match and checked her watch. It was 7:22. She decided to eat. To do it, she rifled blindly through her backpack and ate whatever food her hand happened upon. Luckily it was not the bananas first. When she was full, she felt thirsty, but unless Fernando arrived with the Cokes, there'd be no drinking tonight.

She decided against spreading out her mat. She fished for the light blanket in the pack and, because bugs had started flittering, wrapped it over her head and down around herself. She drew up her legs and covered them, too, leaning finally against the conacaste. She passed the night like that, a tree at her back, the night pressing down.

At dawn, stiff and logy from little sleep, María Mercedes hoisted up her backpack and mat and stumbled out from under the trees. Peering about the hazy clearing, she was stunned to discover she was still alone. She had truly believed that sometime in the night Fernando and Colorado would arrive somehow; that when morning came, she would find him there, miraculously only meters away, stretched out on his petate, Colorado curled beside him. That was the good dream. The bad dream was that he had not come. She hurried down the path to the road. The sky showed pink, and already campesinos were on their way to coffee fields. She was very thirsty. She decided to visit the vendor a distance up the road. The woman had a brazier for making coffee and tortillas. After coffee to revive her, she would go in search of Fernando.

The sun had risen fully when María Mercedes reached the vendor's spot. She waited awhile in a short line, taking in the heady smoke the brazier produced, the smell of tortillas roasting on the tin, the rich aroma of coffee bubbling in the wide-mouth jar set directly on the coals. She bought coffee served in a tin can and two tortillas. She sat under a tree, holding the top edge of the can gingerly so as not to burn herself. It was a little after six. The sun was now brilliant, the air already warm. The trees and scrub sparkled with dew that quickly disappeared. Like Fernando, she thought. She sipped her coffee slowly, blowing into the can to cool it. She fished the remaining cheese from her backpack and savored it with the tortillas. She watched campesinos traipse by. Single campesinos. Campesinos in pairs. Whole families of campesinos. And always the dogs trotting along beside them. Tall dogs and short dogs. All scrawny, nervous dogs. Dogs so different from Colorado. The thought came to her that the road vendor might have noticed Fernando and Colorado. She hastily finished eating and went over and asked.

"Perdone, señora," María Mercedes said when there was a break in the line at the stand. She described Fernando and the dog. "Have you seen them?"

"Not today," the woman said.

"Did you see them yesterday?"

"Por la tarde."

"In the afternoon," María Mercedes echoed. "When in the afternoon?"

"In the late afternoon." The woman was eating a tortilla. She was relatively young. In her forties perhaps, but she had no teeth. She poked small wedges of tortilla into the back of her mouth, past her gums that showed hard and glistening.

"How late was that?"

The woman shrugged and pursed her lips, her mouth collapsing downward.

"Was it still light when you saw them?"

"Of course," the woman snapped. "I can't see in the dark."

"Well that's true," María Mercedes said, taking a quick breath against snapping at the woman herself. "It must have been light if you saw them."

"Al muchacho se lo llevaron."

The bad dream. She was having it again. "What do you mean, they took the boy away?"

"La guardia se lo llevó."

"The guardia took him?" María Mercedes pressed the back of her neck against the sudden chill she felt there.

The woman nodded. "They left the dog over there." She pointed a finger up the road.

"Wait a minute. What do you mean, they left the dog up there?"

"Over there." That same finger, pointing in the same direction as before.

There was a line now. People pushing toward the front. A man behind María Mercedes said, "There's a dead dog up there."

María Mercedes wheeled out of line. She scanned the road for evidence, going off finally, her mouth dry, the blood pounding in her temples. She weaved in and out of campesinos, running at full speed until she came to the dog.

"Ay, Colorado," she said, a hand flying to her mouth. He was like a shaggy piece of red carpet tossed out from some moving thing. Campesinos going past made a wide path around him. María Mercedes crouched beside him. She laid a hand on him. His body was stone. Across his shoulders, his fur was clumped with dried blood. The rest of him was ragged and dirty. As if he'd never been loved. His lips, two delicate black lines, were pulled back over his teeth into a macabre grimace. His eyes were open, staring still.

She took him by the legs and dragged him off the road. People had stopped to watch as she pulled him over brush and scrub. She rested him in a small grassy depression, away from the foot traffic. She patted him on the head. "You were a good dog," she whispered, her eyes filming over with tears. Before she turned from him, she unhooked his collar, hidden in the thickness of his fur. She stuffed the collar in her backpack.

She hurried out into the road again. Addressed a group standing there. "Tell me this, if the guardia took someone away, where would they go?"

The answer came without hesitation. "A Santa Ana. Al cuartel." Again the fingers pointing north.

▼▼

CHAPTER FIFTY-THREE

I t was just past noon when María Mercedes arrived at the Santa Ana police station. She stood before the building, an ochre colonial structure with barred windows, and caught her breath, trying to shake off her apprehension. The station was heavily protected. Police and guardias, uniformed and armed, were posted along the sidewalk and on either side of the massive double doors thrown open to reveal a broad entry laid with tiles the color of old blood.

She stepped inside to cool shadows and eerie stillness, moving slowly past polished empty benches lined against the walls. The entryway divided into a corridor that horseshoed around a sun-splashed cobblestone patio. Slim blades of grass sprouted between the stones. The corridor and the patio were conspicuously empty. In the middle of the patio stood a tall cage, ornate with iron curlicues. What the cage contained, María Mercedes could not make out. A balcony with turned balustrades overhung the patio. Along the rail, sentries kept guard.

María Mercedes entered the first open door she happened upon. She stepped into a room crowded with desks, only one of which was manned. "Where is everybody?" she asked the middle-aged señor with the pressed white shirt behind the desk. He was leafing through a stack of papers, and he did not glance her way when she asked the question, so she asked it again.

"It's lunchtime," he said at length, not looking up.

So it was. She hiked up her backpack, which had gotten heavier over the morning. To lighten her load, she'd given her petate to a woman on the bus. "Excuse me. But I need to know if you're holding someone here."

"Come back after lunch."

"Can't you tell me now if the person is here?"

The man finally looked up. He raked his eyes over her. "Come back at two." He turned to his papers again.

María Mercedes went back to the patio and looked up along the balcony. Were the sentries upstairs guarding the cells? There was a doorway a few meters away. What appeared to be a staircase loomed beyond the door. She hesitated a moment, then went toward it.

She was halfway up the stairs when a guardia materialized at the top of the flight. "Halt!" he ordered, a ready hand on his rifle hanging by a strap.

She stopped short, doing as he commanded, a palm over her heart. "You startled me, mi capitán," she said.

"I'm not a captain, I'm a corporal, and there's no admittance up here."

"I see, but could you please tell me if someone's being held here?"

"For that, you have to see el capitán."

"Where is the captain?"

"He's at lunch."

She shook her head in exasperation and left the building, crossing the street and taking a bench under the olives in the square. She lowered her backpack and sat beside it. For an hour and a half, she kept her eyes glued to the station door.

After lunchtime, she left the bench when people began to bustle about the sidewalks and the square. In the station office, there was someone behind every desk. This time, María Mercedes approached another worker, trusting a new one would be more communicative than the first. "I'd like to see el capitán."

"It's the office next door." Again, no eye contact. Only a raised finger indicating left.

In the second office there was only one desk. A woman wearing milky pink lipstick busied herself there. A closed door was directly behind her.

"Your lipstick's pretty," María Mercedes said, deciding at once to be ingratiating.

"It's called Cherries and Creme," the woman said. "My cousin brought it from los Estados Unidos."

"Well, it looks very good on you. Listen, can you tell me, is this el capitán's office?"

A nod and a broad smile from the full pasty lips.

"I need to talk to him, please."

"El capitán Morales won't be back until three. At three-thirty the latest."

"I see." María Mercedes sighed. "I'll have to return." She was almost out the door, when she stopped and turned back. "Did you say el capitán *Morales*?"

"Sí."

"Is el capitán's name Victor Morales by any chance?"

"Sí. Perhaps you know him?"

"I know him," María Mercedes said. "I'll be back at three."

She returned to the park bench, stunned by the revelation. It had been years since she'd laid eyes on Victor Morales. Since the time when she was eight, the time of Victor's dalliance with Pilar. He'd been Harold's friend. They had gone to military school together. María Mercedes remembered the day the two graduated. She remembered the parade and the reception afterward with the cookies shaped like guns. Her watch said 2:15. She had ample time to eat. She found a comedor a few blocks away. She had a bowl of chicken soup, a cheese pupusa, and a Coca-Cola straight out of the ice chest by the door. After lunch, because she still had time, she dropped in at the cathedral, interestingly positioned across the square from the police station. She descended the aisle, her boots resounding with each step. Like the station had been, the church was cool and still. At the first pew, she genuflected, crossed herself, and then slipped in and knelt down. She unhooked her backpack and dropped it to the tile. She was the only person in the church. No. A woman, draped in a dark tapado, knelt in a side alcove ablaze with rows of candles. María Mercedes lifted a hand to her hair. She had not put on her mantilla, a venial sin. She dug around in her backpack and found it, the new small round kind, and laid it on her head.

The church smelled reassuringly of candle wax and polishing wax, of smoky incense and of hopes and prayers rising up. Magda and don Alvaro had been married here. Her mother and grandmother had bowed their heads before these holy images. María Mercedes patted the agate amulet she wore tied around her bra strap. Fuerza, fuerza, she prayed. Give me strength. After a while, she lit a candle at the alcove containing the life-size figure of the Holy Mother. When her watch showed three, she took off her mantilla and left the church.

"Can I see el capitán Morales now?" she asked the woman still plunked behind the desk. If a meeting with Victor proved impossible, María Mercedes would stand in the middle of the patio. She would yell out Fernando's name up toward the balcony where she assumed the cells to be.

"Who can I say wants to see him?" the woman asked.

María Mercedes was only momentarily taken aback by the fact the captain finally seemed to be available. "Tell him Pilar Lazos," she said. She had decided on this tactic back in the church.

The woman stood and disappeared behind the door. Soon she came out again. "El capitán says come in."

María Mercedes shut the door behind her. He was standing, alert and eager, next to his desk. She didn't recognize him at first; after all, it had been ten years. He wore a brown soldier's uniform, neat and crisp. He seemed taller and was much more filled out than she remembered. His face was dark and jowly. A black, woolly mustache stretched over his lip. "Pilar?" he said.

"No, mi capitán," she said, striding across the room. "Pilar Lazos is my godmother. I'm María Mercedes Prieto, Jacinta Prieto's daughter. Remember me? Remember Nanda? She and I are like sisters."

"You're not Pilar." The ends of his mustache dipped down.

"No, I'm not. I went to your graduation from military school. You graduated with my cousin, Harold Parada."

He went around and dropped into his chair. From the looks of him, he was very disappointed.

"I know you stayed with Harold at Pilar's for a time," María Mercedes said. "As you know, Harold is in La Unión. He's a captain, too."

"Actually, I haven't heard from Harold," Victor said.

"I also stayed with Pilar. For three years, while I went to la Escuela Alberto Masferrer. My godmother is a very generous woman."

He leaned back, a smile flittering in his eyes. "Tell me, what brings you here?"

"A favor, mi capitán. I was hoping you could help me."

"And how's that?"

"Are you holding a man named Fernando Lira? They would have brought him in last night."

He tented his hands against his chest. "Do you know Fernando Lira?"

"He and I work together, mi capitán."

"And what work do you do?"

"We're teachers." The finca story. Time to put it to use again.

"Um. What do you teach?"

"We work at La Abundancia. With la niña Margarita de Contreras. She set up the finca school. We're trying to get all the children not picking to go to the school. As you well know, school is a good thing, mi capitán."

"This Fernando Lira. What does he look like?"

María Mercedes described Fernando. Then she said, "Are you holding him?"

"He's here."

María Mercedes resisted the urge to show great relief. "I'm sure you'll agree there's been some mistake. I was hoping you'd be so kind as to see to his release. Don Neto Contreras and la niña Margarita need Fernando's and my help at La Abundancia. The harvest is starting, and we have to see to many children." A telephone sat on his desk. All he would need to do to verify the story was to lift the receiver and dial the beneficio. Would he do it? If he did, she would have to think of something quick.

Capitán Victor Morales pulled himself out of the chair and rounded the desk. "Come," he said.

She followed him out into the corridor and toward the door

with the staircase. Halfway there, he looked out into the patio. "We have a micoleón living in that cage," he said. He went over and picked up a stick and poked it through the bars. A box with an opening sat in the corner of the cage. He struck the top of the box repeatedly with the stick. The sounds the stick produced were sharp and startling. Soon a kinkajou appeared at the opening. The animal had a sweet face, huge black eyes shiny with fear. It pulled its face back and did not show itself again. "That's our little pet," el capitán said. "Now come."

They climbed the stairs. The guardia who had intercepted María Mercedes a few hours before clicked his heels together and saluted as the captain went by. They went down the balcony, past other guardias who saluted, too. Barred rooms lined the balcony. El capitán stopped at the third room. "Is this your man?" he asked María Mercedes.

She stepped over to the bars and peered inside. There was little light in the room. Except for the figure crouched in a corner, the room was empty. "Fernando," she said, swallowing hard, "is that you?"

The figure stirred and glanced up. She called to him, "Fernando, soy yo, María Mercedes."

He pulled himself up. Stumbled over to the bars. His trousers and shirt were filthy. His cheeks were dark with whiskers. The side of his face was puffy. One eye was swollen shut.

"That's Fernando Lira, mi capitán," María Mercedes said.

Victor Morales still held the stick he'd used in the kinkajou's cage. He thrust the stick between the bars and poked at Fernando's shoulder. "Is it true what this girl says? Is she your partner?" The captain pointed the stick at María Mercedes.

Fernando nodded.

"Now suppose you tell me what you and she do?" the captain asked.

Fernando shot a glance at María Mercedes. Then he said, "We teach the children at the finca."

"What finca's that?"

"La Abundancia."

"You see? It's what I said."

"So you did," the captain said. "Abra la celda," he said to the corporal, who sprung over and unlocked the cell as ordered.

Fernando stepped out. He lifted a hand and shielded his good eye from the glare.

"May we go now?" María Mercedes asked.

Capitán Victor Morales brought his face close to María Mercedes's. On his breath, fried onions. On his ear, a birthmark like the mess you make when you squash a bug. "You can thank your godmother Pilar for this," he said.

"We thank you, too, capitán," she said. You're such a mean son of a bitch, she thought.

"Let me give you both some advice. If I were you, I'd forget this ACUS work. Believe me, it will only bring you trouble." He threw the stick down before escorting them out.

They were too exhausted, too emotionally wrenched to leave town that day. They took refuge in Elena's house, closed up since her move to Magda's after Ernesto's death. Asunta and her husband Gilberto, who'd worked for Elena for twenty years, still lived in the house, which, except for the patio and kitchen, was a desolate repository of old furniture covered with sheets. Asunta herself answered the door and made a fuss over them: María Mercedes because she was Jacinta's girl, Fernando simply because he was María Mercedes's friend. Neither Asunta nor Gilberto asked indelicate questions.

Safe at Elena's, María Mercedes used the phone, and after a number of fruitless calls, she reached Felipe and told him the news. She turned her attention to tending Fernando's wounds: warm cloths to wipe dried blood away. Cold compresses against puffiness. Nose to nose, the two spoke little. Before helping him to bed in one of the servants' rooms off the traspatio, María Mercedes pressed Colorado's collar into Fernando's hand. They held on to each other, remembering.

For a while, they lingered like that. Soon, their closeness gave way to sweet, slow lovemaking. The kind that women dream about when dreaming of their first time.

In the morning, after a reviving shower and a hot meal, they boarded the bus to San Salvador, where, for safety's sake and the good of the cause, they would lose themselves for a few years in anonymity at la Universidad Nacional.

▼▼▼

CHAPTER FIFTY-FOUR

San Salvador
July 1969

Four-year-old Iris Salah came upon great-grandmother crumpled on the floor next to her bed. Iris knelt down, a smooth, pudgy knee jutting out at each side of her. She poked Cecilia on the shoulder. "I found you, mamá Ceci," the child exclaimed, thrilled that, from the look of things, the game between them today would be escondite, hide-and-go-seek. Mamá Ceci and Iris liked to play games. When Iris and her nursemaid, Lety, passed through the gate connecting Flor's and Isabel's gardens, sometimes Cecilia would pop out from behind a tree, her straw hat comical, like a charro's sombrero. Sometimes Cecilia whisked Iris away, escorting her on a fresh tour of discovery in the garden. Mamá Ceci had planted flowers with girls' names: rosa, margarita, violeta, and camelia. In the brunt of the sun by the back wall, a wide bed of irises.

"¿Qué te pasa, mamá Ceci?" Iris asked, nudging great-grandmother again, but more gently this time, alarmed by the garbled sounds coming from her mouth. Lety appeared at the door. "There you are, naughty girl," she said. When she saw doña Cecilia heaped on the floor, she rushed to her side. "Dios Santo," Lety said.

"Mamá Ceci went pum," Iris explained, her bottom lip quivering. To console herself, she toddled over to the dresser displaying framed photographs. "There's me," Iris said, indicating a photo of

Papá, an arm around Mamá. Mamá cradling a scowling baby in
New Orleans.

Magda was unpacking a new shipment of clay figurines from Il-
obasco. Tesoros usually didn't carry many indigenous crafts, but
these featured soccer tableaux—each a domed egg that opened to a
scene. Given that El Salvador and Honduras had recently battled on
the soccer field, the clay figurines were selling as fast as she could
get them on the shelf. Three games had been played in the World
Cup matches. Each country won their home game, but El Salvador
triumphed for the title at the tie-breaker in Mexico City. The rivalry
had brought to a head the grave tensions already existing between
the countries. The Honduran press and radio had inflamed the situation, censuring Salvadorans for crossing over and snatching jobs
away from more deserving countrymen. At the time of the first
match in Tegucigalpa, sixty-three dispossessed Salvadorans had arrived at the border. By the second match, only a week later, the
number brutally evicted by the Honduran government had swelled
to tens of thousands, some said. Newspaper headlines and radio
alerts demanded that Salvadorans go home. Home to solve their
own problems. Priority number one, the media blared, the over-
throw of the Salvadoran oligarchy. In addition, Honduran radio
urged countrymen to "pick up a plank and kill a Salvadoran. Hon-
dureño, coge un leño y mata un salvadoreño."

In El Salvador, newspapers and radios brimmed with accounts
of atrocities committed in Tegucigalpa against Salvadorans by la
Mancha Brava, the Angry Mob, a Honduran organization of political thugs and anti-Salvadoran extremists. At the Universidad Nacional de El Salvador, leftists seized the golden opportunity the times
presented. Revolutionaries thriving underground in both the School
of Medicine and the School of Law disseminated cunningly prepared
propaganda. Capitalizing on the whipped-up mood of the people,
insurgents instigated market women to amass and march to the
gates of the presidential palace. "¡Injusticia! ¡Violación! ¡Genocidio!"
the women bellowed in protest. "Injustice! Rape! Genocide!" The
women, most of them stout-armed and thick-waisted, waved
bloomers over their heads as if they were foul flags. The bloomers

served to shame the president. "Go fight for your country, or wear these!" was the message they conveyed.

The phone rang. It was Flor. She was out of breath. "Ay, thank God you're there. Mamá Ceci had a stroke. She's on her way to la Policlínica. Can I send Iris and la Lety to your house for a while?"

"Virgen Santa. How bad is it?"

"She can't move and she can't talk. But she's conscious. Iris found her."

"I'll be right there," Magda said. "You go ahead. I'll pick the baby up myself."

Flor and Enrique's house was next door to his parents'. When Magda's BMW pulled into her daughter's driveway, Flor rushed out to meet her. She was seven months pregnant, and so big-bellied she was waddling already. "It's terrible. Just terrible." She embraced her mother fiercely. "Enrique and don Abraham are on the way from Santa Tecla. It's a miracle they were both at the factory today." Since graduating from Tulane, Enrique had taken over Júnior Tobar's position as manager of the candle factory owned by Enrique's father and Alvaro Tobar. The business was so successful that a second factory was under construction on the road to La Libertad. These days, Enrique spent his time overseeing this operation.

Iris and Lety came out of the house. Lety carried small overnight bags. "¡Abuela!" Iris cried. She ran over and threw her arms around her grandmother. "Mamá Ceci went pum." To show exactly how, Iris plunked herself down on the driveway and started to stretch out, but Lety pulled her up. "Niña, you'll get dirty."

Magda bent over and brushed off Iris's dress, a celery jumper over an ocher blouse that Pilar Lazos had made at Magda's direction. The colors set off Iris's smoldering beauty: olive skin, round dark eyes, lashes like tiny brushes. Hair as thick as a horse's mane. People frequently commented on her striking resemblance to her father. But Magda knew the added truth. Iris looked like a young Cecilia de Aragón.

When Magda brought her mother the news of Cecilia's stroke, Elena (who two years before had moved in with the Tobars) made a puffing sound, as if loath to believe what she had heard. "According to Flor, tía Ceci's paralyzed and she can't speak," Magda said, but softly because Iris was within earshot and all the child had done on the ride home was chatter on about how mamá Ceci had gone ¡pum! on the floor. "Tía Ceci's in la Policlínica," Magda said.

Elena huffed again. It rankled her that since Flor had cast her lot with the Salahs, Magda used the term "tía" in regard to Cecilia. Try as you might, you cannot maintain the past, Elena thought.

Down a stark hospital hall, in a corner room, the Salah family kept a quiet vigil at Cecilia's bedside. Outside, the city held its breath against rumors of war. In garrisons and barracks, the eyes of fighting men grew bright at the prospect.

The following day, after futile diplomatic attempts to obtain safe-conduct for their countrymen out of Honduras, an exasperated Salvadoran army invaded its neighbor. The first attack destroyed most of the Honduran Air Force on the ground. Next to be hit was the oil refinery at Acajutla, then the highways to Guatemala and Nicaragua. In El Salvador, popular support for the war was overwhelming. The entire country pulled together. People formed bandage-rolling and cottonball brigades. They collected canned food to ship to the border, the focal site of combat. High on all food lists: jars of Café Listo, the Salvadoran coffee in dried and instant form.

In retaliation, Honduras mobilized its depleted forces. Small private aircraft strafed the Salvadoran airport at Ilopango. At the border, the Hondurans did what they could. They launched bombs from the flatbeds of trucks.

The war distracted Elena. She read the newspaper, every word of each edition. She cocked an ear to news updates on the radio. She wrote out a check, ten thousand colones, to help pay for the war effort. The sound of war—faraway bombs and machine-gun fire—was dangerous distant thunder.

Elena snapped fully awake. She had been dozing in the easy chair by the window, a newspaper in her lap. The floor lamp at her side cast a soft light. It was very late. The room was in shadows. The house was quiet. In her head, the rumble of a long-forgotten memory: she and Cecilia sitting on the flat table rock at the finca. Cecilia and she talking in the sun.

"Tell me how you'll feel when I die, Nena."

"I'll be sad."

"Sad? That's nothing."

"Okay. I'll cry when you die."

"Will you cry hard, Nena? Will you throw yourself on the ground? How many handkerchiefs will you need when I die?"

"I'll cry so loud all the world will hear. If you die, I'll never stop crying."

Despite trying to hold them back, tears welled up. Was Ceci dying now? A lump formed in Elena's throat; her mouth collapsed downward, and she began to cry. Softly at first, but then the years of loneliness came crushing down, and she opened her mouth and let loose an anguished wail. The sound she made, loud and bleak and sorrowing, startled her into sudden silence. She looked around the room, a hand over her mouth to stifle herself.

In the corner, from the mahogany dresser it seemed, something called to her.

Elena pulled herself up and crossed the room; she knelt before the dresser that had been hers since her wedding day. She opened the bottom drawer, extracting from the back a silk handkerchief bag. She returned to the chair, lowering herself again into the circle of light the lamp threw out.

She sat there like that, in her quiet room in the quiet house, her hand upon the silk enclosure containing Cecilia's unopened letter.

Over Elena's heart, ice began to crack. At her temples, incantatory memories throbbed.

After a time, Elena pulled Cecilia's letter from the slender bag. The dark blue scrawl over pale blue paper leaped up at her.

For the first time, she ran a nail under the envelope flap. Pulled three pages out. In an interminable moment of revelation, flesh, bone, and marrow soaked up a story thirty-six years old.

Nena, it began. Who had called her this since then? Who would ever do so again?

Nena de mi alma. Remember when we were five? Remember when we sat on your back stoop eating peaches? Two plump, cleft peaches with bright green leaves. Remember how we lifted the fruit from tissue-

paper nests? How we raised them to our noses, breathing in perfume and fuzz? Gilded tissue it had been. A heady golden scent.

Remember your dog, Pirata. How he snatched my peach and ran away? Remember how I cried? How you held me, your skinny arm around my shoulders, both of us sitting on the stoop of the servants' entrance when we were five? Her mother's voice had come then. "Where are you, child? Come here." Off she'd gone, looking for her mother, the peach left behind on the stoop. When she returned, the peach was gobbled up.

Remember you said, Why? Because I couldn't help it, I replied. Because I wanted your peach. Your peach. For only that moment, nothing more. Remember how angry you were? How you gave me two weeks? She'd said, "I'm giving you two weeks, Cecilia Muñoz. In punishment, I'm not speaking to you for two weeks. Two weeks. Then we'll be best friends again."

Nena, for what I've done today, banish me for three years. Set fire to my notes. Burn my photographs. Spit on my memory. Not one word for three years. But after that, allow me to return. Heart in hand, on bended knee, I'll plead for your forgiveness. Like I do now in this letter. Like I will until I die. The letter was signed "Tu Frijol," meaning "Your Human Bean," that old joke between them. The letter spelled out a meeting place, a time, a date: Under the vanilla tree. 3 P.M., November 26, 1936.

In the kitchen, after the stove top and burners grew cool, after pots and pans and the dinner dishes were scrubbed, dried, and put away, after the door to the main part of the house was closed off by don Alvaro, the servants—Jacinta; Tea; Rocío, the inside girl; and Socorro, the cook—sipped a last cup of coffee before heading for bed. Iris's nursemaid, Lety, had joined the group, as had Basilio, an unusual thing. He much preferred to greet the night by playing his flute under the orange trees beside his shed. Sleep came easier after a moonlight sonata. But tonight was different. Chaos reigned, and he needed company. As it had been all day, the radio was on. The midnight broadcast offered no new news at the time, only the drone of a commentator recapping the day's events.

Lety, who would soon slip into the spare bedroom with Iris, was distraught over her father. He'd been working in Honduras for the last six months. For two weeks, Lety had not heard from him. "I'm thinking he's dead," she said to the others. For days, the papers had featured front-page pictures: a body dumped along a road. A body floating in the river. Buzzards, circling.

"You shouldn't think the worst," Socorro said. "Sometimes when there's no news, it's a good thing."

"It's easier to think the worst," Lety said. "I can get used to it that way."

"What's your father's name?" Basilio asked.

"Celestino."

Basilio nodded but did not speak.

Lety, who was nineteen and who'd left home only three years before, said, "We're from Dulce Nombre de María. It's only ten kilometers from the Sumpul. That's the river that borders Honduras." Lety wore a white apron over a blue uniform. She rolled the end of the apron up in her arms, then rolled the apron down again.

"Sweet Name of Mary," Rocío said. "That's a pretty name for a town."

"There's a little church in our town. In it, there's the most beautiful statue of la Virgen. She has eggshell skin and aquamarine eyes. She wears a blue robe with tiny stars sprinkled on it. She's only this tall." Lety held a hand out at the side, palm up, the customary way of indicating people's heights.

"La Virgen will protect your father," Socorro said. Her tightly plaited braids had loosened at the temples, allowing her eyes to relax.

"Ojalá," Lety said. "When my mother was dying, she told me to put faith in la Virgen. She said la Virgen was my second mother."

"Ay, pobrecita," Socorro said, taking pity. "So you see. You must do what your mother said. Have faith in la Virgen."

"Have faith in God," Tea added.

Across the table, Jacinta could hardly place her faith in anything. Like Lety, she was filled with apprehension. Since María Mercedes's return from El Congo, she'd seen little of her daughter. Jacinta knew, of course, that María Mercedes had entered law school at the university, that she was living with a Fernando Lira, also a law student and a rabble-rouser if there ever was one. Just before the market women's march to the palace, Jacinta had dropped by to see them.

They shared a cramped mesón room with a yellow dog named Amarillo. When she arrived, María Mercedes had been practicing aloud a poem she had composed and would soon read at a gathering at the university. The poem's title was "Cambiavidas," "Lifechange." María Mercedes called herself a revolting poet, a term that made both her and Fernando laugh. When María Mercedes talked like that, Jacinta hardly recognized her.

In Magda's kitchen, a sound came at the door leading to the main section of the house. A shaking sound from someone wanting entrance to the kitchen. Jacinta rattled through the keys on her ring and unlocked the door.

It was doña Elena who stood there. Her face was streaked with tears. In her hand she held what appeared to be a letter.

"Is Basilio here?" she said. "Tell him to take out the car. He has to drive me to the hospital."

▼▼

CHAPTER FIFTY-FIVE

Elena slumbered fitfully in a straight-backed chair beside the hospital bed, half slumped against the mattress, her hand molded over Cecilia's. A pillow supported Cecilia's head. A cotton blanket, folded at her chest and tucked under her arms, lay over her body. Feet, knees, and breasts formed small rises beneath the blanket. The early light nudged Cecilia awake. She moved her head, that is to say she cast her eyes about: first up, then down. Then from side to side. Through the hazy scrim of her vision, she identified the ceiling, the corner of the wall, the edge of the window, the curve of someone's head bowed down beside her. In the air, the scent of roses, lilies, jasmine. Was she in her garden now? Cecilia wiggled the fingers of one hand because, next to moving her eyes, it was all she was capable of doing.

Elena started awake. She looked around, disoriented.

Cecilia wiggled her fingers again.

Elena sprung up, the chair bobbling behind her. She reached to steady it, then turned back to Cecilia, who pinned her with sharp, narrow eyes. "Ceci," Elena said, her voice but a whisper. "It's me. I came last night. You've been asleep."

On a fold-out cot, Isabel de Salah stirred under a thin throw. She had refused a nighttime private nurse. It was her mother's long-ago wish: When death is near, don't hold me back. Isabel lifted her head in Cecilia's direction. "Is she awake?" she asked Elena.

Elena nodded, backing away from the bed, allowing Isabel her rightful place beside her mother.

Elena went out into the hall. She sat on a bench just outside Cecilia's door. She had come without her purse. No comb. No lipstick. No money. She had arrived wearing what she'd had on when she unsealed Cecilia's letter: the sensible flats, the linen shift with the side pockets, the cashmere cardigan to protect against night air.

Elena smoothed back her hair. She rubbed her eyes, sandy from tears and fatigue. She watched the hospital come to life. With the dawn, natural light crept in. Medicinal odors began to waft. Nurses, starched hats like tiny galleon sails pinned to their heads, hurried up and down the hall. Doors opened and closed. A physician whom she did not know appeared. He gave a quick nod, then disappeared into the room.

Elena pulled Cecilia's letter from a pocket. She laid the pale blue pages on her lap, passing a hand over them, soothingly, as one might do with an ailing child. She leaned back, resting her head against the wall. Because it was possible, because the molecules of her body had committed every word to memory, she allowed her hand to read the letter once again.

Cecilia's door opened. The doctor and Isabel came out. Elena stood up, then quickly sat down again. She pocketed the letter, looking away from two heads bent in private consultation. Snatches of conversation nevertheless drifted her way. "We can keep her comfortable," the doctor said. "We can do that." "What about an operation? You said yesterday that maybe an operation . . ." Isabel's voice dropped off. The doctor again: "I know it's very sad, but look at the bright side. Your mother's seventy-eight. She's had a full life."

Grief welled up and Elena sobbed silently into a handkerchief. Seventy-eight years. The words fell on her like hard rain, eroding all she'd been: harsh, intractable, unforgiving.

She felt an arm along her shoulder. Ample Isabel, of the untamable hair, the tentlike dresses, the spacious heart.

Elena dabbed her eyes. "Your mother wrote me a letter. I didn't open it for thirty-six years. If I had . . ." Elena shrugged and allowed the sentence to trail off. Truth was, she was an old woman who'd learned nothing of life. What could she say now about what she might've done then?

"Go in again," Isabel said. "It's still early. The family will come soon. There'll be people here all day."

As if to prove it, Magda came hurrying down the hall. "My God, Mamá! I got up and you weren't in the house. Basilio said he'd driven you here." Magda kissed Elena. She held Isabel in a long embrace.

The three stepped into a room bathed in yellow light, dewy with the fragrance of fresh flowers cascading from vases and baskets. Except for the flowers, the room was spare and uncluttered: The clock on the wall showing seven A.M. A few chairs. A cot. The high iron bed. The barred window looking out toward the place where war was being waged.

Elena bent over Cecilia. She caressed her brow, furrowed and sun-browned. Stroked her cottony hair against the pillow. Looked into her eyes. Kissed one cheek and then the other. After a moment, Elena brought the letter out. Held it up. Fanned its three pages accommodating the sprawling handwriting. "Mira, Ceci. It's your old letter. All this time, I never opened it. Until last night." Elena gave an involuntary cry at the thought of wasted years. The edge of a chair was pushed against her knees, and Elena dropped onto the seat. She laid her head beside Cecilia's as if they were small again and sharing a bed. She brought her lips to Cecilia's ear. "No te mueras, mi Frijol. Please don't die, my human bean." Tears rolled down her cheeks and onto the bed. "Perdóname, Frijol. Forgive my unrelenting stubbornness. I wish to God I could turn back the clock. If I could, it would be nineteen thirty-six. It would be three o'clock and I'd be under the vanilla." Elena's voice twisted into a cough. Her shoulders heaved. She threw an arm around Cecilia, holding her down as if she might float off.

Cecilia smiled, though she couldn't show it. She closed her eyes. Moved one finger, then another. No te apures, Nena, she thought. En la eternidad, crecen vainillas. Don't you worry, Nena. In eternity, vanillas grow.

▼▼

CHAPTER FIFTY-SIX

Aguilares
November 1971

María Mercedes and Fernando, along with Diego, Felipe, and Berta from the days in El Congo, allied themselves with the Popular Liberation Forces and formed a new group. They called themselves the Band. They chose the name for one reason, cliché though it was, because they marched to the same drum, a drum banging a steady mighty beat: Sacrificio. Lucha. Liberación. Sacrifice. Struggle. Liberation. They kept the group's name to themselves, performed its work clandestinely, and took cover under their revolutionists' names. María Mercedes became Alma, meaning Soul. Fernando became Martín, after San Martín de Porres. Diego, Felipe, and Berta became Pedro, Pablo, y Judit.

After years of attending the university (which in the end, did not earn them any degrees), after participating in student groups such as JEC, ACUS, and the University Socialist Movement, after countless rallies and marches and demonstrations, most of them netting only clubs against their heads, the Band left the idealistic world of discussions and debates—a world of long nights over countless cigarettes and bottomless cups of coffee—and went out again among the people.

Among the people, they began at the beginning. Among the people, they said: We live in a country of four million souls. Cuatro

millones de almas. Imagínense eso. Imagine that. They made a drawing of the country any way they could: in the dirt with a stick, on a
board with chalk (if they were lucky enough to have a board), or
sometimes in the air with a finger pointed out. They sketched the
country, a figure somewhat like a kidney bean tipped up on an end,
and they said: Our country is very small. This is where you live in
our small country, and they marked a big X on the kidney bean for
the people to see. They said: Look, there are twenty of us here (sometimes there were only five or eighteen or ten, and they said that
number), but there are so many, many more of us in our small little
country that it's a miracle we're not bumping into each other all the
time.

To hear the Band, the people gathered under a tree next to a
cornfield, in the yard of a hut in the shade, or in a church after
mass. Extreme caution was essential. Their enemies were numerous,
well armed, and quick on the trigger—the National Police, the Trea-
sury Police, the National Guard, the army, and since 1968, ORDEN,
a paramilitary unit created for keeping order in rural areas.

In our small country, nobody works harder than you, the Band
informed the people: All year you work, or you work hard at finding
work. They let it sink in, then they said: And for all the work you
do, how much do you get paid?

The people shifted uneasily when posed such a question. The
shift was subtle: a glance turned down, a mouth gone into a harder
line, a defiant hip cocked out. ¿Cuánto ganan al año? How much
do you make a year? Then the Band answered their own question,
because in shame the people never would: Eight hundred colones?
A pause. Then, ¿Más o menos, no? and usually it was the word "less"
that showed in people's eyes.

Four million souls in our little country. How many is that? To
make it clear, they said, If you earned one thousand colones every
day for twelve years, that would add up to four million. It had to
be put that way, the concrete mixed with the abstract, for the people
to really see.

They said, Think of this, and they held two hands up for the
people. Estos diez dedos, these ten fingers, represent all the people
in our country. You, los campesinos, count for seven of the ten. And
they curled three fingers under to make the lesson plain.

▼   ▼   ▼

Alma had opened this evening's meeting—twelve men and women, many children, a few dogs—in an empty classroom of the Aguilares church. She sketched out the country (on a blackboard this time), explained about the four million people, ended the introduction with seven fingers pointing up. While she worked, her belly ached and cramped. She'd had a bad night. Her menses had come and she'd hardly slept, even though she and Martín were staying with Nanda Lazos and Nanda had given them her only bed. Pilar's daughter lived just around the corner from her classroom at the church.

"Coffee harvest's starting soon," Alma said. How many times had she stated this fact? "Cotton harvest, too. How many of you have work?"

Only a few made motions that they did. Not surprising. Since the war with Honduras and the breakup of the Central American Common Market, the possibility of industrialization and more jobs had vanished. Since the war, coffee, sugar cane, and cotton had returned as the cornerstones of the economy. Good news for crop owners. Bad news for workers who had to compete with so many for the same backbreaking work.

"And the rest of you? What?"

No answer to the question. Some looked away. Most looked down.

"Allow *me* to tell you what," Alma said. "The rest will stay home. You'll stay home to agonize about the present. To worry about the future. You'll stay home with no job, little food. Less money than food. It's a disgrace. Una desgracia." Alma shook her head. "Listen to me. Is it too much to ask that God grant us a long life? Is it too much to ask that we see our children grow? That we live long enough to know the children of our children? Is that asking too much?" Alma looked toward heaven. "Please, dear God, forgive the hate I feel. Hate toward a government that shortens lives by allowing people to go without food, without health, without work, to go without education, without self-worth. I'm repulsed toward a class of people that allows this injustice. That condones it. That encourages it. I tell you, something must be done." In disgust, Alma dropped into a chair. Martín's dog, Amarillo, came to sniff around her. He made a quick circle and then lay down at her feet.

Martín took the floor. "So what do you think we should do about all this?" He asked the question, knowing that in the end he would answer it himself. When he did, he kept it simple: "What we do is three things." He ticked them off on his fingers. "One, we organize. Two, we get strong. Three, we overcome."

After the statement, nothing was said. It was always like that. At length, a man in the back spoke up. "It's illegal to organize." He turned his hat brim slowly in his hand. "Only because we're in a church did I come out tonight."

A woman said, "My cousin joined a group. She joined FECCAS. Now my cousin's disappeared." A baby slept in the woman's lap. Because its nose was plugged and dirty, its little mouth was hanging open.

"My brother was murdered," another woman said. "We found his body in a ditch."

Martín nodded. Same as always, fear rose up and took command. To allay it, you had to give it a salute. "People, listen to me. Our fear is real. The enemy preys on it. The enemy loves our fear because it keeps us down. But we must act despite our fear. We must act despite the enemy. We owe it to ourselves. We owe it to the children."

Alma stood again. "Your children. You owe them a future. A future filled with work. With money in the hand. A future of no runny stools. No wormy bellies. No snotty noses. No croup. A future where children don't cry themselves to sleep. Where they don't whimper for a scrap of tortilla, for a ladle of salted beans. For cold coffee, bitter grounds."

Silence. Except for the croupy baby wheezing in and wheezing out. Then a young man in the front said, "How do we start?"

"Three things," Martín said. "Number one: Learn to read and write. You can do it. Right here. In this classroom."

Alma said, "Number two: Next year, when elections come, turn out and cast your vote."

"And number three," Martín said, "make your mark and join the cause."

▼ ▼ ▼

Nanda Lazos's house was cozy. It had a cobalt blue bedroom filled with images of saints. Silver stars were painted on the ceiling. The forest green living room crowded with books and potted plants contained a sofa and two easy chairs draped with Guatemalan blankets. Despite its age, the furniture was surprisingly comfortable. Part of the room, next to the tiny kitchen, was set aside for eating. Tonight, Nanda had concocted a vegetable stew with chunks of beef, yellow rice, and spicy black beans. She was thirty-four and at the height of her beauty: the flawless olive skin, the long face and sensual lips, the wide eyes, ojos rasgados, they were called. Only Nanda's hair was different from what María Mercedes remembered. Cropped short and hugging her head, Nanda's hair made her look sad and waiflike. She bustled in and out of the kitchen; she would not allow her guests to lift as much as a finger.

"Please let me help," María Mercedes said. She and Fernando were already at the table.

"You sit," Nanda said. "It's not every day I get to see my María Mercedes." Finally, she took a seat, satisfied that everything was ready. The stew. The basket of steamy tortillas. The cold pilsners Fernando had brought. The indigo votive candles casting a glow.

María Mercedes laughed. "Your place makes me feel so at home. Like I do at your mother's house and at tía Chenta's."

"How is la niña Chenta?" Nanda asked. She passed around the rush tortilla basket, which had a cover like a sombrero.

"Viejita, pero siempre luchando," María Mercedes said. "She's getting old, but she's still fighting." She helped herself to a tortilla and handed the basket to Fernando. "Last year, Chenta got the market women together. They went to the owners and made demands."

"Sounds like someone I know might have helped her see the light," Nanda said.

"You know how it is," María Mercedes said. She took a bite of stew. It was hot and savory. "Oh, this is so good. Fernando and I, we don't get such food very often. We're always eating on the run."

"A pupusa here and there. A sandwichito if we're lucky." Fernando washed down a mouthful of stew with a long pull of beer.

"Um. This is very good." He tore his tortilla in half, bent his head over the food, and ate with gusto.

"I don't cook much, so this is a treat for me, too. If I'm not at the church teaching morning, noon, and night, I'm out in the country getting people into church."

"You're a saint," María Mercedes said.

"I hardly think so," Nanda said.

"Yes, you are."

"Padre Rutilio's a saint. Or to put it another way, what he preaches is saintly."

"After Medellín everything changed, didn't it, Nanda," María Mercedes said. At the Bishops' Conference in Colombia in 1968, the bishops had proclaimed a new Liberation Theology which urged the poor to take the lead in achieving their own temporal, as well as spiritual, freedom.

"Even before Medellín, padre Rutilio had preached what the bishops finally said. He always denounced inequality and oppression. He always encouraged the poor to seek justice for themselves."

"He was right." María Mercedes said no more. She and Nanda were of different philosophies about what action people should take for change to come about. While Nanda believed liberation would be gained through legal methods such as elections and peaceful strikes and demonstrations, María Mercedes had come to believe that made for little progress. Progress was made through collective action. Action by the oppressed against the oppressors was the only route toward change.

After dinner, the three sat in the living room aglow with candles twinkling from bookshelves, tables, and windowsills. They talked late into the night. About the old days when Pilar lived in La Rábida. About la escuela Masferrer. They talked about the future. How if you sacrificed and struggled you might overcome. Sitting in her living room, her slender legs tucked under herself, the little candles casting highlights on her long sad face, Nanda looked like an angel, María Mercedes thought. It was how she would remember her: Nanda on the sofa. Lit by candles like in church.

The next day, Nanda Lazos went out again to teach in the countryside. She never made it home. For days, weeks, and months people searched for her. María Mercedes. Nanda's brothers. Their wives, their sons. Jacinta and Basilio searched. Padre Rutilio himself. All the people Nanda had touched.

Pilar Lazos searched the longest. She searched even after others said it was no use and gave up.

▼▼▼

CHAPTER FIFTY-SEVEN

San Salvador
May 1975

At forty-four, Victor Morales enjoyed the perquisites of a retired army major. When people addressed him, some still said "Sí, mi mayor" and clicked their heels smartly. Victor Morales liked the sound of that. A few years back, just after his retirement, he'd left Santa Ana, returned to San Salvador, and moved into an aquamarine house in Colonia Flor Blanca. He lived there with his three girls of the nautical names: his wife, Marina (she who comes from the sea), and daughters, Marisa (sea star), ten, and Conchita (little seashell), eight. If he'd had a son, he would have christened him Mario, a name with a prefix denoting both the sea and the bellicose might of Mars.

The army had blessed Victor Morales bountifully. In the army, he lived out his father's dream: rank, promotion, beribboned uniforms. Steady pay, power, prestige. Most important, he received certain bonuses that accrue to men who are shrewd and enterprising, traits his father had lacked. Sheer mental capacity. The clarity to see when he'd reached his limits. The valor to accept ambiguity and adapt to it. The vision to enlist the country's plight in his own cause.

Victor Morales, quick and resourceful as he was, capitalized on the war of oppositions erupting around him (right against left, rich against poor, poor against rich, and recently, left against left). He opened an enterprise offering security to stores and factories and banks. Victor's employees, two dozen eager and steely men, were ex-guardias or ex-police. His offices were on the third floor of the very respectable La Fuente building. The sign on the door read "Seguridad Mayor."

Not surprisingly, business was good. Last week he'd picked up a new account. Fábrica La Luz, a candle factory in Santa Tecla owned by a member of the Big Fourteen, the name *Time* magazine had given the oligarchy, who lived in San Benito, and a turco from Escalón.

From the living room, Victor Morales observed his daughters putting the final touches on the decorations for the wooden cross they'd set up in the yard. Makeshift crosses such as theirs were customarily displayed in gardens for el Día de la Cruz. Years ago, Victor had built their cross himself, fashioning it from two sections of rough-hewn lumber, each as tall as half of him. This year, the girls had draped it with pastel tissue chains, marigold and daisy garlands. Around it they'd piled fresh fruit of the season: anonas and jocotes, paternas and hicacos, arrayanes, nísperos y melocotones.

"Look how pretty, Papá," Conchita said when he came to watch. "We're almost done. Now it's time to put our own crosses on." Conchita turned her back to her father. "Here, Papá. Help me with my chain." Conchita's mother had started the family tradition. For the Day of the Cross, they each hung their jewelry crosses from the family's larger cross.

Victor brushed Conchita's hair off the nape of her neck. He fished out the chain from below the collar of her blouse, a gift to her that celebrated his promotion to major. Each of his girls had received one: thick gold ropes from which dangled heavy Latin crosses. Victor fumbled with the catch, strands of Conchita's hair hampering his progress. After a moment, he said, "Niña, do something with your hair. I can't see what I'm doing."

Conchita reached behind to twirl her hair into a coil, which she held up.

"That's better," he said. His daughter's neck was the color of chocolate milk. Her skin was smooth, unblemished, and beautiful. Victor thought it a miracle that both his children had escaped the curse of a birthmark like the one plaguing him. He undid the clasp and pulled the chain up. "Here it is."

"Now give me yours," Marisa said. Like her sister, she had a pudgy face and soft features. Dark, round, innocent eyes.

"Yes, but you have to promise . . ."

". . . that we'll keep careful watch on all of them," Conchita said. "They're made of gold . . ."

". . . and they cost me plenty of money." Victor Morales laughed because it was the same exchange they had every year. He unhooked his own wide chain, which carried, in addition to a cross, the short length of pita strung with three red agates. The cord and stones were what remained of his natal amulet. Victor handed the chain to his youngest daughter. "You can have it, but only for an hour." In truth, he felt naked without his agates. Since he'd thought to bind them to the chain years ago, he'd worn them daily for cosmic protection. His family had long grown accustomed to this peculiarity.

"Where's your mother? Let's get her cross."

"You better wait, Papá," Marisa said. She had taken her own chain off and had draped it on the cross. "Mami's listening to *Las dos*. You know how she is about that program."

Victor went back into the house and stepped into the room where his daughters did their schoolwork. His wife Marina was next to the radio, glaring down at it incredulously. "Listen to that!" she exclaimed, throwing up her hands when Victor came in. "They interrupted my story. Just when Dulce Alegría is learning the truth about her lover." Marina switched off the radio. It gave an angry little click. "Stupid communists," she said. "Now we'll have to wait until Monday to find out about Julián."

"What about the communists?" Victor asked.

"They interrupted my story," Marina said, her eyes going wide as if she were talking to a dolt. She tossed her thick chestnut hair. Raked it back with a hand. "Did the girls finish the cross?"

"They're waiting for your chain," Victor said. He sat down and turned the radio back on.

"Stupid communists," Marina said, turning heel and marching out of the room.

Victor Morales listened to the news. The red poet, Roque Dalton, had been stood up against the wall and shot. His own Maoist party, the ERP, the Revolutionary Army of the People, had ordered his execution. Chaos brought about by opposing military views within party factions had prompted the shooting. Victor shook his head. The ERP, the FPL, the PRS, the PDC, the PCS. The commies were a bowl of red spaghetti. I hope all the cocksuckers kill each other off, Victor Morales thought. He listened for a while longer, then joined his family to venerate the cross.

That night, across town, María Mercedes Prieto wrote a poem in memory of a fallen poet and a comrade. She titled her poem "Bitter Grounds." By Alma del Pueblo, Soul of the People, she signed at the end.

▼▼

CHAPTER FIFTY-EIGHT

La Abundancia
Santa Ana
August 1976

The order came down by executive decree. A governmental concession toward reform, toward easing escalating tensions that pointed from every direction to the outbreak of civil war. The decree mandated the seizure of properties over five hundred hectares and the turning of the land over to the people.

As fate would have it, La Abundancia was the first property selected for redistribution. "Una finca modelo para modelar transformación," "A model plantation to model transformation." After Ernesto Contreras's death, La Abundancia had passed on to his older son, Ernesto "Neto" Contreras Navarro. Because confiscation did not occur until well after the harvest, the patrón was luckily away at the time. Remaining behind were don Gabriel, el administrador, his five foremen, and his six male clerks, who spent the day stabbing adding-machine keys with fleet fingers. There were others on the finca when the takeover occurred: those laboring under the sun pruning shade trees or transplanting flor de izote to deter soil erosion, those in nurseries nudging coffee seedlings along. And there were women in the kitchens and the laundry. Women tending la casona, though after harvest time, the house slumbered like a hibernating bear.

Against this formidable force of defenders, the army, acting on

orders by the defense minister, launched a full-scale assault. At daybreak two companies of soldiers poured out of a caravan of buses
and massed in a field a kilometer from La Abundancia's gates. Heavily armed and itchy to perform, the men split into platoons, each
led by a lieutenant, and with two captains to oversee strategy. The
prospect of promotion gleamed in the officers' eyes.

To begin, they blocked all roads leading into the finca, estab-
lishing checkpoints at all entrances. Next, they secured the perim-
eters of the property, a ranks-thinning operation given that the finca
extended well up the sides of the volcano. With all in place, a lieutenant colonel gave the order to go in.

At midmorning, a hundred soldiers stormed La Abundancia.
They battered the gates, charged down inner roads and lanes, around
coffee shrubs and under the madrecacaos shading them. Dust billowed as they stormed in. Boots sounded a thudthudthud over the
soft explosions of men's breath. The finca's dogs growled and yelped,
first a single cur, then another, then all the others chorusing in.

Soldiers broke into the house, rammed into cooking sheds and
nurseries. They overran the beneficio. Invaded the office where
twelve paper pushers worked at their desks.

It was a masterful operation.

So swiftly had soldiers come that don Gabriel leaped up, toppling his chair; for an instant, the clatter it made as it struck the
floor was more startling than the swarm.

"Out!" soldiers roared. They used rifle barrels to point the way.

Don Gabriel. Servants, laborers, foremen, clerks. Thirty workers
flew from their violated strongholds like bats out of caves. Two
captains herded them under the spreading ceiba in the yard.

It was the lieutenant colonel who delivered them.

He pointed to the twelve who'd been in la administración.
"¡Fuera!" he bellowed, gesturing toward the road.

"Out?" don Gabriel asked, squinting in the sun, turning up
helpless hands because he didn't understand.

"¡Fuera!" the lieutenant colonel echoed. "Out of the finca!"

Don Gabriel took off first. The others followed. Escorted by
soldiers, the twelve proceeded anxiously, looking back now and
again. They crossed the yard and passed la casona, starting down

the road leading to the gates. Then, because fortune can't be trusted, they broke en masse into a run.

Gerónima, who for ten years had occupied the same spot under the tin roof of the cooking shed slapping masa into wheels against a palm, watched the bosses go with both expectation and alarm. She steeled herself against the sharp report of rifles sure to erupt. When none came, she heard with disbelief the news the lieutenant colonel spoke.

"The rest of you, do not be afraid. By presidential decree this finca now belongs to you."

Eyes widened, but no one moved. Then one of the captains said, "Get back to work. Just because you're landowners doesn't mean you can slack off." El capitán gave a laugh that sounded like a bark. He pointed toward the gates through which the bosses had disappeared. "Don't worry about them. Tomorrow the government will appoint others in their place."

And so it was that the Contrerases' familial grounds were delivered by force into the hands of the people. By late afternoon, when el coronel Manda Todo, the colonel in Charge of Everything, came around for the inspection, he nodded in approval at the splendid military display of soldiers posted along the road, around the house, and throughout the property. He marveled to himself how smooth and uneventful the transfer had been.

A phone call from don Gabriel revealed the news to Neto Contreras, his brother, Alberto, and Alvaro Tobar. Immediately, they jumped in a car and sped to La Abundancia, only to be repelled by soldiers at the gate. It was after five by then, and most official avenues of remonstrance were closed for the day. Their only recourse, for the moment, was to go to their mother's house. There, they would carefully consider their response to the theft of their most precious possession: the land.

Elena, who had moved back home after Cecilia's death, sat silently on the veranda. A maelstrom of enraged voices whirled about her: her sons, their wives. Magda and Alvaro. The grandchildren, all robust women and men, all people of action.

"It's against the law."

"They can't do this."

"How can they do this?"

"Why us?"

"Thank God Papá's not alive to witness such injustice."

"If Papá were alive, this outrage would kill him dead."

Elena's mind turned away from the outbursts, the rantings, the bellowing, the storm. She followed the whim of her mind as it dipped and darted over details in the finca house: the massive sideboard in the dining room, the accommodating table, the dozen matching chairs. All handed down by her mother who had brought them from Spain in the hold of the ship. In the kitchen, the pots and pans, the plates and platters. The green wicker on the wraparound porch. The cherry dressing table in the bedroom. The tall iron bed where she and Ernesto first made love. Elena stopped recounting. The image of her things, of strangers pawing over them, was a blade cutting deep.

Across the veranda, Orlando—Magda and Alvaro's youngest son and for fifteen years an attorney—spoke. "The simple fact is, we can do little against an executive decree."

"Can't someone talk to Molina?" Magda asked. Molina was the president, who had signed the order. "I'll go talk to him. The man doesn't scare me."

"What's there to talk about, Mamá?" Orlando said. "We've been made an example. The president can't go back on what he's decreed."

"But it's illegal, what he's done," Margarita, Neto's wife, said. "Molina's taken property that is our god-given right to own."

"Since when has illegality kept people from doing what they have to do?" Neto said.

Alvaro Tobar thought of his own property. The cotton he'd nursed along with his blood and his sweat. All his haciendas were larger than the hectares proscribed in the decree. And the plantations were spread apart. The largest in Usulután. Two others near Jiquilisco. All separated by other lands, and therefore impossible to reparcel. All falling outside the scope of the decree. If his mother were alive (doña Eugenia had died peacefully in her sleep three years before), his father, too, what would they have done to protect the family lands?

"Well, all that aside," Margarita was saying, "we have to do something. We can't just sit here and take this injustice."

"I second that," Magda said, though she usually did not agree with much Margarita said.

Gradually, from much discussion, an action list emerged: Favors to be called in. Demands to be made. Money to be offered. Throughout the discussion, violence and revenge were two words that did not cross a single person's lips.

After all was said, Alvaro Tobar walked out into the patio. A night with no moon descended. Lit lamps in the house did not make up for the lack. Alvaro sat on the edge of the pila, empty of water for very many years. Soon Neto and Alberto Contreras joined him. The black night lent them anonymity. They were just three men, any men, talking in the dark.

"All those things for us to do," Neto said, "it won't make any difference." He had the most to lose in all of this. Since his father died, La Abundancia had been his.

"I know someone who might help," Alvaro said, because from the start a crystal clear idea had been knocking around in his head.

"Who?" Neto said.

"An ex-army major. A man of connections."

"A man with the right connections, that's what we need."

"He's got them," Alvaro said. "But the right connections don't come cheap."

"If he can help, the cost is not important," Alberto said.

"I'll talk to him tomorrow," Alvaro said. "For now, we keep this to ourselves."

The three returned to the veranda. Because she looked so small and sad sitting in her chair, Alberto bent to kiss his mother. "Don't worry, Mamá. We'll take care of everything."

"What does it matter?" Elena said. "No bad things are left to happen."

She was wrong.

▼   ▼   ▼

Two weeks later, with fifty thousand colones of up-front money paid in cash, Victor Morales sent ten of his most talented men on a mission aimed at making a statement, a mission to teach a lesson, to send a warning, or, put in a way his employers would not dare admit, a mission to extract revenge. Aided by the moon, a detailed layout of the finca, and an up-to-date schedule of current routines provided by an informer, the men stole over La Abundancia's main gate. One of them, in a fleet silent move, slashed the neck of the lone guard posted there. Armed with Uzis and clad in black attire, Victor's men moved on toward their targets: the barracks with the corrugated roof under which bureaucrats slept, the front room of la administración, outfitted since the takeover with cots for the new clerks.

Start to finish, Victor's mission was accomplished in less than six minutes. When the bursts of automatic fire stopped reverberating, when the dust settled and the dogs went quiet, sixteen men lay broken and rent, blood and sinew pooling around them.

The morning newspapers screamed seventy-two-point headlines: MASACRE EN FINCA and ASESINOS ANONIMOS ACRIBILLAN A DIECISEIS and REFORMA AGRARIA—¿A PROPOSITO DE QUIEN? At home, Alvaro Tobar sipped his morning coffee. He did not allow himself to dwell on the largest headlines, so his eyes slid over "Plantation Massacre" and "Anonymous Assassins Riddle Sixteen." The third headline, "To Whose Purpose Agrarian Reform?" he found interesting and so he read the article in its entirety. When finished, he folded the paper neatly, setting it on the table next to his plate. To whose purpose reform? The newspaper's version of an answer was a philosophical treatise. No need for that. Were the question put to him, the answer would be simple: To our purpose, and that was the honest truth.

Alvaro pushed back his chair. He tossed back the last of his coffee, gone cold and bitter now. He checked his watch. He had an early meeting. A delivery to make. A final cash installment of fifty thousand colones. This kind of war was expensive. But war made possible the most difficult things.

▼▼▼

CHAPTER FIFTY-NINE

Left, right. Left, right. Uno, dos. Uno, dos. El Salvador marched down the road to civil war. Sabotage, anarchy. Marxist-Leninist groups, Maoist cells grow and multiply. Kidnapping to make money, to buy arms, to create fear, to subvert the press. Another fraudulent election. General Carlos Humberto Romero wrests power from Molina. Fifty thousand demonstrators crowd la Plaza Libertad. Security forces surrounding the square mow down one hundred protesters. Members of the far right coalesce into the White Warrior Union, the UGB, or la Mano Blanca. At the top of the their long list of ways to stop the left is the elimination of troublesome Jesuits.

Left, right. Left, right. Inhuman acts exact a human toll: The sun rising to mutilated bodies dumped overnight along the streets. The sun setting on bombed-out power and water lines. The stench. The thirst. The filth. In mesones, children wail, beg for food, die slow deaths. In San Benito, children ride to private schools in bulletproof cars. Their fathers drive to work in three-car convoys. Martín drags Alma home. He nurses her leg hit by shrapnel at la Plaza Libertad. It is her thirtieth birthday, but this occasion slips her mind. The government places a moratorium on expropriations. Crying "an eye for an eye, a tooth for a tooth," the UGB demands the government not give in to terrorists. On March 12, 1977, while on his way to celebrate mass at the town where he was born, Father Rutilio Grande and all in his party are assassinated by unknowns.

▼▼

CHAPTER SIXTY

San Salvador
October 1977

Sometimes María Mercedes's leg ached. The whole of her leg, not just the spot where shell fragments had torn flesh. Tonight the back of her thigh throbbed, so she lay, facedown, across the bed while he kneaded the soreness away with a squirt of mentholated balm. "Ay," she said. A long, hissing breath. Amarillo, who loved the tingly taste of menthol, jumped up next to her and tried to get a lick. Fernando pushed the dog aside with an elbow. "Get off. Go lie down." Amarillo slunk to the door. It was chained and bolted shut. When the dog lay down, the crack under the door disappeared behind him.

María Mercedes lifted her head from the mattress. "Good dog."

Amarillo yawned, emitting a half yelp at the end.

"There." Fernando gave María Mercedes's leg a little pat. "All done. It's late. Let's go to bed."

They switched off lights. Turned covers back. Undressed and climbed in. In the middle of the bed, they talked softly, bien bajito. They spoke without uttering names. These days even the walls had ears.

"We're doing it for the poet, for the priest," he said, because he knew she needed reassurance. "We're doing it for all those who've fallen."

410

"I know." She made her own mental additions to Fernando's list: For her grandmother Mercedes. For the ones whose names were scrawled on crosses dotting the family plot. For the lost child Justino, who would have been her uncle.

"And for Nanda," he said. "Wherever she might be."

"For Nanda." At the thought of her friend, María Mercedes's mind filled with the sight of corpses, hacked, burned, dismembered corpses, strewn and stacked at El Playón. She saw herself, her mother, and Pilar, orange halves pressed against noses, picking over bodies in an anguished futile search. She said, "Remember. There must be no killing. Just kidnap, collection, release."

He nodded and the flimsy mattress wobbled. "No killing," he said, but he couldn't guarantee the outcome of anything. So far there'd been no killings in the work the Band had done. Himself. Alma. Pedro. Pablo. Judit. Together, they had paraded, demonstrated, agitated. They had firebombed empty buses and businesses. They had torched rubber tires for the sheer drama of it. Three days ago, through an acrid cloud of burning rubber, armed with only their sorry jamming revolvers, Pedro and Judit had miraculously commandeered a police car. They had come away with a surprising cache of weapons: four Colt M19s, two Browning High Powers, one Heckler & Koch P9S. With arms like that in their possession, they were almost ready for their most daring work.

María Mercedes turned over and stared up at the black void of the ceiling. Six years back, as she stepped gingerly over the corpses at El Playón, something inside her began to change. After El Playón, the image of corpses sprung up in her head by day and filled her dreams at night. Something huge and silent and dark expanded in her, nudging aside her tender sensibilities. Slowly, she turned away from her mother and Basilio, from Pilar and from Chenta. She loved them; that would never change. But she was no longer the person they had loved. She was someone else entirely, which was not to say she did not at times feel the pull from the one she once had been. Her old self tugged at her now. She trembled thinking of what she owed her family. What she owed the Tobars.

She rolled over and faced Fernando, though she could only make out his shadow in the dark. "Remember what you promised. Remember the man who must not be touched."

"How can he be touched when he's off tending cotton? You yourself said he spends the harvest in Usulután."

"That's true. I just want it to be clear." She was pushing her luck. She had gone against the group when they'd targeted Alvaro Tobar. That they had settled for his partner, Abraham Salah, was something she could not help.

"Don't worry. I know what you want. Kidnap. Collection. Release." He cupped her face between his hands. "Mi Alma," he whispered. "My courageous Alma."

"My handsome Martín."

▼▼▼

CHAPTER SIXTY-ONE

La Banda met at a place that Pablo had found, an abandoned hut with a cornfield gone to seed down a path off the road to Santa Tecla. The group had been meeting there for a month, using the field for target practice. As in the ACUS days, they built a fire; it was small, lanternlike, showing just enough light to distinguish faces. The topic for discussion was Operation Absa, code name for the kidnapping of Abraham Salah.

Judit, who since she'd given up the name Berta was less of a joker, gave a detailed recap of the target. All facts she'd committed to memory. "The subject is a sixty-eight-year-old male turco who lives by San José de la Montaña with wife and servants; a total of six in the household. He's a member of ANEP, the National Association of Private Enterprise. His family owns Textilos, S.A., the largest manufacturer of textiles in the country. He's part owner of La Luz, a candle factory headquartered here, in Santa Tecla. As you know, we pass the site coming here. There's a second factory in Quezaltepeque, twenty kilometers to the northeast. Subject has three children, the youngest a male in his thirties who manages both factories and travels frequently between them. Subject owns land, comprised mostly of real estate for lease. He's on the board of two banks, el Banco Salvadoreño and el Banco Agrícola. So much for subject's qualifications."

Pablo, who when not on La Banda business was Felipe, took his turn. "Subject drives a four-door, dark blue 1975 BMW. Placas P-three-one-two-nine-seven. The car is not bulletproof. No body-guard is employed, however the subject appears to be armed. He's a man of regular habits. Each Tuesday and Thursday, after having lunch at home, he pulls out of his driveway at one-thirty. He arrives at La Luz in Santa Tecla at approximately two o'clock."

"A most worthy subject, our man, don't you think?" Judit said, her true nature presenting itself. "He's rich. He's old. He's a man of habit who prefers traveling alone."

Pedro, known also as Diego, said, "If he leaves his house at one-thirty, that places him at the ambush point at about quarter to two."

"Exactly," Pablo said.

"Let me go over those details," Pedro said. "The ambush site is on the road from San Salvador to Santa Tecla, at the place where the road branches left and descends toward La Libertad. As we know, there's a sunken median there in the form of a *Y*." He lifted his hands, right one higher than the left. "To go to Santa Tecla, you stay right and follow the climbing road." Pedro made a going-up motion with his right hand. "If you're going to La Libertad, you stop before crossing left." He made a downward motion with his left hand. "The subject's car will be intercepted as it starts its climb toward Santa Tecla. There's a grassy knoll at that spot in the median. We'll take him there. Force his car against the knoll."

"We'll need two vehicles for that," Martín said. "One to follow. One to intercept. We'll take the cars the previous night. Change the plates before they're used."

Alma said, "A panel truck is a must. That and maybe a pickup. We can't depend on the subject's car."

"That's right," Martín said. "The panel truck will follow the subject out of the city. The pickup will intercept at the crossroads. One vehicle in front. One vehicle in back. After the ambush, only the panel truck will continue on."

"So now let's say the subject's captured," Alma said. "Go over what happens next."

"We haul his ass to jail," Judit said. "The People's jail, that is."

"There's a place in Colonia Utila," Pablo said. "I found a small house there. It has a garage connected to the house. Two of us will move in before the operation. We'll keep a low profile and establish a presence before we begin."

"Colonia Utila," Pedro said. "That's a quiet, family neighborhood. It's not more than five minutes from the median. That's perfect. Who would guess we'd hide the target so close to the scene?"

"Not the police," Judit said. "They're too stupid."

"What about Morales and the security people from La Luz?" Alma asked.

"There's no reason for factory security to be involved," Pablo said. "We're taking the subject before he reaches the factory, not while he's in it. By the time the news of the abduction gets to the factory, we'll all be safe and sound in the People's jail." He smiled at Judit, showing he could joke.

"So," Martín said. "We have the guns. We have the method. We have the place. Now let's settle on the day."

"Just a minute," Judit said. "First let's settle on the war tax. How much ransom will we ask?"

▼▼

CHAPTER SIXTY-TWO

November 17, 1977

Socorro was at the stove sautéing onions and tomatoes to top the filet she would grill for Magda's lunch. She shook the black-bottomed pan back and forth across the burner. She made quick, rasping sounds that were annoyingly satisfactory because they matched her mood. Last night, a group of guerrilleros—who could keep them straight?—had assaulted YSU and taken over the station. The attack had wiped out all the regular programs. Including *Las dos*. "Beasts," Socorro said. "Now the brutes have left us between chapters."

"It's not the end of the world," Basilio said. He was at the servants' table, waiting for lunch.

"Yes it is." Socorro flicked off the heat under the pan. She set it with a clang on a back burner. She gave the soup in the big kettle an exasperated stir. "Today's Tuesday, isn't it? Well, today was the day Julián and Dulce Alegría were running off together."

"I thought you told me they couldn't get married because they were related," Basilio said. Who could understand these far-fetched, convoluted stories?

Socorro rolled her eyes, squinting as always because of her tight braids. "¡No, hombre! That's what la Bárbara said. She said Julián was a long-lost son. She said it because Julián thought he was an

416

orphan. She said it because she's selfish, and wanted Dulce Alegría all to herself. But then Julián saved everything. He had his blood tested and proved la Bárbara wrong."

"That's ridiculous. Why would anyone say something like that? And who'd believe it if they did?"

"La Bárbara said it because she's evil and conniving. Dulce Alegría believed it because she's an angel and as good as Inocencia ever was. Pobre Inocencia, dead before her time."

"I thought Inocencia was in a wheelchair?"

"Well she was, but now she's dead. She had a murmuring heart. Remember?"

Jacinta strode in. "El señor just came in from Usulután. You'll need to make lunch for him, too."

Socorro poked fists into the plump flesh of her waist. "Why didn't someone tell me he was coming?"

"Because we didn't know," Jacinta said. She took a chair next to Basilio.

"What's a murmuring heart?" Basilio asked her.

Before Jacinta had a chance to answer, Magda popped her head into the kitchen. "Socorro, open a can of mushrooms for don Alvaro's filet." Magda went back through the house and into the bedroom, where her husband stood in his closet. He had unlocked the built-in cabinet where his guns were stored. Magda went up behind him and circled him with her arms. "Mmmm. What a surprise. I'm so glad you're here." She laid her head against his back, warm and smelling of musky lotion.

"Wait. Let me get this off." Alvaro peeled off the shoulder holster with his revolver and placed them beside the other weapons stashed in the cabinet. He locked them up and hooked the key on the nail set in a board at the back of the shelf that held his ironed shirts. He turned back to Magda. "Now," he said. "Where were we?"

"Right here." She embraced him again, but around the chest this time. She looked up at him. "I was saying how glad I was to see you. My phone call this morning must have been very persuasive." She gave a laugh, recalling how she'd described how much she missed him. How she'd told him, softly, very softly, what she'd do if he came home.

"Who can resist a woman in need?"

She pressed her lips to his. Parted them as he did. Ran the tip of her tongue against his. He gave her tongue a playful little nip. Patted her on the rump.

She pulled away. "What's wrong?"

"Nothing's wrong. I'm hungry."

"Well, so am I."

"But right now I want food. Then we'll take a siestecita." He wiggled his eyebrows. Made a motion toward the bed.

"Promise?"

"Promise."

They were halfway through lunch—these days, when he was home, it was just the two of them at the table—when the phone rang. Jacinta answered it. "Un momentito, señor," she said, setting down the receiver on the little table in the hall. She came to the dining room. "Don Alvaro, don Abraham wants to talk to you."

Alvaro dabbed his mouth with the napkin and went to get the phone. Soon, he was in the chair again, turning back to his lunch.

"How did Abraham know you were home?" Magda asked. She used her knife to mound onions and tomatoes on a slice of filet she'd speared with her fork.

"He called El Porvenir."

"So what does he want?"

"He wants me to go with him to Santa Tecla. Looks like that property in Zaragoza we want is suddenly available. If we're going to get it, we have to move fast."

"When are you going?"

"He's coming by in fifteen minutes. Enrique's already at the factory. We'll meet him there at two."

Magda put down her knife and fork. "But what about our sies-tecita?" She turned down her lip. Blinked her eyes to complete the sad effect.

"I'll be back soon." He leaned over and blew her a kiss. "Any-way, a little waiting heightens passion. Isn't that what you always tell me?"

"Well, all right. But don't you let me wait too long."

▼   ▼   ▼

The BMW had started to climb the road to Santa Tecla when Alvaro spotted the gray Toyota pickup pulling out ahead. "Abraham," Alvaro said, interrupting their conversation about the new property. Reflexively, he laid a hand on his partner's arm. "Watch that pickup . . ." Alvaro's next words were swallowed up by the squeal of skidding tires, by the braking of the pickup leaping out in front of them.

Abraham jerked the wheel to the left. Alvaro braced himself for impact. He was tossed hard against the door frame when the BMW struck the curb. They rolled up and over it. He bounced off the dashboard, then hurtled back against the seat when the car shuddered and stalled out.

Alvaro winced at the pain in his neck and shoulders. The pickup had stopped perpendicular to them. Doors were flung open. A man and woman charged out, revolvers drawn and ready.

"Start the car!" Alvaro yelled. "Back up now!" He thrust a hand into his jacket, reaching for his weapon, and found to his horror he had left the gun at home.

Two guerrilleros yanked open the back door and burst in behind them. Two more stormed toward the front of the car. All wore ski masks over their faces. "Out! Out! Out!" Commands rained down from all directions.

Abraham Salah threw a shoulder against the door and hurled himself from the car, reaching at the same time for his pistol. When his feet hit the ground, he stumbled a bit and turned, his gun hand up. A woman rushed toward him, wide eyes framed in the mask opening. The woman fired. He squeezed the trigger. Felt the recoil when firing back.

A guerrillero yanked Alvaro by the arm from the car. Gunfire, close by, echoed in his ears. The stench of sulfur stung in his nose. He hopped a little on one foot, thrown off balance by a man who had hooked a hand inside his collar and was trying to pull him down. To square himself, Alvaro dropped into a crouch. Sprung up. Took the man out with a swift right punch. Another shot. A low, stinging blow that buckled his knees.

"Go! Go! Go!"

Rough, grasping hands under his armpits dragging him.

"She's dead. Get her in the panel truck. But the old man's still alive."

¡Pak! ¡Pak! Two more shots.

Grass blurred beneath him. A shove over a steely edge of something. His cheek hard against a rumbling.

"Let's go! Let's go!"

The long scrape of a closing door. Motor revving. A forward jerk.

Two pairs of feet clattering beside him.

"Let's go! Let's go!"

Tires screaming.

Something wet, like blood, seeping.

▼▼

CHAPTER SIXTY-THREE

To the man on the Vespa it was like watching a movie. He saw the gray Volkswagen panel truck tear off down the street. Inside, three masked guerrilleros. Also in the truck, but out of view, one guerrillera who appeared dead. More important, a man who struggled fiercely when they hauled him in. The man on the Vespa scanned the vehicle for license plates but glimpsed none before it careened around the corner. Twenty meters away, the Toyota pickup was hiked over the curb, motor running. The BMW sat behind it, all doors flung wide. Don Abraham, the factory patrón, lay belly up on the grass, the top of his head destroyed.

From nowhere and everywhere, what seemed like all the people in the world materialized at once. They came running over the median and down the street. Cars screeched to abrupt stops. In a long hiss of brakes, a bus pulled up, too.

The man on the Vespa stepped on the gas. He navigated around the astounded, milling crowd. He turned the corner where the panel truck had crossed, and rode down a street lined with small tinted houses, one-storied, flat roofed. He went up one street and then another, whizzed past rows and rows of boxy pastels. No panel truck in sight, not on the street or in any driveway. He stopped to take a breather and to digest all he had seen and not seen. Then he headed for La Luz, the place of his employment. He dashed into the office, startling don Enrique at his desk.

"Balearon al señor," is what the man blurted.

"They shot what señor?"

"El patrón, patrón. Don Abraham. Su papá."

Enrique made a choking sound that turned finally into a word, "Where?"

"Back at the crossroads. On the grass, beside his car."

In Enrique's ears, a surging rush like an incoming wave. He rounded the desk. "Find el mayor Morales. He's somewhere in the plant. Meet me there the both of you."

It was twenty minutes after two.

In the rose-tinted house, a few neighborhoods away, Alma was peering under the garage door she'd lifted only high enough to watch for the panel truck. When it lurched into the drive, she raised the door fully. Closed it swiftly when the panel truck rolled inside. The garage filled with engine roar, with the heated smell of exhaust, with the vehicle itself.

Alma lowered her ski mask. She scooted around the truck as the motor cut off. The driver's door creaked opened. Martín stepped out. He wore his mask; his gun was tucked into his waistband. He pulled her swiftly through the side door into the house's tiny kitchen.

"It didn't go well. Judit's dead. Her body's in the truck."

"¿Y don Abraham?" Through the eyeholes of his mask, the dark bright pupils. Like targets they were.

"Dead, too. We left him behind."

"What now? Now we have no one."

"Yes we do. The old man had a passenger in the car. We took him."

Out in the garage, the panel truck's side door slid open with a grind. Soon, Pedro and Pablo hauled the prisoner in. He was slumped between them, his arms slung around their necks. As they went along, the tops of his shoes trailed against the floor.

Seeing him, Alma felt the blood drain out of her head. She steadied herself against the wall. Laid a hand on her ski mask for assurance she had it on.

"What's wrong with him?" Martín asked the others as they dragged the prisoner past.

"He says he's wounded," Pablo remarked.

Martín said, "Get him in the bedroom."

Alma slid slowly down the kitchen wall. It was don Alvaro they'd taken. She watched them all disappear into the room.

The room had only one window that looked out to an inner hall. A plywood square sealed the window opening. A one-hundred-watt bulb, wired at the switch to stay on, was screwed high on the ceiling and provided the only light. There was a cot with a pillow and a blanket. A single wooden chair.

They dumped him on the cot, and he let out a yowl. Sweat slipped down his forehead, blinding him.

"Shut up! Remember the turco. What happened to him can happen to you."

"Get a doctor." Alvaro wiped his eyes, but still the room swam. His belly ached profoundly. He swallowed hard to keep from vomiting. He rolled on his side, yowled again against the stab of pain in his buttock. He lifted himself up gingerly. Reached back to touch. "Look," he said, raising a red palm so they could see what he felt.

"Puta. Sangre," Pedro said. He helped turn him over. Saw the spreading stain on the back of his pants. "He got it in the butt."

"I need a doctor," Alvaro said.

"Get him some water," Martín said.

Alma pulled herself up. She went to the sink and turned on the tap. Let the water run cold before filling up a glass. The room was tilting. The refrigerator was humming. In her ear someone was whispering, What is it you have done?

It was thirty minutes after two.

The Santa Tecla police—three cars, six officers—attempted to disperse the crowd, but to no avail. The people stood silently, gawking at the crazily juxtaposed vehicles, at the body, covered now respectfully with a sheet.

Though the police had not allowed him so much as a touch, an officer lifted the edge of the sheet so Enrique could make an identification. "It's him. Put it down," he said, turning away from blasted bone, from clotted shiny tissue, from his father's beloved face.

Victor Morales held an unsteady Enrique by the elbow and led him a few meters away. "What will happen to him now?" Enrique asked.

"They'll take him to the morgue."

"In San Salvador?"

Victor shook his head. "No. In Santa Tecla."

"Can you do something about that? I want him transferred to the capital."

"I'll take care of it," Victor said.

They joined the man with the Vespa, who was talking to an officer who took down notes: A Volkswagen panel truck. Gray. No plates. Three men. All masked. Two others inside: One, a woman clearly wounded, and also masked, which meant a guerrillera. The other, a man fighting for his life.

The news was an explosion going off. "What are you saying? Enrique asked. "Are you saying someone else was in my father's car?"

The man with the Vespa nodded. "Sí. Un señor bien vestido."

"A well-dressed man?"

"Sí. Y así de alto como usted."

Someone else in the car. Someone well dressed. Someone as tall as he. Enrique started down a mental list of people he knew who might fit the description.

"The truck turned that corner," the man went on, pointing to where. "I tried going after it on the Vespa, but so many people came. Then it was too late."

"I have to get home," Enrique said to the police. "Mayor Morales here, whatever you need from me, you can get from him."

Victor Morales squeezed Enrique's shoulder reassuringly. "Leave everything to me," he said.

It was fifteen minutes until three.

▼   ▼   ▼

When he walked in, Flor knew something was terribly wrong. For one, he was home at just a little after three. For another, his face was gray. "What is it?"

His daughters, Iris, Jasmín, and Lili, were home on school vacation. They gave a delighted whoop when he appeared on the porch. "¡Papi!"

He kissed them, lowering lips to their unmarked perfect faces. How he loved them. Their dear tender bodies. Their eyes, thick-lashed and large as almonds, like the eyes of that Bambi he'd once had as a pet.

"Mamá and I. We have to go over to Abuela's," he said. "For now, you girls stay here with la nana."

Flor called out for Lety; then she took her husband's hand. She walked with him over the thick grass, through the opened inner gate into Isabel's garden. Going under the lush trees, around the pretty flowers, she clasped his hand tighter, then tighter as they went.

Isabel was in the house. Enrique called her name, and she came strolling out to the glass table with the wrought-iron chairs, a look of pleased surprise spreading over her face.

"What?" she said, her expression collapsing at the sight of them standing so close together, their breath held in as if there wasn't any air.

"It's Papá," Enrique said.

Isabel dropped down heavily into the nearby chair. She placed a hand on her heart, as if to hold her heart in. "Is he dead?"

"Sí," he said, his own face crumpling.

"What happened?" Flor asked, her voice a mere sigh.

"La guerrilla."

"No," Flor said, dropping down beside Isabel's chair. She threw her arms around her.

Isabel felt the ferocity of Flor's embrace. It strengthened her somehow. "¿Dónde? ¿Cúando?"

"About an hour ago. At the Santa Tecla crossroads. The police say someone was in the car with Papá. Someone the guerrillas took away."

"Holy and powerful God," Isabel said. She laid a cheek against the top of Flor's head.

▼▼

CHAPTER SIXTY-FOUR

Alma and the others, ski masks cuffed in a band around their heads, were hunched down in the middle of the living room as if gathered around a cook fire. The house was sealed tight: windows closed, shades drawn. Everywhere, there was the cheesy stench of raw nervousness. The prisoner lay in his cell. Before Martín had turned the key, he'd gulped down two glasses of water. Swallowed three aspirins. Wadded toilet paper hard against the wound.

"I don't like what's going on with him," Alma said. "There's more to it than meets the eye."

"He'll be all right," Pedro said. "He just got it in la nalga. It happened when we were scuffling. It's just a little flesh wound."

"It's a war wound, is what it is," Pablo said, snickering.

"Stop it," Alma said, batting her comrade in the arm. She had not seen the prisoner. She did not want to see him. One look at him and she'd be lost. Bad enough she could see his wallet, curled under at two corners, his wedding ring, his thick gold watch on the floor before them. Inanimate objects shouting out accusations.

"What shall we do with la Judit?" Pedro asked. "It's hot in the truck."

The thought of the effect heat could have on dead flesh silenced all of them for a moment. Weeks and weeks of preparation, yet they'd not envisioned a catastrophe like this. Martín said, "There's a shed out back. When it gets dark, we'll put her in there. Later, we'll have to dig a spot for her in the yard." The house had a small backyard bordered on three sides with tall ficus hedges. "For now, our main concern is the prisoner. He's not who we figured on. We need a new plan."

"Whatever we decide, we'll have to hurry," Alma said. "The prisoner's wounded. That changes everything."

"It's not like he's dying," Pablo said.

"Listen," Alma said. "Let's not assume anything. Look how all is changed from the way we planned it. We have to contact the family. Make our demand. The sooner we collect, the faster the release." She tapped her watch. "It's already four-thirty."

"By noon tomorrow all this can be concluded," Pablo said.

"We're still asking the four million, right?" Pedro said.

"No," Alma said. "From this prisoner, we'll never get that."

"So how much should we ask?"

"The most, a million." (*He* would never know how much she'd saved *them*.)

"No!" growled Pablo. "That's not enough."

The change started a row. They had expected so much. How would they manage with so much less?

Alma sprang up, the heat in her eyes. The heat throbbing at her temples. "You listen to me, cabrones. We're playing with fire here, understand. We ask a million, we get it. We ask for more and we don't. It's as simple as that."

The men said nothing. Sitting on their haunches, one rocked back on his heels; another wiped the sweat beaded above his lip; a third lowered his hand from the handle of his gun.

"So who do we contact?" Pedro said.

"Who do you think?" Martín asked her.

She dropped down again beside them and nodded her head in the direction of the prisoner's door. "Go in there. Ask him."

Martín went in, the mask over his face.

The prisoner was on the cot curled into a ball. He'd raised the blanket over himself. Had tried to tuck it in. "I'm cold," he said, hearing the door open.

The room was simmering.

"Get a doctor. I'm not well." His heart galloped.

"We'll get someone for you soon." Martín pulled up the only chair and sat down. "But first there's the matter of the war tax. The sooner the levy is paid, the faster your release."

"Call my family. They'll give you what you want." He tried straightening his legs, but he could not. The light had gone fuzzy, like when he was coming out of sleep.

"Who shall we call?"

"Call my son, Alvaro. He's named after me, but we call him Júnior. Júnior Tobar. He lives in San Benito. Calle La Revolución." When he was born, his son was slippery and slender like a fish. Alvaro could see him resting in the curve of Magda's arm. "No, wait. Don't call Júnior's house. Call mine. Júnior's sure to be there with his mother." The dark froth of Magda's hair. The fragrance when he buried his face in it.

"Júnior Tobar. At your house."

"I'm going to be sick."

"I'll get you water in a minute. Better yet, a Coca-Cola. A Coke's good for the stomach."

"Please get a doctor."

"I'll get a Coca-Cola."

Pedro slipped out the back of the house and went around to the sidewalk. As if out for an evening stroll, he started toward the corner, keeping his pace slow and easy. Hands thrust into pockets, he breathed deeply, taking in the sweetness of the night air. The freshness of mid-November, the greenness of pepetos set along the sidewalk, their branches laden now with roosting guardabarrancos and dichosofuís. Pedro went down the quiet street, past houses and the amber squares of light that were their windows. He crossed the street at the corner. Two blocks ahead, the Esso station glowed like a neon ship in the night.

He strolled past the gas pumps, continuing for two blocks more. He cut across the parking lot of el Hospital San Rafael. Half a dozen cars dotted the parking lot. He weaved among them, heading for the lighted canopied entrance of the emergency room. He walked into the lobby lined with chairs, only two of them occupied: an old woman holding a sniffling child, a young woman holding her belly. At the back of the room, two nurses talked avidly behind a long counter. Pedro went to the pay phone set in the corner. He dropped a coin in the pay phone slot. Got a signal. Dialed a number, then turned around and faced the room. After the second ring, someone picked up.

"¿Bueno?"

"Is this the house of don Alvaro Tobar?" He spoke, holding a hand up to his mouth and around the mouthpiece.

There was a pause, then, "Sí."

"I want to speak with his son, el Júnior Tobar."

"Un momento, por favor."

Another pause. "¿Sí?"

"Are you el Júnior Tobar?"

"Do you have my father? Is he all right?"

"Here's a message: All information will come tomorrow." The second call he would make from the Esso station.

"Who are you?"

Pedro laid the phone softly in its cradle. He started back toward the house.

It was nine o'clock.

Dear God, what is happening to me?

It was seventeen after two.

At three, Martín went in to check the prisoner.

The prisoner was dead.

▼▼

CHAPTER SIXTY-FIVE

Magda's house was a command post. The family huddled inside. Only Elena, because of fragile health, had remained in Santa Ana. The Tobar brothers had established a cordon of security around the house, around the Salahs' compound in Escalón as well. At Magda's, Victor Morales's men were posted beside the front gates, along the driveway, and around the garden. They guarded the entrances, seven doors in all. Powerless to do anything else, the family men joined the major's force. With pistols tucked in waistbands, they kept watch, helped attach clumsy recorders to telephones, they fine-tuned radios to stations that might carry new developments. Magda's two brothers contacted the bank in anticipation of the ransom demand that was sure to come soon.

The news had first aired at four o'clock: "We interrupt this program to announce the murder of the industrialist Abraham Salah and the abduction of his partner, cotton baron Alvaro Tobar. At this hour, no group has identified itself as holding him. No demands have yet been made to the Tobar family." Within minutes, friends began arriving at Magda's gate. All were courteously turned away.

At a little before nine, Magda was in the family room slumped on the sofa beside Flor and the phone. Since the horror began, the phone had rung intermittently. Each time it did, Magda gave a jump and had to hold herself back from lunging for it. This time, it was not she who was in charge of things.

The phone rang again.

Orlando Tobar picked it up. "Un momento." He gave a quick nod, then started the recorder and signaled to his brother. Júnior took the receiver. "Do you have my father? Is he all right?" After a pause, he said, "Who are you?" Soon after, Júnior hung up.

"Is he alive?" Magda asked.

The others who had gathered in the room—brothers, sons, in-laws—leaned toward Magda as if to catch her when Júnior spoke his reply. Even the old santos sitting on the lighted shelves lining the walls seemed to incline themselves in her direction.

"It was a man. All he said was, 'Information to come tomorrow.'"

"When tomorrow?"

"He didn't say."

The night stretched interminably. Few slept as lamps burned in rooms, in the garden, and up the drive.

In Magda's room, she and Flor lay on the bed, forehead to forehead, arms extended around each other's shoulders. It was the middle of the night, and the two had not changed out of their clothes. A box of Kleenex sat on the bed between them. Periodically, one plucked a tissue and wiped her eyes or blew her nose. Light from the dressing room cast a glow over the lush carpet, along the dresser, over one wall studded with studio-framed photographs: Magda and Alvaro at the lake, their golden faces looking out. Magda and Alvaro bundled up against the winter in New York. Magda and Alvaro, smooching for the camera like two silly clowns.

"You should be with Enrique," Magda said. She'd made this comment a dozen times before.

"Enrique's with his mother. He told me to stay here. It's where I want to be." Flor thought of her daughters, all tucked safely into beds down the hall. If this had been Enrique, she would have needed her girls a handspan away for the rest of her life. That this was happening to her father made her need her mother more.

"I'm glad you're here." Madga squeezed Flor's shoulder, and

Flor began to weep again. Magda patted her daughter's back. For a time they were like that: two women grappling with calamity. Two women discovering there was no antidote for grief.

Flor blew her nose again. She said, "Have you thought of anything more to ask?" When the second call came, Júnior would pose two questions to the abductors for proof her father was alive. Questions requiring answers only a family member would know.

"I have one," Magda said. " 'What do fifty-nine and seventy-five make?' I'll have them ask your father that."

"Ay, Mamá," Flor said, tears spilling again. She saw all those eighty-threes on all those letters she and Enrique had exchanged.

Magda kissed her daughter's head. "Help me think of a second one," she said.

When the telephone in the family room shrilled at eight A.M., everyone near it gave a jump: Júnior and Orlando on the sofa. Their brother Carlos at his mother's desk. Their wives curled up in chairs. Orlando pressed the recorder as Júnior picked up.

"Júnior Tobar here."

The same voice as the night before came over the phone, "Good. Listen carefully. We want one million colones in hundred-colón bills."

"Wait just a minute. First I want to know about my father. Is he all right? Is he alive?" Júnior's chest tightened. His mouth went dry.

"He's alive."

Júnior moistened his lips with his tongue. "You'll have to prove that. We won't turn over any money until you do."

"And how do we do that?"

"We have two questions for you. Have my father answer them. If you provide the correct answers, we'll proceed as you ask."

A hesitation. "What are the questions?"

Júnior gave the first question.

"What is the total of fifty-nine and seventy-five," the man repeated.

"Yes. Here's the second one." Júnior gave that question, too.

"What was buried under the vanilla tree," the man echoed.

"That's right," Júnior said.

"Did you hear what I said about the money?"

"You want one million colones in one-hundred-colón bills."

"Exactly. Place the money in a duffle bag. The kind soldiers use. The bag must be ready for delivery at eleven. That's in three hours."

"Where do we deliver the bag?"

"Never mind that for now. We'll call back at eleven to give you a location."

"You give the answers, then," Júnior interrupted. "No answers. No money."

"Sí, sí. Another thing, the courier with the bag. He must not be a family member. Don't try to trick us. We know your family. You're all under surveillance. If you send a family member, the prisoner is dead."

"One more thing, when will my father be released?"

"We'll let you know where he is after we get the money."

"Tell me who you are."

"Let's just say we're the Soul of the People."

The phone went dead.

Basilio stood in the doorway of his shed and watched Jacinta cross the garden toward him. All these years and she was still as slender and lovely as when a girl, as when he'd first surrendered his heart to her. They were both old now. Dos viejos going on sixty, the chasm between their ages miraculously narrowing over time. He had never laid his mouth on hers. Never once held her. Only twice had he been privileged to spread a hand over hers: on the day they buried Mercedes and just after María Mercedes's birth. These deprivations others might have found pitiable, but to him they were unimportant. What truly mattered was that every morning when the sun rose beyond the garden wall, Jacinta rose not far from him. For this he gave daily praise, because her nearness counted for everything.

Jacinta came up carrying Basilio's laundry in her arms, the laundry an excuse to have a talk with him. There were eager armed men patrolling the garden. She felt their eyes on her as she stepped over the lawn. "Were you at the gate this morning, Basilio?" Jacinta asked. She handed the laundry over.

He set the clothing on his cot and turned back to her. "She hasn't come," he said, cutting to the heart of Jacinta's inquiry. It was María Mercedes she was asking about.

"Maybe she's on one of her church trips," Jacinta said. "God knows she goes on plenty." Half the time her daughter was away. She and that Fernando. The yellow dog, too. Off in the country. Up in the mountains. Taking the word to the people, María Mercedes said. This matter Jacinta discussed only with Basilio. These days church work was very suspect.

"She must be," Basilio said, believing it was only a question of time before María Mercedes showed up. If she didn't, how long before people noticed it? What would the family make of her absence?

"The second call came in," Jacinta said. "They want a million colones." She had been serving coffee in the family room when she overheard the conversation.

"Who's asking for all of that?"

"I heard don Júnior say, 'It's the Soul of the People.' "

In Basilio's head, a memory. María Mercedes riding in the car with him. María Mercedes reciting for him a poem she had written. "It's by Alma del Pueblo," she had said. "That's me."

"What's wrong, Basilio?" Jacinta asked.

For the third time in his life he reached out and took her hand.

▼▼▼

CHAPTER SIXTY-SIX

They called back. At eleven, the same male voice.

"Is the money ready?"

"It's ready. It's in an army duffle bag. The green canvas kind."

"One million, correct?"

"One million in one-hundred-colón bills."

"Good."

"Before we continue, though, let's have those answers. Like I said before, no answers, no money." Júnior was sitting on the sofa next to his mother. Magda held his hand tightly.

The man on the phone spoke.

Júnior drew in a sharp breath and repeated, "Eighty-three and Elena's ring." Magda gave a small involuntary cry and crumpled against the back of the sofa. Flor threw a hand up to her mouth to stifle a gasp. She fell against her mother.

"Bueno," Júnior said. "Tell me where you want the money."

"You have someone to carry it?"

"We have a man."

"Remember, no family members."

"I understand." Júnior glanced at Victor Morales, who was across the room. The major stood beside a bulging duffle bag. His own army bag, in fact. He wore a blue baseball cap for ease in identification. "Tell us where our man should go. He'll be wearing a blue cap."

"The man must be alone. Send him up the Paseo Escalón to the Redondel Masferrer. It's across from la Iglesia Cristo Redentor. He's to pull into the church parking lot, then cross on foot to the traffic circle. Tell him to walk around the redondel once. He should be carrying the money. At noon, someone will approach him."

"Redondel Masferrer. At noon."

"Remember, he comes alone. No family members, no police, no clever tricks or the prisoner is dead."

"I understand."

There was the sudden hum of the dial tone.

The phone still in his hand, Júnior allowed himself to collapse against his mother, too. "Papá's alive," he said.

Pablo watched the church lot from the small park across the street. The church had stone walls and wide windows. A bell tower with a single bell rose up on one side. Pablo checked the time. It was ten minutes to noon. At twelve the bell would begin clanging the hour. Because it was a weekday, the front doors of the church were closed. Only two cars were parked in the lot. The traffic circle—a grassy rise ringed by a narrow walk—was off to the right. Pablo kept an eye on it, too. He watched cars roll periodically up the avenue, proceeding halfway around the circle before continuing on.

The park was shaded by mango trees. Six of them, to be precise. There were two benches: one near the sidewalk, the other, where he sat, farther back, beside a space with a teeter-totter and two swings. A few children were on the swings. Young boys with dirty knees and, because school was out, with plenty of time on their hands. Pablo patted his shirt pocket, feeling reassuringly the folded paper inside. He pulled it out, unfolded it, and scanned the note again.

The note read: "Drive back down Escalón eight blocks to la Plaza Alegre. Stand with the duffle bag next to the bumper car ticket booth. You have seven minutes. No stopping. No phone calls. No contact with anyone. Seven minutes, or we'll be gone and he'll be dead."

Across the street, a maroon Buick pulled into the church lot.

Pablo refolded the note. He watched the car nose into a space and stop. Soon the car's door swung open. A man stepped out. On his head, a blue cap.

Pablo plucked two five-colón bills from his trouser pocket. "Tsst, cipote," he called, crooking his finger at the nearest boy, the one who appeared to have come alone. "Come here, kid," he repeated. The boy stopped swinging. Pablo motioned again and the boy started over.

Across the way, the man in the blue cap stood at the curb. Hanging from a strap over his shoulder was a duffle bag bulging and stiffened by its contents. The man had slung an arm around the bag, but the bag was so stuffed, his arm did not fully encircle it. He crossed the street and headed for the traffic circle. When he stepped onto its walk, the church bell began to peal.

"What do you want?" the boy said. He looked to be seven. Maybe eight. He had a round face. A smudge on one cheek.

"You want to make ten colones?"

The kid's eyes widened for an instant. "How?"

"See that man going around el redondel?"

The kid looked in that direction. "Yes."

"The man and I, we're playing a game. When I tell you, go across the street and hand him this note." Pablo raised the paper and one of the bills. "I'll give you a five for that."

The bell continued clanging.

"What about the other five?" the boy said, pointing to it.

"I'll give you that one if you wait on the redondel until the man leaves. After he leaves, come back here and you can have the second five. But don't look this way when you're with him. If he asks you any questions, don't answer them. I'll be watching from here. If I see you look this way or talk to him, kiss this other five good-bye."

The boy frowned and looked across the street. The bell stopped, the last stroke reverberating for a moment in the air. "You're playing a game?"

"Yes. We're playing a game." Pablo held out the note and a bill. "Here. Walk slow. Don't look back. Remember, I'll be watching."

The boy took the note and the bill. "This game," he said, "who's winning?"

"I am," Pablo said. Then the kid set off.

▼   ▼   ▼

Noon at Plaza Alegre and the arcade bustled with commerce and gaiety. Sheltered under corrugated tin roofs, a line of pupuseras stood beside braziers and comales turning lunch against their palms. They greeted and chatted with customers creeping up in lines toward them. At tables, clients spooned relish from wide-mouthed jars onto pupusas and tortillas. They blew across their coffees, steaming and strong.

On the giant slide, children exclaimed clambering up and shrieked whooshing down. In the bumper cars, they squealed when whipping around curves or when their cars collided against others or when they glanced off the rubber railings of the big round track. At pinball machines, intense types with twitchy gunslinger fingers poked and thrust and jabbed buttons, sending lights flashing, signals chiming, and bells dingdingdinging.

From the shooting gallery came the pop pop pop of air rifles aimed at a steady parade of tin bunnies marching in and out of sight.

When they first arrived, Alma and Martín had slid into a picnic table with a clear view of the bumper cars and the ticket booth. Their coffee cups sat before them, cooling even in the sun. Alma lifted her cup and took a swallow, choking it down. Martín patted her on the back. "Steady," he said.

"I'm all right." She set the cup roughly on the table again, sloshing its contents onto the oilcloth when she did. She glanced at her watch. It was ten minutes after twelve.

They had a plan. When the courier showed up at the bumper cars, it was she who would approach. Stationed at the shooting gallery, Martín would cover her. Pedro was in a car waiting across the street. She caught a glimpse of the car now through the people milling under the arcade.

"We'll stay till twenty after," Martín said. "Not a minute longer."

She tried another swallow, needing this, something, anything, to brace her. In her life, she could never have dreamed up such disaster. Don Alvaro's rigid body curled up as if just born. Pedro rushing in from the call with proving questions. That her life with the family had given her the answers was an irony she could not dwell upon for even one moment.

"You have the address, right?" Martín asked. Now he glanced at his watch. "It's thirteen after."

"I have it." In the pocket of her trousers the square of paper with the message: "Pick up prisoner in Santa Tecla, at two-thirty-five Calle Delgado, Colonia Utila." In the right pocket of her vest, the Makarov revolver. For assurance, she slipped a hand around it.

"Here comes our man," Martín said.

Coming across the arcade dodging people, a man in a blue cap and clasping a canvas bag. The bag looked formidable. She could feel its weight already pulling at her shoulder. When this was over, she would disappear. Make her way to Cuba somehow. Fight for the cause from there.

"Let's go," she said, sliding out from the table, forcing herself to be methodical and slow. She turned back to Martín as he slid out, too. "You in position first," she said. She watched him stroll over to the shooting gallery, his hand thrust into the pocket where his revolver was stashed.

The courier walked up to the ticket booth. He wheeled slowly, raking his eyes over the crowd. After a moment, she stepped toward him. When she neared, she almost lost control. She knew this man. This man knew her.

They stood face-to-face, not speaking for a moment. Then Victor Morales said, "Isn't this interesting, not that I'm surprised. Where's your friend el catedrático? I see the two of you have graduated from church work."

"Just put it down," Alma said. I'm going to have to kill him, she thought. "Come on. Put the bag down. Unzip it. I want to see inside. And don't try anything. There's plenty of people covering us."

"First give me the man's location," Victor said.

"Oh no. You put the bag down. I look inside. Then I give you a location."

Victor unzipped the bag at his shoulder, then lowered it to the floor. He crouched beside it and spread it open just enough for her to glimpse the banded stacks of bills.

"Bueno," Alma said. "Zip it back up. Push it over." On the

bumper track, little cars careened and crashed. One headed their way. When it hit the railing just behind him, she would do what she had to do.

Still kneeling, he pushed the bag toward her. "Where's the location?"

"Here. In my vest pocket." She slid a hand over her gun. He saw the way her eyes shifted. The way her hand widened in the pocket. He was onto her at once. Fleetly, from years of practice, he drew a pistol from the waistband under his jacket. While she aimed, he fired. One good shot to the chest. When she fell, he aimed at her head. Squeezed the trigger once again.

At the shooting gallery, Martín heard the bumper car carom hard against the railing. He heard two reports. Watched his comrade's knees buckle. Watched her crumple to the ground.

Victor Morales grasped the bag handle, heaved it up and over his shoulder. This is mine now, he thought. He pivoted, turning on a heel, lurching through the bystanders shocked stiff, hands bunched over mouths in disbelief.

Martín pulled out his gun and pushed through the crowd after Victor, keeping his eye glued on his bobbing blue cap. Around the bumper car track, past the pinball machines, Martín darted around people, knocking some aside as he gathered speed. People pointed at the revolver in his hand. Back at Alma's body, a woman screamed: "¡Está muerta! ¡Está muerta!"

Victor was lumbering with his load across the lawn toward the sidewalk when Martín came up behind him. At close range, he planted his feet, held the gun with two hands, and pumped out two shots. Pak! The first one entered the nape of the neck. Pak! The second one, because the target was dropping down, entered the middle of the skull.

There was a common intake of a multitude of breaths; then pandemonium erupted. People screamed. People ran. People took cover by diving under tables. The toppling of a brazier and comal intensified the commotion.

Martín dashed up to the bag. He tugged at the strap with his free hand, yanking it out of the target's death grip. At the sidewalk, Pedro was in the car. The motor was running. The side doors yawned open. Martín half lifted, half dragged the bag to the car. He heaved it into the backseat, gave it a push until it was completely inside. He slammed the door. Pedro was already pulling out when Martín jumped in front.

They were only a block away when the sirens started up. Pedro drove at normal speed going up Escalón. When he got to the church lot, Pablo was waiting. They stopped and Pablo climbed in back. "¡Puta!" he said when he saw the bag. "What happened to Alma?"

"She didn't make it," Martín said. When he spoke, something ached behind his eyes.

"It was either her body or the money," Pedro said.

"Long live the cause," Martín said. "Long live those who die for it."

▼▼

CHAPTER SIXTY-SEVEN

T he heart has four small chambers, but it can hold a world of grief. To what purpose recounting the blows fate dealt: the impact bullets made against flesh, the staggering realization loved ones are lost for eternity, the terrible betrayals they are capable of. To what purpose retelling, except to say horror came visiting and left in its wake regret and guilt and not a small amount of bitterness.

December 5, 1977

The family was gathered under the portico of Magda's drive. The servants were there, too. Júnior Tobar's big car was parked by the door, and Basilio loaded luggage into the trunk. Three suitcases for Magda, two for Elena, the last one, a medium cloth case packed with Jacinta's things. Basilio closed the trunk lid. He went up on the portico and stood beside Pilar. He would not be driving the car today. A blessing, really. Today he was not capable of attentive efforts, like driving Jacinta to the airport so she could fly out of his life.

Júnior guided Elena into the front seat and sat her down. Flor came up and knelt beside her grandmother, speaking gently to her.

Magda made her rounds among the group, pressing this one's hands, kissing that one on the cheek. When she drew up to Basilio, she said, "Take good care of everything."

"Please let me come, too," Basilio said, the words sputtering out in his despair. "I'm sure you'll need a driver over there."

"This won't be forever, Basilio. I promise you."

When Jacinta walked up, he stiffened his sagging legs, taking in the sight of her face, her charcoal gaze turned hollow now.

"I have to go," she said. "You know how much I do."

He nodded. It was all he was capable of doing.

She circled her arms around him. Brought her lips to his cheek. "Hasta luego, fiel compañero. Until later, faithful companion," she said, before letting him go.

He took a step back and walked unsteadily toward the garden.

Pilar sobbed uncontrollably. She fell into Jacinta's arms. Held her in a fierce embrace. "I'll come see you in Miami."

"I'll be waiting."

Time came for them to go. Jacinta slipped into the back beside Magda. Before the car had started down the drive, Basilio came around the house again. He hurried to Jacinta's side of the car. "Para ti," he said, extending a small package wrapped in brown paper through the window.

They all stood under the portico, and they didn't stop watching until well after the car disappeared from their view.

The airplane climbed over the countryside. Jacinta sat next to the window, contemplating the startling geometry of greens and browns, the concert of blues slipping under them. Beside her, Elena and Magda had rested their heads against seat backs, closed their eyes to the harsh world they were attempting to leave behind.

Lying on Jacinta's lap were the contents of Basilio's package. Five sealed envelopes addressed to her. Each a letter from Miguel Acevedo.

The dates on the envelopes read March 1945, November 1945, August 1952, January 1964. All had been posted in El Salvador. The fifth envelope told a different story.

Jacinta unclasped the pocketbook she'd tucked between herself and the side of the seat. She extracted from it a little box. In the box were six burned matchsticks, the soot worn off years ago. Also in the box was a length of jute studded with three red agates. At the morgue, she herself had untied the amulet from around the strap of her girl's bra. A second matching amulet had been discovered on Victor Morales. Was it not certain, then, that her long-lost brother had killed her daughter moments before he died? The irony of this thought brought new tears to Jacinta's eyes. Mamá, give me strength, she thought, rubbing the smooth ancient stones her mother once had held.

Jacinta looked out the window again.

Down there, so far away, her past reduced to a still life: The black cone of the volcano. A flock of wild birds. A path winding its way toward a stream. A girl tagging after her mother. A devoted boy trailing behind.

For a long time, Jacinta fixed her eyes below. Then she stashed away her treasures in the little box. Slipped the box into her purse.

She turned back to Miguel's letters, still lying in her lap.

The last one he'd written was dated December 1975. The return address read Miami, Florida. She opened it first.

▼▼▼

The story continued, as all stories do until life itself is done.

In a country named The Savior, 1980 brought full-scale civil war.

By 1992, when peace was signed, seventy-five thousand had died, three hundred thousand had fled, and five million remained, these filled with hope on bitter grounds.